PRAISE FO[R]

THE BONE S[PINDLE]

An INSTANT Indie Bestseller!

★ "Vedder weaves compelling character backstories into a complex plot, rich with detail and magic, and balances heart-pounding action with romance, travel, and thorough worldbuilding. This gender-flipped retelling effortlessly melds romance, adventure, and fantasy. Highly recommended."
—*SLJ*, starred review

"Packed with fully fleshed-out characters and lots of adventure, this book is a fun read that will easily draw fairy tale lovers. Vedder's first novel nicely balances its exciting plot with touching matters of the heart."
—*Booklist*

"An enchanting read for fans of fairy-tale romance and girls with battle axes."
—*Kirkus Reviews*

"[An] action-packed, gender-flipped 'Sleeping Beauty' reenvisioning . . . Video game–style fantasy tropes and energetic plotting provide an alternative to Forgotten Realms and David Eddings for new readers of epic fantasy."
—*Publishers Weekly*

PRAISE FOR

THE SEVERED THREAD

"Both the action and the romance are heart-pounding, but perhaps the most touching aspects are the friendships among the characters: Their world is full of magic, mysteries, and danger, and they support each other through it all with love and compassion."
—*Kirkus Reviews*

"This flipped fairy-tale series is too fun to miss. Highly recommended."
—*SLJ*

ALSO BY LESLIE VEDDER

The Bone Spindle
The Severed Thread

MIDDLE GRADE

The Labyrinth of Souls

THE CURSED ROSE

LESLIE VEDDER

putnam

G. P. PUTNAM'S SONS

G. P. Putnam's Sons
An imprint of Penguin Random House LLC
1745 Broadway, New York, New York 10019

First published in the United States of America by Razorbill,
an imprint of Penguin Random House LLC, 2024
First paperback edition published 2025

Visit us online at PenguinRandomHouse.com.

The Library of Congress has cataloged the hardcover edition as follows:
Names: Vedder, Leslie, author. | Title: The Cursed Rose / Leslie Vedder.
Description: New York : G.P. Putnam's Sons, 2024. | Series: The Bone Spindle ;
volume 3 | Audience: Ages 12 years and up. | Summary: Trapped in a tower with
Briar Rose, Fi faces the Spindle Witch's threat and the imminent discovery of
Siphoning Spells, while Shane seeks a weapon to save Andar and contends with
the danger of Red's betrayal and the ruthless Spindle Witch's executioner,
leading them to unravel the secrets of the Tomb of Queen Aurora.
Identifiers: LCCN 2023055318 (print) | LCCN 2023055319 (ebook) |
ISBN 9780593625569 (hardcover) | ISBN 9780593625583 (epub)
Subjects: CYAC: Magic—Fiction. | Witches—Fiction. |
Good and evil—Fiction. | Fantasy. | LCGFT: Fantasy fiction. |
Novels. Classification: LCC PZ7.1.V427 Cu 2024 (print) |
LCC PZ7.1.V427 (ebook) | DDC [Fic]—dc23
LC record available at https://lccn.loc.gov/2023055318
LC ebook record available at https://lccn.loc.gov/2023055319

ISBN 9780593625576

1st Printing

Printed in the United States of America

LSCC

Design by Suki Boynton | Text set in News Plantin MT Std Regular

For my partner, Michelle,
who fills my life with love and makes coffee

THE CURSED ROSE

PROLOGUE

IN THE FIRST blush of dawn, Camellia Rose crept down the silent halls of the sleeping castle. Her velvet cloak whispered around her feet as she slipped into the Great Witches' chamber. The room was thick with shadows, the air rich with the scent of smoke and wormwood and magic.

As long as Camellia could remember, she'd been sneaking into this forbidden chamber. Only it wasn't forbidden anymore. Now it was as much hers as anyone's. The soft leather spines crackled as she ran her finger down a row of old spell books, the smell of ancient paper tickling her nose. Her reflection stared back at her from the frosty window: a young girl with fair cheeks and a crown of braided willow branches nestled in her golden curls, the soft buds unfurling into delicate white blossoms. Camellia blew gently against the icy glass and traced her name into the fog.

The curling letters of the Divine Rose script looked strange there. As strange as they'd looked etched into the white marble tree in the castle garden, where her name was now sealed away forever. The name of the new Rose Witch.

At eleven, Camellia was the youngest ever to hold the title of Great Witch. Though she wasn't *Camellia* anymore, she supposed. She wasn't a princess, or a daughter. When a Witch gave up their name, they were supposed to give up their birthright, and all their old loyalties as well, and devote themselves only to magic. But she had always loved the name her mother had given her, after the pale flowers that grew wild and strong, shining like stars against the dark hedgerow.

"You'd better get rid of that before the others arrive."

Camellia whirled, her breath sharp in her throat. "Spindle Witch."

She had missed the woman in the shadows of the room—sitting silently at her spinning wheel like a spider patiently weaving her web. Her long ebony skirts rustled as she teased out a bobbin of golden thread.

A shiver tingled down Camellia's spine. Many in Andar feared the Spindle Witch—even Camellia's father, who made the sign to ward off evil whenever the Spindle Witch passed. But Camellia had always been fascinated by this woman of immense, unrivaled power. She admired how effortlessly the Spindle Witch wielded her magic—and how little she cared for those who feared her.

The Spindle Witch's eyes gleamed behind her veil. "Breaking the rules already, my dear?"

Camellia blushed. "It hardly matters. The Great Witches already know my name." But she did as she was told, wiping

2

away the whorls and loops on the window. "It's a little silly, isn't it? It's not like everyone will just forget."

"You'd be surprised how easily people forget things." The Spindle Witch beckoned her close and pulled a shivering flower from Camellia's willow crown. "Memories spring up all at once, like the seeds you grow in the garden. Forgetting, on the other hand, is a slow, inevitable decay." The Spindle Witch closed her hand, crushing the petals into her black glove. "Your name is merely an echo now, a remnant of who you were. It does not do for a Witch to cling to such sentimental things."

Camellia bit her lip. Her mother's words had been different, softer, as Camellia traced her name onto the Tree of Roses, the monument to all the Rose Witches before her. Though she only used her fingertip, the letters cut deep into the marble, like they'd been carved centuries ago. *From now on, your name is a sacred treasure,* her mother whispered against her ear, *meant only for those who love you most.*

"My mother—I mean, the queen." Camellia caught herself. "She says Rose Witches give their names to their loved ones, who engrave them on their hearts."

The Spindle Witch gave a creaky chuckle. "Who will you give your name to, then?"

"My brothers."

The old Witch's head tilted, almost imperceptibly. The golden thread shivered in her fingers. "*Brother*s," she breathed, the *s* lingering on her tongue. "I wasn't aware the queen was expecting."

"She's not . . . yet," Camellia admitted, her voice hushed with excitement. "But it's been foretold."

The Spindle Witch's eyes glittered. "Now, that is something to celebrate."

Camellia leaned close as the wheel began to churn again, the wooden pedal creaking against the floor. "You could tell me your name. The one you gave up. I can keep a secret," she whispered.

The Spindle Witch's lips twitched, her hand carding softly through Camellia's hair. "It's been so long, my dear, I'm afraid I've quite forgotten it."

Camellia frowned. She could never tell whether the Spindle Witch was telling the truth. The veil hid everything but her ruby-painted smile.

Camellia's attention drifted to the book on the table beside her. It lay open to an ink-and-color picture of a young girl with golden hair, her long braid dangling out a window and a crow perched on her finger. Camellia bent close, surprised.

"This isn't a spell book. It's a children's storybook." She traced her finger over the flaking silver ink. "I've never heard 'The Eye of the Witch.'"

"It's a very old fable—as old as the kingdom itself." The words were sharp and eager, like they'd been inside the Spindle Witch a long time. "It tells the story of a monster born in the shape of a little girl, who devoured the lives of others. In the womb, she devoured her twin sister. When she was born, she devoured her mother, and then years later her father, and still she hungered, devouring more and more."

The dawn light had crept into the stained-glass window beside them, illuminating the roses red as drops of blood. The Spindle Witch's fingers twirled the golden thread faster and

4

faster, the blur of the wheel almost lulling Camellia into a trance as she spoke.

"The people of the land locked the girl away in the only prison that could hold her: a tower carved from a spire of black stone. There the girl wept and wept, with only the crows for company. Her cries drew the creatures of the forest, and she devoured them, too, until the whole forest was just a wasteland of bone."

Camellia flipped to the last page, a picture of the black tower rising above piles of bleached white bones.

"Night after night, she peered out her glowing window at the dark world, until her window became the moon and her long golden hair the moonlight, the Witch locked away forever with her insatiable hunger."

"That's an awful story," Camellia said, crossing her arms. "That poor girl. They just locked her away."

The Spindle Witch gave a wispy laugh. "Such a soft heart, little Rose Witch. Perhaps if you had been there, the story would have ended differently. But then again . . . perhaps some things are simply fate."

Camellia closed the book and held it out.

"Keep it, dear," the Spindle Witch said, pressing the book into her arms. "Engrave it onto your heart for me. Some stories should never be forgotten."

1

Fi

DARKNESS PRESSED IN around Fi like a cold frost, making the hair stand up on her arms and stealing the breath from her lungs. She blinked, unable to tell whether her eyes were open or closed. Everything was just blackness. The smooth stone floor was like ice under her bare feet, and she shivered in her nightgown, wrapping her arms around herself. She had a feeling that if she could see anything, her breaths would be white clouds in front of her face. The silence was so oppressive it echoed like a ringing in her ears. Fi squeezed her eyes shut, trying to get her bearings and figure out where she was.

A sharp tug on her hand made Fi's eyes spring open. She looked down to find a shining golden thread looped around her fingers, glowing over the Butterfly Curse mark on her palm. The thread spiraled off into the gloom like an invitation. Fi lifted the golden string and began pulling it in, hand over hand, following the unspooling thread deeper into the blackness. A pit of dread opened in her stomach, gnawing at her insides as she went on. She had a feeling she had been here before. She knew where this path ended.

Fi began to run, her bare feet slapping against the stone. The golden thread was so light it felt like nothing in her hands. Something rattled ahead of her, concealed by the dark. Fi gripped the thread like a lifeline.

Suddenly, she was face-to-face with two gleaming red eyes. The darkness shrank back as a bone creature surged up in front of her, spiral horns rising from its bleached skull. Its spine was a twist of disjointed vertebrae, and its arms were ropes of sinew ending in jutting bone claws. It was a monster with red eyes—but still Briar's eyes.

The creature seized Fi by the arms, those sharp claws so long they dragged against her back as its massive bat-like wings unfurled above her. Its red eyes burned like fire. They were so captivating it took Fi a moment to notice that the end of the golden thread disappeared into the empty space in the creature's chest, where its heart should be.

Terror made everything slow down—the shiver in her lungs, the clench of fear in her gut. Fi was frozen. The skull face was close enough that she could make out the tiny imperfections around the eye sockets. Close enough to kiss. A thrill of horror slid through her as the skull tipped toward her, but in the end, the creature only lifted one gruesome hand, clutching the golden thread.

There was a voice in her head suddenly—Briar's voice.

Where does it lead?

FI SHOT UP from the nightmare, panting and sweating. She scrambled to her feet so fast she knocked the chair she had fallen asleep in to the floor. Her hand slid across the battered desk, scattering papers and quills as she blinked the dream away. It took a moment to recognize the things around her: the small, round room of gray stone, her lumpy pallet on the floor, the arched window that let in the only light.

Suddenly, Fi needed air. She stumbled over to the wide sill, perching carefully on the edge and digging her fingers into the rough stones. There was no glass or shutter on this window. Cold sweat had made her blouse damp under her black vest, and the breeze chased goose bumps up her arms. It was a warm, sunny afternoon, but there was always a chill here, in the Spindle Witch's tower.

Fi looked out at the landscape she'd studied a hundred times. High, dark mountains ringed the valley, their slopes so steep it looked like they'd been shorn away. A dead forest lurked at the base of the tower, which wasn't so much a building as a jagged spire of stone piercing the heart of the valley, sheer and unyielding. Instead of carefully smoothed arches and polished flagstones, everything in the Spindle Witch's tower was narrow and rough-hewn, and the doorways were so low Fi had to duck to get through them. There were only three rooms, stacked on top of each other at the very tallest part of the tower, all the windows facing the same direction.

There were no stairs to the base of the tower—no way out at all, except the same way she'd gotten in: Briar.

Briar. Just thinking of him made Fi's heart stutter. It wasn't the first time she had dreamed of the bone creature bound with golden thread. She was sure it was Briar, but she was less sure whether he was really in the dream, trying to tell her something, or if it was just her mind tormenting her with her worst fears. She wouldn't be surprised. This place was enough to drive anyone mad. She had only been here a few weeks, but it already felt like an eternity.

Fi leaned as far as she dared out the window, searching for movement below. The forest around the tower was long dead, the bristling white trees calcified like stone. It reminded her of the Forest of Thorns, but where that had been a knot of oppressive black, the trees around the tower seemed to shimmer, their branches thick with delicate golden threads that danced in the breeze. The whole valley glittered like sunlight on the top of a lake.

The ground beneath the trees was blinding white. For the first few days, Fi had thought the valley was full of bleached rocks, or maybe crusted in salt or some other mineral. Then she realized the truth. The entire valley was carpeted in the bones of animals, years and years of skeletons layered over each other. The only creatures that lived in the forest now were the crows, the dark blotches of their feathered bodies stark against the glittering woods as they laughed and called to each other, pecking at the bones.

Fi's fingers clenched the windowsill. Briar Rose was perched in the highest branches of a skeletal tree below the window, staring up at Fi. The great juts of dark wings curved from his back, and his ivory horns gleamed in the sunlight, but he was still mostly Briar, not yet the skull monster she saw in her dreams. Desperately, she traced the pale skin of his face and the vee of his neck with her gaze—still flush, still real. Still alive.

Fi swallowed down his name. For the first few days, she had screamed herself hoarse calling for him, praying that she would see some spark of recognition in his gaze. He never so much as stirred. Fi was beginning to worry she might never see her Briar again. And yet every time she sought him out, he was always looking back at her, gazing up at the window, following her every movement with his empty red eyes. It was the tiny spark of hope she held on to late at night, when the dark tower seemed to close in around her and it was hard to remember why she was doing this.

Fi's hands curled into fists. She stepped back from the window, forcing herself to look away. Briar was why she had allowed the Spindle Witch to take her to this bleak place, why she spent every day poring over Camellia's book and code. She had to deceive the Spindle Witch into thinking she was working for her—at least until she found a way to save Briar Rose.

It was the biggest gamble Fi had ever taken, and the one with the worst odds. The more she found out about the Siphoning Spells the Spindle Witch was after, the more Fi was sure she could never be allowed to get her hands on them. The devastation she'd wreak would be incalculable—for Briar's people scattered across Andar; for Fi's partner, Shane, out there somewhere; even for her home kingdom of Darfell.

Guilt roiled in her gut at the notion of what she was risking, and a pang of longing seized her heart at the thought of her own family in Idlewild. She imagined her mother in the garden, clipping the last summer stalks of her golden orchids, while her father wandered the yard with his hands clasped at his back, forever obsessing about the drooping tomato plants. So many lives just like theirs hung in the balance.

Fi took a deep breath. What was done was done. The only way out of this—for any of them—was for her to follow through and figure out how to stop the Spindle Witch.

She turned back to the room, stepping around her pallet and a stack of clothes in a basket, plain blouses and pants that Fi traded out beneath her vest. Her old, tattered glove lay at the bottom, torn and discarded. Sometimes the sight of the Butterfly Curse on her tan skin surprised her; she had become so used to the black glove. But there was no one to hide from here, and no one to hurt.

The Spindle Witch had laughed at the mark when she had first seen it—*such a tiny thing*, she called it. Fi had never felt smaller or more insignificant than in that moment, listening to the Witch laugh away the curse that had taken everything from her. Why did the Butterfly Curse only seem to be able to hurt the people who didn't deserve it?

Her small cabinet held a jug of water, a string of dried jerky, and a knot of hard bread that only the Spindle Witch could replenish. Fi had no idea when the woman came and went from the tower, only that sometimes she was there and sometimes she was gone in a cloud of beating black wings.

The desk was a mess from when Fi had jerked up from her nightmare, and she winced, realizing Camellia's precious book had fallen to the floor. She scooped it up, smoothing the bent pages. The book had fallen open on a picture of a girl with golden hair staring longingly out the window of a dark tower.

The book Camellia had hidden away was a collection of

children's stories. Fi recognized most of them, like "The Ghost in the Well" and "The Girl in the Forest of Wolves," but these were ancient versions, all of them with dark, unhappy endings. Instead of trapping the ghost in the well and escaping together, one child pushed the other to his death in order to replace the lid. The brave huntsman fought the wolves of the forest to save his true love, only to find they were actually the missing villagers under an enchantment and he had slaughtered them all. It cast a sinister pall over the folktales of Fi's childhood, like she was seeing the dark seeds at the centers of the stories.

Over the last few weeks, word by word, she had pieced together Camellia's code, but she was starting to think that wasn't the only secret Camellia had hidden in this book. There were notes scrawled in the margins, too, all of them surrounding one particular story: "The Eye of the Witch."

Like the rest of the stories, this was a particularly bleak telling, but with every word, every faded illustration, Fi had become certain of one thing. The Spindle Witch was the girl in the story, and this was the tower she had been imprisoned in.

Camellia must have figured out the Spindle Witch's true identity and left this book as a message to Briar, but Fi wasn't sure what it meant. The girl's real name wasn't in the pages, and the whole story was written like a fable. Had the girl in the story really eaten her twin, or had she just survived when the other baby didn't? Had she killed her mother, or had the woman died in childbirth? As someone who studied history, Fi knew better than to put much stock in the specific details of old stories.

On the other hand, this valley was filled with a sea of

bones, and Fi had nearly been devoured by the Spindle Witch herself. Her hand rose unconsciously to her neck, remembering the golden thread twisted around it and draining away the life inside her. It wasn't hard to imagine the Spindle Witch as a monster locked away for the safety of all.

Fi rubbed at her eyes, frustrated. She'd read the story so many times the words practically blurred when she looked at them. Camellia's vague notes were no help. On one page, *long golden hair* was circled twice, and on another, Camellia had underlined *devouring life*, with the word *Time?* scrawled in the margins. Maybe it had meant something to Camellia, but it didn't mean anything to Fi.

At least not yet. She needed more information, and there might be a way to get some.

Fi glanced behind her at the aged wooden door, her eyes flickering up to the ceiling. The whole valley was quiet, with no birdsong, no animals, no rustling leaves, just the howl of the wind and the irregular screech of the crows. Most of the time, it made Fi feel like she was losing her grip on reality, but it also meant she'd learned to recognize all the sounds of the Spindle Witch moving around the room above her: the sharp footsteps, the scritch of a pen on parchment, even the little hiss and whir that meant the Witch was spinning. Right now, everything was silent.

There was one place in the tower Fi had not been yet. The room at the very top—the Spindle Witch's room. If there was anything to be found, that would be the place.

Fi didn't wait. She didn't want to give herself time to rethink this. She glanced briefly at her rope with the metal ring, which was coiled around one leg of the desk. She passed it, grabbing a single sheet of stiff paper instead. If it came down to a fight with the Spindle Witch, Fi had already lost. The point was to be smarter. Fi folded the paper between her hands with a sharp crease.

She opened the door cautiously, stopping again to listen as she looked up the curving staircase. It was so steep and the steps so narrow it was almost more like a ladder, and Fi often had to hold on with both hands when she climbed down to the small washroom below, the ice-cold water pumped in from a cistern.

Fi turned the other direction, climbing slowly and silently. Her heart thudded dully in her chest like it was beating through a block of ice. This wasn't the first time she had climbed to the door at the top of the tower, but she had hesitated each time, afraid of what would happen if she was caught. The Spindle Witch wanted the code Fi had memorized and whatever it led to, but Fi wasn't foolish enough to think she was anything more than the most convenient means to that end. That could change fast.

She forced herself to go on. The way things were going, she would have to give the Spindle Witch the code soon, anyway, and then she would become just as expendable.

This was why Fi hated gambling. Her brain incessantly fed her worst-case scenarios one after another, threatening to paralyze her.

She stood before the Spindle Witch's door, staring at the flaking wood. Dread settled over her shoulders like a cloak. Fi shook it off.

It's just like a ruin, she thought, steeling herself. *Keep a level head, and you can figure your way out.*

The last time she had come up these steps, Fi had studied the door carefully enough to know that there was no lock on the tarnished handle. Instead, it seemed to be held shut by a hook slid into a ring on the other side. That was what the piece of paper was for. Fi lifted the folded sheet, pressing her fingers along the crease to make it crisp. Then she slid the stiff paper between the door and the frame, under the hook. She lifted it up carefully until she felt it tap against the hook.

If she yanked up with all her might, she would just rip the paper, but Fi knew how to be patient. She raised the fold, tapping at the hook little by little and working it loose. Her palms were sweaty and her shoulders tense when the piece of metal finally popped free. Fi stuffed the paper into her pocket, turning the handle and pushing the door inward slowly.

No tripwire snapped, and the figure of the Spindle Witch didn't loom out of the shadows. There was just the soft swish of the door closing behind her, and before she was ready, Fi found herself walking into the heart of the Spindle Witch's tower.

Fi honestly didn't know what she had expected, but it wasn't this. It looked like a child's room—or at least a prison that had held a child. There was a small, half-sized bed in a metal frame crowned with polished knobs and a tattered blanket that looked more like a spiderweb. On the pillow lay a twisted burlap sack in the shape of a doll, with large button eyes and a jagged smile that had clearly been cut and resewn. There was also some kind of pattern or writing on the wall, low to the ground.

Fi knelt to get a better look. It wasn't a message at all. Instead, Fi ran her fingers across childlike drawings carved into the stone. Crosshatches and grooves showed where careless little hands had scraped something dull and metal over and over into the hard rock.

There was nothing special about the pictures themselves. They were just like the ones Fi had scratched into the dirt with sticks, mostly rabbits and dogs and other animals, but there were hundreds of them, painstakingly scored into the stone line by line. Fi's stomach did a little flip-flop as she thought of the monster born in the shape of a girl, locked in a tower. How many figures were carved into the walls—hundreds? How many years would it have taken a lonely child to carve them? And could it really have been the Spindle Witch?

Fi traced a crow with an over-wide smile and then stood up with a shiver. She didn't have forever to look around. A spinning wheel sat by a large open window so tall Fi thought she could stand upright in the frame. Beneath it lay a basket brimming with tangles of gold, which Fi assumed was unspun thread. There was an armoire on the other side of the room, and next to it a vanity with a tall rectangular mirror.

She headed to the armoire but was distracted by the movement of her fractured reflection in the mirror. The glass was scarred by long cracks that ran its entire length, splintering her image into an unsettling patchwork. Her broken reflection turned with her as she moved toward the vanity.

Only three things sat on the smooth surface: a little dish stained the deep red of the Spindle Witch's lips, an ancient brush with a tarnished silver handle, and a gleaming pair of scissors. There was something important here, Fi thought, her hand hovering over the scissors. This was a clue, and her brain was desperately trying to put it together.

She reached up to tug on her ear, distracted. Dread slithered through the pit of her stomach, a foreboding feeling she couldn't place until she realized that her reflection hadn't moved when she did.

Fi's head shot up. Her reflection was gone, and there was someone else in the mirror.

A figure with dark brown hair that fell around him like a tangle of spider threads sat on the other side of the vanity. He reached out, almost as though his hand would stretch through the fractured glass. "You have something of mine," he whispered. A strange smile twisted his lips as he lifted his face just enough for her to make out his features. One deep green eye fixed on her, the other closed under a crisscross of scars marring his tan face.

Fi leapt back, adrenaline pounding through her veins. *Something of his?* Even as fear prickled her skin, her mind was whirring. The man inside the mirror—could it be . . . ?

Then, all at once, the man surged forward, his long hair wild, his face so close his scratched-out eye reflected in every crack of the broken mirror.

"Get out," he warned, his expression dark and sinister.

Fi felt as though those words had knocked the breath out of her. She stumbled back.

"Get out!" the man said again, and this time something slammed into her, like a gust of wind that hurled her backward.

A gasp ripped from her throat as she plunged toward the wide-open window. She tripped over the basket, and the backs of her knees hit the edge of the rough stone sill. She made one last desperate effort to catch herself, grabbing at the edge of the window as her back arced over the dizzying drop. The high wind whipped at her hair, and she felt like a thread as thin as the one from her dream was all that held her up.

The last thing she saw was the dark-haired man smiling in the broken mirror. Then she felt phantom hands on her shoulders, shoving her out of the tower into the empty air.

Fi screamed, but the sound was swallowed by a sudden cacophony of crows, black wings beating in a thundercloud as all the birds in the valley rose at once. Her body seemed to hang in the sky for one impossible moment, and then she was falling, careening headfirst toward the bone-covered ground far below. Black feathers filled the air. Fi's chest clenched so hard that her heart must surely have stopped beating. She squeezed her eyes shut, not wanting to see the crash.

Then there was a rush of air around her, and her body jerked as she stopped falling, something sharp digging into her back. At first, Fi thought she'd been impaled on one of the skeletal trees. Then she recognized the feel of the arms around her. Her eyes shot open. She surged up, exhilarated, desperately searching the face of her savior, hoping to meet beautiful blue eyes.

The pale face above her was slack—empty eyes bloodred. The calcified forest rose around them. Briar had caught her scant inches from the ground.

Fi gaped at him, queasy from the fall and the feel of Briar's sharp claws digging into her skin. His arms were warm where they were still flesh and horrifyingly cold where they had turned to bone, but it didn't stop her from holding on as tight as she could, winding her arms around his neck. They hadn't been this close since their last night together under the stars. She twined her fingers into Briar's golden hair. The soft strands felt so familiar, but his face was an expressionless mask, his lips thinned into a frown Briar had never worn.

"Briar," she whispered. She could have sworn those red eyes flickered to her for just a moment, but she lost him again in a beat of his powerful wings, the air surging around them as he soared back up the tower.

Her hopes of reaching Briar, at least right now, shriveled when she saw what was waiting for her. The Spindle Witch had appeared in the highest window, and she was calling Briar to her, summoning him with a crook of one long, thin finger. The Witch motioned for her pet to bring Fi up to the forbidden room, and Briar obeyed. He had still been there to catch Fi, though, and she would hold on to that.

The Spindle Witch watched their approach, her red lips pressed together under the black veil. The wild rise of the crows had been a sign of her coming back, Fi realized. The man in the mirror had pushed her out just as the Spindle Witch returned. That couldn't be a coincidence.

Fi was disoriented and shaken, but she tried not to let that show on her face as Briar flew through the giant window and set her down before the Spindle Witch. Then he left her, moving away to hover outside the window.

The Spindle Witch's dark eyes fixed on Fi through the lacy

veil. Fi couldn't tell if she was smiling cruelly or if the natural curve of her lips just had a sinister lilt. Her mind raced as she tried to figure out how to explain what she had been doing in the Spindle Witch's room, to calculate whether begging for mercy would have any effect on the Witch who stood over her.

"I do hope that pathetic sight wasn't some sort of escape attempt," the woman said, clicking her tongue. "It's quite a fall from your window, dear, and I thought I was clear when I warned you there's no getting away."

Fi bit her tongue, trying not to react. The Spindle Witch must think she had fallen out of her own window. But even if the Witch hadn't seen her sneaking around, at the very least, the hook on the door should still have been open. Fi's eyes cut over to the door, only to find that the hook was properly in place once more.

A flicker of movement drew her gaze to the mirror. The image of the one-eyed man flashed into the surface for a moment, his finger held over his lips. *Shh.*

Fi's mouth went dry.

The Spindle Witch tapped her nails impatiently. "What are you looking at?" she demanded, turning around. The man was already gone.

"Nothing—and I didn't try to escape," Fi said. It wasn't hard to fake the shaking in her voice. "I just fell. It was an accident."

If the man in the mirror had gone so far as to fix the lock on the door, then Fi was sure of it: he had pushed her out of the window to keep the Spindle Witch from finding her. But why?

The Spindle Witch hummed thoughtfully, twirling a little piece of golden thread between her fingers. "I'll have to keep a closer eye on you, then—just to make sure there are no more *accidents*." Her eyes glittered with an unmistakable threat, and Fi swallowed hard, taking it for the warning it was. "Now . . . do you have my code yet?"

"I'm close," Fi said, her voice carefully flat. "I've almost got it unscrambled."

There had been times in her life when Fi regretted not being a more emotive person. Her ex, Armand, had certainly never tired of needling her for keeping her feelings buried when other people's were right at the surface. Right now, though, she was just grateful.

In truth, she had already unscrambled the book code and Camellia's message. She just hadn't worked out what it meant yet. She had to hide that from the Spindle Witch for as long as possible to buy herself more time.

"I certainly hope you're *very* close, and not just for my sake," the Spindle Witch crooned, her finger crooked. Suddenly, Fi was very aware of Briar still waiting for orders in the window. "My patience is wearing quite thin. Better get back to it, hadn't you?"

The Spindle Witch sent Briar off with a dismissive wave, his wings heaving as he flew back to his perch in the dead forest. With her other hand, she gestured to the door. Fi hurried to escape before the Witch changed her mind.

She couldn't help but shoot one last look at the mirror as she passed. It was empty of everything except her own ashen reflection, but she did notice something she hadn't the first time. There was a subtle pattern of butterflies engraved along the edge of the mirror, beautiful stylized swallowtails.

Her head swirled at the possibilities of just who was hiding in the mirror, who the Spindle Witch really was, and how Camellia had expected an old storybook to save an entire kingdom. Fi had come up here searching for answers, but all she had were more questions, and the feeling she was running out of time.

2

Red

EVERYONE WAS WATCHING her.

Red hunched into the hood of her feather-gray cloak, keeping her face in shadow as she walked between the decrepit buildings. It didn't matter. Everyone in the Everlynd camp knew who she was. The girl who'd served the Spindle Witch. The monster.

As a thief, Red knew how to disappear when she needed to. But there was no hiding among the Witches of Everlynd. Even without a stitch of red in her clothes, her favorite color traded for a black skirt and blouse that laced up the front. Even with her eyes cast away and her face hidden. Even with her wolf, Cinzel, left behind at her small camp on the edge of the woods. The shadow of who she had been clung to Red like a bloodstain she could never scrub off.

She deserved the cold stares. The whispers. All of it. She wasn't the reason Everlynd had gone up in flames—they had

Fi's Butterfly Curse to thank for that. But Red had certainly done more than her share of ugly things.

She picked up the pace, heading for the center of camp, where a cluster of three gray towers stood out against the dark green of the soaring fir trees. That's where Perrin would be.

The people of Everlynd had taken over the ruins of a large town tucked into a pine forest, what had once been an outpost to the east of Andar's castle city. If she peered through the trunks, Red could see the black wasteland, and beyond that, the Forest of Thorns, just a dark smudge like a distant thundercloud. It was closer than she'd ever wanted to be to that place again.

The town itself was a sprawl of squat houses with decayed roofs and a few mossy towers that weren't sturdy past the second level. Perrin's people were hard at work bolstering and repairing what they could, and the air was loud with the bang of hammers and the shouts of workmen patching the walls. Weathered sheets of burlap flapped on new roofs like blank flags.

Red's chest squeezed as she passed the little stone house where Perrin and Shane and the Paper Witch were staying. The descendants of the Great Witches had been given the best Everlynd had to offer: an old, wobbly shell of a house with a leaky roof and canvas stretched over the gaping hole in one wall, its slanted windows glittering with warped yellow glass. Shane kept badgering Red to move in with the rest of them. But Red wasn't interested in sleeping so close to people who despised her.

She fisted a hand in her skirt. The ugly wound on her palm throbbed, threatening to break open and start bleeding again. The thorn rod was gone, all of its power ripped away from her when she'd turned on the Spindle Witch. But sometimes Red swore she could still feel it, like a splinter of dark magic festering under her skin.

The memory of the Spindle Witch's voice whispered in her mind.

A little bit of me, a little bit of the Forest of Thorns, and a little bit of you, Red.

Red grimaced. Once you'd let something that dark inside you, maybe you never got it out.

Through a ragged curtain doorway, she caught a glimpse of people moving inside one of the cottages. A young woman with dark ringlet curls stood with her bare arms outstretched, while three other women circled her, painstakingly binding line after line of ink onto her tawny skin. Red could see the black strings of letters curling up from the faded pages of crumbling old books singed along the warped spines.

Red shivered. She couldn't get used to the way the Witches of Everlynd used magic as if it were nothing. She'd spent a lifetime hating and fearing magic—her own most of all. The Paper Witch had explained that they were preserving books rescued from the fires of Everlynd. Red had bitten her tongue before she snapped that they needn't bother.

The Spindle Witch had Briar Rose. Soon she'd have the Siphoning Spells. And then the whole world would be cracked and withered at her feet. Who would care about a few old books then?

Something hurtled through the air. Red jerked out of her thoughts as an overripe tomato smashed against the wall beside her, splattering her face. She whipped around, but she couldn't tell who had thrown it—no one would meet her eyes, everyone on the street pointedly looking away.

"Hey! Who did that?"

Suddenly, Shane was beside her, stepping between Red and the crowd. Red didn't know where she'd come from, but she wasn't surprised. The huntsman was always good at sniffing her out. Shane's worn red coat was dusty, her short hair tousled and her fair face flushed like she'd just come from sparring. Red had liked the way Shane's ash-brown hair looked twisted up in a braid, but she had to admit short hair suited Shane, too, bringing out the sharpness of her features.

Shane's eyes blazed as she glared out across the street. "If you have something to say, come right out and say it!" she shouted.

No one took her up on the offer. But Red could just imagine what they were thinking. The same whispers she'd heard a hundred times before.

She's a traitor. A monster.

She'll bring the Spindle Witch down on us.

Shane looked like she was about one second from shaking everyone in the street down for their vegetables. Red made a disgusted sound in her throat.

"Just let it go." She ducked under Shane's outstretched arm, marching off before the huntsman could make a scene and worsen her already rotten reputation.

"Red, wait up!" Shane caught her at the corner, tugging her by the elbow into a narrow alley with ivy-choked walls. "Are you okay?"

Red shot her a withering look. "It's a tomato. I think I'll survive."

The ax strapped between Shane's shoulder blades glinted as she crossed her arms. "Still. Fewer people would throw stuff if you brought your guard dog along."

In spite of herself, Red's lips twitched into a little smile. "Probably. But I haven't taught you to come when I whistle yet, so . . ."

"Hey." Shane scrunched her nose. "I told you to stop comparing me to Cinzel."

"And I told you to stop growling at people," Red returned.

For just a second, tucked up close to Shane, she could forget it all: the whispers, the cold knot in her chest as she walked this place she didn't belong. But as soon as she turned her head, it was right there again. A cluster of soldiers in Red Ember cloaks threw Red a dirty look, but they hurried on when they caught sight of Shane right beside her shooting them an even dirtier look in return. Red pushed her hood back, scrubbing at the slick splatter of the tomato on her cheek.

"That's not a very good way to make friends, you know. Siding with the traitor." She tried to keep her voice light, but if Shane's expression was anything to go by, she failed miserably.

"They're wrong about you," Shane said, her voice serious and soft.

Red's smile turned bitter. "Oh, no, Shane. Never forget— I am a traitor. Just because I'm here now doesn't mean I don't deserve everything they throw at me."

Shane pulled her sleeve over her palm and wiped the

tomato splatter off Red's face, her knuckles lingering soft against Red's cheek. "Just give them time. They don't know you like I do."

Red laughed hollowly. Who did Shane think she knew? Red didn't even know who she was anymore. She'd lost herself up in that tower. In one fell swoop, she'd lost her past, she'd lost her future—she'd lost the shackles that bound her, too. But she didn't feel free. She just felt empty, some great cavern inside her filled with nothing but ash and acrid smoke.

She'd left the Spindle Witch. She'd done Shane's *right thing*. But doing that hadn't made her into Shane, eternally brave and selfless. Red was still afraid. She was still weak. She still wanted to crawl away and hide with the few things she treasured.

And here Shane was, still looking at Red like she saw something beautiful in her, when Red felt like she was just scars and bruises and open wounds.

She wanted to lean into that touch, to put her hand over Shane's and surrender to the heat of the girl's fingers against her face. Instead, she flinched away, walking fast down the alley in the direction of the tower. She wasn't at all surprised when Shane fell into step beside her.

Whoever Shane had fallen in love with—the daring relic hunter, the playful thief, the mysterious stranger in the scarlet dress—Red wasn't that person anymore. And she didn't think she could take the moment Shane realized that and walked away.

"So where are you headed?" Shane asked as they ducked under a sweep of ruined tarp.

Red's face twisted, a sour taste in the back of her throat. "Perrin called me to the tower."

Shane looked grave. "I'll go with you."

"Of course you will," Red muttered. Shane never missed an opportunity to stick her nose in Red's business. But she didn't protest. Where she was going, she didn't really want to be alone.

They walked in silence until they reached a wide-bottomed tower with dark lichen crawling up its thick walls. Red could see Perrin waiting for her, leaning back against the door in a cream-colored tunic with billowing sleeves. His short dark hair had grown out into curls, and his brown skin glowed in the warm afternoon light. He offered Red a strained smile.

"You're taking guard duty now?" Shane asked.

Perrin shook his head. "I sent the guard away. I thought Red could use a little privacy—and a friendly face."

Shane snorted. "Yeah, no one's ever accused Ivan of being friendly."

Red's heart guttered at the thought of the man imprisoned inside that tower. Ivan, her father's right hand.

After the fight in the rain, Red thought she'd seen the last of Ivan forever. But a few days after she and Shane and Perrin arrived, Everlynd's scouts had found him holed up in an abandoned Witch Hunter outpost, feverish and clinging to life, and dragged him back to the camp for questioning. Red had kept her distance—until now.

"Why did you call me here?" she demanded.

Perrin scrubbed a hand through his hair. "He's asking for you. You don't have to see him, but I wanted you to have the choice. Before it's too late."

Too late? Red crossed her arms tight, holding herself against the instinct to run. "And the council's going to let us traitors talk?" she bit out. The steward, Nikor, had warned Red in no uncertain terms to stay away from the prisoner. Not that she was eager for a reunion.

Perrin's face turned grim. "I thought you knew." He threw a glance at Shane. "He's dying, Red. Very soon. They've gotten all they can from him. They don't care what he does anymore."

"And he's asking . . . for me?"

Perrin nodded. "All night."

Red bit her lip, warring with herself. She had nothing to say to the man who'd ruled her nightmares for so many years. She couldn't imagine what he had to say to her. And yet some horrible curiosity kept her rooted there, her eyes fixed on the door.

Shane took a step toward her. "You don't have to do this. You don't owe him anything." Her voice was quiet, though her fierce eyes never left Red's.

Red took a deep breath. "It's not for him. It's for me."

She had so many ghosts. Maybe she could lay this one to rest.

Shane scowled, but she didn't say anything as Perrin swung the door open, leading them up the rot-chewed stairs to the second floor. Shafts of sunlight stabbed through the slit windows into the dark belly of the tower. Red felt her heart knocking against her chest, her skin prickling with fear and revulsion.

There was only one door at the top of the steps. Perrin hesitated, his hand on the ornate knob. "The Witches have done what they can. He's not in any pain."

"Too bad," Shane muttered as they stepped inside.

The room beyond had been modified into a prison. The giant metal bars of what had once been a gate were braced between the stone walls to make a cell. Each rusted iron bar tapered to an elaborate spear point, and their sharp tips dug into grooves in the floor. Red peered at a small pallet, a chair, and a few other amenities the right hand of the Witch Hunters didn't deserve. The sour smell of sweat on the air made her want to gag.

Ivan was already on his feet, as though he had known she was coming. He was as tall and horrifying as she remembered, but his body had turned gaunt, his pale skin sunken and deathly white under his scars. His chest and left arm were wrapped in coarse bandages, and she caught streaks of dark bruises between them, his veins purple and swollen under the skin. He should have been too weak to move. But he'd dragged himself up so he could look down at her through the bars.

"Well, well." Ivan's face split in a hooked grin. "The little Witch. I thought you'd be too scared to face me."

"I have nothing to fear from you anymore," Red bit out. She forced herself not to flinch as Ivan limped toward her, leaning his bandaged shoulder against the bars.

"You're very brave with these foul Witches behind you. But I don't think the marks I left come off that easy."

His eyes slid to the collar of her cloak. Red couldn't stop herself from slapping a hand over the sealing tattoo. The two snakes seemed to burn and writhe under her fingers— just as hot and painful as the day he inked the mark onto her neck.

"Hey!" Shane banged the bars, forcing Ivan back a step. "You asked to see her. Whatever you want, spit it out."

Red felt Perrin move to stand beside her. Ivan glowered at Shane, his fingers twitching as if missing his saw-toothed blade. His eyes flicked back to Red.

"You're a witness to your father's death." Ivan wiped at a crust of blood around his mouth. "Is what they said true? The Spindle Witch killed him and took his place?"

Red lifted her chin. "Yes. She killed him. And she manipulated you, and all the other Witch Hunters, for years and years."

Ivan slammed his hand against the wall. "That's why he sent me away from the Eyrie. The Witch knew I'd uncover her deception."

Watching his face contort, Red felt a rush of something sick and hot in her chest. It was power, she realized. For the first time, she had the power to wound him the way he'd wounded her.

"You lost, Ivan." Red threw her hands out, gesturing to the cell. "The High Lord is dead, and you're dying. Everything you worked for has come to nothing. You promised to kill me—but in spite of everything you did, I'm still alive. And now it's my turn to make you a promise. You're going to die alone in this cell, nothing but a pawn for the Witch you hated. And not one single person is going to mourn you."

The words came sharp and venomous. She felt Perrin's soft hand on her arm like a warning, but she shook it off.

"The Spindle Witch used you," Red taunted. "How does that feel? Bitter? Painful?"

Ivan's mouth twisted in a sneer. "You tell me, little girl."

The words hit her like a slap. Red pulled back, realizing suddenly what she must look like to Shane and Perrin. Standing there goading him, every ugly part of herself on display. She backed away from the cell, clenching one hand into her skirt—the hand scarred by the Spindle Witch's rod.

Ivan had been her father's right hand. And Red in turn became the right hand of the Spindle Witch. He had done cruel and horrible things to her, and she'd grown up to do things that were just as horrible and cruel to someone else. Looking at him was like looking in a monstrous mirror.

Ivan's eyes glowed in the sickly light as he bent toward her, heavy with menace. "We're not so different, are we, Assora?"

Red shook her head hard. "That's not my name anymore."

His laugh rattled in his throat. "It will always be your name. It's in your blood. Did your father ever tell you where it came from?"

Red's lip trembled. "It was the last thing my mother said before she died."

She had heard the story many times when she was little, and then one day, her father abruptly stopped telling it, his face curdling in fury whenever Red asked. Her beautiful mother had carried Red through a difficult pregnancy with the grit of a warrior and survived for three days after, holding Red close and crying. With her last breath, she'd named the baby Assora. In the loneliest hours of her childhood, Red had clung to the scraps of that story and the mother she had never known. The one person who hadn't lived long enough to despise her.

"So he never told you the truth."

Red's head snapped up.

Ivan spat onto the floor, a rust-colored stain. "He didn't find out until later. *Assora* was the name of your mother's ancestor—the true name of the Snake Witch. You're descended from her, one of the vilest creatures that ever lived."

Perrin stiffened, and Shane sucked in a surprised breath.

"What?" Red whispered. She felt ice-cold, her skin prickling as the words raced through her head. *Assora . . . the Snake Witch . . .* "You're lying," she choked out. But the horrible gleam in his eyes said otherwise.

"Your mother wasn't using her last breath to name her precious child. She was confessing to her monstrous lineage." Ivan's brutal gaze burned into her. "I only regret I didn't kill you right then, as soon as I knew what you really were."

Blood roiled in Red's ears. All the pain and bitterness rushed up in her like bile, and she threw herself around Shane, bashing her hands into the bars. "Whatever I am, you made me!"

Then Shane's arms were around her waist, wrenching her backward out of Ivan's reach. "Red!" Shane shouted. But it was too late. The damage was done.

Red tore herself away from Shane and ran. She didn't look back, almost slipping on the narrow stairs as she fled from the monster in the cell and the monster he reflected back at her. She didn't care who saw her running through the Everlynd camp with tears streaming down her face. No one could imagine worse than the truth.

She'd been born a monster. Lost part of herself to Ivan.

Sold part of herself to the Spindle Witch. Maybe no part of Red really belonged to her anymore.

Distantly, she realized her palm was slick, the bandage stained with blood. She must have split the scab open on the bars of Ivan's cell. Or maybe the Spindle Witch's mark was a wound that would simply never heal.

3

⟶⟫⟫⟫—✦—⟪⟪⟪⟵

Shane

SHANE STALKED ACROSS the Everlynd camp, stomping through the remnants of a fallen scaffold and banging the splintered boards out of her way. She longed to put her fist through something more substantial—like Ivan's skull.

Her head was still reeling from everything she'd heard in the tower. And she wasn't the only one. From the way the blood drained out of Red's face as Ivan poured out the truth about her bloodline, he'd cut her deep. Shane had hesitated only long enough to trade worried looks with Perrin, and then she'd taken off after Red, her guts in a knot. She lost the girl in the crowded streets. But she knew where Red would go. The only place she ever went.

Shane kicked a dusty bucket into the wall. She hated being stuck in this camp, just waiting for something to do. Her whole body felt tense and useless. And she was so angry.

At Ivan. At herself. And at her partner, too, for getting them into this mess.

Shane still burned with rage whenever she remembered Fi framed in the window of the watchtower, looking back at her with that resigned expression as she told Shane there was no other way. There was *always* another way. There was no *working with* a monster like the Spindle Witch, not even to save Briar Rose. Shane was going to have to save her partner from the worst enemy Fi had ever had: herself.

Even if she had to do it alone. The people of Everlynd were preparing for battle at the speed a whole kingdom moved. By the time they actually decided what to do—assuming they did anything at all—it would be too late to save Fi. And probably the rest of them, too.

She drew up short as she reached the edge of Red's little camp, tucked just inside the trees. Everlynd was admittedly short on supplies, but still Shane couldn't help thinking Red's camp was sadder than it needed to be. Just a scrappy sheet of canvas fashioned into a makeshift tent, a dented cookpot beside the stream, and an uneven stone ring around the charred hunks of her last smoky fire.

Red wasn't hard to spot. She sat hunched on the decaying log beside the stream, turning something in her hand. Her father's Witch Hunter pendant, Shane realized, as the topaz gem caught the light. Red pushed her curls away from her tan face. She wasn't crying anymore, but Shane's heart twisted at the tearstains on her flushed cheeks. The wolf lay at her side, his massive head pressed against her thigh. Shane didn't think she was imagining the reproachful look in his yellow-gold eyes.

Red turned the amulet over, her fingers tracing the name engraved into the back. *Assora.* Her bloody bandage left a dark smudge on the beaten silver chain.

As Shane stepped into the camp, Cinzel growled—the first warning growl she'd gotten from that mutt in a long time. She stopped a foot short of the log, as close as she dared without getting nipped.

"Are you okay?" Shane asked. Red shot her a venomous look. "Well, you're obviously not *okay*, but . . . you're bleeding."

Red glanced down at her palm. Her lips curled in a sharp, humorless smile. "This? Trust me, I've had worse."

Shane swallowed, remembering all the *worse* Red was probably talking about. Since the first time they met, Shane had been trying to mend those old wounds, all the hurt Red wouldn't let her touch. She wondered if Red would ever run to her instead of running away.

She cleared her throat. "Well, it'll be no problem for me to take care of, then. Where are those bandages the Paper Witch gave you?"

Red arched an eyebrow, nudging her pack with her toes. "You should know. You're out here often enough, begging me to patch you up."

Shane didn't remember doing any begging, but she bit down the urge to argue about it. She'd been sparring her way through the warriors of the Red Ember, just to blow off a little steam. Red complained every time Shane showed up covered in cuts and bruises, but she never turned her away. And if Shane sometimes let herself get roughed up a little more than necessary so she had an excuse to come out here, well . . . that was between her and the last guy who'd chipped a tooth on her fist.

She dug into Red's pack for the linen bandages and the squat little jar of salve. It smelled earthy, like oak and juniper, and stung like seawater on split knuckles, but the Paper Witch swore by it. Cinzel was taking up the best spot, but Shane wasn't tactless enough to try to move him off Red's lap. Gingerly, she knelt next to Red, watching the girl's face as she unwound the stained bandages.

"Let me know if it hurts."

Red gave her a flat look. "It's an open wound. Of course it hurts."

"I meant let me know if I hurt you . . . you know, more than I have to."

Red's eyebrows shot up, confirming exactly how ridiculous that sounded. Shane grimaced. In moments like these, she wished she had a little more of that tact and delicacy that just oozed from people like the Paper Witch. But all she had was herself—blunt and honest. She smoothed salve into the jagged gash, Red's soft hand flinching in hers.

Red let out a long breath. "I understand it now. What changed my father. Why he turned on me."

Shane's head jerked up. But Red wasn't looking at her. Her eyes had turned distant, locked on the pendant gleaming against her skirt.

"My father always feared the magic inside of me. He was strict—so angry whenever he caught me playing with the ancient relics in the Eyrie or paging through the stolen spell books." Red shook her dark curls out of her face. "I can't even remember how many nights I spent down in the dungeon, begging him to let me out, promising I'd never do it again. But he could be kind, too, when he wanted to be. Until the day I found the wolf pups."

Shane swallowed hard. She remembered Red saying she and Cinzel had been together for years. And something else, something she'd whispered while staring at the saw-toothed swords strapped to Ivan's broad back: *I had two wolf pups. Now I have one.*

Cinzel whined. Red blinked her wet eyes, digging her fingers into the thick fur of his ruff.

"I found them crawling in the bracken—orphaned, starving. I sang to them. I took them in. And I made them my own." Her lips twisted in a bitter smile. "Of all the Great Witches, the Witch Hunters hated the Snake Witch most, so terrified of her connection with beasts. My father must have seen it in me then. Her blood. Her magic. After that, he gave up on torturing me, or saving me, or whatever he was trying to do. He ordered Ivan to kill me and the wolves."

Shane's eyes widened. "How did you get away?"

"Well, we didn't all get away, did we?" Red murmured, tracing a soft thumb down the wolf's ears. "My father didn't have the stomach to kill me himself. He drugged me, and Ivan carried me into the Forest of Thorns. But I woke up. Cinzel's brother, he tried to protect me, and . . ." Red choked on the rest, her face twisted in disgust. "And all of it. Everything— it was because of this name and this legacy. A legacy I don't even want!"

She yanked her arm back and threw the pendant with all her might into the woods. They both flinched at the crack of something breaking.

If Ivan was still alive when this conversation was over, Shane was going to march back to that tower and kill him herself. She had to concentrate on not binding Red's hand too tight. "Your father," she said through gritted teeth, "he was—"

"A monster?" Red cut in, with a mocking smile.

"You're nothing like him," Shane insisted. Red threw her a look, like that wasn't so clear from where she was sitting. Shane's temper flared. "Look, if it hurts that much, just forget it. Your father, and the Snake Witch—leave it all behind."

Red's eyes flashed. "Like you did, you mean? It must be so easy when there's an ocean between you and everything you want to forget." Then her mouth fell open, as if the words had come out a little crueler than she intended. She grabbed Shane's wrist before she could pull away. "I didn't mean that."

But she was right, Shane realized. The things she'd left behind in Steelwight—she hadn't really forgotten them. She'd just turned tail and run.

She had never regretted giving up her birthright and leaving Steelwight behind. Leaving had been the right choice. But she'd done it the wrong way, disappearing in the night with no word to her brother. She hadn't given Shayden a chance to understand, or even to say goodbye.

For the first time, she found herself thinking that maybe when all of this was over, she'd go back to Steelwight—not as the heir of Rockrimmon, but as a hero of Andar, a wandering warrior just dropping in to scandalize the gossips. She wanted to feel the sting of the salt air on her cheeks again, to see the heir's iron circlet on Shayden's head, to know if he and Kara were as disgustingly happy together as she'd wanted them to be. It would be just like old times, with her grandmother shouting in one ear and Shayden crying in the other. And then she'd kick her muddy boots up on the long feast table and tell her stories, like all the grizzled warriors who used to come through her father's hall, every adventure life or death, every battle a great victory.

And Red would be there, too—slipping Cinzel the best morsels under the table, splashing in the moss-ringed tide-pools and shrieking at the cold water on her bare toes. Shane would take Red to the ocean, just as she'd promised, and show her how the waves sparkled like liquid silver at first light. Watch the red sun come up in beautiful brown eyes no longer haunted by pain or anger or fear or regret.

Shane scraped a hand through her short hair. "You're right," she admitted, holding Red's gaze. "I got to run, and you don't get to. Right now, the only way out is through. But I promise, on the other side of this, I'll take you away, and you'll never have to look back again."

Red sighed. "You do love making those impossible promises." But there was a little warmth in her eyes again, her lips pursed into a tiny smile.

Right then, Shane wanted to close the distance between them and kiss Red, like she hadn't since the night before the battle for the Eyrie. There had been a promise in that moment, too, a delicious possibility of forever. One that had made Shane determined to save them both at all costs.

But all costs had turned out to be more than she ever could have imagined.

"Red," Shane started. "Listen. I—"

Cinzel's ears flickered suddenly, swiveling toward a sound in the trees—the crackle of a stick breaking underfoot. Then he bounded out of Red's lap, lunging into the bushes to slobber all over the intruder. It was Perrin. He stumbled, tripping over the wolf's big bushy tail.

"Guess there's no sneaking up on you two," Perrin joked. The Paper Witch followed him out of the brush, looking remarkably dignified for someone who'd just been eavesdropping behind a tree. His silver-blond hair was tied back from his pale face by a simple white ribbon adorned with a tiny silver bell that tinkled above his sky-blue robes.

Shane shot Perrin a look. "You have the worst timing."

"Sorry," Perrin said sheepishly. "We were going to wait until you were finished, but Cinzel had other ideas."

Red got to her feet, scowling again. "I should have known you'd run straight to the Paper Witch and tell him—"

"That you'd just been to see Ivan and this isn't a good time," Perrin rushed out, his eyes wide as he cut her off. "I know. But it's urgent."

"Not that," Shane snorted. "That she's actually—ow!" She broke off as Red's heel came down hard on her toes. Red and Perrin were both glaring like they wanted to brain her with one of the sooty rocks from the campfire. Shane rubbed her throbbing foot against her calf. "I mean . . . yeah. That Ivan thing," she muttered. Apparently, Red's connection to the Snake Witch was a secret—and a sore subject.

The Paper Witch looked utterly unconvinced. "Whatever you are all trying to conceal from me, it will have to wait. We have more pressing matters."

He reached into his sleeve, pulling out the butterfly pin and dangling it between his fingers. It had been a while since

Shane had seen that annoying little relic she and Red had retrieved from the study of the Lord of the Butterflies. Three tiny chains dangled from the end, one empty, while the other two held delicate butterfly charms that clinked softly together.

"I took this to the Seer Witch," the Paper Witch explained. "She had a vision as she has not in many years. One of the Spindle Witch's demise."

Shane crossed her arms. "I hope she told you how it works."

"That, unfortunately, was not part of the vision."

"Figures," Shane muttered.

Perrin and the Paper Witch were trading looks in that annoying way people did when they'd already been talking and planning behind other people's backs.

"There is one person who certainly knows how to use it," the Paper Witch said.

Perrin's face stretched into knowing smile. "That would be the Witch who originally constructed the pin."

"Wait a minute . . ." Shane said suspiciously.

"I believe you met him once already," the Paper Witch said mildly.

"Impossible," Red scoffed, shaking her head. "The Lord of the Butterflies disappeared from that mirror after he gave us the pin."

"Exactly." The Paper Witch's eyes twinkled. "He disappeared from *that* mirror, so we will simply have to find him in another. We'll need to go back to Everlynd."

"Everlynd." Red crossed her arms. "Didn't the scouts say that place is still crawling with Witch Hunters?"

"I'm in," Shane said. She didn't care how dangerous it was. If there was another shard of the Lord of the Butterflies out there, she'd find him, even if she had to kick her way through every vault, storeroom, and root cellar in Everlynd to do it.

4

Fi

FI STOOD AT the window, holding a single flickering candle and watching the roiling night outside. Breathy wisps of fog slid over the windowsill, hissing as they met the warmer air beyond. It was time.

In the late afternoon, mist had rolled in over the great cage of mountains, slithering between the jagged peaks like an unwinding snake. By the time the sun set, the mist blanketed everything, sinking into the valley until the Spindle Witch's spire was shrouded in fog, the view from the windows an unbroken wall of white. As though the tower were cut off from the rest of the world.

Fi had been waiting for a moment like this since her ill-fated trip to the Spindle Witch's chamber three days before. The Witch had been watching her closely, and so had all of her crows. Fi had seen them flying around the tower, sometimes perching on the wide windowsill, tipping their heads and studying her with impenetrable black eyes. But there was no way anything could see through this haze, and the room upstairs had been silent all day. This might be her only chance to get back to the mirror.

The swallowtail engravings on the mirror were the last hint Fi had needed to put the clues together. Especially with what Shane had told her of the Witch who hid his knowledge by leaving pieces of himself inside mirrors.

Fi traced the butterfly on her palm and then squeezed her hand into a fist. She retrieved the folded paper from the small desk. Her single candle shivered in the dark.

The mist was spreading softly across her floor, bringing the chill with it. Fi left her feet bare, letting the prickling cold keep her alert as she crept up to the Spindle Witch's room. She popped the little hook easily this time. As the door swished open, the mist swirled and churned around her. The fog had beaten her to the Spindle Witch's room, and the tower was thick with it, the heavy air making it hard to breathe.

Fi's candle burned a path through the silvery cloud as she crept to the vanity. This time, she sat carefully on the padded stool, setting the candle next to the brush and scissors and looking into her fractured reflection. Her face was shadowed in the firelight.

"You're the Lord of the Butterflies, aren't you? Or at least a piece of him," she said, lifting her hand and uncurling her fingers to reveal the swallowtail mark. "This is what you meant when you said I had something of yours."

"Clever little visitor." Fi's reflection disappeared, leaving the one-eyed man sitting just as she was at the vanity. Long strings of unbrushed hair fell around his face, and his black-and-red robes stood out against the same mist that seethed behind Fi. "Glad to see you survived the drop." His smile grew wider, distorted by a crack in the mirror.

"Did you know someone would catch me?" Fi asked.

There was something careless about the man's expression as he shrugged. "I knew it was a kindness either way."

The thought made Fi's chest tighten. The Lord of the Butterflies had been perfectly willing to kill her. He had also implied there was a fate worse than death in this tower. Fi didn't want to dwell on either possibility. Instead, she held the butterfly mark close to the mirror.

"This curse—it's the same one that was cast on you. Can you remove it?"

The Lord of the Butterflies leaned forward with an intense look of interest. "Mm . . . I'm afraid this was after my time." He lifted both of his hands, revealing smooth palms empty of curse marks. "You see, I'm only a fragment of myself left in this mirror, frozen at one particular moment like a fossil trapped in amber. That curse, though . . ." He reached forward, and for a fleeting moment, Fi felt the phantom sensation of fingers running across her palm. "What a clever bit of spell work. The magic used to create it is definitely mine, but why would I cast a curse on myself?" He paused to fix Fi with an amused smile. "On the other hand, I do know of two Witches powerful enough to use my own magic against me."

"Queen Aurora and the Spindle Witch," Fi filled in. She had gathered as much from the letters she'd pieced together in the library of Everlynd, which had given her a glimpse into the relationship between the Lord of the Butterflies and the first Queen of Andar. From what she'd gleaned, it hadn't ended particularly well.

"She was *Princess* Aurora when I first met her," the man said. His expression softened, almost fond.

Fi felt a curl of disappointment that it wouldn't be so easy, but she should have realized that if the Lord of the Butterflies had been able to remove the curse himself, he probably wouldn't have disappeared into exile. Besides, she had far more important things to worry about right now. Fi shot a glance at the ghostly room behind her, the child's bed veiled beneath a shroud of silver mist.

"The Spindle Witch was the girl locked in this tower, wasn't she?"

"Of course," the man said. "We found her here. Aurora and I. Long ago."

Fi filed that little tidbit away for later. "If that's true," she pressed, leaning forward over the vanity, "then why are you hiding from her?"

The Lord of the Butterflies sighed heavily, his face turning so that all Fi could see was his lips thinned beneath a curtain of hair. "The two of us can't meet anymore," he said. "She hunted down this mirror and dragged it back here many years ago, seeking my knowledge. But I'm afraid she wants something that I cannot give her."

"The Siphoning Spells," Fi guessed.

The Lord of the Butterflies didn't answer, but the tight line of his lips said it all.

"Why is she so desperate to find them? She's so powerful already," Fi whispered. The Spindle Witch had crushed the Witches of Andar, left the kingdom in ashes, and come through without so much as a scratch. Fi thought about the monster girl in the story, trapped in a dark spire. "I mean, she's clearly able to leave this tower . . ."

The Lord of the Butterflies held up a finger. "Not fully," he said with a shake of his head. "A part of her will always be trapped here . . . a very *small* part."

He looked unbearably sad as he said the last, and Fi felt cold, just as she had when she ran her hands over the carvings on the wall. She didn't need to know the whole story to know that whatever was dark and terrible about the Spindle Witch had been born here, in this awful, lonely prison. But Fi was just as sure that the Witch had to be stopped now, before she wrought more horror and destruction.

Suffering begets suffering. That was what the Paper Witch had warned Fi just after she ended up with the Butterfly Curse. *Hurt has a way of consuming from the inside out when left to fester in dark places.*

Fi sucked in a breath, making the flame of the candle shudder. "Do you know how to kill her?" she asked quietly.

The Lord of the Butterflies fixed Fi with a disappointed look. "That is entirely the wrong question."

Whatever else he might have said was interrupted by a great gust of wind. Black feathers surged out of the mist as a flock of crows burst through the window, cawing and scratching. They knocked over the spinning wheel, sending the basket of golden thread tumbling across the floor, and then suddenly the Spindle Witch was rising from the haze, striding forward with an expression of pure rage beneath her veil. The train of the long black dress followed her like a shadow, and her long nails shredded the delicate lace of her skirts. All the mist in the room seemed to burn up at once.

"I knew you were still in there," she hissed, stalking toward the vanity. Fi stumbled to her feet, kicking the stool away and trying to escape, but the Spindle Witch wasn't even looking at her. She was looking at the now-blank face of the mirror. "I should have realized you'd reveal yourself to a girl like her." The Witch's nails raked against the glass. "Come out," she crooned, dragging her fingers over her own splintered reflection.

Fi's back hit the cold wall. All of her limbs felt numb. She held her breath, praying she'd go unnoticed.

"Come out," the Spindle Witch beckoned again. Then she wrenched away from the mirror, seizing Fi by the back of her neck. She hadn't even used her thread—her sharp nails cut into Fi's skin as the Spindle Witch dragged her forward, her grip so strong Fi could barely struggle.

Bony fingers dug into the flesh at the base of her skull until she felt like her neck would snap. Then the Spindle Witch whipped around and slammed Fi's head against the mirror. Another crack slid across the surface. Fi gasped, dizzy and disoriented as the Spindle Witch ground her face into the cold glass.

"Come out," the Witch warned, "or watch her die from in there!"

There was a hint of warm air on Fi's cheek for a second, like a breath, and then the sensation of a strange hand carding through her hair. She was still hazy, but it was no longer her own reflection she was pressed against. The Lord of the Butterflies had returned.

"Temper, temper, little spider," he mocked.

Just as suddenly as the Spindle Witch had grabbed Fi, she released her, tossing her aside. Fi managed to catch the edge of the vanity, stumbling but staying on her feet. The Spindle Witch rose before the mirror, a victorious smile splitting her painted lips. "I've waited a lifetime for this, and now you're going to tell me everything."

The Lord of the Butterflies didn't seem fazed. He just shook his head with a knowing look. "Oh, my sweet little Witch," he murmured, "you've never had the power to make me do anything."

His green eye flickered to Fi for one moment, his expression piercing into her. Then the black veil over the Spindle Witch's head burst into flames, a crimson fire that enveloped her and chewed through the curls of black lace. At the same time, the Lord of the Butterflies in the mirror seemed to shimmer, fading and turning to smoke.

"There," he said, just a wisp of a ghost. "Now you look like the girl I remember."

The crimson fire burned itself out at the same moment as the Lord of the Butterflies disappeared, leaving the reflection of a young blond woman in the mirror. Fi stared. The Spindle Witch was painfully beautiful right now, clearly flush with magic. Her skin was pale as porcelain, and her blue eyes were wide with long black lashes—just like the girl in the pages of the storybook.

The Spindle Witch let out a shriek of fury as she pounded on the mirror. She dragged the bone drop spindle from her sleeve and drove it viciously into the surface of the mirror, shattering it out of its frame.

Splinters of glass crashed to her feet. The golden hair that had been coiled around her head like a crown ripped free, and a long golden braid slithered over her shoulder, falling almost to the floor. So long that once it might have trailed from the window of the tower . . .

Fi gasped as the pieces came together. The brush, the scissors, the girl in the story, and most of all, the spindle and the golden thread. It wasn't thread at all. It was golden hair—the golden hair of the Spindle Witch, which she had learned to twist and spin to make her spells. Those thousands of strands of gold in the forest below were from the girl who had dangled her hair from the tower. That was how she had stayed alive for centuries, sucking the life from the creatures of the forest. And if she'd had this terrible power from the moment she was born, maybe she *had* killed everyone who had ever loved her . . . whether she was a monster or not.

Fi's heart warred between pity and horror.

"You!" The Spindle Witch rounded on her. "I knew you were working against me, but I didn't care as long as you were useful. You've just outlived that usefulness."

Golden thread gathered at the Witch's fingers. Fi stepped back, cornered against the cold stone of the tower with nowhere to run.

"The code—Camellia's code—" she stuttered.

"Don't think you can keep playing that card." The Spindle Witch wrenched up her hands, throwing out her fingers. The golden thread shot toward Fi, winding around her arms, pulling tight and slicing into the skin around her wrists. A single thread that shone like a piano wire looped around her neck.

"I've solved it!" Fi said desperately, as she felt the thread tightening. "I have the whole code!"

The Spindle Witch stepped forward with a swish of black skirts. Without her veil, it was easy to see the malice shining in her eyes. The thread had stopped squeezing Fi's neck, but it remained painfully tight.

"Then give it to me right now. The whole code."

Fi's first instinct was to try to make the Spindle Witch some kind of deal, or at least beg for her life. She swallowed it down. She had a feeling that if the next words out of her mouth weren't Camellia's riddle, she would be dead.

"In the forest of spines
Where the thorns gather
The shine of Andar's most precious rose
Reveals the hidden butterfly."

The thread slid against Fi's neck, and she closed her eyes, wondering if those would be her last words. Instead, she felt the slither of the thread coming free, and she gasped, able to breathe again.

"It's a riddle," Fi hurried on, bracing herself against the sudden weakness in her knees. "I haven't solved all of it, but I know what one of the lines means. 'Andar's most precious rose' has to be the ruby in Queen Aurora's crown, buried with her in her tomb."

The Spindle Witch wound her thread back, the golden loops slowly tightening around her drop spindle. Her gaze never left Fi. "And I suppose you *coincidentally* happen to know where this tomb is."

"I know how to find it," Fi admitted.

Just giving the Spindle Witch the code would have been meaningless, after all, with nothing else to offer. The riddle alone would have saved Fi's life only for as many seconds as it took her to gasp it out. Fi had to keep something back, something to make sure she was still useful.

"There are old maps, scores of them, in the library of Illya on the border of Darfell," she went on. "They map out all the ruins in Andar. One of them points to Queen Aurora's tomb. With that, I'm sure I could get there."

"How very irritating that you remain just useful enough to keep alive," the Spindle Witch said. She clicked her tongue. "Very well. I'll let you out of your cage to fetch me the ruby."

Fi wanted to sag with relief, but she was careful to keep her expression neutral. She didn't want to give the Witch any reason to change her mind.

"But . . ." the Spindle Witch said, drawing out the word with a smile that made Fi's neck prickle. "It seems you need a reminder of what's at stake."

She crooked her fingers. In a second, Briar appeared in the window, the fog churning around his dark wings. Fi's heart plummeted at the sight of him. Briar landed obediently at the Spindle Witch's side, waiting for a command, his face blank as if he couldn't see the wicked smirk on the woman's red lips.

Fi was shouting before she even knew why. "No! Please!"

The Spindle Witch reached out and tugged, yanking a thread Fi couldn't see. Suddenly, Briar was on the ground, writhing and screeching, clawing at the stones as pain tore through him. Fi's ears rang with his screams. Briar hadn't

56

said a word to her in weeks, and now his voice was all around her, pounding in her head until she thought she'd start screaming, too.

One wing crashed into the armoire and splintered the door, chunks of wood exploding across the floor. The Spindle Witch just laughed. When Briar tossed his head, Fi could see the knobs of his spine jutting up against the skin, his bones growing sharper under the ragged velvet coat. The skull-headed monster from her dreams flashed through Fi's mind.

For one second, fear held her in place like a chain. Then she shook free and ran for Briar, dodging the Spindle Witch's outstretched hand.

"Stop it!" she shouted. She caught one handful of Briar's coat before a leathery wing struck her in the shoulder, throwing her across the room. Fi groaned in pain but forced herself up on her elbows. She looked desperately at the Spindle Witch. "I understand. I won't try anything else. Just stop, please—you're torturing him!"

The Spindle Witch's eyes glittered. Then she twisted her fingers as though tying an invisible knot, and instantly Briar collapsed, his body heaving. Fi scrambled to his side. Golden hair hung into Briar's face, and she pushed it back from his sweaty forehead, careful of the horns. His cheekbones were sharp against her hands. But his face was still covered in smooth, pale skin, and she could feel his heart beating just as fast as hers. He was still Briar, underneath it all. Still alive.

Fi blinked back tears. "Briar . . ."

Briar stared at her. Then he wrenched away and flung himself from the windowsill, vanishing into the night. Fi raced to the window, too, but caught herself against the frame. In his current state, she wasn't at all sure Briar would save her from a second fall. The mist swirled where his wings had swept through it.

Bony fingers seized Fi's wrist. She whirled to find the Spindle Witch sneering down at her. "Continue defying me, and there will be nothing left of Briar Rose—at least nothing you would recognize. Never forget his life is in my hands. Don't disappoint me again."

"I won't," Fi promised.

The Spindle Witch released her, and Fi fell back against the wall, rubbing her wrist.

Her fingernails dug into her palms at the memory of Briar writhing on the floor. Fi hadn't forgotten the stakes. She'd left her partner, abandoned her friends, joined the Spindle Witch, and been locked away in this sinister place—and all of it, every sickening choice, was to get Briar back. Their last night, under the stars, Fi had looked into Briar's eyes and promised they would be together forever. She didn't take that promise lightly.

It was time to start fighting back against the Spindle Witch, and the Lord of the Butterflies had given her an idea how.

5

⤜⤜⤛ ⤛⤜

Shane

WITH A GROWL of frustration, Shane kicked the shelf she had just finished searching. She should have known nothing could ever be easy when it came to the Lord of the Butterflies— not even finding a little mirror where he'd supposedly left another scrap of himself.

At the impact of her foot, hand-painted porcelain vases teetered precariously, and a delicate-looking glass ball rolled off its base, tumbling toward the floor. Perrin darted forward, reaching out his long arm and snatching the bauble out of the air. Shane shot him a grateful look. It was probably those dagger-throwing reflexes that made him so agile, she decided—or maybe he just stretched a lot.

The Paper Witch gave a very disapproving cough. "We may not have found what we are looking for yet, but there are still many important and valuable items here," he admonished.

"So don't kick 'em?" Shane guessed.

Perrin laughed. "No harm done," he said, setting the glass ball back on its stand. "I think you just kicked loose a decade of dust."

As if on cue, Cinzel sneezed, snuffling and smacking his jaw unhappily. Red shot Shane a dirty look.

The hidden storeroom the five of them were currently packed into looked like it hadn't had any visitors in Shane's lifetime, if not longer. There hadn't been a single footprint on the silt-covered floorboards when they arrived, which was probably a good thing, since it meant no Witch Hunters had gotten here ahead of them. Shane almost wished someone *had* tossed the place. Finding something in the chaos left by a looter might have been easier than figuring out some batty Witch's system of organization.

Rickety shelves leaned against the storeroom walls, filled to the brim with every trinket imaginable, from jewelry to glass baubles to stone figurines, and then more mundane things, such as brass bowls and teapots. There was even a dish full of what looked like pearls, glistening and swirling with their own inner light—though the second Shane had picked one up, the spark of light flittered away like a fish disappearing into deep water. The room's dark corners were piled high with ornately carved chests and wooden crates, some of them bound with chains and sealed with sinister iron locks. At the Paper Witch's suggestion, they'd left those alone.

Something had glittered tantalizingly when the Paper Witch first lit his small lamp, but it turned out to be a piece of stained glass in a frame—not a mirror at all, much less the hand mirror they were looking for, which would have swallowtail butterflies engraved into its silver handle.

Shane supposed, ungratefully, that she ought to be happy the Witches of Everlynd had been able to give them any kind of lead at all. Scouring three hidden vaults was a lot easier than searching aimlessly through the vast ruins of the entire city of Everlynd, even if Shane was starting to think that these *treasure rooms* were mostly just filled with odds and ends nobody could figure out the purpose for, plus sentimental junk from the old days of Andar that they just couldn't bear to throw away.

Crystal goblets and delicate sculptures wobbled on the shelves every time she took a step, and Perrin had nearly suffocated when he was buried under a heap of musty tapestries. Red had been hanging back since the first silver box she opened turned out to be a music box, the sudden tinkling sound making all of them jump out of their skins while Cinzel snapped at the empty air. Now the wolf hugged close to his human, growling distrustfully at everything knee high. Shane herself had a line of red welts across her knuckles from a trick chest snapping closed on her fingers. Only the Paper Witch was unscathed.

The man sighed heavily, replacing the sapphire-studded lid of an empty container. "I do hope the Stone Witch's recollection has not led us astray," he said, guiding them back toward the sliding wall that concealed the door. Shane caught a glimpse of his worried face before he extinguished the lantern. "He was quite a bit younger when the vaults were sealed. Well, no matter—we only have one more to search."

The ancient Stone Witch looked like a fossil forgotten for more than a hundred years himself, and while Shane didn't doubt the solemn man's power, she was starting to have serious doubts about his memory. She held her tongue only because the Paper Witch had already opened the secret passageway, and if she yelled or kicked something again, she might bring Witch Hunters down on them.

Since losing their High Lord and his right hand, the Witch Hunters were in disarray. The different sects that had banded together under Red's father had severed their tenuous alliances, and infighting had broken out. Which was good, except for the part where, in the chaos, a whole mess of them had taken over giant swaths of Everlynd. From the hill above the city, with the waterfalls pounding down below them, Shane had watched the dark smoke of greasy fires rising from the ruined buildings. They were definitely not alone, and if they weren't careful, they'd be outnumbered in a hurry.

The late evening air was crisp as they tramped back up the ruined stairway, sticking close to the wall. Shapes loomed out of the dark, mangled statues with char streaked down their arms and faces. The Paper Witch paused in the burnt-out husk of the entryway, little flecks of ash raining down as he gripped the blackened doorway.

"The final vault is in the very heart of Everlynd. Shane and I will go alone," he said. "Perrin, take Red to the Reflecting Chamber at the edge of the city and keep watch there for us."

"But . . ." Perrin started to protest. Whatever he saw in the Paper Witch's expression stopped him. "Fine. Looks like you're with me, cutie," he said, tickling Cinzel under his furry chin. "And your human, too." He gave Red a wink.

Red rolled her eyes fondly. Shane was a little jealous Perrin had been able to get a genuine smile out of her.

"Be careful," Shane said, as Red slipped past her.

"Me?" Red quirked her lips. "I've got the very dangerous job of hiding. You're the one walking straight into the teeth of the Witch Hunters."

"Worried about me?" Shane asked, raising an eyebrow.

"Just whether I'll die of boredom waiting for you to finish your *very thorough* storeroom excavation," Red said. "Yet another exciting day in the life of a treasure hunter."

There she was—just a glimmer of the old Red. Shane laughed in relief and then smothered the sound at the Paper Witch's reproving look.

"I'll hurry back," Shane promised, brushing her knuckles against Red's. Red didn't say anything, but her fingertips caught Shane's, squeezing for the barest moment. Then she and Perrin ducked out into the street, heading one way while the Paper Witch led Shane in the other, her skin still tingling from that fleeting touch.

The Paper Witch pressed a finger to his lips as they crept deeper into the city. Shane nodded, unslinging her ax just in case. The overlapping shouts of Witch Hunters were growing closer, putting Shane on edge. As silently as possible, they navigated toward the center of the city, ducking between piles of rubble. Everlynd had been beautiful, with its golden buildings and overgrown gardens shimmering in the mist of the waterfalls. Now it was hard to see anything except the scorch marks and shattered windows. Some of the structures seemed untouched, while others were nothing but blackened rubble, their doors sagging from broken hinges.

Shane shook her head. Typical Witch Hunters. They hadn't even sacked the city properly—they'd just taken what they wanted and moved on, like a roving pack of dogs.

Luckily, the Witch Hunters seemed to have settled in for the night. Shane and the Paper Witch stuck to a narrow pathway off the main roads, their footsteps echoing eerily in the empty streets. At one point, they passed close enough to a rowdy camp that Shane could hear jeers and raucous laughter rising up over the low roofs, only one stone wall separating them from the Witch Hunters' roaring bonfire. Her lips turned up in disgust, and she spat as she passed—the least she could do to get the foul taste out of her mouth.

At last, they reached a wide building with a rounded face and at least a dozen windows stacked in two glistening rows. Most of the lower ones were broken.

"Quickly," the Paper Witch said, motioning her inside.

Shane didn't need to be told twice. She ducked into the crumbling building, careful of the glass underfoot. Two long tables cluttered the back of a room studded with an array of chairs. Some were overturned, and others were missing legs—probably yanked off for firewood.

"This one's hidden under the floor," the Paper Witch explained, peeling back a richly woven rug that had seen better days. Together they rolled the rug up, tossing it aside. Shane frowned down at the wooden floor. The boards were laid tightly, and there was no obvious seam between the planks.

The Paper Witch reached into the deep pocket of his blue robe, pulling out a handful of paper scraps so small they seemed more like dust. He closed his eyes, his blond hair almost translucent in the last rays of the evening sun pouring through the windows. Gently, he blew on his hands. The paper scraps flitted down like a gust of snow, swirling one direction and then the other and finally settling into an almost invisible groove in the floor, outlining a trapdoor.

Shane whistled, impressed, leaning down to slip her fingers into the hidden groove and pry up the door. A ladder disappeared into a square of darkness below.

Something glass shattered outside, close enough to make Shane's teeth rattle. She tucked her ax back into its straps and then jumped down the ladder, not bothering to climb. It wasn't a very long drop, and in a second, Shane's feet hit sand—soft sand. A whole mound of it.

She slipped trying to get out of the way, stumbling in the dark until she caught herself on a shelf. It shook ominously, and she had a horrible vision of something old and clunky careening down on her head.

The Paper Witch clambered down the ladder in his long robes, closing the trapdoor and plunging them into darkness.

"Watch out. The ground is . . . sand." Shane didn't get it out in time. The Paper Witch gasped, clutching at the ladder rungs as his feet tried to slip out from under him.

Something jagged poked into her side. Shane felt around in the dark, trying to imagine what she was leaning against. The distinctive curve told her it was most likely a stone bust of some old Witch's head, replete with beaky nose. She ran her hand along the warped wooden shelf, her fingers sliding through piles of sand.

There was another rattle from the shelf, but this one was different, faster, almost a clicking sound. Could it be a clock, still working after all this time?

"How 'bout some light?" Shane called impatiently.

"A moment," the Paper Witch promised.

Shane felt a strange weight and tickle on her elbow. Had a lump of sand just fallen on her from somewhere? She lifted her arm, trying to peer at it through the dark. Then light sprang to the Paper Witch's lantern, and Shane came face-to-face with a scorpion, its segmented tail raised as it clicked its way up her arm.

Shane yelped, covering her hand with her coat sleeve and flinging the creature away.

"Shane! Above you!"

Shane's eyes darted up in time to see a second scorpion on the shelf next to her head, poised to strike. She let out a string of curses and grabbed the first thing that came to hand, a hunk of crystal carved into a swan. She brought the pink quartz down as hard as she could, crunching the scorpion under the base. Shane leapt back, statue at the ready.

And she called herself a treasure hunter! What kind of amateur went fishing around with their bare hands in the dark?

"Are you all right?" the Paper Witch asked.

Shane poked the body of the scorpion, only setting the crystal aside when she was sure it was dead. "Fine," she said gruffly. "But I flung one more of those things somewhere, so watch out."

"That might not be our only problem," the Paper Witch murmured, looking around with a frown. The storeroom's far wall was split by a long fissure, as though the foundation had been yanked in different directions. Sand had spilled in, burying at least half the room and blanketing most of the shelves.

"Can we even search it through this?" Shane asked.

"We'll just have to try," the Paper Witch said, sighing and rolling up his sleeves.

Shane had some unfinished business first. Ax in hand, she stalked around the room, scanning the ground for any sign of the first scorpion. Movement caught the corner of her eye, and she spun, bringing the blunt end of the ax down onto the deadly creature before it could scuttle into an overturned pot. The Paper Witch jumped at the crash.

"Scorpion's dead," Shane told him, returning the ax to its braces. "We should probably be careful, though. If those things came in with the sand, there could be more."

The Paper Witch nodded, kneeling down to blow the soft grains away from the carved lid of a gilded chest. Shane went back to the shelf she had run afoul of. She wasn't looking to pick a fight with any more scorpions, but she thought she'd seen a number of things glittering just beneath the sand.

They were silent as they searched, tension hanging over them like a held breath. Their position felt more precarious in the center of the city—and every shake, every rattle of treasure felt like it could be another scorpion. Twice Shane reached for her ax only to realize she was facing off with a painted mask or a glittering obsidian hairpiece. She felt like a fool, but she was not going to let some ugly, poisonous crea-ture get the drop on her—not a second time, anyway.

Shane searched the lower shelves, finding only knick-knacks and baubles. She paused over a little box made out of two polished shells, which held a pair of dangling ruby ear-rings. It was impossible not to imagine dark curls and flash-ing eyes. Shane was sorely tempted to pocket them until she remembered she wasn't a looter and that she wasn't supposed to be thinking about anything except the butterfly mirror.

All she had left was the highest shelf. Shane considered calling over the tall, reedy Paper Witch, but there was nothing she hated more than being reminded how short she was. She scowled, casting about until she spotted the overturned pot that had almost become a scorpion hideout. It might be just tall enough if she turned it upside down.

Shane dragged it into place, stepping up and balancing her weight on the thick clay base. She still had to push up on her tiptoes, and the pot shifted unsettlingly in the sand, but she was high enough to peer over.

The top shelf was mostly empty—a couple of bejeweled sheaths, a set of polished wooden rods wound with braided rope, and there, in the back, something shiny with a silver handle. It could be the back of a hand mirror.

Shane stretched as far as she could. Her fingers closed around the handle. Elation surged through her. She tugged it toward herself and then sucked in a horrified breath as it flipped up to face her. It was indeed the hand mirror, and right beside her in the reflection was another scorpion, its black tail taut as it scuttled straight for her.

Shane jerked backward just as the stinger flashed out. It hit the mirror with a *ping*. The pot underneath her tipped, rolling over and dumping Shane into the pile of sand beneath the ladder. Her back hit the metal rungs hard enough to knock the wind out of her. The clang echoed around the room.

"Shane, are you hurt?" the Paper Witch asked, whirling around.

"Scor . . ." she tried to wheeze out, fighting against the pressure squeezing her lungs. "Scorp . . ."

"What?" the man said. He was right next to the shelf now, and tall enough to be in range of the scorpion at the top.

"Scorpion!" she managed finally, her breath coming in a surge. "Get away from there!"

The Paper Witch ducked. The lantern swung wildly as he threw himself into the sand beside her. A tense moment passed, until Shane let out a sigh, deciding the creature had better things to do than chase them down. The Paper Witch relaxed at her side.

"I'm afraid I must agree with Red," he said, sounding a little winded. "This is a very unpleasant profession."

"It has its moments," Shane conceded with a grin. "But I found it." She lifted the mirror, waving it in the air between them. The swallowtail butterflies etched into the handle flickered in the firelight.

"Well done, Shane," the Paper Witch said, though his face said he didn't approve of the careless way she was swinging the precious relic around.

"You really think the Lord of the Butterflies is in here?" Shane asked as she handed the mirror over, happy to let the Paper Witch be the one to tuck the legendary Witch into his shirt.

"It's difficult to be certain," he said. "But this is not the place to find out."

"True," Shane agreed, with a dirty look around for more scorpions.

They stopped at the base of the ladder while the Paper

Witch put out the light. Shane climbed the rungs carefully, pausing at the top and easing open the trapdoor.

Before she'd gotten it two inches up, she was stopped by a sudden clattering of boots as someone stumbled into the room right over their heads. Shane froze, lowering the trapdoor again and listening. There was a crash, like a body being thrown into one of the giant tables, followed by raised voices and the sounds of a fight.

Shane didn't want any trouble, but she wasn't about to leave some innocent person to be slaughtered by Witch Hunters. With a quick glance down at the Paper Witch, she cracked the trapdoor just enough to get a view of what was going on. It was almost entirely dark now, the room lit only by the afterglow of the sun, but she could just make out two figures, one picking herself off the ground while the other cracked his knuckles. They were both Witch Hunters.

Shane was about to close the trapdoor and just let them have it out when she caught a snatch of what they were saying.

"After everything the High Lord worked to build, you would turn and serve the Spindle Witch?" The man who'd cracked his knuckles was speaking, his face twisted in disgust.

"I'll serve any master who can pay," the other Witch Hunter, a woman with a long braid disappearing beneath her cloak, sneered.

"I ought to gut you for that."

The woman laughed mirthlessly. "Kill me, don't kill me—it's all the same. Some have gone to her already, and more will follow."

The man let out an enraged snarl, lunging for the other Witch Hunter. A punch across the jaw sent her stumbling into the tables. The woman got up slowly, spitting blood from a busted lip. It hit the floor with a wet smack.

"Think it through, fool," she hissed. "Whoever we're serving, it's a chance to keep fighting the accursed Witches of Everlynd. To get revenge for the High Lord."

Down in the hole, Shane swallowed a curse. She had always known most Witch Hunters were no better than mercenaries. For every true believer, there were at least two vultures just in it for the coin and the blood. But they hadn't worked so hard to fracture the Witch Hunter alliance just to send them into the arms of the Spindle Witch.

The moon slipped out from behind the clouds. The man staggered back in surprise, staring at the dark hood of the woman's cloak. "You . . ." he breathed out, so low Shane barely caught it. "What happened to your eyes? They're glowing." He reared back, snatching for his sword. "This is witchcraft—"

There was a sudden wet noise. The Witch Hunter's words cut off into a gurgle. A heartbeat later, his body slumped to the ground, a knife embedded in his chest to the hilt.

"Pity you noticed that." The woman planted the toe of her boot into the fallen man's jerkin, her long fingers wrapping around the bloody dagger. "No matter. I'll find someone more receptive to my message."

Her . . . eyes? Shane's head jerked back. She'd never heard of magic like that.

Someone or *something* was up there recruiting for the Spindle Witch. She could let it alone—report what she'd heard to Everlynd and hope for the best. Or she could handle this herself, right now.

Shane surged out of the trapdoor, rolling fast across the glass and lurching to her feet. The woman's head whipped around. Her eyes were silver—a color Shane had never seen before—and they seemed to glow malevolently in the dark. Shane sucked a breath in through her teeth.

"What are you?" she growled.

A strange smile stretched across the woman's face. "Right now?" she asked. "I'm just some nameless Witch Hunter. After that? Who knows."

Shane felt a prickle on the back of her neck. What was that supposed to mean? She hated creepy Witch riddles—especially from silver-eyed murderers apparently loyal to the Spindle Witch.

The huntsman unslung her ax, hefting it between them. "I guess I'll just have to end you right now, then, nameless Witch Hunter. And after that, you can be a corpse."

The woman tipped her head back in a guttural laugh. Then all at once she jerked the knife out of the corpse and flung it at Shane, forcing her to scramble out of the way. The blade hit the wall in a spray of red. A broken chair hurtled past Shane's head. She swore, throwing herself down as splintered wood pelted her arms.

The woman was fast—faster than Shane had expected—leaping at her and stabbing viciously with her saw-toothed sword. Shane flipped over and slammed her heel into the soft part of the woman's knee. She felt the bones crunch. In one move, she swept the woman's legs out from under her, smashing the nameless Witch Hunter to the floor.

Slivers of glass from the shattered windows stabbed into the woman's arms. But her sickening smile never faltered, not even a flicker of pain crossing that leering face. That definitely wasn't normal.

Shane heaved herself up, her hands tensed and ready around her ax. The Witch Hunter uncurled slowly, staggering as she tried to stand and her knee bent at an unnatural angle. The woman scowled and leaned heavily against the wall.

"So fragile, these little bodies," she lamented. "And they wear out so quickly." Her head tipped back, silver eyes gleaming greedily as she studied Shane. "Though yours looks nice and sturdy."

Shane's guts gave a sickening lurch. "You're some kind of ghost possessing that body, aren't you?" she accused, trying to remember any of the signs her grandmother had taught her to ward off evil spirits.

"Ghost?" The woman wheezed out a chuckle. "How deliciously superstitious. I'm just a Witch, and this is nothing more than a little trick. I know all about you—Shane, the huntsman—but I had no idea you'd be so amusing."

"So you know me," Shane said through gritted teeth. "But I would definitely remember if I'd met a body-snatching creeper like you."

"Would you, really?" the woman asked. "I've been so many people. Maybe I'll try on your skin next."

Shane shuddered, imagining her body acting on its own while some Witch crawled around in her head. "Come and get it," she dared.

"I'd love to," the woman said, flashing a hint of teeth. "Unfortunately, I have other priorities tonight. But I'll see you again." Those uncanny eyes glowed like tiny moons in her shadowed face. "Tell Red she's a fool for betraying the

73

Spindle Witch. And that her days are numbered." Then the Witch Hunter slumped down the wall, crumpling into a boneless pile in the remnants of the broken chair.

Shane's heart surged into her throat. She kicked the splinters of glass aside, lugging the trapdoor open and heaving the Paper Witch up.

"What was that?" the man asked, clearly shaken.

"Bad news," Shane muttered. "We've got to get to Red and Perrin."

She just hoped they got there first.

6

Red

RED SAT ON the edge of a reflecting pool, trailing her fingers along a trellis of vines so overgrown they hung down like a heavy curtain.

The Reflecting Chamber wasn't a chamber at all, but a secluded courtyard tucked into one of the buildings untouched by fire. Glassy pools of dark water rippled under rustling trees, and the air was sharp with the tart smell of ripening limes, the first ones falling unpicked onto the stones. The rush of the nearby waterfalls filled her ears. Scarlet-winged hummingbird moths flitted between the bright trumpet flowers, so close that Red felt the buzz on her skin. Cinzel snapped at the moths as they passed, but he hadn't caught one yet.

Red braced her chin on her knees. Here in this garden, it was almost possible to imagine Everlynd wasn't half in ruins. That the entire world wasn't hanging by a tenuous spider thread.

What would it have been like to grow up here instead, Red wondered—to be descended from the Great Witches in a place where that birthright was full of promise? Would she have joined an Order of Magic, like Perrin? Impressed the other children by singing to her wolves while the pups rolled on their backs, happily crooning along? She could have learned the magic languages that were just scribbles to her. She certainly still would have broken a few hearts with her looks and her charm.

And then, one day, when a mysterious warrior with an ax strolled into town, Red would sweep forward in her scarlet cloak and offer to show her around. Buy her a drink. Maybe even use her great gift of magic to save Shane for a change.

Their first kiss would be in a garden like this one, not out in the cold and forbidding wastes with the hungry wind howling in her ears. And when they promised to be together, Red would have no doubts and no fears and no uncertainties. She wouldn't be the one flinching back every time Shane reached for her hand.

The truth made her feel worn and brittle as an old bone. The stars above her were hazy with the smoke of dozens of fires set by the Witch Hunters, each new plume just one more reminder of how impossible the odds were.

Red was no Great Witch. And she knew better than to indulge in fantasies.

She reached down to run her fingers through Cinzel's fur only to find the wolf had wandered away. He was lounging on his white stomach next to Perrin, who crouched beside a small fountain, studying the trickle of water dribbling from the carved copper spout. The entire wall above him was a mosaic of shell and glass and glimmering chips of tile forming the image of a woman wrapped in long, lustrous robes, her arms spread as if arising from the water. Her hair unfurled around her like seaweed, but all Red could see were coiling snakes.

Cinzel whined, tipping his head curiously as Perrin held up a tiny hourglass in one hand and a palm of clear water in the other. Red had seen the tiny glass bauble before. Perrin wore it on the end of a strap around his neck, the golden sand inside shifting and spinning whenever it fell out of his shirt.

"What are you doing with that?" Red asked, curious in spite of herself.

"Just a bit of an experiment." Water dripped off the ends of Perrin's fingers, sending ripples across the fountain. "I'm trying to figure out the best medium for my magic."

"You don't already know?" Red asked. She had the barest knowledge of how powerful Witches worked their spells, and she'd never been interested in learning. Most of her life, magic had only meant pain. Her hand curled unconsciously around her scarred palm.

Perrin lowered his hand to the basin, tracing a finger over the surface. "I'm thinking it might be water. The Paper Witch says I should actually be much stronger and I've been limiting myself by using the hourglasses. But the golden sand was my great-aunt's medium. It makes me feel closer to her."

Red's face pinched in confusion. "Didn't she die a long time before you were born?"

"She did," Perrin confirmed. "But dream magic is special. Sometimes, when I'm asleep, I see little pieces of the lives of Witches who came before me."

"You share their memories?" Part of Red was in awe, and

part of her shrank away from the thought of that kind of power. Or what someone might see if her memories were on display.

Perrin seemed to guess what she was thinking. He gave her a lopsided smile. "It's not always the good moments. But it makes me feel like I'm part of something bigger than myself. She's my family."

Red couldn't help flinching at the word *family*. Ivan's voice haunted her, his cruel smirk as he ripped away her last delusions about her mother—and her bloodline. There was the Red that existed before that moment, and the pieces of Red that existed after. If she could even put those pieces together again, what would they make? A Witch like Perrin, descended from a legend? Or would she still just be an outcast and a traitor, ruled by a fear of her own power she could never overcome?

"Maybe you should just keep using the golden sand," Red said, her mouth dry. "The Paper Witch could be wrong."

"But he's not," Perrin said with a sigh. He cupped both hands in the fountain, lifting them high and watching a trickle of water fall from his palms. "I've been afraid of letting go— and of where following my magic might take me. But I can't just shut that possibility out because it scares me."

"Why not? Maybe you don't have to know everything. Maybe you're fine as you are," Red protested. She wasn't even sure why she was arguing—just that her heart was beating too fast, her fingers clenched on the pool's stone rim.

Perrin's expression softened. "But if I stay this way, I'll never know who I really am, will I?"

Suddenly, Red realized they weren't just talking about his

medium. She scoffed, looking away. "You're not as subtle as you think."

"Really?" Perrin laughed. "Because I feel like I delivered that perfectly."

He stretched out his long legs, leaning back against the mosaic. One of his cream sleeves was rolled higher than the other, and the water had left a wet splotch on his coat, but somehow he looked far too wise in that moment, his brown eyes unbearably kind.

"I'd like to think we've gotten pretty close." Red shot him a look, and Perrin grinned. "Me and the wolf, I mean."

"Well, he's a lot easier to bribe than I am," Red said with a fond eye roll, watching Perrin slip a little nub of jerky out of his pocket and toss it to Cinzel. The wolf snatched it out of the air.

The boy shook his head. "You look a bit like her, you know—the Snake Witch, I mean."

Red stiffened.

"That was a compliment," Perrin assured her. "In Everlynd, there is no higher honor than being compared to one of the Great Witches."

Red knew that. In the stories of Andar, the Snake Witch was one of the great protectors—a Witch who stood guard over the castle, gave her life for the tragic prince, and died a hero's death.

But that wasn't the story Red had grown up with. The Snake Witch had been called something else among the Witch Hunters, mostly before they spat on the ground: the Monster Witch. On winter nights, when the cold wind sliced through the cracks in the old walls, Red had crouched close to the

Eyrie's watchfires and listened to tales of this ancient Witch who ensorcelled snakes and serpents and all manner of other vile beasts, bending them to her will.

"She actually had a snake familiar," Perrin continued, oblivious to Red's dark thoughts. "A lot of people think the snake that's wrapped around her arm in paintings is just a symbol, but it was her lifelong companion. Kind of like you and Cinzel." Perrin massaged the fur around the wolf's ears.

Red bit her lip. "What could I possibly have in common with a Great Witch?"

"She was a lot more than just a Great Witch," Perrin told her. He hummed thoughtfully, tipping the tiny hourglass on his necklace back and forth. "Most of the memories I see belong to the Dream Witch, but the Snake Witch is in a lot of them. Would you like to see her?"

"How?"

Perrin smiled, like it was nothing. "With dream magic, of course." He held out a hand.

Red hesitated, looking back at the curtain of vines and the burnt city beyond. This probably wasn't what Shane had in mind when she'd sent them to keep watch, but they were well hidden here. And Red was tired. Tired of being scared. Tired of not knowing. Just tired.

"Okay." She got to her feet, dusting off her skirts and walking over to Perrin. "Do I just take your hand?" she asked, uncertain.

"You'll probably want to sit down first," Perrin suggested wryly. "So you're not as far from the ground."

Red dropped down next to him and leaned back against the wall, patting her thigh to call Cinzel close. Then she reached out and slipped her hand into Perrin's. His fingers squeezed hers, warm and sure.

"Look right here." Perrin lifted the tiny hourglass around his neck and spun it between his fingers, turning it over and over and over, never giving the sand a chance to settle.

Red found herself blinking heavily. She was about to ask Perrin what was supposed to happen next when she realized the garden had vanished. Everything was black around her, like she had plunged into the darkness of her own mind. Fear rose in her chest. Was this what was inside her? Just darkness and emptiness and . . .

Perrin's hand squeezed hers again, and suddenly she found herself somewhere else. This dream felt warm and hazy, surrounding her in a soft golden glow.

"The happiest memories only get more beautiful with time," Perrin whispered.

The edges of the scene around Red were fuzzy, like a running watercolor, but the woman at the center was crystal clear. In a wild garden edged by a high stone wall, a woman with tan skin and a long dark braid sat in the crook of a tree branch, ignoring at least half a dozen empty benches. Her jacket was piled in her lap, and as she made a quiet shushing sound, Red realized there was some kind of small creature cupped in her hands.

Red stared, fascinated. This had to be the Snake Witch. She looked to be in her early twenties. Her eyes rose warily as someone approached: a woman with brown skin and bouncy curls held back by a bright blue scarf that matched her silk dress.

"The Dream Witch," Perrin said. "She's just a few years

younger than the Snake Witch. This is when they were both in training, before either of them had chosen an Order of Magic."

"Did you catch the little biter?" the Dream Witch asked, her voice light and amused. "Aloysius made it sound like it was quite a fearsome beast that got him."

"It's a tiny stoat," the young Snake Witch said flatly.

The Dream Witch chuckled as the little weasel-like creature popped its head up, giving her a wary look—much like the one the Snake Witch had shot her moments before. The white fur on its throat rippled as it peeped and trilled, burrowing back into the Snake Witch's hands with a flick of its black-tufted tail.

"So, not terrifying at all," the Dream Witch filled in, grabbing a tree branch and leaning close to get a better look.

"Most *terrifying* creatures are actually just *terrified*," the Snake Witch murmured, petting the stoat kit's rich, dark fur. "And it's almost always humans that made them that way."

She shot the Dream Witch a look, as though to say she was no exception.

The young Dream Witch leaned in, hands clasped behind her back. "So how should one approach a dangerous beast, then?" she asked playfully.

"Not at all," the Snake Witch said, tossing her braid over her shoulder. "They prefer to be left alone."

"All of them? In every circumstance?" the Dream Witch pressed, her lovely dark eyes twinkling. "No matter who's asking?"

The two women stared at each other, the moment hanging.

"Maybe not," the Snake Witch said finally. "Approach

slowly, then. Softly. With no expectations. And preferably not empty-handed."

The Dream Witch laughed. "I'll keep that in mind for next time," she said, throwing the Snake Witch a wink.

The Snake Witch blushed.

Red felt like she was intruding on an intimate moment. But she couldn't look away, watching the Snake Witch whispering into the stoat's rounded ears. She didn't look like some magical figure of legend. She looked like a person—not so different from the girl Red saw in the mirror.

The edges of the image started to blur, and suddenly Red was swept into more memory fragments. They came so fast they were almost dizzying—just flashes of the two women laughing together over open spell books, holding a lantern between them and walking side by side through deep snowdrifts, following a horned owl through the forest to a hollow tree. Red watched as the Snake Witch transformed into a giant white snake for the first time, only half as tall as a person, and twined around and around the Dream Witch, who laughed at all the pranks they could pull with this. The Snake Witch simply flicked her forked tongue in disapproval.

The Dream Witch slept in a hundred improbable places, and the Snake Witch dutifully covered her with a blanket or pried away the scrolls she'd fallen asleep on, or, in one moment that sparkled like gold, held her close while the rain pattered down a long gray window.

Soon a snake began to appear in the memories, its scales the brilliant green of new leaves. *If that ever winds up in the bed, I'm moving out*, the Dream Witch declared, her voice just a soft ripple on the surface of the memory. But still Red watched her setting up a warm rock on the windowsill in the best sunlight, then falling asleep over that rock herself and waking up with a face full of snake.

These memories weren't actually in her head; Red was sure of it. She never stopped feeling Perrin's hand in hers or seeing the streaks of wavering emptiness where the images were incomplete. But somehow the feelings had gotten inside her, a big, warm rush of longing that was familiar and foreign all at once. What had the Snake Witch and the Dream Witch been to each other?

"It's the stories from the big moments, from the end, that everyone always remembers," Perrin said.

Red glanced at him. He looked every inch a Dream Witch, his simple clothes replaced by a glittering golden robe. The sand at his feet wavered and rippled like water, and suddenly Red thought she understood what he'd been telling her about his medium. Perrin smiled as the scene changed again.

"But I like to think of them this way. As people, with doubts and insecurities and triumphs and a thousand other things you can only experience in a whole lifetime."

The two women stood on the edge of a lake with their hands intertwined, the city of Everlynd spread out behind them. The rays of the dying sun turned the lake to molten gold so their bodies were just dark silhouettes against the water.

The Snake Witch looked out across the waves. "I'm taking my Witch title tomorrow."

"I knew you'd be chosen to head the Order." The Dream Witch's lips bent in a soft smile. "It's a shame, though. Your name is so beautiful—I hate for it to be lost."

The Snake Witch turned to her, pulling her close by their entwined hands. "Then I'll leave it with you, Evista."

The Dream Witch pressed their foreheads together. "And I'll keep it safe for you forever, Assora."

She said the name with love. Reverence, even—like it was a spell, a secret word that when whispered just right put a little more magic into the world. Eyes closed, she began to recite an old rhyme, one Red had heard many versions of, borrowed ages ago from ancient wedding and bonding ceremonies.

"Through meetings and partings. Traced in our palms, traced in the stars. An unbreakable promise."

The waves lapped at the shore as the memory began to fade. Red turned to Perrin in his sparkling robes. "Were they in love?" she asked.

"I don't know," Perrin said, looking wistful. "And she's certainly not telling." He gestured to the Dream Witch, who was laughing now and whispering something Red couldn't hear into the Snake Witch's ear. "But I'd like to think so."

Red wanted to think that, too. She looked back at the image of the Great Witches, the image of her ancestor, so different than Red had imagined. So brave and bold and yet so timid with her heart—right up until the very end.

"Thank you, Perrin," she started to say. Then, suddenly, the dream shuddered around them, and the image vanished. Red jerked awake to find Shane grabbing her none too gently.

"Red? Red! Are you okay? Tell me that thing didn't get you!"

Red had no idea what *thing* Shane was talking about, but whatever it was, it couldn't be worth shaking her like this.

She scowled up at the huntsman's chin. "You know, this is a very rude wake-up call. Especially when Perrin was just taking me on a dream walk—"

She barely got the words out before Shane hauled her to her feet, crushing Red into a tight hug. "Don't scare me like that," she hissed into Red's hair. Red's heart fluttered as Shane pulled back, glaring between her and Perrin. "For the record, this in no way counts as keeping watch. If I were a Witch Hunter, you'd both be dead."

"Did something happen?" Perrin asked, sitting up and stretching. Cinzel twined around him, agitated by all the excitement.

"We found the mirror," the Paper Witch said, helping the boy up. "But I'm afraid that's not all we found."

Shane still hadn't let go of Red's shoulders. Red could feel the tension in her grip, her gray eyes unusually serious as she searched Red's face. "There was something—a Witch, I guess—possessing the body of one of the Witch Hunters and recruiting on behalf of the Spindle Witch. We got into it a little before it . . . ghosted off." She flapped a hand in the air.

A chill like a cold wind slid down Red's spine. She seized Shane's arm. "This *thing*. Did it have silver eyes?"

"Yeah," Shane said, brow furrowing. "Friend of yours, Red?"

Friend. Red could have choked on the laugh stuck in her throat. But she was frozen, gripping Shane's arm hard enough to bruise.

"Red?" Perrin asked softly.

Red was suddenly deathly cold. Even Cinzel, whining and bunting his cheek against her hip, barely registered as she pictured icy silver eyes staring at her, never from the same face twice.

"We served the Spindle Witch together," Red finally managed. "I was her right hand, her relic hunter and thief. He was her left hand, her assassin and killer."

"So he's a Witch, like you?" Shane asked.

"Not like me." Red clenched her hand into Cinzel's fur. "He's ruthless and powerful. I don't know his real name, or if he ever had a Witch title, but the Spindle Witch calls him her Wraith. He can project his will into the minds of people who are sleeping and take over their bodies."

Perrin's mouth fell open in horror. "That sounds almost like dream magic," he said, a deep frown marring his features. "But suppressing the will of another person—that's an unbreakable taboo. Any society of Witches would expel him for using magic that way."

Red flinched. "The Wraith doesn't care about things like that. Or who he hurts. He's . . . cold."

Cold. That was what Red had felt whenever she and the Wraith crossed paths. A tiny prickle at the back of her neck, like something trying to get in. Red had detested the Spindle Witch's dark magic and wielded the thorn rod only when she had no choice. But there was no escaping how the Wraith relished it—or how those eyes had glittered when she recoiled from the sight of his bloodstained cloak, whatever face he'd borrowed twisted into a cruel and satisfied smile.

The Paper Witch looked troubled, his gaze distant. "I have heard rumors—mysterious deaths among some of the strongest descendants of Andar. Witches who died behind locked doors, surrounded only by their closest companions."

Red shrugged. "It could be him. The Spindle Witch calls him the Wraith because he kills like a vengeful ghost. He takes over people's sleeping bodies, turns them into his puppets, and uses them to kill. When he's finished, he slips back out. Sometimes, they don't even know what happened."

"How can you tell when he's inside someone?" Shane asked.

"You've already seen it. It's the eyes," Red whispered. "The Wraith's eyes are silver, and the eyes of anyone he's possessing turn silver, too."

"That's it. We're never sleeping again, any of us," Shane declared, pinching the flesh between her thumb and forefinger hard enough to leave a mark.

Red huffed out a laugh, feeling the tiniest bit of warmth return to her at Shane's antics. "Don't be ridiculous. I doubt he'd be able to control someone as stubborn as you for more than a few seconds. Sooner or later, even a sleeping person wakes up and reasserts their will . . ."

"I'm sensing an enormous *but*," Shane said.

The Paper Witch drew in a sharp breath. "The people in the castle of Andar."

Red nodded grimly. "They're still under the sleeping curse. They can't wake up, no matter what he does. They're the perfect puppets. His own personal closet of people to wear. Who knows how many of them he could control?"

"That's a cheery thought," Shane muttered.

"But one we will have to contend with later," the Paper Witch said firmly, laying a hand on her shoulder. "For now, it must be enough that we have found the mirror. And with it, a connection to the Lord of the Butterflies."

Shane wrinkled her nose. "Fantastic. More creepy Witches."

"At least this one's trapped behind glass," Perrin offered, leading the way out of the garden. Cinzel trotted after him, crooning for more treats.

As they followed the Paper Witch, Shane grabbed Red's hand, twining their fingers tight. "You don't leave my side," she warned. "Not with some vengeful ghost Witch out there making threats against you."

Red shivered. With Shane's hand warm around hers, she tried to hold tight to the memory Perrin had shown her, the two women on the lakeshore with their palms pressed together. But Red's palm was just a crisscross of pale scars, the skin ragged from all of the mistakes of her past. Whatever lines of fate or love she'd once had, they'd probably been obliterated.

7

Fi

BRIAR'S GREAT BLACK wings folded as he touched down in a small clearing with Fi held tight in his grip. Slowly, she unwound her arms from his neck. The midday sun winked at her through the rustling green leaves of a small glade of aspens. A bird with a striking yellow breast darted into a thick elderberry bush, making the bright red berries quiver. Somehow, Briar looked even more like a monster here.

Fi slipped out of his arms, loss warring with relief. Nothing was more reassuring than the heartbeat she'd pressed her cheek against while he carried her, still sure and strong. But it couldn't erase the queasy feeling of holding on to the sharp, segmented bones of his shoulders or the icy claws that dug into her back.

Briar had appeared twice more in her dreams as the creature of nothing but bone and skull, tugging endlessly on a thread that led into his missing heart. Fi still didn't know what it meant. She straightened her vest, checking that her rope still hung from her belt.

As she stepped back from Briar, she startled a cloud of milky butterflies perched on a lavender bush. Suddenly, the air between them was full of whispering white wings. Through the swarm, she caught flashes of Briar, his golden curls, his ragged blue coat, and for one aching moment, Fi was swept away in a perfect memory—Briar smiling at her through a storm of butterflies, a symphony of light magic and all the stars shining in his beautiful blue eyes. She knew better, but she couldn't stop herself from peering up at him, hoping to see that same soft memory reflected on his face.

"Briar . . ."

His face was empty, his red eyes blank. The memory vanished like he'd ripped it from her, leaving nothing but a gaping hole in its place. Fi turned away. Her last image was of Briar's hulking black wings and golden hair bathed in the rays of the sun, a single white butterfly perched on the curve of one gleaming horn.

Fi forced her thoughts to the city ahead. She knew this area well. For the first time in months, she was back in Darfell, on the outskirts of the border city of Illya. She'd traveled there many times growing up, often for festivals just like the one being held this week.

Today was the first day of the end-of-summer festival, when the trade caravans gathered to hawk their wares before heading back to the sea for the winter. The roots of the celebration went all the way back to the Renewal Festival of ancient

Andar, when Witches with powerful earth magic would feed the chaff from the harvest into great crackling bonfires that burned for nights on end and then spread the fine gray ash across the fallow fields. Most of the old ritual had been forgotten, but bonfires would still burn in the town square for the next three days. More importantly, Illya would be busy and full of people, making it easy for Fi to slip in unnoticed.

Ahead of her, the town gates were thrown open, the yellow-and-red sun banners of late summer flapping against the weathered wood. Even before she got inside, the noise broke over her like a wave: the trill of pipes and people laughing and the booming voices of merchants shouting over one another, each offering to beat the best prices by a few coppers. Fi's eyes watered with the delicious smell of roasted tomatoes and fried yams and hot apples broiled in sweet cinnamon brine. It felt like a lifetime since she'd had anything but bread and water.

Fi could just imagine Shane with a skewer of potatoes in one hand and a buttery roll stuffed with almond paste in the other, probably heading straight for the bonfires and trying to jump them all. Even though some were for fertility and some were only for couples, she had a feeling Shane just wouldn't be able to resist the challenge of leaping over the flames. She shook her head at the thought of her absent partner, suddenly feeling very alone.

She moved slowly with the crush of people passing the main square, where the festival was going on in earnest. She paused to watch the musicians playing and dancers twirling with brilliant red streamers while play-actors performed for a group of delighted children. Fi got lost in it for a moment, remembering when she'd been small enough to attend the festival with her parents, her mother's hand tight around hers as Fi watched the fire dancers with wide eyes.

Flapping black wings brought her back. Three crows were fighting over a scrap in the road, screeching at each other and ripping the sliver of blackened meat with their long, sharp beaks. Fi felt like she'd been doused in icy water. She looked around slowly, noting the dozens and dozens of crows perched on the roofs of red-clay shingles and wheeling overhead like circling buzzards. Some of the birds must be native to Illya— it was a big city, and the festival meant plenty of trash and food scraps to draw the local scavengers. But . . .

Fi shivered, thinking of the crows that perched on the Spindle Witch's fingers while she whispered into their glossy feathers. At least some of them had to be her spies. All of Fi's good feelings evaporated, and she kept her head low, snaking through the crowd. Beady eyes seemed to follow her as she hurried on.

At last, she reached the old library. Uneven stone steps led up to an ancient two-story building with ragged gray walls, the plaster flaking away like dry scales. Vines bulged in the cracks, and a burst of bright pink bougainvillea had overtaken an upper balcony.

She pushed the doors open and was all at once over-whelmed with a feeling almost like coming home. The inside was just as she remembered it, old but well taken care of and well loved. She looked over the glistening floors of bare wood and the leather-bound books stacked on battered old shelves, which leaned in toward each other like they were whispering secrets. Shafts of sunlight through the narrow windows sparkled with dust motes.

Fi moved confidently through the stacks. It had been a while, but she had spent a month one summer practically living here, and she still knew where the most ancient texts were kept.

It was Lillia's tireless quest for the hidden city of the dream Witches that had brought Fi and her mother to Illya the summer she was thirteen, when she was too old—or almost too old—to be awed by the dancers and acrobats at the festival. The border town had more than its fair share of ancient maps, many of them drawn by the cartographers of Andar centuries ago. She and her mother hadn't found Everlynd, of course, but they had stumbled on something else: an ancient map with crumbling yellowed edges that held a different secret—one about Andar's first Witch Queen. That was how Fi had known about it, and why coming here had been her first thought when the Spindle Witch uncovered her deception.

Always play your trump card last. Fi had managed to delay coming here until the start of the festival. She was still one step ahead of the Witch, even if it was just a small one.

She took one last wistful look around and then made for the back room. She could almost smell the musk of the old texts already and feel their delicate curling pages beneath her fingers.

"That area of the library is not open to the public."

A blue-robed library attendant swept out from between the shelves. She was plump, with thick black hair and crow's feet around her eyes from decades of peering at tiny text, along with smile lines from a lifetime of answering the questions of curious children. One of whom had been Fi.

"Ninette!" Fi said, recognizing the old library keeper.

The woman peered at her and then lifted a pair of glasses that hung around her neck on a chain. "Is that little Filore Nenroa?" she asked, delighted.

"Not so little anymore," Fi said, as they clasped hands warmly.

"It's been too long," Ninette agreed. "I didn't know Dom and Lillia were here for the festival."

Fi held back a flinch. "They're not. It's just me," she said. With everything that had happened in the last few weeks, the Butterfly Curse had almost become an afterthought. Being here, where she had so many memories, was a painful reminder that being alone wasn't something that had started when she lost Briar and left Shane. She curled her hand over the curse mark on her palm.

The woman tutted, her eyes glistening with memory. "I can't believe you're old enough to be off on your own already," she said fondly. "Well, enjoy the library—and don't forget to poke your nose out at least once and take in the festival, too."

Fi nodded as the woman hurried off, swallowing down the lump in her throat.

The special collections room was small, with books crammed shoulder to shoulder on every available surface. A sliding ladder of dark polished wood offered access to the highest shelves. The only light came from a circular window in the ceiling, and the golden sunlight pooled on a wide oak table at the center of the room, its rough surface etched with the careless marks of quills and compasses from visiting cartographers. The drawers beneath were stacked full of maps and scrolls with pages too delicate to even bend or fold. Fi made her way across the room, kneeling beside the table and pulling out the bottom drawer to reveal a familiar map.

It was a map of ancient Andar, inked in swirls of black and painted with now-fading colors. It made the great kingdom of magic look like a land of fairy tales. The white castle in the center was surrounded by lush weeping willows, and the rest of the kingdom was awash with green and gold, dotted with countless landmarks named things like the *Wandering Meadows* and the *Tower of Dawn*. It was fantastically detailed, the spindly ink lines drawn so finely they looked like wisps of spiderweb pressed into the page. To the south of the castle, the cartographer had drawn a little white entryway surrounded by blue water above the couplet:

TO THE FALLEN, WE BEQUEATH OFT THE ERA UNMOOR

The first time she read it, Fi had thought it was nonsense, or perhaps some fragment of a forgotten poem. But her mother had known better.

She brushed her fingers over the parchment. A warm feeling rushed up to meet her—the memory of lying on the floor of this very same room with the map unrolled before her, elbows sunk into the ornate pile rug, and her dignified mother sprawled out right next to her, their laughter filling the tiny sunlit room as they tried to guess where the secretive dream Witches had hidden their golden city. She had loved playing that game, giggling as her mother made wild, fantastical guesses: veiled behind a waterfall in the Glade of the

Fire Flowers or high in the Silver Peaks among the rocks and woolly mountain goats.

"How about here?" young Filore asked, pressing her finger down onto the ancient map where the strange couplet was written. "Maybe it's nonsense because it's from a dream."

Lillia laughed, pushing back a curl of dark hair that had fallen out of her braid, thick with frizz. Her eyes held their familiar sparkle as she examined the spot under her daughter's finger.

"That's not nonsense. It's an anagram," she explained, copying it onto a scrap of paper and then crossing out the letters one by one as she unscrambled them. "It's written that way to deter strangers from disturbing the first Witch Queen's final resting place."

BEQUEATH OFT THE ERA UNMOOR *was actually* THE TOMB OF THE QUEEN AURORA.

Filore traced the small white arch at the bottom of the map. The illustration of the tomb was surrounded by tiny red roses, each one smaller than the tip of her littlest finger.

"Have you been there—Aurora's tomb?" she asked.

Lillia smiled, her voice hushed, like she was sharing a wonderful secret. "Not yet. But it's supposed to be one of the most beautiful places in all of Andar. When Queen Aurora died, the Witches of Andar transformed this whole valley into a breathtaking garden, with reflecting pools and wild roses and thousands of tiny silver bells hung in the willow trees so that those who came to visit Aurora's tomb could hear her laughter singing in the wind. Aurora's king-consort was a great sculptor, and it's said he carved her memorial statue himself out of the living stone, working alone in the valley for ten years until every detail was perfect."

Filore looked up, enthralled. She was fascinated by everything her mother knew and all of the places she'd been. She wanted to do that, too—to travel all over Andar and Darfell and Pisarre, and even to the kingdoms beyond, peering into every crevice of the world until no corner of the map was a mystery anymore. Maybe she'd even reach the secret city of the dream Witches that had eluded her mother.

"I'm sorry we didn't find anything," Filore said.

"Nonsense," Lillia told her with a smile. She snagged her traveling hat from a stack of books, dropping it onto her daughter's head at a jaunty angle. "We found a hundred things—just not the one thing we were looking for." She slipped the map back into its drawer, smoothing her hand over the soft colors. "No knowledge is ever wasted, Filore. Maybe the next thing you're looking for will be right here."

How right her mother was. Fi's lips tugged into a smile at the memory. She pulled the map gently from the wide drawer, laying it across the table. Then she reached into her shirt and pulled out a folded piece of parchment, smoothing it down.

It was an exact copy of the map, one she'd drawn painstakingly from memory, though hers was plain and unadorned with pictures. Fi had always had a knack for memorizing things, able to recreate maps she'd barely glanced at. She looked between the two, making sure she hadn't mistaken a single detail.

Fi's hand cramped at the thought of the nights she'd spent under the desk in the Spindle Witch's tower, hiding the flame of her single candle as she drew in secret. It had to be perfect, because she would have to show it to the Spindle Witch to justify the time she spent in Illya. The map was just her ruse, though. In truth, she had come here for something else.

Satisfied, Fi folded the map back into her pocket. She snagged a cloak forgotten over one of the ornate chairs, throwing it over her shoulders and slipping out the back door.

On the street, Fi pulled the hood of the cloak close around her face. Even amidst the music and laughter, she could still hear the cawing of the crows. She kept a steady pace, moving like a ghost through the crowds.

At the main square, she peered down the side streets until she spotted the painted wagons that belonged to the performers. There were a few men and women drinking on the roof of one, and a burly man who looked like a guard outside another, eating a skewer of roast tomatoes and tapping his toes to the jaunty tune from the square. It was just the first day of the festival; no one was flush with coin yet, so no one was keeping too close an eye on their wagons.

Fi ducked into one lavishly painted in red and gold. Inside, boxes and chests were stacked precariously to the roof. Provisions in brown canvas sacks hung from nails on the wall. Tucked into one corner was a pile of soft blankets and a few toys that clearly belonged to a child.

Fi passed it all, heading for the mirror with the colorful masks and scarves hanging from the frame. It only took Fi a moment to pick out a costume; after all, she didn't care how she looked as long as she didn't look like herself.

She changed quickly, trading her plain clothes for black pants and a long-sleeved top, both accented with bright strips of red and yellow cloth. Even the black glittered like it had been painted with gold dust. Fi sat down in front of the mirror, looking through the vials and pots strewn around it. She'd never really learned how to apply makeup properly, so Fi just slicked her hair back into a tight ponytail and then painted black onto her eyelids, using her fingertips to brush swoops of yellow and red at the corners like tongues of flames.

When Fi looked in the mirror again, she hardly recognized herself. She looked like one of the fire dancers she had watched so many times at this very festival, whose spinning ropes had made her heart pound with excitement.

The fire dancers were the reason she had first wanted to learn how to wield a rope. She had spun and twirled and clocked herself in the head countless times figuring out how to master the rope in a dance long before she realized how useful it could be as a treasure-hunting tool. She hadn't actually danced with the rope in a long time, and she had never quite captured the grace and bend of a real fire dancer. But Fi had fought with her rope, practiced with it, used it as an extension of her own body. Her control was perfect, and that would have to be enough, because Fi would have to put on quite a show to pull this off.

She picked up one of the performers' dance ropes, unhooking the ragged ball at the end blackened with oil, and fixed the ball to the end of her own rope instead, testing the new weight. Then, with a last glance at the stranger in the mirror, Fi darted out into the crowds.

Now dressed as a performer, Fi could move more easily. She passed right through the heart of the square, even stopping at the tents to buy a few things. Then she made her way to the foot of a tall white-plastered inn richly decorated with lavish silk curtains and gold filigree around the dark-framed windows. In its shadow stood a pair of women, one playing a pipe and the other strumming a mandolin, a four-stringed instrument Fi recognized from Pisarre. Luckily, they seemed to be short a dancer. Fi spun her rope and tossed them a smile.

"How about something a little more lively?" she asked.

The older woman smiled back, nodding to the girl next to her. "As long as you're not expecting more than a third of the take," the girl said.

"Wouldn't dream of it," Fi agreed. She didn't plan on taking any of the coins they raked in. Turning away, Fi pulled out the only items she had bothered to shove into the pocket of her new costume: her flint and tinder. In a moment, she had the ragged ball on the end of the rope lit.

It hissed, throwing bright sparks, and Fi's heartbeat kicked a little faster. She spared one look up at the inn, and then the music started.

The tune was one from Pisarre, Fi noted with pleasure— one she knew. Along with the mandolin, she had noticed the colorful sashes wrapped around the women's waists, which was the fashion in the coastal kingdom. She had always loved the music, the way it meandered and swelled, drawing the audience in. Fi would have to do the same.

The flame at the end of her rope threw off brilliant sparks, and Fi could feel the blistering heat as it hung by her side. She began to swing it gently from one side to the other, tracing a blazing arc through the air. Just like when she used it to fight, the goal was for the rope to never stop spinning, one motion flowing seamlessly into the next. The momentum would keep the fire from burning her, and as long as her fingers didn't slip, the flaming ball shouldn't come flying back to clock Fi in the head, as it had when she was little.

A small audience had gathered already, a little boy tugging

on his mother's skirts and pointing toward the flames. Fi smiled at him. On the downbeat, she let the rope fly, spinning it over her head and out toward the crowd before yanking it back. The music swirled around her, the fiery rope circling her like a burning star. She remembered how effortless the fire dancers always made this look, and she hoped she looked half that impressive. The fire hissed close to her ear as she caught the rope around her elbow and whipped it over her head, drawing a gasp from the crowd. Fi couldn't stop her smile. That move was more suited to a fight than a dance, but no one seemed to be complaining.

More people gathered around her, and Fi scanned the audience as best she could, looking for one particular figure. She twisted and whirled, her hips and the flame matching the rhythm of the song. She could only imagine the look on her mother's face if Lillia could see her now—or Shane's, for that matter. *Or . . .*

Her heart bucked, her throat closing as she imagined Briar standing among the awed crowd, his blue eyes shining with wonder. Briar, who loved every new thing and had wanted to travel the world with her more than anything. Briar, who would insist on trying the rope himself and would absolutely brain himself with it. She choked on a tiny laugh, and then she whipped the cord over her shoulder and breathed in the sizzling oil and smoke as the ball hurtled past her face, pushing herself faster and harder. When this was all over, when she got Briar back, she would do this dance one more time, just for him.

It was as she came out of a spin, half-dizzy and exhilarated by the blazing fire, that she finally saw the person she'd come all this way for. He was unmistakable in his crimson coat, his dark hair feathering around his tan face.

Now to get his attention.

Fi sucked in a breath, quieting her galloping heart. She slid her hand up the rope, whipping it in frenzied circles that showered her with red sparks and had the spectators gasping. Fi threw the rope out, using her boot to kick the flaming ball skyward in a high arc. She ducked forward at just the right moment and let the cord wrap around her neck.

It was a hard move to pull off even when it was just a ring on the end of the rope. As the cord wound over her flesh, it was hard not to remember the crawling feeling of the Spindle Witch's threads closing around her throat. This was different, though—this she was in control of. She let the rope loop around her once before jumping into a quick turn and throwing it the other way, the fire safely at arm's length once more. Cheers and claps erupted from the audience. It was a thrill to be the center of attention, with so many eyes on her, but one Fi would be just as glad never to experience again.

As the song ended, she slowed the rope down with a few lazy circles, her eyes scanning for the flash of red in the crowd. She needn't have bothered—the figure was already pushing his way to the front. Fi smiled, catching the rope against her elbow to stop it. She took an elaborate bow, turning to the left and right, trying to mimic the easy moves of a real dancer as coppers were tossed into the musicians' bowl.

When Fi finally rose from her last bow, her eyes traveled over an expensive pair of boots that shone with polish, up black leather pants, a silk shirt under a vivid crimson coat, and a myriad of silver rings and necklaces, including a ruby the size of a robin's egg on the boy's finger. Armand Bellicia clapped faintly, staring right at her.

Fi hadn't seen her ex since he'd tried to separate her and Shane at the border of Andar after his disastrous masquerade party. The mark on her palm tingled, but for once, Fi refused to be drawn into the agonizing memory of the moment Armand had forced the Butterfly Curse on her. Right now, the curse was the least of her problems.

Fi locked eyes with Armand, feeling more confident than she ever had staring him down. She could see the moment he realized who it was under the costume and makeup. His eyes widened, his jaw going slack and leaving his usually sneering mouth open.

"Fil—" he began.

"Did you enjoy the performance, your lordship?" Fi cut in. "Enough to grant me a private audience?"

She arched an eyebrow in warning and in offer, and wasn't surprised at all when Armand agreed. She knew him well enough to predict what he would do. Armand Bellicia was going to be her trump card in this game against the Spindle Witch.

8

Fi

FI SIPPED LEMON tea out of a delicate teacup painted with marigolds. She sat on the edge of a cushioned wooden chair, looking absently out of a towering window hung with rippling blue silk curtains. The seat across from her was empty.

Armand had quickly agreed to Fi's offer for a private meeting, taking her back to the very inn she had been looking at from the street, where the Bellicias always rented out the entire top floor for the Renewal Festival.

It was at this very festival that Fi and Armand had met for the first time years ago. Fi had just turned fifteen and was itching to step out of her parents' shadow. Armand was seventeen and handsome—and best of all, he'd had a mystery.

She'd stumbled on Armand wandering the city's oldest district with a scrap of paper cupped in his hand. He'd been pickpocketed—probably quite easily, given his level of distraction, and though Fi hadn't caught the thief, she had saved

Armand from becoming a criminal himself by paying for his lunch. He'd returned the favor by sharing the piece of ancient map that had brought him to Illya. It turned out to be a dead end, nothing but directions to a cave of raw sapphires that had long been mined out. But Fi hadn't been disappointed, far too enthralled by the hunt. And by Armand.

Armand had been her first treasure-hunting partner, her first love, her first heartbreak, and her first brush with hate all wrapped in one person. It was strange and disorienting to be here with him again, where it all started.

As soon as they arrived at his quarters, Armand had sent a servant scurrying for tea, lemon for Fi and jasmine for himself. Then he had disappeared to freshen up and left Fi alone in the sitting room. It was a little power play that Armand liked to use—keeping people waiting for him. Fi had watched him do it many times back when they were partners. Another time it might have annoyed her, put her on edge, but today it had given her exactly the time she needed to prepare.

Her arms felt stiff inside the tight black costume. She hadn't had the chance to wash off her eye makeup, and her fingers trembled around the handle of the teacup. Fi set it down in the saucer with a little clink. The room's furnishings were made of sturdy wood, highly practical and plain, but everything had been dressed up for its current guest with fancy lace doilies and silk runners. There was even a delicate-looking vase full of marigolds tucked into the corner and a bowl of expensive imported nuts on the table. Armand always did enjoy his little luxuries, Fi mused coldly.

The last time she had seen her ex, her heart hadn't been

as ready as she thought, and he'd almost beaten her. Today, she had come prepared.

As though summoned by her thoughts, Armand appeared in the doorway, leaning in to study her before sauntering into the room. He had changed into a rich red tunic with a high collar embroidered with golden lilies. Dozens of rings glittered from his fingers, and a gold pendant with the mark of Bellicia hung from his neck. He was still good-looking beneath all the arrogance, but Fi found it easy to see past that.

He wanted to impress her—he'd always wanted to impress her. But looking at him now, utterly absorbed in his own theatrics, Fi could see what a child he was, preening and bullying and sulking for attention. Compared to the Spindle Witch, to the loss of Shane and Briar, everything about Armand just seemed so small.

Armand slung himself into the seat across from her, regarding her with a smug smile. "I'm sorry; did I keep you waiting?"

Fi bit the inside of her cheek. "Your tea is getting cold," she said flatly.

Armand seemed disappointed by her answer, lifting his teacup carelessly and taking a gulp. His lips turned down. "These little backwater towns just don't know how to make a good cup of tea." He shook his head dramatically. "Not like some of the places we used to go. Which reminds me, how was your little trip across the border? I don't see your *maid* . . . Lost another partner already?"

Shane's absence hit her like a gut punch. She could just imagine what her partner would have to say if she could see

Fi sitting here having tea with *that arrogant little slug-weasel*, as Shane had so colorfully named him. But she hadn't forgotten her promise never to agree to one of Armand's little arrangements again. Even without Shane here shouting it in her ear, she had no intention of breaking that promise.

"Save your snide comments. I'm here to talk about something important," Fi said. "Something that affects Bellicia and all of Darfell."

Armand frowned at her serious expression, finally deigning to lower his cup. "Fine. I'm listening."

"The Spindle Witch is moving again. I can't explain everything, but she's about to get her hands on a vast power—something that will make her completely unstoppable," Fi told him.

Armand didn't seem impressed. In fact, he was chuckling. "You sound like a doomsayer on the corner. The Spindle Witch is just an old story. That monster died a hundred years ago with the rest of the dried-up kingdom of magic."

Fi dug her fingers into the arms of her chair. "You're wrong, Armand," she said coldly. "I've seen her, and what she's capable of, with my own eyes. I have no reason to lie to you about this."

That shut Armand up. He studied her for a moment, as though he were swishing the words around in his mouth, tasting them. "If that's true, Filore—*if*," he said, holding up a warning finger, "and I would need some proof—then I hope you're not here expecting me to marshal the Border Guards. You know my father will never allow them to march into Andar."

Fi shook her head. She was well aware that the Duke of

Bellicia considered his problems to stop at his border. "I don't need an army. I have a plan to stop her before it comes to that. I just need your help, Armand."

He looked so pleased that Fi immediately wanted to take the words back. Nothing had ever delighted him more than when she *needed* him. Fi steadied herself before she did something she regretted. This was for Briar, and Shane, and everyone standing in the Spindle Witch's path. Armand was just a tool, and this time, Fi was going to be the one doing the discarding when it was over.

Armand swigged down the last of his tea, all the way to the bitter dregs—no doubt just for the show of it. Then he leaned over the table, bracing his cheek on a careless hand. "What makes you think I'll help you?" he asked. "You weren't very receptive to my last favor, after all."

Favor? She remembered when he'd tried to trick her—to tear her away from Shane and force his way back into her life. She didn't remember receiving any favors.

"This isn't about us, Armand," Fi ground out. "There is no us. I'm here because you're heir to the house of Bellicia, and as selfish and arrogant as you are, the one thing you always cared about was taking your father's place someday as Border Master. So earn it." Hesitantly, she reached out and laid her hand over Armand's on the table. An olive branch. "Prove you deserve it by doing the right thing now."

Armand turned his hand over beneath Fi's, squeezing her fingers. His expression softened.

"I will do the right thing, Filore," he said slowly. "But I have some conditions."

Fi yanked her hand away from his in disgust. She didn't

even have to ask—his predatory smile said it all. She shouldn't have expected anything else. Armand was a man who couldn't be reasoned with, not even when the lives of his own people were at stake.

"You would risk letting the Spindle Witch destroy Darfell just to get back at me?" Fi spat.

"Of course not," Armand said with a little wave of his hand. "But I don't see why I shouldn't take advantage of the situation to get everything I want." He chuckled, bracing his chin on his steepled hands. "You never could tell when you were in a weak bargaining position."

He looked expectantly at Fi, like he was waiting for her to crumble—to end up on her knees in front of him, as she had before.

Fi took a deep breath. "Actually, you taught me a lot about bargaining and power, and I think you'll find I'm a very quick study. How was the tea—a little bitter? Are you sure you know what was in there?"

The victorious look on Armand's face twisted into something dark. "What did you do?" he demanded, snatching up his teacup. He brought it up to his nose, sniffing it, and then dragged a finger through the dregs at the bottom. It came away coated with a film of white powder. "What is this, Filore?"

Fi pushed herself up from the table to look down on Armand for a change. "It's poison, Armand—a brew I picked up from an ancient Witch's spell book." She enjoyed the look of shock that marred his handsome features. "Slow acting, of course, since I still need your help." She had bought the ingredients from the apothecary and spice shops at the festival and mixed it in this very room with all the time Armand had given her.

Armand's chair clattered to the floor as he surged to his feet, his surprise melting into rage. He seized Fi by the collar and dragged her forward. Her knees banged into the table, overturning both cups. "How dare you," he hissed.

Fi reached up and pried his fingers away. "I don't think I'll be taking any more threats from you," she warned coolly. "Because no matter what you try, I'm not going to tell you what I gave you, and I don't have the antidote on me. So now it's your turn to listen."

Armand's face was still curdled with rage, his eyes flashing. But she could see a little fear there, too. Fi wondered if this was a first for him—feeling so powerless in front of someone.

Armand had taught her exactly how it felt to have your own power ripped away. But he'd taught her other things, too. With his cruelty, his selfishness, he'd made her determined never to be like him, never to revel in the power she held over someone else. Not even this boy, who had taken so much from her.

Armand backed away, slumping into his chair. "I guess your position wasn't so weak after all," he murmured.

Fi breathed out and felt something deep inside of her uncurling. She had finally left the girl he cursed behind. Like a butterfly emerging from a chrysalis, Fi was something new, utterly beyond his reach.

She turned to the window, the sheer blue curtains whipping around her. "Since we've established that I can't trust you, here's what's going to happen. I'll be waiting with the antidote where I need you to meet me in five days—which will give you just enough time to get there and save yourself before it's too late. But only if you do exactly as I say."

Armand nodded grudgingly. "What do you want me to do?"

"Do you still have the letter opener with the Curse of the Wandering Butterfly?" Fi asked, holding her breath. "Did you keep it after you used it on me that day?"

Armand gave her a strange look. "Yes," he admitted.

"Good," Fi said, flexing her palm over the swallowtail mark. The movement made the black wings seem to shiver. "I'll need it."

9

---»»»—•—«««---

Shane

"THIS BETTER WORK," Shane muttered, backing up and admiring her handiwork.

The butterfly mirror winked back at her, perched in a high stand at the center of one of the Everlynd camp towers. All of the windows had been covered and blacked out. Braces of lit candles lined the round walls, throwing off dancing shadows and muting all of the colors. Shane's dark coat looked almost black, Red's dress a burgundy wine, and Perrin's stark-white shirt a lustrous gray. Cinzel hadn't been allowed in, so at least there was no wolf underfoot—probably a good thing, since the long bookshelves were overflowing with inkwells and delicate vials and a hundred other things Cinzel's bushy tail could bring to a sad end. A small writing table bristled with quills ink-stained at the tips.

The whole room had clearly been knocked together hastily from the odds and ends in the camp, but somehow the

Paper Witch had managed to give it the same comfortably cluttered feeling as his ramshackle tower.

Shane dug a toe under the thick purple rug. The Paper Witch had brought them to his new little workshop and set up the hand mirror before he'd gone off to retrieve something and left them here to die of anticipation.

Shane had peered into the mirror many times on their journey home. Perrin had polished it till it shone, and even the patient Paper Witch had laid a charm across its surface, the little scrap of paper fluttering as he whispered over it. It all got them nothing. At this point, Shane was just hoping this whole thing hadn't been a colossal waste of time—they couldn't afford to be wrong. Her eyes slid over to Red, who stood with her hands on her hips, frowning.

The girl had been acting squirrely since Shane had shaken her and Perrin awake from their ill-advised dream jaunt in the middle of enemy territory. Neither of them seemed interested in explaining what was so important they had to go fishing around in Perrin's memories right there in Everlynd. The one time Shane had tried to bring it up, Red had ducked away from her, moving to walk next to Perrin and directing question after question at a bemused Paper Witch.

Shane was usually the first one to write off secretive Witches as just being needlessly secretive. But Red kept shooting Shane strange looks whenever she thought the huntsman wasn't watching, a faint thoughtful frown tugging at her eyebrows. Still, anything was better than the bitter, wounded expression Red had been wearing when she told them about the left hand of the Spindle Witch. The Wraith.

Shane bit down a shudder of revulsion. *One Witch problem at a time*, she reminded herself, turning back to the mirror.

"Show him the pin," Red suggested.

"Sure. Couldn't hurt," Shane said, holding out her hand to Perrin and wiggling her fingers expectantly. Perrin's look said he didn't think this was a good idea, but he passed the butterfly pin to Shane anyway.

"Hey, you in there," she growled, dangling the pin in front of the glass. "Recognize this? It's yours." She shook it, brandishing the little butterflies on their delicate chains.

The three of them paused, holding their breaths. Shane and the flickering candles remained the only thing reflected in the surface.

"Hit him a few times," Red suggested with a toss of her hair. "Maybe he just needs a wake-up call."

Shane eyed the stand thoughtfully, wondering if a little rap of her knuckles would knock the mirror off.

"Or," Perrin suggested, "maybe we should wait for the Paper Witch."

"A wise choice," the Paper Witch said drily.

Shane turned to find the man had reappeared in the doorway in a long silver robe. His pale blond hair hung loose except for a single gathered strand wrapped round and round with blue thread, the little silver bell tinkling as he moved. His expression was half exasperation, half fondness as he looked at Shane, dangling the precious hairpin like bait in front of the mirror.

"That, I assure you, will not work," the man promised. Shane stepped back, allowing him to take her place. "This hand mirror belonged to Queen Aurora," the Paper Witch continued, running his hand along the silver rim. "I'm afraid there's only one way to awaken the magic for certain." He lifted one hand into the air, raising a small sharp knife in the other.

"What are you doing?" Shane hissed. The Paper Witch slid the knife across his palm. Red gasped as he fisted his wounded hand over the mirror and squeezed.

Perrin's eyes were wide. "He carries the blood of the Rose Witches. It might work." As Shane watched, a few red drops splashed onto the top of the mirror, sliding into the grooves of the butterfly engraving.

"If this mirror was enchanted for Aurora, he should respond," the Paper Witch explained. He let a few more drops fall until the butterflies were outlined in red, the hint of color staining their wings dark like the painted wings of monarchs.

This time, Shane felt the change in the air, a shivery feeling like eyes on the back of her neck. The candles flickered madly in their braces, the flames whipping and dancing as though caught in a sudden gale. The mirror went dark and then light as all the candles flared at once.

Shane blinked spots out of her eyes, and when she could see again, there was a different face in the mirror: a familiar brown-haired man in brilliant red-and-gold robes. His hair was pulled into a half ponytail streaming down his back, and somehow he seemed far less wild and intimidating than the figure Shane and Red had met in the study. Maybe it was his soft expression.

The last time they'd met a version of this Witch, he'd told Shane these were little slivers of himself, a single moment and emotion trapped in time. Shane shivered, wondering exactly who they were talking to this time and what kind of knowledge he was safeguarding.

The Lord of the Butterflies looked them over. "A descendant of Aurora," he greeted, eyes fixing on the Paper Witch. "I did promise to come whenever she called me to this mirror. I suppose you're close enough."

The Paper Witch inclined his head. "Lord of the Butterflies," he said respectfully. "We need your knowledge."

"It's about the Spindle Witch," Shane cut in, trying to speed things up a little. The Paper Witch shot her a warning look.

The Lord of the Butterflies didn't look angry, just amused. "I don't know any Witch with that title," he said simply.

Shane gritted her teeth. "Think hard," she suggested. "Cruel, powerful, uses golden threads . . ."

A strange smile crept across the man's face. "I just met a girl like that—so lonely and desperate, whispering to all her little crows. So she'll be called the Spindle Witch . . ." He said the name as though he were savoring every syllable.

Shane felt like something slimy was crawling down her spine. There was something deeply unsettling about this man, and Shane was glad they only had to deal with little pieces of him. Even if they were all out of order in time. Shane just hoped this one wasn't from too early to help them.

"Maybe you can tell us something about this, then." Red reached out, closing her hand over Shane's and holding the butterfly hairpin up in front of the glass. Unlike the rest of them, the pin reflected in the mirror. The delicate butterflies swayed in front of the Witch as though it were in both places at once.

"Fascinating," the man breathed as Red twirled it around, making the butterflies clink and glimmer. "I never would have thought to construct a spell that way."

"Well, you did," Shane snapped. "You made this pin, and when you gave it to us, you—well, another mirror you—said it was a very powerful weapon, but only *under exactly the right circumstances*. We need to know how to use it."

Shane's stomach clenched at the sudden sensation of ghostly fingers brushing over hers. The pin seemed to move on its own as the Lord of the Butterflies reached up to study it. Red jerked away like she'd been burned. Shane tensed the muscles in her neck, but she forced herself to remain still.

"It's a tool," the Witch said finally, sitting back. "For severing someone from their magic. Though it's incomplete."

Severing the Spindle Witch from her magic sounded like an excellent plan. Shane suspected a nine-hundred-year-old woman *without* powerful magic wouldn't be nearly so difficult to defeat. That still left one little problem.

"Incomplete," Shane repeated. "That sounds fixable. Is there a way to complete it?"

"When I said 'incomplete,' I meant literally." The man reached out, tapping the empty chain on the pin reflected in the mirror. "One of the butterflies is missing. It would have to be replaced with another of my butterflies. I gave one much like it to Princess Aurora before her coronation—it was fashioned into a ring. She kept it with her always. As her descendant, perhaps you have it."

The Paper Witch's shoulders slumped. "Thank you, great lord, but I do not. If it is as powerful as you say, it was no doubt buried with Aurora in her tomb."

That still sounded fixable to Shane. Tomb robbing was not her usual gig, since disturbing dead Witches seemed like just asking to be cursed, but it couldn't be that different from treasure hunting.

Perrin seemed to be thinking along the same lines. "So, if we get this ring, we can complete the pin?"

The Witch hummed thoughtfully, tipping his head. "Let's just say you definitely can't complete the pin without it. How's that?"

It sounded suspiciously like a devious Witch leaving himself a loophole. Still, Shane wasn't going to waste any time trying to squeeze the truth out of the Lord of the Butterflies. This version of him was much more obliging than the one she and Red had met before—probably because he was a well-dressed sliver of himself tucked inside a princess's hand mirror. They were all parts of the same whole, though. The one who'd had a falling-out with Aurora. The one who had been enthralled by the Spindle Witch's power. The one who had ultimately been cursed and banished.

Shane nodded to the Paper Witch. "So, if I take the mirror to Queen Aurora's tomb, we might finally have a weapon to use against the Spindle Witch. Even if it is in the shape of a hairpin."

The Witch in the mirror clicked his tongue in disapproval. "I wouldn't recommend it—taking me along, that is." His eyes glittered in the light of the flickering candles as he looked at the small space around him. "This mirror is very old and well used. I don't have much strength left. You'll probably only be able to call me one more time."

"What?" Shane demanded.

"So make it count," he suggested warningly. "Have everything in order—and have it absolutely right. No second chances."

"Well, that's clear as mud," Shane grumbled, before the Paper Witch swept between them.

"Of course, great lord," he said with another bow.

The Lord of the Butterflies smiled fondly, his eyes tracing the blond wisps of the Paper Witch's hair. "I'm glad to see so much of Aurora lives on," he murmured. Then his smile took on an entirely different edge. "Oh, and to the hothead: I never did anything by accident. If it's in the shape of a hairpin, it's in that shape for a reason."

He was gone before Shane could even squawk in indignation at being called a hothead. *The shape of a hairpin . . . for a reason?* Shane wasn't even going to guess. She'd let Perrin and the Paper Witch and other people whose job it was to untangle ancient Witch gibberish puzzle on that one.

Of course, there was one person Shane would have given anything to have at her side right now, and not just because she was the best historian and Witch puzzler Shane had ever met. Because Shane had a ruin to take on and she could have used her treasure-hunting partner at her back. She curled her fist. She'd just have to go it alone this time.

"Well, I guess I know where I'm headed," she said.

The Paper Witch shook his head, pinning Shane with an exasperated look, the one that usually preceded her getting her way. "You want the location of Aurora's tomb," he guessed.

Shane grinned. "Unless you have some other treasure hunter in mind. We need that ring."

"Whoa, whoa, back up," Perrin broke in. "Queen Aurora's tomb is the most sacred and protected ruin in all of Andar. Plenty of grave robbers have tried their hands, and it's thwarted every one—for *centuries*. Not to mention there are some nasty rumors about that place, like people disappearing, never to be seen or heard from again. Some even say it's cursed."

"Perrin," the Paper Witch admonished. "That is nothing more than gossip." He turned back to Shane. "Little is known about the inside of Aurora's tomb, but she was the greatest light Witch in our kingdom's history—a queen who ruled with compassion and wisdom. She would not leave any dark curse, I assure you. I can arrange a guide from among the Everlynd scouts to take you—"

Shane shook her head. "Nope. I'm going alone. Anyone who's not a treasure hunter is going to slow me down."

The Paper Witch looked like he wanted to argue, but Shane was prepared to dig her heels in on this one. Aurora's tomb was infamous among treasure hunters, too. Shane had heard her own nasty rumors about people who entered the tomb and then were found months or even years later wandering the valley with no memory of who they were. Aurora might have been good and noble and whatever in the storybooks, but her tomb was the resting place of a powerful dead Witch. Whatever happened to people in there, it was *real* magic—*big magic*. The kind that Shane couldn't risk facing with someone who had no idea what they were doing.

"You can't be serious about this," Perrin started. Red looked like she had some objections herself—actually, Red looked like she had a lot of objections, her mouth twisted in a deep scowl.

Luckily, Shane didn't need their approval. The Paper Witch's robes swished over the rug as he moved to stand in front of her, his blue eyes searching hers.

"I have known you for a long time, Shane, and I trust your judgment," he said. "If you say you must do this alone, then you must. But know that I will help you any way I can." He rested a hand on her shoulder, squeezing softly.

"Thanks," Shane said, her throat feeling a little thick. She could still remember when the Paper Witch was just a stranger in white reaching out to some washed-up mercenary in a backwater bar. The Paper Witch had seen something in her then that she couldn't see—even if he had taken a few precautions at first, like putting locks on everything down to his silverware drawer. He'd given her a second chance to find herself. It meant a lot to know he trusted the person she'd become.

"Perrin, fetch a sheet of parchment from that shelf beneath the window, would you?" the Paper Witch said. Then he turned to the small writing table.

"You're going to draw me a map by hand?" Shane asked, trying not to sound ungrateful. She had figured finding the tomb would take more than a few scribbled directions.

"That would be far too imprecise," the Paper Witch said. The bell in his hair tinkled as he swept quills and brushes out of the way, making a space on the cherrywood surface for the cream-colored sheet of paper Perrin had retrieved. Then he lifted a hand, gently tugging free the crystal earring that he had worn as long as Shane had known him. He held it up in the wavering light. If she looked closely, Shane could just make out the tiny pattern of a rose inside it, a deeper curl of red within the pink crystal. She'd never noticed that before.

"Queen Aurora's resting place is a sacred location, one guarded by all the Roses of Andar. The pattern inside this crystal is made of ink," the Paper Witch explained.

He lowered the earring until it dangled right over the smooth surface of the paper and then lifted his empty hand, twirling his finger around the crystal like he was coaxing an errant thread. To Shane's amazement, the tiny rose began to uncoil from the crystal, sliding down onto the parchment in spindly lines. Even though there had only been the barest hint of a rose inside the earring, the tendrils of red ink just kept unspooling, like a tiny trickle of blood draining from the crystal's heart. As the lines crawled across the page, she realized it was the beginnings of a map.

"This will take a while," the Paper Witch said absently, his eyebrows furrowed in concentration.

"Let me help," Perrin offered. He studied the uncoiling lines for a moment before resting his fingertips on the paper and beginning to turn it gently. The map emerged beneath their hands, slowly spreading onto the mottled parchment.

Shane felt a flicker of movement as Red sidled up to her elbow.

"You're really going alone. You don't need a partner?" Red asked. Her voice was painfully hopeful.

"Not this time," Shane said. Then, softer, she added, "It's too dangerous, Red. No room for amateurs on this one."

Red crossed her arms. "And what about the Wraith? You're just going to traipse around in the forest alone while he's out there, after all of us?"

"He's not after all of us. He's after *you*, Red." Shane caught her by the elbows, squeezing softly. "You're the one he wants. You'll be safe here with the people of Everlynd." The girl opened her mouth to argue, but Shane shook her head, cutting her off. "I can't risk something happening to you."

"But I'm supposed to be okay with something happening to *you*?" Red demanded hotly.

Shane grinned. "You don't have to worry about me. I'm not that easy to kill, remember?"

Red didn't smile back. Her eyes flared as she wrenched away, jabbing her sharp finger into Shane's chest.

"I don't know why I bother with you," she bit out. "Maybe I'm not worried. Maybe I just didn't want to be left behind. But fine, Shane—do it your way." Then she whirled around and stormed out of the tower, slamming the door so hard three scrolls toppled off the shelf.

Perrin caught Shane's eye and winced. "Maybe she'll have cooled down by the time you get back?"

Even Shane wasn't that much of an optimist. But she'd have to deal with that later. Right now, she had a tomb to raid.

10

≫≫≫—⋘⋘

Red

DUSK WAS FALLING as Red stole through the Everlynd camp, silent as a shadow in her long gray cloak. Cinzel padded ahead of her on soundless feet. The wolf whined low in his throat, a warning, and Red ducked out of the road, pressing her back to a wall of chipped yellow stones. She counted her fast breaths until the figures had passed: two men wearing the sigil of the Red Ember. Then she hurried on, listening in between heartbeats for anyone coming after her.

Soon, they would be lighting the torches, ringing the chorus of little chimes that called the soldiers of Everlynd to watch. But for once, Red wouldn't be around to hear it. She was going after Shane, and no one was going to stop her. Not the council with their rules. Not the Paper Witch with his gentle reminders to be patient. And certainly not Shane, looking at her with those serious eyes when she told Red she *couldn't risk something happening to her.*

Her cloak snagged in the outstretched fingers of a thorny bush, and Red ripped it free. Shane was the only reason Red was willing to be in the Everlynd camp in the first place, and she had no interest in staying without her. She could see the line of dark firs in the distance where the southern edge of camp bled back into the forest. That was where she'd pick up Shane's trail.

Against the pale green twilight, the crooked little houses looked like a row of jagged teeth. It reminded her far too much of the last place she'd called home: the ruined carriage house inside the Forest of Thorns, where the Spindle Witch had kept her like a pet until she was old enough to be useful.

Red had hated that place almost as much as she'd hated the Eyrie. She hated the splinters of the rotted doors she had to creep over in her bare feet once she grew out of her shoes. She hated the skeletons of ancient carriages hulking in the corners, the shredded fabric of their painted hoods clinging to the wooden ribs like dried skin stretched over bones. She hated filling her stomach with warm water from the river and watching her supplies dwindle while chubby Cinzel got thinner and thinner until she could feel the outline of his ribs when she ran her hand along his coarse fur.

The Spindle Witch only came when she felt like it, and she never seemed to show up before Red was down to her last moldering apple. During the day, Red wandered the crumbling outbuildings, catching glimpses of a white castle so pristine and cold it seemed carved out of ice. And then, at night, when the forest was full of creaking and moaning, Red imagined monsters all around her—the ghosts of Andar wailing in the trees or packs of hideous half-dead wolves stalking her through the thorns. Too numb to cry, she would cover her ears and bury her face in Cinzel's flank and dream of a day when she'd be somewhere safe and warm, somewhere she was wanted.

Now Red knew what a lie that had been. She wasn't wanted anywhere. She had been an abomination to her father, a pawn to the Spindle Witch, and to the people of Everlynd—a traitor, an agent of the enemy. That was all they'd ever see.

Shane had tried to convince her to tell everyone she was descended from the Snake Witch, but Red flat-out refused. Her whole life, Red had been hated and reviled for something she had no control over, magic she didn't want and didn't ask for. And it had been meaningless. Being loved and accepted for something just as out of her control, some accident of her birth—that would be equally meaningless. She wouldn't give them the satisfaction of changing their minds about her that easily.

She had just slipped into the forest when she heard something—hushed voices coming through the copse of pines ahead. Red shushed Cinzel and crept forward, peering between the bristles. Moonlight spilled into a clearing where two figures were standing close together, speaking urgently. Perrin's arms were folded over his embroidered coat, and he faced a pale blond man with the white tower rippling on his red cloak. A soldier of the Red Ember, Red realized, though he only looked a little older than Perrin. His handsome features were cut by sharp worry lines.

The stranger's voice was cold. "If you and the Paper Witch keep openly defying Nikor like this, he's not going to let it go. First a search for some mirror, and now a fool's errand to Aurora's tomb?" He shook his head in disgust. "When will you stop chasing the Paper Witch's flights of fantasy?"

"When he's wrong," Perrin said with a shrug. "The way I see it, he's the only one still trying to save Andar."

"Wake up, Perrin. He's been wrong every step of the way," the man spat. "First it was some girl who was going to save us, and then Briar Rose. Now you want us to trust a couple of outsiders—one of whom worked for the Spindle Witch?"

"Leave Red out of it," Perrin said sharply. "This isn't about her."

Red felt a strange little flutter in her stomach. Perrin didn't have to defend her—he didn't know she was here. Cinzel's ears flicked, and Red laid a calming hand over his neck, her breath tight and shallow in her throat.

"You're right, Perrin," the man ground out. "It's not about her. It's about you and your obsession with Andar and the Great Witches. There was never room for anything else with you—especially not me."

"Soren," Perrin said softly. Red's eyes widened, the scene in front of her taking on a new edge as Perrin tentatively reached for his hand.

"Don't," the man suggested. He flinched away, taking a moment to collect himself. "I didn't come to talk about that. Your voice still has sway around here, Perrin—at least as much as the Paper Witch's. It's time we think about abandoning Andar and saving ourselves. And I'm not the only one saying that."

Perrin shook his head. "Abandoning Andar and the people in the castle will never be the right answer."

"Fine, don't listen to me." Soren tossed his cape back angrily. "But eventually, you're going to have to pick a side. I just hope you pick the right one." He turned on his heel, stalking away into the trees. Red froze, praying he wouldn't look left and spot her in the shadows.

She let out a silent breath as his footsteps receded. When she turned back to the clearing, she found a different set of eyes fixed on her.

"Red?" Perrin said in surprise.

Red flushed at being caught so obviously eavesdropping. Cinzel broke away from her and bounded through the bushes, greeting Perrin enthusiastically and snuffling at his pockets. Those bribes were certainly getting the job done.

"Sorry," Red huffed. "I was . . ." She bit her lip. It wasn't like she could tell him what she was really doing out here.

Perrin looked her up and down, taking in her sturdy boots and the worn pack over her shoulder. Then his face lit up with a grin. "Out for a walk, I take it."

Red clenched her hand around the strap of her bag. "You can't stop me."

Perrin's eyes sparkled. "From going for a walk? In the same general direction that Shane went when she headed for Aurora's tomb? Why would I stop you?" He slipped his hands into his pockets. "In fact, I wouldn't mind a walk myself—at least as far as the perimeter."

Red felt a little off balance at Perrin's offer and at the fact that he didn't seem intent on stopping her. She nodded hesitantly, and the two fell into step together, ducking under low-hanging branches and picking a path through the trees. Cinzel padded cheerfully between them, his tawny fur glossy with moonlight.

Red threw Perrin a sidelong glance. It wasn't her business, but she couldn't pretend she wasn't dying of curiosity.

"That guy you were arguing with . . ."

"My ex, Soren," Perrin filled in, rubbing the back of his neck. "He was always pretty rigid and uncompromising—probably why it didn't work between us. Also, he's Nikor's cousin, which was almost a dealbreaker from the start."

"*That* Nikor?" Red asked incredulously. Now that she was thinking about it, she could see a certain family resemblance in the way he'd flung his cape and stormed off.

Perrin laughed. "I do seem to have a knack for picking the wrong guys—and girls, for that matter." He pushed back a springy pine branch and shot Red a conspiratorial look. "When I was younger, my first crush was on the Paper Witch. So tragic and good-looking, riding away from Everlynd forever to fulfill his destiny . . . I pined for years. Don't tell him that, though."

Red couldn't help smiling at the thought of a young, starry-eyed Perrin writing the Paper Witch's name in the sand between magic lessons. "Very bold, trusting your secrets to a known thief."

Perrin winked. "I'll take my chances."

Red kicked a rock out of the path, her thoughts drifting back to the argument she'd overheard. "What did he mean, anyway? *Pick a side?*"

Perrin sighed. "Between Everlynd and Andar," he

explained. "But the thing is, I already picked a side a long time ago."

He went quiet for a moment, fidgeting with his hourglass necklace.

"My parents were part of the rangers, the Red Ember squad that tried to rescue Witches trapped outside Everlynd. They died rescuing two young boys from the Witch Hunters." Perrin scuffed his boot hard against the ground. "That was the last mission the rangers ever took. After that, Nikor said the losses weren't worth it. He disbanded the rangers—turned his back on everything they stood for. And there weren't many people who disagreed with him."

"That's . . . I'm so sorry," Red whispered, swallowing hard. His parents had died trying to rescue people like Red. And Perrin had grown up alone—a feeling Red knew all too well.

Perrin shook himself, managing a small smile. "My parents were the strongest voices on the council for Everlynd using its power to do more. They believed in Andar. If we give up on it now, their sacrifice will have been for nothing."

Red didn't know what to say to that. They walked in silence until the trees broke away and they stepped into moonlight once more. Below them, where the ridge sloped down, the black wasteland was just visible, spread out like a pool of vast still water, the pearl of the full moon gliding through an equally black sky. The last traces of twilight had disappeared.

Red turned away and looked south instead, toward slopes of waving grasses and soaring pines. The direction Shane had gone.

"I guess this is where my walk ends," Perrin said. "But

if you and Cinzel want to go a few more miles, you might just catch up with Shane." Then his expression softened, and he reached out a hand, touching her lightly on the shoulder. "Never think you don't belong here, Red. There was a special connection between the Great Witches, and I'd like to think that could extend to their descendants."

"Are you asking me out?" Red teased, giving her skirt a flirty swish.

"Oh, no—you aren't nearly wrong enough for me," Perrin chuckled. "But the descendants of the Great Witches is a pretty exclusive club these days: membership three. As far as I know," he added, looking thoughtful.

Thinking of the Snake Witch made Red's insides twinge, but she couldn't tell why anymore. Ivan's sneering face and the stories her father had told her, stories of the Monster Witch he'd reviled, those memories still haunted her. But with them came the memories Perrin had shown her: the Snake Witch and the Dream Witch with their hands intertwined, their foreheads together, their lips curled with the secret promise they'd whispered on the shore.

Red shook her thoughts away. "I doubt I belong in any club. I'm nowhere near as strong as you or the Paper Witch."

"I still have a ways to go myself," Perrin admitted, looking sheepish. "The Paper Witch is appalled by how little progress I've made and is determined to teach me personally."

Red blinked, suddenly realizing something. "You're hiding from him, aren't you? That's what you're doing out here!"

Perrin flashed her a grin. "I won't tell if you won't."

Then he turned for the Everlynd camp, walking backward and waving. "If anybody asks, I fell asleep out here and never saw anything. I'll see you when you get back."

"When I get back," Red repeated. And even though, just minutes ago, she would have been glad to never see this place again, the thought wasn't as awful as she'd expected. Red wondered, not for the first time, if Perrin had some kind of magic beyond his dream magic. How else did he always seem to know exactly what to say?

Cinzel nuzzled her and tugged playfully on her burgundy skirts. With one last look back, Red let the wolf lead her across the moonlit field, feeling lighter than she had in a long time.

IT WAS PAST midnight when she finally reached Shane's camp, her gray cloak pulled up against the night chill. At least, Red thought it was Shane's camp. Cinzel had stopped sniffing and was circling her legs, flicking his tail like he did when he'd found the source of a scent. But the fire in the little ring of stones looked like it had been hastily doused, and while there was a heavy pack leaning against one tree, the bedroll beside it was empty, the blankets tossed aside.

The camp seemed deserted. Red moved cautiously into the circle of pines, intent on kicking through the abandoned pack for proof she was in the right place. She was tired and hungry from her long hike, and she'd been sorely hoping for a warm fire and bite to eat from Shane's provisions.

Red was only two steps in when she was suddenly tackled.

She shrieked as a dark figure slammed her into the dew-wet grass, wrestling with her cloak and flipping her onto her back. Red sank her teeth into her attacker's wrist.

"Ow!"

That voice was all too familiar—as was the colorful string of curses that came after it. Red fumbled the cloak out of her face and found herself staring up at Shane, who had pinned her to the ground. The huntsman looked wild-eyed, her ash-brown hair a sleep-addled mess.

Shane's mouth fell open. "Red?" she demanded, sitting back and letting her up. "What are you doing out here? I thought you were a Witch Hunter. I could have killed you!"

"A Witch Hunter?" Red repeated indignantly. "*That's* how I come off to you?" Shane was still hovering over her, close enough that Red might have felt her pulse pounding for an entirely different reason if she wasn't so insulted.

Cinzel surged forward, sticking his nose against Shane's and greeting the huntsman with a lick right down the center of her face. "Good to see you, too, mutt," Shane said, pushing the wolf's head away from her mouth. But it was an affectionate push, and Red's heart swelled listening to Cinzel's happy crooning. He always knew exactly what she was feeling—and he was far too honest about it.

Red looked away, rubbing at her wrists. "Even if I was a Witch Hunter, in what world would it make sense to tackle me to the ground? Without a weapon, I might add." Red cast about, finally spotting Shane's ax partially buried in the bedroll by the smoking remains of the fire.

At least Shane looked a little embarrassed as she got to

her feet, offering Red a hand up. "I heard noises coming from the trees. I just . . ."

"Acted without thinking," Red filled in. She smoothed out her skirts, throwing Cinzel a dirty look for letting Shane get the jump on her. "This is the kind of thing that wouldn't happen if you had someone to split the watch," she pointed out.

"Red," Shane warned. Her arms were crossed, her lips pressed into a frown. "I already told you . . ."

Red tossed her disheveled curls out of her face. "Yes, yes. You decided this ruin is too dangerous for me. But guess what? I decided traveling alone is too dangerous for you." At Shane's stubborn look, she huffed, throwing up her hands. "Just because I can't be your treasure-hunting partner this time doesn't mean I can't watch your back and tend the fire and . . . cook or something."

"You can cook?" Shane asked, sounding skeptical.

"That's beside the point," Red snapped. "The point is . . ." There was a little catch in her throat, a sharp sting that made her voice waver. "Don't send me away."

The words came out more vulnerable than she meant them to. Red bit her lip to keep the *please* down. Her heart was beating too fast, some small, quivering part of her hanging on Shane's answer.

Shane looked down at her, lips parted, her gray eyes searching Red's face. And then she caved.

"You can come with me as far as the valley. But you absolutely can't follow me into that tomb. Promise me, Red."

Red scoffed, relaxing. "Believe it or not, I have no interest in going into some ancient tomb that robs people of their memories. But if you want to be absolutely sure, there is one way." Tentatively, she traced her hand down Shane's wrist, her fingers slipping in between the other girl's. "Come back safely, and I'll have no reason to go in after you."

Shane squeezed her hand. "You've got yourself a deal."

Her grip felt so warm and strong. Red looked down, studying their laced hands, and thought again of the two women on the shores of Evista Lake, their silhouettes shimmering against the mirror-bright water.

Traced in our palms, traced in the stars. An unbreakable promise.

The lines of Red's palm were barely there anymore, covered up by all her scars. But Shane's palms were scarred, too, and rough with calluses from the handle of her ax. Maybe Red had been wrong, worrying that she'd worn those lines away. Maybe she'd just been making them, all this time, in all the good and bad ways—the grooves in her palm, the places where they fit together.

Shane obviously wasn't on the same page, or that brainless oaf wouldn't have dropped her hand so fast.

"Well, the fire's too wet to light again," Shane said, making a face at the damp logs. "It'll get pretty cold tonight. And it looks like you brought exactly no supplies. Guess you'd better . . . I mean . . ." Shane trailed off, scrubbing a hand through her hair and throwing Red an awkward sideways glance. Then she kicked out of her boots and crawled into the bedroll, holding the blankets open. "Well? Are you coming?" she asked, her voice brusque.

A little thrill rolled down Red's spine. "How very forward of you," she teased, batting her eyelashes.

"Not like it'd be the first time," Shane grumbled, very obviously fighting a flush.

Red faked a gasp. "Scandalous. Just how many treasure-hunting partners have you lured into your bedroll with the old douse-the-fire routine?"

Shane spluttered. "That's not— I meant it wouldn't be the first time for us! I don't . . . Ah, shut it," she grumbled, as Red lost control of her giggles. She lumped her cloak into a pillow and toed off her own heeled boots, lining them up neatly next to Shane's. Then Red wiggled down into the bedroll next to her, a spark racing along her skin at every accidental touch.

Even as short as they both were, it was a tight squeeze—much tighter than the luxurious bed in Everlynd where Red had first fallen asleep with Shane's arm around her. She rested her cheek against her balled-up cloak and counted every little breath, the two of them nose to nose. She could feel the ridges of Shane's knuckles against hers, their ankles brushing, their knees softly knocking—all the funny little imperfect parts of them trying so hard to fit together.

And those fierce gray eyes fixed on her, heavy with longing. Red stared back into those eyes and wondered if that was what the ocean was like, so deep and endless it would pull her under.

She had felt this in Everlynd, too—the heat, the soft shudder as Shane's hand slid down her arm. But this was better. This wasn't a fragile dream of a moment, something Red was just stealing for a little while. This was hers. She had fought for it—betrayed for it—faced her oldest and her deepest fears for it. And now she got to keep it, as long as she was brave enough to lean in.

"Red," Shane murmured, so close she felt it against her lips.

Red's heart rocked like an unsteady boat. Then Cinzel flopped down right on top of them, his heavy paws digging into her stomach, and Red burst out laughing, the sweet tension of the moment disappearing as Shane groaned and rolled onto her back.

"Great. Now I'll wake up smelling like dog."

"Are you implying that's how *I* smell?" Red demanded, appalled.

"Well, I wasn't going to say anything."

Shane yelped as Red's cold toes dug into her calf. Still, Red couldn't fight a smile as she closed her eyes, drifting off faster than usual squished between Shane and Cinzel.

It wasn't what she'd imagined as a little girl in the Forest of Thorns. But she'd finally found that place she'd been searching for. Somewhere she was wanted. Somewhere safe and warm.

Fi

AURORA'S TOMB WAS breathtaking.

Fi stood at the edge of a shimmering lake, looking across the water at the doorway to the tomb. Pillars of white framed a cavern cut directly into the stone of the southern hills, which rose around her, forming a summer valley speckled with wildflowers. The lake was shallow, barely deeper than Fi's hand, and the shore was thick with weeping willows, their sweeping boughs inclined as if forever in mourning. Though it had been hundreds of years, Fi still caught the glimmer of tarnished silver bells twined through the branches.

She held her breath as a soft breeze rolled through the valley, the music of the bells surrounding her with a sad, sweet song. Even wild and overgrown, it was more beautiful than she'd imagined.

The peace of the moment was broken by the flap of rustling wings. It was just a pair of starlings taking off, but Fi shivered, remembering the great black wings that had borne her here. She resisted the urge to turn around and try to pick out Briar's form through the trees. Watching her and waiting.

She had no time to waste.

White stones made a path to the tomb. Fi stepped across them carefully. The reflection of the clouds in the shallow water was so clear she felt like she was walking across the sky.

There was no door to push aside. Fi ducked inside the cavern and had to pause to let her eyes adjust to the sudden dim. A vast space stretched out before her, its thick walls carved into false columns veined with streaks of gold.

At the center stood a statue of Aurora. It was tall, at least twice the height of a person. The king consort who carved it had obviously dearly loved the queen, and he'd captured her smooth face tipped serenely to the side with just a hint of a smile on her lips. The crown on her head made her look regal, but the image was softened by the long-stemmed roses spilling out of her arms. The wall behind her was carved into an enormous relief of a rose garden.

Legend said that on the day Aurora was laid in her tomb, the Witches of Andar brought thousands of roses to lay at her feet, enough to fill this entire chamber. Fi almost imagined she could still smell the sweet fragrance of crushed petals clinging to the rocks.

Fi took a deep breath, tucking her copied map back into her pocket. She had managed to keep the Spindle Witch in the dark about the real reason for her trip to Illya, and if Armand had done as he promised, everything was ready. She felt the squeeze of anticipation in her chest. There were so many moving pieces to keep track of and so many ways this plan could go wrong—but if it worked, this could all be over soon.

Concentrate, Fi thought, shaking her head before she got too far ahead of herself. Solving the riddle of Aurora's tomb came first. This was one of the most dangerous ruins that had ever existed—any distraction here could prove fatal.

That was when she heard it—a noise from deeper in the chamber.

Someone else was in this tomb. The figure was partially hidden by the statue of Aurora, moving slowly along the back wall. Fi darted forward, stepping up on the statue's pedestal and pressing herself against the carved skirt. The cold rock sent a shiver down her spine. She inched around the base, angling her head just far enough to get a view of the person.

Fi's stomach swooped, and she had to hold on to the pedestal to keep from falling.

Shane!

The girl's gray eyes were scouring the wall, and her short-cropped hair was messy, as though she had been tugging on the ends in frustration. Fi could see the hint of an Everlynd-blue shirt underneath her dusk-red coat. An open-sided lantern dangled from one hand, and Fi couldn't hold back a smile as she watched Shane swing the flame carelessly, nearly lighting her own elbow on fire. The huntsman let out a few loud, creative curses.

A wave of longing swept through Fi so fast it made her eyes prickle. Suddenly, she missed Shane more than ever—more than she had locked in the Spindle Witch's bleak tower, or poring over books in the oppressive silence of her little room, or any of the long nights she'd spent talking to the empty air after Briar flew away. She wondered if that longing had been there the whole time, held back by a carefully propped-up dam of plans and distractions, waiting to burst the moment she saw her partner again. Fi dug her fingers into the statue, biting back the urge to shout Shane's name.

Fi was at a crossroads. She could race across the cave, throw her arms around Shane, and tell her partner everything. But she had a feeling Shane would not approve of her plan to take on the Spindle Witch. Or her choice to use Armand. Or the fact that she was still willing to risk a lot of lives for a gambit that she herself gave at best fifty-fifty odds.

Fi had never met someone who could dig their heels in like Shane. If she didn't like Fi's plan, she would do everything in her power to derail it. The Spindle Witch's patience with Fi was already hanging by a thread—one more delay, one wrong move, and she would lose Briar forever. She couldn't gamble with that.

With a silent apology, Fi turned away from her partner to study the giant relief carved on the back wall depicting a wild, overgrown garden filled with exquisitely carved roses. Shane was tugging at all the stone flowers, searching for a hidden door.

Fi and her partner were clearly working off of the same information. There were only fragmentary accounts of the treasure hunters who had entered the depths of Aurora's tomb and lost their memories, written mostly by the people who found them wandering in the woods, or, in a few cases, the companions they left behind. But there was one common thread: every account described the treasure hunters disappearing through a door in the wall of roses.

Shane, in spite of her impatience, had clearly been methodically making her way across the room, trying every one. Though she wished it were under better circumstances, Fi felt a little thrill in her stomach at the thought of going head-to-head with Shane in a treasure hunt. Fi had confidence in her knowledge, but Shane had a way of pushing through things, and if it came to an actual fight, Fi would definitely be at a disadvantage.

She had to take the lead right now. What were the clues? What didn't fit?

Fi studied the relief. The first details her eyes were drawn to were the soft lines carved down from the ceiling over the tangle of roses. Sunbeams, maybe? They were all at the same angle, too. Fi let her eyes settle back over the tangle of roses that seemed to sprawl in every direction.

No. Not in every direction. Fi's fist curled in excitement. Most of the roses were bent over or tipped away from the carved rays. Only one blooming rose had its face tipped directly toward the sunbeams. Aurora had been named after the dawn, and her reign had brought the dawn of a new kingdom. The way forward would be facing the sun, just like Andar.

No details in ruins were ever by accident. Fi smiled faintly, remembering another ruin where she had said almost those exact words to her foul-mouthed partner.

Shane hadn't reached the rose that would open the hidden doorway yet, but she was close, and as thorough as she was being, there was no way she'd miss it.

Fi weighed her options. Taking Shane in a fight was out. Her best bet was to get through the door first and then block the passageway behind her. She felt around in her pockets for something heavy. In truth, she was woefully unprepared, armed only with what she could smuggle out of the Spindle Witch's tower. She had a single rag-wound torch that wouldn't last long once it was lit, and her flint and tinder, which she'd managed to hang on to for the entire journey. Her rope hung from her belt in a tight coil. Beyond that, all she had was paper, charcoal, Armand's antidote, and one short dagger.

Fi pulled the blade from her belt. It was ancient, just like everything else in the Spindle Witch's tower, with a worn handle and a dull blade. It was her only weapon, and she was loath to lose it, but she'd be no match for Shane with a dagger anyway.

Fi steadied herself, then pulled back her arm and threw the dagger toward the entrance of the tomb. It was one of the oldest tricks in the book, and also one of the most effective, because people always felt compelled to investigate strange noises—especially hotheads like her partner.

The dagger cracked against one of the stone pillars and then clattered to the ground. Shane stiffened, whirling with the lantern raised.

"Who's there?" she called out. There was a beat of silence, and then Shane unslung her ax, stalking toward the front door. "Red, I swear if that's you . . ." she grumbled.

Fi held her breath, sliding around the statue as Shane passed on the other side. For one moment, they were only feet apart, one slab of stone and a whole rash of decisions separating them.

Fi dropped soundlessly off the pedestal and ran quickly and quietly toward the hidden door. Shane's heavy bootsteps didn't immediately pound after her, and Fi let out a sigh of relief, skidding to a stop beside the wall. She reached out, tracing her fingers over the stone and examining the rose. It was beautifully wrought, with delicate petals carved mid-bloom. It was also more worn than the stone roses around it—no doubt smoothed by the hands of a hundred treasure hunters who had come before her. Close inspection revealed an almost invisible seam where it attached to the wall. It was meant to be turned to the same angle as the sunbeams.

Fi reached out, closing her hand over the rose. The stone was stiff, and she had to use both hands to wrench it free from years of grit and dust. After a half turn, it clicked into place, almost jumping out of her hand. There was a deep rumble in the wall, and the room began to tremble, followed a second later by an angry shout.

"Hey! Fi!"

She shot a glance over her shoulder. Shane was running straight for her, lantern swinging wildly.

Fi turned back to the door, willing the old mechanisms to turn faster. "Come on, *come on,*" she whispered, pressing against the wall as hard as she could. She could hear the angry thud of Shane's boots getting closer. The hidden door had slid aside far enough to reveal a strip of darkness, a corridor of some kind, but it was still too narrow to squeeze through.

"Don't you dare!" Shane was shouting. The girl was close enough that Fi could see the whorls on her lantern and the anger snapping in her eyes. Fi turned desperately back to the door. She could get her arm in all the way to the shoulder. If she just wiggled her hips a little, she might be able to push through.

Fi threw herself into the gap. Her hips caught between rough jaws of stone, and for a sickening moment, Fi thought maybe she was stuck. She gave a hard kick, heels pushing off the ground, and then suddenly she was through.

"Oh no you don't!" Something heavy slammed into Fi from behind. She flew free of the doorway as Shane seized her arm in a death grip. "Gotcha!"

They stumbled together into the dark. Shane's lantern banged against the wall, hissing and sputtering. Through the wild shadows, Shane's blazing eyes locked on hers. Then she felt the ground slope beneath her, and her stomach lurched with horror. This wasn't a passageway after all—it was a trick floor tipping them down into a chute.

It was too late to stop their fall. Already, Fi could feel the treacherous gravel slithering out from under her boots. Shane hadn't loosened her tenacious grip, so Fi did the only thing she could—she grabbed Shane's hand and thrust the lantern as far away from them as her arm would reach. Hopefully it would be enough to keep them from getting brained by the metal casing or setting their clothes on fire. Then the ground vanished, and she and Shane plummeted down into the blackness.

Fi had thought she was ready, but she still found herself shouting in surprise as they careened down the chute. At least Shane was yelling right along with her. The lantern ripped out of her hand, tumbling down the chute ahead of them with a bang and clatter as it bounced off the walls.

This is why you never rush a ruin! Fi berated herself.

Then suddenly she and Shane were in free fall, spat out into the air for just a moment before they hit a soft floor of sand. The lantern rolled away from them, the flame sputtering angrily. For a long moment, the two of them lay side by side, Shane groaning and Fi just trying to get her breath back.

At last, Shane pulled herself onto her stomach, crawling to the lantern before it went out. As soon as she righted it, she turned back to pin Fi with a searing glare that probably would have turned her into a smoking pile of ash if Shane were a Witch.

"I can't believe you just tried to ditch me," she ground out. "Again."

Fi ignored that, slowly getting to her feet and peering around. They had tumbled into some kind of smooth cylindrical shaft, maybe ten feet across and at least thirty deep, almost as if they were at the bottom of a giant well. Fi could think of a lot of reasons to make a room this shape in a ruin—most of them unpleasant. The musty air hit the back of her throat.

It was hard to see in the dim, with only a single sputtering lantern, but if she tipped her head back far enough, she caught the glimmer of glowing crystals embedded high above her, little pinpricks of light that seemed to be growing brighter. *Like the crystals in the ancient forge.* Fi could just make out the flicker of shapes carved into the smooth stone walls, each one winking with lustrous gold.

"Are you listening to me?" Shane demanded. A second later, Fi found herself backed against the wall with Shane's fist in her collar. Something hard dug uncomfortably into her back. Shane's eyes burned into hers. "How could you leave with the Spindle Witch like that? What the hell were you thinking?"

Shane reached for her again, and Fi wondered if she was about to be on the receiving end of Shane's *aggressive* brand of justice. Instead, she was yanked into a bone-crushing hug. It felt like all the fight was squeezed right out of her along with her breath. Her eyes slid closed, and she wrapped her own arms slowly around Shane's back, hugging back just as tight.

"I'm glad you're in one piece," Shane said gruffly. "But I'm still extraordinarily pissed at you." She pulled back but kept hold of Fi's shoulders, as though she were afraid Fi might disappear the second she let go.

"I'm glad to see you, too," Fi whispered, her throat a little thick.

Shane scowled. "Yeah. I could tell by your big happy greeting and the way you tried to ditch me in the entry hall." She finally let go, shooting Fi a sideways glance. "What are you doing here, anyway?"

There were so many ways to answer that. So many things she could tell Shane—and so many more she couldn't. Fi swallowed hard. "I'm here to retrieve something for the Spindle Witch."

Shane stiffened, her eyes turning flinty.

Fi hurried on before Shane could change her mind and throttle her after all. "Look, I have a plan to stop her, okay? I can't tell you what it is yet, but—"

Shane crossed her arms. "Forget it. *I can't tell you my plan* is something people only say when they have a bad plan."

Fi couldn't really disagree with that, but . . . "Shane, you're just going to have to trust me."

Shane scoffed. "Oh, that's rich coming from—"

Whatever else she wanted to say vanished into the piercing shriek of stone moving against stone. Fi jerked her head up. A thick stream of sand hit the floor right behind them—so hard the sharp grains pelted their legs. Fi stumbled back, throwing a hand up to shield her eyes.

"What the . . . ?" Shane swore, choking and coughing on the dust.

Sand was pouring out of a dark hole in the ceiling, puddling and slithering out across the floor. Fi's stomach plummeted as she realized exactly why this room was fashioned like the bottom of a well. If they didn't escape fast, they'd be buried alive.

The crystals had brightened to blistering clusters of blue-white light, just enough for Fi to pick out details of the shaft. There was some kind of a door set into the wall at the very top, but it was barred shut, the old wood blocked by rusty iron rods. Even if they could get there—and that was a very optimistic *if*—she had no idea how they'd get through.

Shane growled in frustration, kicking at the swiftly piling mountain of sand before rounding on Fi.

"This isn't over," she warned. "But temporary truce?" She held out a hand.

"Just for the one ruin," Fi agreed, feeling a rush of nostalgia as Shane's crushing grip closed over hers.

"I'm not going to let you go again," Shane promised. Then she turned back to the cascade, stamping down the sand that was already up to her toes. "So, what have we got . . . partner?"

"Give me a sec." Fi dusted herself off, spinning a slow circle.

The round walls were smooth as though they had been sanded down, leaving not a single toehold, but there were pictures carved into the rock, all painstakingly filled in with delicate gold that glistened like molten fire.

At the bottom of the shaft were twelve figures about as tall as she was, each dressed in sumptuous robes. Fi's eyes traced each one. Instead of being adorned in jewels, they seemed to be decked out in natural elements. One woman wore a coronet of glittering wheat stalks, and the man beside her carried not a scepter but a slender branch of flowers carved so exquisitely Fi could tell they were plum blossoms. The woman across the well held a crystal of frost in one hand, her cape sewn of bristling feathers.

Above them, so high Fi could barely make it out, another shiver of gold circled the room—lines of ancient runes scratched deep into the stone. It didn't look like a Witch language, but she recognized the shapes of a few of the letters. This must be an even older alphabet, a language that preceded Andar's founding.

"Any idea who these people are?" Shane asked. She stuck her hand into the cascade of falling sand and jerked it back just as fast, the force nearly enough to knock her over. "This is filling up in a hurry," she warned, sizing up the stone walls. "If we need to do something down here, we'd better do it quick."

Fi was barely listening. There was something about the twelve figures and the old runes written above them—something that niggled in the back of her brain, a snatch of an old story she couldn't grab hold of. She found herself unconsciously tugging at her earlobe, backing up to study the barred door at the top. Her back hit the wall, that same hard something jabbing into her spine as when Shane cornered her a moment ago.

"I think I found something," Fi called excitedly. Shane crowded in next to her, peering over her shoulder.

There was a metal lid sticking out from the stone, tucked into the curl of one carving's cloak. At one point, it may have been painted to blend in with the rock, but now it was rusted over. Shane dug her fingers under the flaking edge. The hinges creaked against her grip, but then they gave, the lid banging down against the wall. They blinked through the sand cloud to see what they had uncovered.

A jagged hole was cut horizontally into the stone. It looked just big enough to slip a hand through, but it was utterly dark, and deep enough that Fi couldn't see exactly what was down there. Shane grabbed the back of her collar before she got too close.

"Be careful," she warned. "Looks like whoever buried Aurora wasn't playing around."

A ring of razor-thin blades lined the edge of the hole, glittering wickedly in the lantern light. Fi was willing to bet the wrong move would make them constrict. Someone could literally lose a hand in this trap.

Shane reached out a finger, gingerly testing one of the blades. She yanked her hand back with a hiss.

"Still sharp," she confirmed, wiping the thin streak of blood on her pant leg. "Surprisingly nasty trap for this peaceful lot."

"What?" Fi asked, confused.

"The people on the walls." Shane waved around. "Not a

single one of them has a weapon—well, unless you count that guy with the flowering tree branch."

Trust Shane to be clocking whether the decorations were armed. Fi's head shot up, her gaze traveling the room again. Twelve figures. The ancient writing from before Andar was united. And now this bladed trap.

She sucked in a breath. "I know who these people are and what we have to do. But you're not going to like it."

"Shocker." Shane stomped her feet again and glared at the sand falling endlessly, like a ticking clock. "Tell me, but make it fast—you know, like we're stuck in the bottom of an hourglass."

"Right," Fi said, pinching her temples. Her knowledge of the founding of Andar was a lot spottier than her knowledge of the Witches who came later. But the story painted out in this room was one she could never forget—not since she first heard it from her father as a wide-eyed child, mesmerized by the iron will of Andar's first queen.

"The people on the walls are the twelve warring lords Aurora united to create the kingdom of Andar. Some she defeated in battle, some she negotiated with, and some she helped with great feats of magic. The man with the flowering branch—he must be the lord of the southern duchy, which was known for vast groves of plum trees. The woman with the feathers is probably from the owl forest—"

"Less of that, more of whatever will make the sand stop," Shane demanded. Behind them, the lantern sputtered and went out as the sand gushed through the metal frame. Luckily, the crystals were as bright as lamps now, illuminating the whole well with an eerie glow.

"The important part is the end of the story," Fi said in a rush. "It's said Aurora convinced every single lord to take the knee willingly by offering her arm."

"Her arm?" Shane repeated, her forehead bunched in confusion.

Fi nodded. "As a gesture of trust, when she asked to speak to a lord, she would take off her gauntlets and lay her bare arm out beneath an ax so that if the lord felt betrayed, they could take her arm as recompense."

"Hearing that makes me like Aurora more, but I think I like this trap less," Shane said, looking askance at the arm-sized hole in the wall.

Fi's stomach fluttered, the excitement of the ruin finally taking hold of her. "This is Aurora's trap. Aurora's tomb. To get through, you have to be willing to risk at least as much as she did."

"Fine," Shane said. "But it should be me."

Fi bit her lip, glancing between the wall and the gushing sand. The insidious hiss rushed in her ears. "Okay. But you should probably take your coat off so your sleeve doesn't snag on the blades."

Shane nodded, slipping the ax and its harness off her shoulders. Fi waited until her back was turned. Then she shoved Shane hard, making her stumble across the piles of sand.

Shane was the best warrior Fi had ever met. There was no way she was going to let Shane lose an arm—not in a mess Fi had gotten them into.

"Sorry, Shane," Fi whispered, as she thrust her own arm into the wall, right between the blades.

12

---✦---

Shane

FOR A SECOND, neither of them breathed. Shane stared at her partner's wide eyes, waiting in horror for the sound of screeching mechanisms or a nasty squish. But it never came. Fi's shoulders slumped, and her head sagged back against the wall.

"It's okay," she rasped. "I think there's something in here—feels like a lever."

Well, that was luckier than Fi had any right to be. Shane balled up her coat, tossing it angrily aside.

"I'm thinking of revoking your position as the brains of this partnership." She couldn't believe Fi had pulled another fast one and stuck her hand in there—or that Shane couldn't yank her back out without lopping Fi's arm off. "Your list of offenses is mounting," she said, fixing her partner with a hard look.

"Put it on my tab," Fi suggested drily. She turned sideways, sliding her hand farther inside until the blades were flush against her upper arm. "I think I can just reach it . . ."

The telltale groan of mechanisms sounded inside the walls, and for a second, Shane thought she saw a shiver of movement around the golden figures. Then it died out.

"Shoot," Fi said under her breath. "This is the kind of lever that won't stay down without constant pressure. As soon as I push this, I'm going to have to keep holding it. I'll be stuck here." Both their gazes dropped to the sand that was already over Fi's boots and still falling fast. Shane had dug herself out, but her partner wouldn't be able to anymore.

"No time to waste, then," Shane said. "Just do it."

Fi nodded. "All right. Three, two, one!" She twisted her arm, and the mechanisms sprang to life.

Shane threw a hand over her mouth as a thick cloud of dust dislodged from the shaking walls. Something rustled and shivered in the cracks between the stones. Tiny platforms no wider than Shane's hand were sliding out of the wall, spiraling upward like an impossibly narrow staircase. About halfway up, the platforms stuttered out, giving way to four thin steel beams on rusty chains that had dropped from the ceiling, clanking above her. Shane couldn't tell what those were for yet, but she wasn't looking forward to finding out.

"Guess I'm going up." Shane made quick work of strapping her ax over her shoulders and then picked up her jacket, which was half-buried already. She shook it off and threw it at her partner. Fi caught it with her free hand.

"Hang tight," she told Fi. "Cover your head with that if you, you know . . ."

"Start to get buried alive?" Fi guessed. She crooked an

eyebrow. "Hey, at least this time you don't have to worry about me going anywhere, right?"

"I didn't miss that terrible sense of humor," Shane grumbled, but she couldn't help trading a smile with Fi before turning for the wall. The first of the little platforms was waist high, and they were set about a leg span apart—maybe a little farther than Shane's legs, honestly. If she took it at a run and didn't miss any jumps, she should be able to make it up using the platforms like steps.

Tiny, treacherous little steps.

"Here goes nothing," Shane muttered, and raced for the wall.

Her boot hit the first platform too hard, her shoulder banging the wall and almost throwing her right back into the sand. She lurched forward instead, landing on the next step and the next. The rickety wooden platforms groaned under her boots. Some were worn down to nubs, like scrawny mushroom caps she could barely get a toe on. Shane swore, digging her fingertips desperately into the gold engravings of a woman's plumy crown as one of the platforms crumbled under her boot. The groove was so tiny she felt like her fingernails were going to rip out of the nail beds.

"Shane!" Fi shouted.

Her toe caught the next platform, and Shane threw herself forward, every muscle in her gut clenching. Her fingertips were raw and throbbing when she finally let go of the wall.

Somewhere beneath her, she heard Fi gasp in relief, but she couldn't spare her more than a glance. It was still enough to tell that the sand was already to Fi's thighs.

Shane wiped her sleeve across her sweaty forehead. The platform behind her was kindling, nothing but busted-up sticks poking out of the wall where the step had been. If she fell, she wouldn't get another shot at this. She was more than halfway up, but the last couple of platforms were farther apart. She was going to have to jump.

There was no point in calculating or overthinking it, or in wondering how many ways screwing this up could kill her. Shane got as much purchase as possible with her boot and then trusted her body and leapt. She almost overshot the mark, bashing her shoulder painfully into the wall to stop her momentum. That whole arm was going to be black and blue tomorrow. Two more jumps brought her face-to-face with the final platform and the first steel beam swinging above it.

Shane's lungs were on fire. She could feel her pulse thumping under her skin. She pressed her back to the cool stone wall and pushed off hard. Her boot hit the final platform—then suddenly there was a crack, and the rotted wood snapped, plummeting out from under her.

Shane's heart swooped into her guts. All instinct, she slammed her boot against the shorn rock, kicking off the wall and throwing herself bodily toward the steel beam swinging on its chain.

She heard Fi scream her name. Shane swore as one foot kicked into the stream of falling sand. She barely got a hand around the swinging chain before her body torqued with the force, the whole cascade trying to drag her down. Her bruised shoulder screamed in protest, all of her weight hanging from one hand.

Shane dangled there for a moment, scrabbling at the chain crusted with sand. Then she swung her legs up, wrapping them around the beam and pulling herself on top of it.

She wanted to collapse there—maybe for several years. Instead, she rested her forehead against the cool metal for three quick breaths, just enough to stop her head from spinning. Then she sat up and looked around. From this close, the falling sand looked like a giant waterfall, and it was just as loud, the current rushing in her ears. It was harder to see through the dust, but Fi looked at least half-buried now. Maybe more. She had to hurry.

The hanging beams wobbled as Shane walked across them, but she would take a little wobbling over the dilapidated platforms any day. Each beam tilted up toward the next one, making a little walkway around the streaming sand. It would have been pretty straightforward except that the last beam, nearest to the ceiling, was dangling from one chain. The other had clearly snapped at some point, leaving it hanging like a big useless pendulum.

One problem at a time. Shane made her way along the swaying beams, her hands outstretched for balance. She still had to leap between them, and the ancient chains creaked and groaned under her like they were all one bad step from snapping and sending her tumbling down to join Fi in her sandy grave.

Shane inched along the next-to-last beam. She was high enough now to see that the bars over the little door had slid back into the rock, leaving it unlocked. That had to be the way forward. But something seemed off. Shane had no doubt Fi was right about the overdressed folks on the walls, and right about the willingness to sacrifice an arm. But was that what Aurora's trap was really about—sacrifice?

She squinted down the shaft. Fi was buried up to her chest, desperately holding Shane's jacket up to shield her face from the spray. Shane could tell she was breathing hard as the sand pressed in on her ribs.

She let her eyes sweep the whole of the well. Through the glittering cascade, she caught a glimpse of something on the opposite wall from the door—a narrow hollow cut into the stone, and inside, a jagged hole exactly like the one Fi had stuck her hand into. With the final beam broken, there was no way Shane could get to both sides. She'd have to jump and use the chain to swing to one side or the other.

It was the easiest choice she had ever made.

Speckles of sand ghosted around her. Shane took three running steps and then launched herself into the air. The drop yawned beneath her. Her hands closed around the chain, her boots clanging against the dangling steel beam.

Shane let out a whoop of exhilaration as the whole contraption swung toward the far wall. At the last possible second, she let go, careening toward the little hollow. A cloud of sand rose up around her as she landed. She couldn't even see Fi anymore, but none of the mechanisms had retracted, so she was still down there somewhere, holding on.

Shane checked the hole for blades and then shoved her hand inside. She had to stick her arm in all the way to the shoulder, but her fingertips ghosted over something—cold metal, the crank of a lever. Shane yanked it down. The mechanism nearly sprang out of her hands. Apparently, this one didn't require somebody to hang on to it like Fi's did. The cascade of sand slowed to a trickle as the fissure in the ceiling rumbled closed.

Shane spun around and gripped the wall of the hollow, peering down. The sand hadn't just stopped pouring in from above. Some kind of grate had opened in the floor, and right before her eyes, the sand was pouring away, hissing down into the bowels of the ruin. A second later, Fi appeared, coughing and spluttering, throwing Shane's coat and a mound of sand away from herself.

Shane's shoulders slumped in relief. She eyed the swinging beams for a second before jumping onto the lowest one, the metal shuddering under her weight. Then she slid carefully over the side, dangling from her fingertips for a second before dropping, using the quickly dwindling pile of sand to cushion her fall.

Her boots slipped out from under her in the slick pile, and she ended up on her backside—but luckily, that was somewhat cushioned, too.

"Shane!" Fi choked out, but it came out more like a garble.

Shane scowled, glaring up at the ceiling. "You know, for a supposedly peaceful Order of Magic, these Rose Witches sure spend a lot of time coming up with inventive ways to kill people." She bent to dig Fi's leg out of the sand, though she regretted that a second later as Fi pulled her boot free and almost kneed Shane in the chin.

Fi was still blinking at her, sand-crusted and bewildered. "What about the door? Why didn't you just take the chance and go?"

Shane snorted. "First of all, I'm insulted. Second, you

misunderstood this trap in a big way." She shook out her jacket and slipped it back on, resettling the ax on her shoulders. "That's not the right door up there—probably just a one-way ticket back to the mountains. And the way I read it, that story about Aurora isn't just about sacrifice. It's about trust. Nobody who would ditch their partner in a sand avalanche is going to make it through Aurora's tomb."

Shane glanced back to see whether that bit about trust had landed. Fi's face was certainly pinched into a frown, but Shane couldn't tell if that was guilt or the excessive amount of sand Fi was shaking out of her hair.

"Guess we're done with this lever, then." Still, Fi hesitated before she relaxed her grip, pulling her arm out of the hole fast as the mechanisms groaned again. But it was the good groaning this time—a half-sized door grinding open at the bottom of the wall, still partially covered by a mound of sand. Shane kicked it out of the way while Fi picked up the dark lantern and hooked it on her belt.

"Think it's safe to say the worst is over?" Shane asked.

Fi rolled her eyes. "Not if experience is anything to go by."

Shane took the lead this time, crawling on her hands and knees through the opening. It was roomy enough that she wasn't worried about getting stuck, but she was glad not to be all that broad-shouldered. She could hear Fi behind her, the lantern clanking against the ancient stone walls.

It felt like it took forever, but it was probably just half a minute before Shane felt empty air in front of her and slid out into a vast, open space, the darkness pressing in from all sides. Fi's boot lodged in her back as she scooted out of the passage right on her heels. The door snapped spitefully closed behind them.

Shane huffed out a laugh. "Just like old times, huh?"

She couldn't tell in the dark, but she had a feeling Fi was rolling her eyes. The girl knelt down, and Shane heard the scrape of her flint and tinder as the sparks flew once, twice before the lantern finally caught, casting a yellow glow.

Fi's features leapt out of the dark, her expression of apprehension turning to one of wonder as she stood, holding the lantern aloft.

They were in a wide rectangular room with sheer walls and no windows or doors. The floor was stone, but with patches of sand here and there, probably swept in from the previous room. At first, Shane thought the walls were covered with the same rose carvings as in the first chamber, but when she looked closer, she realized there were no flowers in bloom among these vines—just unopened buds and roses puckered at the tips, forever closed. A shiver crawled up her spine. It was eerie how much the rose-less vines looked like the wicked Forest of Thorns.

"Shane, look at this," Fi said, pointing. In the very center of the chamber, a great black slab of stone rested in a pool of dark sand. It was definitely in the shape of a coffin, but it looked like something that would be more at home in a haunted crypt than the tomb of a beloved queen.

"You think she's in there?" Shane asked. She pinched the skin between her thumb and forefinger just in case.

Steelwight had a lot of stories about angry ghosts and souls dragged to the other side for trespassing on the realm of the spirits. Shane had spent countless childhood nights lying awake in terror of those stories—mostly because her grandmother insisted that Shane could offend all the War Kings of Rockrimmon, living or dead, with her stubbornness and liked to finish her ghost stories with a jump scare, grabbing her grandchildren with her bony fingers so they wouldn't sleep a wink.

"There's no way to know for sure without checking," Fi said, not sounding the least bit concerned about stepping on any ghostly toes. "But . . . does this feel like the end of the tomb to you?"

"No," Shane agreed. "Plus, we're not currently standing on a pile of skeletons, and I don't see a place for dozens of treasure hunters with no memories to have escaped back to the forest. Which I guess makes this another—"

"Trap!" they finished together.

The word hadn't even stopped echoing before the air around them filled with a hissing noise. It sounded like a hundred snakes moving at once. Only there were louder noises, too, grating and grinding.

"The walls!" Shane shouted in warning, practically ripping her ax from its straps. Fi swung the lantern around, the light spinning dizzily as she scrabbled for her rope.

It was like all the walls had come alive, the rose vines writhing across the bare rock like a mass of snakes twisting over and through each other. Shane felt her heart slam into her throat. This was no trick or illusion, no ancient mechanism. This was real magic. Her knuckles curled over the ax as she watched the vines slither down from the walls, crawling toward them through the dark.

Shane had no idea how effective her ax would be against

a magic snake, but it would be pretty hard for those things to keep moving once she'd pulverized them. The lantern light flickered, the shadows growing and shrinking as Fi turned in a circle.

For just a second, the flame was hidden behind her partner's body. Suddenly, the uncurling vine in front of Shane had a second shadow splashed against the wall—one that wasn't cast by their lantern.

"Watch out!" Fi screamed, yanking Shane backward by her coat.

A wisp of light, ethereal as a ghost, rushed past them like a warm breath. It looked like one of her grandmother's will-o'-the-wisps, darting into the corners of the room and disappearing in the shadows.

"What is that thing?" Shane demanded.

Fi's eyes shone as she set the lantern on the ground, unspooling her rope. "I think it's our next clue," she said.

Shane felt Fi's back thump against hers, solid and steady. Then the snakes were on them, and she threw herself into the fight.

13

Fi

FI SET A length of rope spinning, trying to track the slithering vines while still keeping one eye on the little ball of light. It had retreated to a high corner of the ceiling, waiting. Fi would have to worry about that later. The first of the vine snakes was getting close, its stone leaves crackling as it plowed through the sand. Fi squared her stance, trying to recall all of the details of the room at the same time. There had to be a way out—a way forward—and a hint buried somewhere in the chaos around them.

A violent crash behind her signaled the beginning of the fight. Bits of broken stone skittered across the floor as Shane cracked her ax through the first vine.

With a rush of sand, another vine sprang at Fi, twisting around her wrist like a shackle. The hard stone cut into her skin as it cinched tight and then froze, turning back to unyielding rock. Fi yanked at her hand, but it was locked in place.

Two more of the vines were already racing toward her. Desperately, Fi let her rope fly. The metal ring bounced off the writhing vines with a loud *ping!* and then lurched out of her grip. The rope had snagged on one of the stone thorns. Another stone vine hurtled at her, and Fi ducked just in time, nearly wrenching her arm out of its socket. She didn't miss the way the little wisp of light jumped, like it was waiting for just the right moment to strike.

"Shane!" Fi yelled. Behind her, she could hear the grunts and crashes of the huntsman dealing with her own problems.

"Little busy here, Fi!" Shane called back.

"The vines are trying to trap us so that light—*whatever it is*—can attack."

"What?" Shane demanded.

Fi tugged desperately against the stone shackle, kicking at one of the vines slithering around her feet. Her toe throbbed like she'd kicked solid rock, but at least she'd tossed it back a few inches.

The vine coiled again, the stone rippling like a viper as it readied to strike. Fi stretched as far as she could, struggling to grab her fallen rope. The vine launched at her. Instinctively, she threw her free hand up to protect her face, aware even as she did that she was about to be completely trapped.

The stone never reached her. Shane let out a great shout as her ax smashed into the vine, shearing it in half and leaving it a crumbling stump writhing on the ground.

"Keep your eyes covered," Shane warned. Then she spun the ax in her hands and slammed the blunt end into the vine trapping Fi's wrist. The stone shattered, bits of rock flying in all directions, and Fi stumbled free. The skin of her wrist was scraped raw. She grabbed her rope and turned to join Shane, only to find her partner shoving her toward the black coffin instead.

"This is a job for a huntsman," Shane growled. "Figuring a way out of here—that's a job for a bookworm."

Fi wanted to protest. Blood was already running down the side of Shane's face, her messy hair studded with shattered chips of gray stone. But her partner was right. Fi shot one last look at the strange wisp of light hovering at the edge of the room. Then she snatched up the lantern and rushed to the black coffin.

In the wavering light, the stone gleamed as though the entire thing had been carved from obsidian. The surface was smooth, and it was thick enough that Fi couldn't even hear a hollow echo when she rapped her knuckles against it. There was nothing else in the room—the clue she was looking for had to be here. But it was hard to focus with Shane locked in battle behind her.

Fi jumped as a torn-off hunk of vine smashed into the coffin inches from her.

Focus! Fi told herself. She sucked in a deep breath of dusty air. There was a seam running around the top edge of the coffin—invisible to the eye, but Fi could feel it with her fingertips. *A lid.* Fi forced her shoulder against the edge, using all of her weight to try to force it open. The stone didn't budge. Clearly, it wasn't a matter of brute force. She had to find a way to unseal it.

"Anytime, Fi!" Shane growled. Her voice was closer,

close enough that Fi could feel the shards of broken vines striking her calves as Shane hacked away. It really was just like old times.

Fi closed her eyes and pinched her earlobe. Hard.

This was the tomb of Aurora, the first Witch Queen and the founder of the Order of the Divine Rose. But there were no roses in this room, deliberately so, and unlike the sunlit statue and the garden of weeping willows, this place was dark and menacing, with a cold, forbidding coffin. It was the most unfitting place possible to be the resting place of a Witch like Aurora, the greatest light Witch Andar had ever known.

All at once, she was lost in a memory of Briar Rose, sparks of white light dancing between his fingertips. Briar, who had the same magic as his powerful ancestor.

This wasn't a trap at all—it was a test. Fi's eyes sprang open in time to see a stone vine flying toward her. Shane seized her by the collar and dragged her to the ground.

"I can't hold them off any longer!" she warned.

"It's okay." Fi squeezed her partner's shoulder. "I know what I have to do." Then she stood up, walking purposefully toward the ball of light. The vines snapped at her feet, leaves and bulbous rosebuds gliding through the sand.

"Fi!" Shane shouted. "Get back here!"

"Trust me," Fi said, throwing a look over her shoulder.

"I *really* hate it when you say that," Shane grumbled.

Fi just smiled. Then the little wisp of light darted forward, straight at her. Fi threw her arms wide and let it in.

It was like being hit by a blast of air, or a rush of mist if, instead of icy cold, the feeling was warm like the sun. At first, it felt like all the life was being sucked out of her,

her knees buckling, her breath stuttering and shallow in her chest. Then a different kind of power filled her, searing and bright. Fi looked down at her hands in wonder. They were glowing a silvery white.

On its own, her body turned back toward the obsidian coffin. Fi's first instinct was to fight it—to try and regain control of her body—but she didn't, because this was the test.

Aurora Rose was the most powerful light Witch of all time. The little ball was a fragment of the queen as surely as the Lord of the Butterflies hid pieces of himself in mirrors. Aurora was the guardian of her own tomb and the judge of who could enter. In the end, a trap, no matter how clever or carefully set, could only test a person's wits, or strength, or luck. The only way to know what was in a person's heart was to look inside them. Whenever treasure hunters broke into her tomb, Aurora's spirit had possessed them and simply walked the unworthy back out into the forest, leaving them with no memories of her.

And now? What would she do with Fi?

Fi felt herself take another step. The vines calmed around her feet, the stone rosebuds unfurling in the radiant white light. Fi closed her eyes. The glow that had filled her didn't feel as frightening when she imagined it was really Aurora, who looked so much like Briar Rose.

Please, she begged silently. *I may not be worthy, but my cause is. Briar is. Your descendant needs you*. At the thought of him, a tide of memories rushed over her, and Fi let herself get swept away in them—Briar carrying her piggyback, Briar swirling in his Red Baron costume, Briar's blue eyes sparkling like a deep, warm ocean, Briar kissing her under a sky of stars. Briar, who was the light burning in the center of her, chasing away all of the darkness and the fear and the loneliness she had gotten so used to. It made her ache and ache and ache, remembering how much she loved him and how he'd been ripped away from her.

Fi didn't know if Aurora could see those memories, too, but she tried to concentrate on that love, on her desire to save him and all of Andar. *If you ever loved someone like this*, she thought, *please help me get him back.*

Her body had reached the coffin. Shane was shouting her name, but it sounded distant and hazy. Aurora raised Fi's hands. Light gathered at the tips of her fingers, sparks of pure white magic. Fi gasped, a tear sliding down her cheek at the light that felt so familiar.

The Witch gathered all the magic into a single finger and then pressed it against the seam of the coffin. Light spilled out, running like water down the black stone, pulsing and bright. She could feel Aurora's presence like a warm sunlit day full of the soft scent of roses.

Suddenly, Fi's ears rang with a voice. It whispered with the rustle of the wind through the willows outside, the tinkling song of silver bells.

I've waited so long for this day.

It was Aurora, inside Fi and all around her. Light filled her vision, blinding white like she was looking directly at the sun, and when she blinked it away, she was somewhere else. The spire of the Spindle Witch's dark tower rose from the carpet of white bones—but for one instant, one second between blinks, it had looked inverted, as if she were seeing Briar's white tower rising from the black thorns instead.

Two lonely towers. Two Witches waiting for a rescue. Just as Fi had always suspected, these stories were infinitely more tangled than they first appeared.

Yes, Aurora breathed, close in her ears. *We found her in the tower. She was all raw magic at first—no skill, only instinct. But she learned fast. So fast.*

The scene had changed. They were inside the tower— the same empty tower Fi had wandered for weeks. Except it didn't look so lonely or empty. She recognized the Spindle Witch's room from the pictures scratched into the wall, but now it was crammed with Fi's unsteady desk and some other furniture, all laid out together as if to make a worktable. The surface spilled over with heavy leather-bound books, some wide open while others bristled with so many bookmarks and scraps of notepaper Fi doubted anyone could find what they'd marked.

The Lord of the Butterflies and Aurora sat on the floor, poring over a line of glowing runes that seemed to be shimmering on the surface of the stones.

The Lord of the Butterflies had his hair pulled back into a half ponytail, the rest of his long brown locks spilling over his neck and into the folds of his sea-green robes. Beside him, Aurora chewed thoughtfully on the tip of a quill. She was wearing a fine red velvet dress with sweeping sleeves, but she'd pushed them back to her elbows, straggles of her golden hair escaping from a messy bun. She had kicked off her boots and left them in a pile in the doorway, her crown with its gleaming ruby rose carelessly tossed onto a heap of cloaks.

Fi swallowed. They didn't look regal or imposing. They looked . . .

Happy.

"Are you feeling any of this, dear?" Aurora asked, and Fi's eyes were drawn to the last figure in the room.

It was the Spindle Witch, but not as Fi had ever seen her. The girl sat in the wide window with her long golden braid dangling over the sill. At Aurora's question, she lifted her head and reached dutifully out the window.

Her body jerked unnaturally, her fingers curling and flinching away as though she'd been pulled back by some invisible force. The runes beneath Aurora and the Lord of the Butterflies flashed at the same moment, a pulse running through them like a ripple across glassy water. Now that Fi was looking, she could see the runes weren't so much a language as a spiderweb of crisscrossing threads and whorls.

The phantom voice filled Fi's ears again. *An ancient and powerful enchantment ran through the entire tower, imprisoning the Witch and her magic forever. It stood unbroken for centuries . . . until we came along.*

Fi shivered, watching Aurora and the Lord of the Butterflies pulling and tugging on the lines of the spell. Sometimes the girl's body jerked in response, her head snapping like a puppet's.

She paid them no mind, all her attention focused on something in her lap. Her fingers flashed with gold as she tied it together with strands of her hair. Fi wasn't sure if the uneasy feeling rising through her was Aurora's or her own, but all she could do was watch.

In the folds of the young Spindle Witch's skirt lay a dead crow. Part of it was still covered in a tatter of black feathers, and part had been picked down to the bone. Both eyes were gone, and one foot was mangled and gnarled. Still, the Witch worked over it tirelessly, knotting each broken bone back together. When she was finished, she slipped down from the windowsill and set the corpse on the floor, sitting back on her heels.

Fi couldn't tear her eyes away. Brows knit in concentration, the Spindle Witch lifted one hand and then pulled, as if on an invisible thread. The bird twitched, one glossy wing quivering.

The Spindle Witch yanked again, harder. The crow let out a harsh squawk, hopping on its gnarled foot as it was dragged back to life. Black feathers drifted onto the girl's skirt as it flapped its mutilated wings.

"Stop that," Aurora warned, her voice sharp.

The Spindle Witch ignored her, cooing and coaxing the bird toward her. It hopped once. Twice.

Aurora's finger flashed with light. She brought it down quick, snapping the golden threads of hair that held the bird together. It collapsed into a pile of feathers and brittle bones.

"Ow!" the Spindle Witch cried, jerking back as though she'd been singed. "That hurt," she hissed, wrapping an arm around her waist.

The Lord of the Butterflies chuckled. "I've warned you many times, little spider. You have to learn to sever that magic from yourself before you use it, or whatever happens to that magic happens to you. Knots, twists, braids—tie it off. Otherwise, it's still connected to you. And a clever Witch like Aurora can use that to hurt you and teach you a lesson."

The Spindle Witch shot Aurora a venomous look, yanking more threads of gold from her hair. She stretched them between her fingers, tying a series of messy, ugly knots as she bent to repair the bird.

Aurora sighed, rubbing her temples. "You shouldn't encourage her like that."

The Lord of the Butterflies smiled, enigmatic. "I'm a teacher, Aurora. It's what I do."

The crow flapped to life again, hopping desperately across the threadbare rug. The Spindle Witch held out a hand, but the skeletal creature tried to take to the air, flapping unevenly. The Lord of the Butterflies rose and snatched it in one hand.

"Better," the man praised. "But there's another lesson here. Your hair is a powerful conductor of your magic, a medium like no other—but it is still a part of you. Like an offering of blood, it is a conduit through which magic can flow both ways." He gestured to the broken pieces of hair on the floor, the ones Aurora had snapped. "Once you've severed it, it's no longer part of you. That protects you. But you don't exactly have control of it anymore, either."

The bird in his hand struggled, driving its razor beak into the hand that squeezed it.

The Spindle Witch's eyes were bright with awe. "Like you and your mirrors," she said.

"Precisely," the man agreed. "That is why they are free to do as they choose and we don't always agree anymore. To give something its own magic is, in essence, to give it life."

The Lord of the Butterflies let go of the patchwork bird. The creature screeched and dove for the window. The bones sticking out of its wing caught the sill, and it unraveled before it even hit the ground.

"It's not true life, though." Aurora scooped the bird gently into her hands, straightening out the bent body. "It's a facsimile at best."

The Lord of the Butterflies clicked his tongue in disappointment. "Oh, Aurora. Who are we to decide what *true life* is?"

The man's eyes were fixed on the Spindle Witch as he said it. The gleam there reminded Fi of the man who'd written the letters she found in Everlynd's library—the Witch who had excavated the deepest places of the earth in his pursuit of magical knowledge, who had severed an entire family line from magic forever just to see if he could. A man who knew no boundaries.

Aurora's eyes had turned hard. "Why don't you wrap this up, and I'll bury it for you," she suggested, handing the crow's corpse to the Spindle Witch. The girl hurried away, fondly smoothing the short contour feathers around its rotted head.

Aurora swung her cloak onto her shoulders.

"I have to get back to Leonesse," she told the Lord of the Butterflies as she stepped into her boots. "The lords of the council are in an uproar again. But I'll try to make time to come back soon."

"You won't be missed," the man informed her coldly. "In fact, you've wasted so much of your time and talent trying to keep hold of this"—he held out her crown, the winking circlet dangling from the end of his finger—"I hardly recognize you as my assistant. Let alone my best student."

Aurora ignored the barb. Still, she hesitated as she reached for the crown. "I've begun to have doubts about her," she whispered, glancing over his shoulder to the girl spreading the crow out on her vanity, humming as she wrapped the dead bird in pale blue cloth. "That magic she uses . . ."

"It's magnificent," the Lord of the Butterflies said, his lips curled into a sharp smile. "In fact, she's given me a whole new perspective. Those little threads of life our friend manipulates, the ones she says run through everything—I wonder if the same is true of magic. Witches, their spells, the objects they create—even the earth itself. If I could learn to manipulate the threads of magic the way the little spider tugs at threads of life, there would be nothing I couldn't do."

Aurora's hand tightened to a fist, the crown digging into her skin. "That's a dangerous idea. Magic should have limits. You taught me that."

"Did I?" the Lord of the Butterflies asked airily. "Maybe I was thinking too small."

The memory ended there. White light fuzzed at the corner of Fi's vision, the images fading into the soft glow. But beyond her, somewhere inside Aurora, she knew there was more. An argument and a battle of iron wills. The creation of the Siphoning Spells, and the breaking of a dear and trusted friendship. But that moment—that had been the crack opening between them that yawned into a chasm.

Fi thought of the letters she'd found in the library of Everlynd. The veiled messages the Lord of the Butterflies had sent to Aurora as he detailed his twisted experiments and his admiration for the *little spider*—each letter more contemptuous and spiteful than the last. Why had Aurora shown her this particular memory? So she would know how dangerous the Spindle Witch was? Or was it the Lord of the Butterflies she was warning Fi about?

Fi almost toppled over as she found herself thrust back into her own body. The last of the light left her in a blinding flash. For just one moment, she thought she could see Aurora herself, more beautiful than she had been in any statue or picture book illumination, smiling with a spark of magic in her crystal-blue eyes. She reached out soft hands, laying them on either side of Fi's face.

You are worthy, Aurora whispered.

Then Fi blinked, and Aurora was gone, and so was the lid of the coffin. The vines had returned to the walls, just stone carvings once more. Fi's legs felt a little wobbly.

Shane grabbed her by the shoulders, less to hold her up than to shake her. "Are you okay? What was that?" she asked, clearly unnerved.

"Aurora," Fi said, barely a whisper. "And I think we've been invited to enter her real tomb."

With the lid gone, the coffin revealed not a body, but a set of stairs leading down, farther into the mountain.

"After you," Shane muttered.

Fi nodded, slipping over the edge of the coffin and leading the way down the stairs. She didn't know what Aurora had hoped she'd understand from the memory, but she'd have to ponder it later. She had a feeling she and Shane had almost reached the end of the tomb . . . and their briefly rekindled partnership.

14

~~»>>>~ ~«<<<~

Shane

SHANE FOLLOWED FI down the stairs with more than a little trepidation. She was still trying to wrap her head around everything that had just happened—particularly the part where her partner had apparently been possessed by the spirit of an ancient Witch. Right before the coffin sprang open, Shane could have sworn she saw the image of a golden-haired woman with a kind smile flash over Fi's, but it had been Fi's hands doing the magic.

Watching her, Shane had felt like she was about to lose Fi to magic the same way they had lost Briar Rose. Now, staring at the back of Fi's head, Shane promised all over again that she wasn't going to lose her partner—not to magic, and not to Fi's own ridiculous stubbornness.

The lantern swung back and forth in Shane's hand as they moved down the cramped passageway, the light bobbing over the narrow stairs. Shane had no idea what was waiting for them at the bottom, but after the dark chamber above, she wasn't getting her hopes up.

Fi stopped abruptly as the steps came to an end, blocking the way as she gaped in awe. Shane gave her a hard nudge. "This is a bad habit of yours," she pointed out. Then Fi moved aside, and Shane was the one left speechless.

They stepped out into sunlight. They had emerged in a niche cut into the wall of a high cliff, and at their feet lay a vast sea of roses. Water trickled down the cavern walls and gushed out of gaps in the sandy white and yellow rocks, forming a clear stream that rushed off the edge of the cliff as a waterfall. Rose vines spilled all around it, trailing down the rock wall as though the whole niche were a hanging basket of flowers. They had passed all the way through the mountain and come out the other side, where the high cliffs cut over a great rushing river that flowed to the southern sea. The air was full of flitting butterflies in a rainbow of colors and dust motes sparkling like gold in the sun. A few songbirds trilled from nests tucked into the walls.

Now Shane understood what Fi had meant when she called this Aurora's *real* tomb. This was the final resting place of a beloved queen.

"There she is," Fi breathed. Shane followed her partner's gaze.

There was no coffin, not even a platform of stone. Aurora's gleaming white skeleton lay in the grass among a tangle of roses and thorns. Green vines twined through the bones, and a haze of yellow butterflies had alighted on the rounded ribs. *Swallowtails*, Shane noted distantly.

Aurora had rested here so long that even her golden hair

was gone, and not a single scrap of her dress remained—only the gems that must have been sewn into the gown, now scattered through her bones like winking stars of sapphire. Her hands lay by her sides, buried in the blooms. On her bone brow rested the golden crown sparkling with the ruby rose.

Shane traded a look with Fi. She couldn't tell yet if the ring was even there, but she knew this was the end of their truce.

Fi seemed to have the same thought. She backed away slowly, curling her rope around one fist. "I don't suppose I could convince you to back off and let me get what I came for."

Shane snorted, sliding into a fighting stance. "Not a chance," she promised, eyeing the ring on the end of Fi's swaying rope. "The treasure is coming back with me, and so are you, whether you want to or not."

Shane locked her hands, cracking her knuckles. It wasn't an empty threat. She was beginning to think it might take a few knocks to the head to make Fi see reason on this subject—or, if that didn't work, Shane was confident that she could drag Fi's unconscious body out of here. One way or the other, she was getting her partner back.

"You can't beat me," she pointed out. Even with the rope, Fi was no match for her.

Fi sighed, swinging the ring up to catch it in her hand. "You're right," she admitted, dropping her gaze. "I could never take you." She took a step forward. "At least . . ." Fi's eyes shot up defiantly. "Not in a fair fight."

Shane saw it coming too late. Fi dropped low, sweeping her leg and taking out Shane at the knees before racing toward the skeleton. All Shane's reservations evaporated as she went down in the roses and got an armful of thorns. She tore free of the leaves and vines, sprinting after her partner and cursing herself for letting her guard down. She should have expected a cheap shot like that. Fi always had a backup plan.

Flower petals and butterflies scattered as Shane and Fi ran through the hidden garden, birds crying in shrill warning. Fi reached the skeleton first, dropping to her knees in the deep red blooms and stretching out her hands.

Shane launched herself at her partner, tackling her away from the bones and sending them both tumbling into the roses. Fi gasped as Shane's shoulder drove into her stomach, forcing the air out of her lungs. Shane tried to follow up the move, pinning Fi as she had Red, but Fi slid her knee up between them, forcing Shane off with a sloppy kick to her gut.

They both scrambled to their feet. Fi was panting hard, her arms scratched up and bleeding a little. Shane wiped a sleeve across her bleeding knuckles, where the thorns had dug deep into her skin.

"I have a plan to stop the Spindle Witch," Fi said slowly, her eyes boring into Shane.

Shane found that even less convincing the second time. "Yeah, so you said. But does the first part of your plan involve giving her everything she wants? Gambling with countless lives to save *one boy*?"

"If it was Red, you would be doing the same thing," Fi countered, her voice a little desperate.

That thought had occurred to Shane, but so had another one. "And if I did, then it would be your job to stop me from making that mistake." Slowly, she unslung the ax from her back.

Fi's face paled as she studied the weapon, trying to gauge how serious Shane was. "I'll stop it before it goes too far," she promised.

That was the last straw. Shane swung down her ax, burying it into the roses between them. "It's already gone too far!" she shouted. "She's too close to everything she wants. This right here, this is me stopping the Spindle Witch by stopping you."

She'd learned when she first came to Darfell how seductive that little bit of logic was, doing the wrong things for the right reasons. There was no end to how dirty you could get thinking that way—or how fast you could lose control.

"You're on the wrong side, Fi," Shane warned. "Now it's time for you to trust me."

Fi's squeezed her eyes shut like she was in pain. When she opened them, she was smiling, a soft, sad smile that made Shane ache. "I do trust you," she said. "More than you could ever know. That's why I can take this risk. Because I know you'll be there to stop her if I can't."

"That's not the kind of trust I meant!" Shane growled in frustration.

"I know," Fi said, and then all at once she moved, feinting one way and then spinning on her heel to try to get around Shane.

She should have known the same trick wouldn't work twice. Shane used the handle of her ax as a pivot and swung her body into a high kick. She caught her partner right in the chest with full force. Fi gasped in pain as she was thrown backward, skidding through the dirt. A part of Shane cringed, but she forced herself to keep going.

Fi was bent over clutching her chest, but as soon as Shane

got close, she shot up, whipping out her rope. The metal ring hit Shane's shin so hard it buzzed against the bone. Shane gritted her teeth. A few inches higher and the ring would have crushed her knee.

Shane wasn't the only one fighting for real.

Her leg throbbed, but she wasn't going to let that stop her. Before Fi could pull back, Shane stomped down and caught the ring under her foot. Fi jerked forward, still tangled with the rope. She had no chance to wind it back before Shane was on her, smashing her boot into Fi's shoulder.

Fi went down hard. She leveled a kick at Shane's stomach, right at the floating rib—always wickedly clever, but not fast enough. With a silent apology, Shane caught Fi's ankle and flipped her face down into the roses, hearing the other girl hiss as she got a face full of thorns. Fi thrashed, tangled in her own rope, managing to smash one boot out wildly enough to throw Shane off balance and break her grip.

They were right by Aurora's skeleton, close enough that Fi rolled over into the bones as she squirmed away. Shane used the ax to catch her balance while Fi scrambled forward, grabbing the Rose Crown with her free hand. Then Fi leapt to her feet, backing away toward the edge of the cliff.

Shane straightened slowly, her fingers clenched around the ax's worn wooden handle. She didn't know what Fi planned to do with that crown, but she'd lost any chance of escaping. Shane was between her and the only way out.

"It's over," she said, resting the ax against her shoulder.

"It is," Fi agreed. Then she turned—not toward the door, but toward the cliffs. Without looking back, she took a few running steps and threw herself over the waterfall.

"Fi!" The name tore out of Shane's throat. She ran for the edge, far too late to do anything. Falling from this height—even into a river—would kill her.

Shane skidded to a stop at the cliff's edge, searching desperately for her partner in free fall. Or worse, her broken body on the rocks far below.

Great bat-like wings stretched across the chasm as the creature that had once been Briar Rose caught Fi in midair, pulling her to his chest and flying sharply upward. Shane gaped. Bone horns protruded sharply from Briar's head, and even at this distance, Shane could see the glimmer of red in his eyes. He was even more monstrous than when she'd last seen him, his ragged coat no longer able to hide the twisted bones of his tortured form. Only his golden hair glittering in the sunlight reminded her of the boy prince she'd known.

"Damn it!" Shane screamed in frustration, kicking a heavy rock into the rush of the waterfall. Hadn't she warned herself that Fi always had a backup plan? Now her partner was flying away with the Rose Crown of Aurora, and all Shane could do was watch her disappear in the arms of a monster. Again.

Breathing heavily, Shane turned back to the ruined garden, kneeling by the skeleton and pushing aside the thick undergrowth to reveal the delicate bones of the hand. A black ring encased Aurora's middle finger. A metal butterfly perched on the band, sparkling. Shane set her ax aside, using both hands to work the ring free. Then she laid the hand back down gently, staring at the queen in her eternal rest.

If it really had been Aurora's spirit that possessed Fi, Shane sincerely hoped that crusty old ghost knew what she was doing. Because Shane wasn't sure her partner did.

At least she had gotten the butterfly ring.

Shane looked at the skeleton's brow, empty now of the legendary Rose Crown. Shane had just assumed she and Fi were after the same thing. She had no idea what Fi and the Spindle Witch wanted with that crown. But maybe that meant Fi didn't know what Shane was up to, either. She spun the little ring around in her fingers, looking up into the sky where her partner had disappeared.

Maybe Shane was one step ahead this time. But the price had been far too high.

15

Fi

COLD AIR WHIPPED through Fi's hair as Briar flew over
Andar, the wind whistling in her ears. Fi shivered, pressing
herself closer to him for warmth. The Rose Crown was tucked
carefully into her vest, and her heart was still galloping in her
chest. The memory of her wild jump played over and over in
her head.

It had been unlike her to take a risk like that. An act of
total desperation.

When she'd realized Shane had her cornered, she had only
one thought: *Briar*. She couldn't let it end there, not when
she was so close. She remembered the way Briar had caught
her when she fell from the Spindle Witch's tower, and the
way his eyes seemed to follow her everywhere, always keeping
her in sight. In spite of everything that had happened, she
couldn't banish the foolish hope that there was still a connec-

tion between them. So she had taken the chance, throwing herself over the cliff into the swirling white mist.

She had believed he would catch her, and he had.

Briar's arms wrapped around her, snatching her from free fall, and for just one second, they fit together again, perfectly in sync. Fi felt relief and hope surging up through her chest like a rising tide. Finally, she had the first desperate glimmer of an idea about the bone creature in her dreams, always tugging at the thread in his heart and asking where it led. Maybe it led to Fi. Maybe he was trying to tell her that the connection the bone spindle had forged between them was still there. That it was their destiny to be together.

It certainly felt like destiny, weaving through the wispy white clouds with Andar racing by far below. A dark malaise hung over the Forest of Thorns and the castle, a vicious blight, but from this high, she could also see the gold and green and sparkling blue at the edges of the kingdom, the parts of Andar that were still alive. Andar hadn't given up the fight yet. The battle had just been on pause for a hundred years—a whole kingdom trapped in the base of an hourglass, being slowly swallowed by sand.

But that was about to change.

Briar's wings surged around her, shimmering as they broke from the clouds. Dead ahead, she could see the little forest where she'd made her camp near the base of a much smaller waterfall. She felt a rush of exhilaration as Briar swooped, scarlet wildflowers whipping beneath them.

Of course, she would give it all up to be walking next to Briar again in the mud and dirt, tired and worn and itchy, forever side by side. Right now, she was as close to the prince as she had ever been, but his heart was miles away. She wanted those sparkling blue eyes back, and his teasing, mischievous smiles. She wanted the future they had imagined together, standing on a starlit hill. She wanted to kiss him and taste roses.

"Soon, Briar," she promised, whispering the words against his jaw. His face remained impassive as he descended, setting her down in a clearing of scrubby grass. Fi untangled herself gingerly from the long bone claws. With no orders to follow, Briar stood motionless beside her like a pretty porcelain doll: hollow on the inside and so very breakable. Fi forced herself to turn away.

Her camp was little more than a pile of ragged blankets, a brown sack with a few provisions, and a fire ring she'd set up the night before. She had picked large rocks, piling them high so that they would be noticeable, because the ring of stones was the sign—along with the little waterfall splashing through the mossy rocks and the scarlet fire flowers. Enough signposts to point even the rusty, out-of-practice Armand Bellicia here.

Fi's pulse pounded in anticipation as she moved toward the crooked willow tree hanging over the waterfall's glistening pool. She ducked beneath the sweeping branches—but there was no one waiting for her next to the knotty trunk.

Fi's heart plummeted. Her entire plan hinged on Armand bringing her the cursed letter opener. She'd thought she had him with the poison, but she wouldn't put it past him to have cured himself somehow and abandoned her at the most critical moment.

Fi cursed and knelt before the tree, searching frantically for any sign he'd been here.

"Looking for this?"

Armand ducked under the curtain of willows, flicking the branches aside with one hand. In the other, he held the letter opener that carried the Butterfly Curse, twirling it carelessly between his fingers. He was immune to magic, after all, so he had nothing to fear from cursed relics. Fi even knew how that particular Bellicia family trait had come about, now that she'd read the Lord of the Butterflies's letter detailing how he'd severed Armand's ancestor from his magic—and all magic—forever.

Armand was dressed in a red tunic and black pants, with a rich travel coat flowing from his shoulders. He had clearly been watching her from somewhere, waiting to make his entrance until she was on her hands and knees in the dirt. Probably a little payback for their encounter in Illya. Fi had no time for his games. She held out her hand for the relic.

Armand pulled it out of reach. "Antidote first."

Fi frowned, but she lifted the little vial, pinching it between her thumb and forefinger so he could see the liquid inside. "At the same time?"

Armand licked his lips and nodded. Fi extended her hand slowly, only for Armand to suddenly snatch the vial and lurch back out of her reach.

"What are you doing?" Fi hissed.

"Just making sure you kept your word." Armand yanked the cork out with his teeth, spitting it aside and downing the vial all in one go.

"You can't be here, Armand," Fi warned. "Just give me the letter opener and get away as fast as you can."

Armand sneered. "And leave you to face this *great threat to all of us* alone? I think not. You've had your way quite enough."

Fi clenched her fists, anger warring with fear. Armand was about to mess up weeks and weeks of planning—and for what? His egotistical need to always show her up.

Anger won out. Fi lunged forward, shoving Armand hard enough to make him stumble backward out of the curtain of willows. Fi followed.

"If the Spindle Witch sees you, it'll ruin everything. And whatever happens, it will be on you."

"I don't see any sign of a world-ending evil Witch," Armand said, waving lazily around the clearing. "And I looked hard."

Not hard enough, Fi thought, if he'd missed the way she'd been flown here by a creature that was as much bone as human. Even now, Briar was probably just standing on the other side of camp, barely blocked by the trees.

"I don't have time to explain everything to you," she bit out, looking at the letter opener in Armand's hand and fingering her rope. She'd take it by force if she had to. She hadn't survived Aurora's tomb and faced down her own partner to have the likes of Armand Bellicia stand in her way.

"Luckily for both of us, I'm not interested in your explanations," Armand said. His free hand settled on the thin rapier at his waist, tracing the marigold engraved on the pommel. "I am the Border Master's son, and if this threat is as dire as you insist, I will deal with it myself. Properly."

Fi could have strangled him for his overconfidence, but she didn't have time. "Please," she begged, not for herself, but for Briar. "Before it's too late—"

The screech of a wild crow split the clearing, its voice shrill in warning, and then a gust as strong as a whirlwind rushed through the forest. A thousand wingbeats like an army of crows. Armand's coat flapped madly, and a rain of leaves and dust whipped around them.

A moment later, the Spindle Witch strode through the trees, the layers of her dark skirts dragging in the dirt. Her veil was a wisp of black that barely covered her eyes, sweeping down the back like a cape. The Witch's face looked young today, but her limbs were twisted and withered with age. She would be hungry. Fi looked around desperately, trying to salvage her plan.

She had known the Spindle Witch would come—she had been counting on it. After Fi's last betrayal, there was no way the Witch would leave the Rose Crown in her possession. The youth had faded from her hands as she wrapped bony fingers around Fi's wrist, crooning that she would come to retrieve the rose *personally*. A warning. A threat. And a chance.

This was supposed to be her moment. Fi had not been idle in the Witch's tower; she had been watching the woman closely, gathering all the information she could, and she had worked out a few things. Like the fact that the Spindle Witch's golden thread wasn't actually infinite. And that she only used the pieces she had already spun. Never just her hair—and after what Fi had seen in Aurora's memories, she supposed she knew why.

It was a distinction that was practically meaningless in

191

places like her tower or the castle of Andar, where she'd had hundreds of years to spin her threads, covering them with traps. But out here in the woods, whatever thread was on her spindle would be all she had. It wasn't much of an advantage, but it would have to be enough.

Fi shot a look at Armand frozen by her side, his eyes wide in disbelief as the Witch bore down on them.

"My, my," the Spindle Witch hummed, twisting a golden thread between her fingers. "More treachery, and so soon. I find I'm growing fond of your futile little rebellions."

Fi didn't say anything. She glanced at the letter opener in Armand's hands, trying to decide if she could grab it before the Spindle Witch realized what she was doing. The Witch followed her gaze, studying the dark-haired boy.

"Spindle Witch," Armand hissed out. He pressed the letter opener to his chest, his right hand gripping the hilt of his sword.

"I see you've brought another little friend for me to play with," the Spindle Witch said, looking down at Armand like he was nothing more than an irritating bug. Then her gaze focused on the letter opener, and Fi could see the way she stiffened. Her eyes glittered with sudden anger. "Now, where did you get a dangerous thing like that?"

Armand's rapier leapt out of the sheath with a scrape. He leveled it at the Witch, though the tip was shaking.

This was not the way Fi had wanted this to go down. She'd planned to have the letter opener hidden in her sleeve so she could stab the Witch in the heart at the same moment as she handed over the Rose Crown. Now they would have to improvise.

She'd gotten the idea from the Lord of the Butterflies.

When she'd asked him how to kill the Spindle Witch, he'd warned her that was *entirely the wrong question*. Fi didn't know if that was because the Spindle Witch was immortal or because she was simply too powerful for a mere human to kill. But she wasn't the first Great Witch brought low—the Lord of the Butterflies was.

From what she knew, the Butterfly Curse hadn't just banished him. It had turned his own magic against him. And now Fi was going to do the same to the Spindle Witch.

"Armand," Fi hissed. If he was here, then she would use him. "Her threads probably can't hurt you. Use the Butterfly—"

A golden thread snapped forward, twisting around Fi's neck in the span between heartbeats. "That's quite enough of that," the Witch warned. Fi choked, scrabbling at her neck.

Armand looked between them in horror. As if mesmerized, he reached out, brushing his fingers over a few lines of golden thread. The thread seemed to lose its power under Armand's fingers, instantly withering and turning back into dead hair.

Fi snapped it from her neck and shook it off, panting. The broken strands fluttered to the ground.

Maybe Armand would be more useful than Fi thought. She had known he was immune to magic and curses; she just hadn't been sure how far that power extended. Armand looked disgusted.

The Spindle Witch yanked her thread back, spinning it angrily between her fingers. "Don't think that little parlor trick will save you," she spat. She lifted her hand high, tugging at the empty air. Fi had a bad feeling about this.

"Armand—the Butterfly Curse—" she tried again.

This time, it was not a golden thread that cut her off, but a gleaming bone claw. Briar Rose cut through the air on his dark wings, swooping down and dragging Fi away. Her boots skidded through the grass and mud. She struggled against his tight grip, trying to twist free.

"Filore!" Armand yelled, his thin rapier jumping to stab at Briar's side. Briar let go of Fi long enough to knock the sword away. Fi took the opportunity to seize his hand, yanking one of the claws backward at the joint. The overextended finger cracked like it was about to snap, and Fi felt sick.

"I'm afraid she can't help you anymore. Your opponent is me, little boy," the Spindle Witch said, the words poisoned by a laugh.

Fi tried to crane her head around to see what was going on, but she was forced to throw herself backward as one of Briar's claws sliced through the air right where her neck had been. She could only hope the Bellicia bloodline would keep Armand alive long enough for him to figure out to use the Butterfly Curse.

Fi's rope was still wrapped around her arm. She let the ring fall, spinning it quickly and then flinging it forward with all her might. It slammed into Briar's ribs with an awful crunch that he didn't even seem to notice. Was he unable to even feel pain anymore?

Fi looked up at him, the hulking wings and horns glinting as Briar advanced on her. There would be no stopping him now without killing him.

"Briar," she tried. "Please . . ."

That was all she got out before Briar leapt at her, his claws plunging straight for her chest. Fi ducked and rolled out of the way. Out of the corner of her eye, she could see Armand fighting a mass of crows, the black wings beating at him as he slashed his sword wildly. The Spindle Witch's golden threads gleamed in the air around him, waving like tentacles, searching for a weak point. One got too close to him, the end going suddenly slack.

The snap of wings was the only warning Fi had that she'd taken her eyes off of Briar for too long. She scrambled up to her feet, not even looking back before whipping the rope up in a high arc. It caught one of Briar's wrists, wrapping around and around his forearm. Fi threw herself forward, yanking the rope with all her might and dragging Briar to the ground. He came down hard, raking deep grooves into the dirt as he landed. Then he launched himself at her on all fours, like an animal.

Fi didn't have time to dodge. She dropped to the ground as Briar's claws ripped through the air over her head—and then she was all out of moves. She panted, bruised and breathless, as Briar loomed over her, claws poised to strike.

Armand screamed in pain. Through the flare of Briar's wings, Fi watched in horror as the rapier and the letter opener were yanked from his grip by shimmering golden threads. The sharp blade of the sword gouged deep into his shoulder as the Spindle Witch disarmed him, flinging the weapons away. The letter opener sailed in a wide arc, disappearing into the long grass.

Armand's face and arms were scratched up from the

crows, blood streaming down into his eyes from a cut on his forehead. The Spindle Witch bent down to pick up the sword with the bloodstained tip.

One of Briar's hands pressed painfully down on Fi's chest, trapping her in place. The claws of his other hand rested against her throat as he waited for a command. Fi heard a clank as the Spindle Witch threw Armand's sword aside.

"Such an unwieldy instrument," she murmured. "Briar, my pet, kill him."

Briar's jagged claws slid away. For a second, Fi felt like he was staring right at her, those red eyes locked with hers. Then he stood up, dutifully turning on the weaponless lord. Armand lurched backward, his usually arrogant face pale with terror.

"No," Armand begged, shaking his head. "This can't happen. Not to me."

Briar lunged, his great wings flapping as he dove straight for Armand Bellicia. He had forgotten one thing, though— Fi's rope was still tangled around his arm.

It took all of Fi's strength to rise to her knees. She wrapped the rope around both hands and then yanked back with all of her might. Briar jerked backward midflight.

Fi's shoulders screamed with the effort of holding him. Briar was strong, and the rope tugged hard, the rough coils ripping into the skin of her palms until they bled. She didn't let go. She wasn't going to let Armand Bellicia die—but she especially wasn't going to let Briar Rose become his murderer. She just had to hold on—

Briar's bone claws flashed, slicing through the rope. He

and Fi flew in opposite directions. Fi tumbled into the dirt, and when she raised her head, something glittered right in front of her. The letter opener. Briar's leathery wings flailed as he desperately tried to keep his balance, one hard joint smashing into Armand's chest. The boy flew off the bank and splashed into the river. His head broke the surface with a gasp, and he bobbed once before vanishing with the current.

"You won't get away so easily," the Spindle Witch promised. She lifted her hand, gathering golden threads in her fingers, her hateful gaze locked on the spot where Armand had disappeared.

In that moment, Fi saw the opening she had been waiting for. She abandoned her rope, gripping the letter opener in both hands and racing forward. The Spindle Witch turned just in time for Fi to drive the blade with the Butterfly Curse directly into her chest.

The Witch's eyes filled with pure shock. Briar crumpled into a heap on the river's edge, and Fi held on, pushing forward with every ounce of willpower until she had driven the blade in all the way to the hilt. Blood slicked Fi's hands, staining the swallowtail butterfly on her palm a deep red.

Fi staggered backward, losing her grip as the Spindle Witch doubled over. Fi's breaths were coming hard, the tight feeling in her chest easing for the first time since the moment Briar had been taken. She had done it. Somehow, she had outsmarted the Spindle Witch. The woman clutched at her chest, wheezing and choking—

With laughter.

Slowly, the Spindle Witch straightened. Her red lips

were curved into a cruel smile. The letter opener still stuck straight out of her chest, right over her heart, and Fi felt like the world was tilting under her.

"Fool." The Spindle Witch closed her hand around the letter opener, yanking it free. "This hasn't been a weak spot of mine in a very long time."

"But the Butterfly Curse . . ." Fi protested weakly. "Anyone who touches it . . ."

The Spindle Witch laughed again, sickeningly sweet. "I see you put some thought into this," she said. "But not enough. How many people has this wretched thing cursed already?" She held up the letter opener. "At least two, perhaps more? There's not enough magic left in this relic to be a threat to someone like me. It's used up—and so are you, my dear."

The Witch's fingers curled around the little dagger, snapping it in two. Fi flinched as the bloody pieces hit the ground. This was the curse that had ruined her life, the curse that had defeated the Lord of the Butterflies, the most powerful curse Fi had ever known—and the Spindle Witch had tossed it aside like it was nothing.

She hadn't saved anyone. She'd played right into the Witch's hand. Shane had been right all along.

The Spindle Witch clicked her tongue. "I thought I warned you what would happen if you defied me again."

She raised her hand, and Briar staggered up from his heap, moving dutifully toward his master even though all she was going to do was torture him. The Spindle Witch took hold of that invisible thread, and this time, she spared Fi a vicious look as she began to turn it slowly, like she was twisting a dagger sunk into his very heart. Briar screamed—the only time Fi ever heard his voice anymore.

Fi couldn't stand it. She couldn't watch this happen again. She was beyond thinking; she had no plan. Fi threw herself at the Spindle Witch, grabbing for her arm. She was caught immediately in a web of golden threads, the sharp strands jerking her arms up above her head.

"You won't win in the end," she shouted. Her fingernails caught in the Spindle Witch's veil, wrenching it back to reveal those hard eyes, that golden hair, the monster born in the shape of a girl. "I may have failed this time, but I won't stop—I'll never stop! I'm going to save Briar and Andar. We have a destiny, a bond that can never be broken. I was chosen for this."

The Spindle Witch released Briar all at once, rounding on Fi with delight. "Chosen?" she repeated. "Is that what you believe?"

Something dark hung in the air, a sudden weight that settled on Fi's chest.

"I know all about the silly little spell the Rose Witch cast on my bone spindle," the Witch said, leaning forward so she and Fi were eye-to-eye. "The magic was meant to find a savior for Briar Rose—a Witch with magic powerful enough to defeat mine. And it did."

"I don't understand." Fi sagged as the threads loosened around her. She wasn't a Witch—she had no magic at all.

"Oh, I know, dear," the Spindle Witch said with a condescending smile. "Spells aren't intelligent. They simply do what they've been crafted to. That spell wasn't reacting to you. It was reacting to this."

She seized Fi's wrist, jerking it up to reveal the butterfly mark on her bloody palm.

"A little piece of the Lord of the Butterflies—the only Witch who has ever been more powerful than me." The Spindle Witch tightened her grip, her nails cutting into Fi's skin as she squeezed tighter. Her red lips curved into a ruthless smile. "You weren't chosen. You're not the savior of Briar Rose. You're nothing. Just the mistake of a foolish Witch and the foolish spell she died for."

Every word flayed Fi open. *It couldn't be.* If she hadn't been chosen, then what had all of this been for? By waking Briar, she'd put him directly in the Spindle Witch's grasp. She had entered Everlynd and doomed the last survivors of Andar with her curse. She'd abandoned Shane and wound up giving the Spindle Witch exactly what she wanted. And for what?

Fi was no savior. Her chest felt like it would cave in, her ears still ringing with the last of Briar's screams. She had tried to defeat the Spindle Witch and failed. The words echoed in her head. *A failure. A nothing. A mistake.*

"Though I must admit you've been unexpectedly useful to me." The Spindle Witch yanked Fi closer, reaching into her vest and pulling out the Rose Crown. "Just what I was looking for," she purred.

"No . . ." Fi's vision wavered, the whole world blurry through a film of tears. Her head was full of memories—Shane's blood-streaked face, her determined expression, and her warning that Fi was on the wrong side.

The Spindle Witch let go of her, tossing Fi aside to admire the ruby crown, which shone in the sunlight. Fi fell to her hands and knees before the powerful Witch. She didn't think she could get up even if she wanted to. She felt drained and empty, as hollow as the puppet Briar, who stood next to her. She didn't have any more cards to play. She had finally outlived her usefulness.

The Spindle Witch looked down at her as though sensing her thoughts. "Don't worry," she said. "I won't kill you yet. Either of you." She beckoned Briar closer with a crook of her finger, grabbing his chin. "You're mine, and he's mine, until you've solved the Rose Witch's code." The woman began reciting Camellia's riddle, the same words Fi had repeated in her head over and over.

> In the forest of spines
> Where the thorns gather
> The shine of Andar's most precious rose
> Reveals the hidden butterfly

She shoved Briar to his knees beside Fi. "You've brought the crown. Now bring me the rest, and maybe I'll put you out of your misery . . . together."

Fi barely heard the Witch's final command to Briar—*Take her home*—or felt Briar's cold touch as he lifted her into his arms. It was only after Briar scooped her up and they were in the air that she realized they were heading the wrong direction to be returning to the Witch's tower.

Not that it mattered. Nothing mattered anymore. She had been utterly defeated by the Spindle Witch. This was the end, for her and for Briar Rose. Fi buried her face into his unfeeling chest and sobbed.

16

⋙⟶ ⟵⋘

Red

IT WAS RAINING when they trudged back into the Everlynd camp. Red peered at the rows of shuttered windows and
covered tents from under the lip of her gray hood. She was
cold and hungry and generally in a damp mood.

Shane wasn't in any better spirits. The huntsman had
barely said two words to Red since coming back from Aurora's
tomb. Shane preferred to throw herself into chopping firewood that was too wet to use and kicking apart the remains
of stone walls that were barely in their path. Red watched her
put a fist through a cracked branch as they broke trail, and
she couldn't help but wonder whose face Shane was imagining under her knuckles.

Shane had returned from the tomb dirty and ragged, with
such a grim expression that Red had felt a moment of panic.
But Shane hadn't been dying, and she hadn't failed. Instead,
the huntsman wrapped one arm around Red and pushed the

butterfly ring into her hands, whispering that she'd lost her partner again.

The rain started a few hours later. It had followed them for days, sometimes coming down in sheets, sometimes just a foggy drizzle that left Red shivering by a weak fire, holding Cinzel close and watching Shane hurl wet pine cones into the flames. So many times, Red opened her mouth to say something—that it wasn't Shane's fault, that she'd done everything she could, that she'd come back with the ring and her life, and maybe that was all they could ask for right now. She stopped herself every time. She already knew it wasn't what Shane wanted to hear.

Red desperately wanted to help Shane. To be there for her the way Shane was always there for Red. She just didn't know how.

The Paper Witch and Perrin were waiting for them when they reached the little stone house. Cinzel immediately plopped down in front of the fire, leaving a big wet wolf splotch on the nice rug. The Paper Witch suggested they could take their time to warm up, but Shane just shot him a dark look.

"Let's get this over with," she said.

Which was how Red found herself in the tower again, a few straggling curls stuck to her face. They'd changed out of their soaked traveling clothes, but the chill had gotten into Red's bones, and the hem of her crimson dress was already damp and discolored from the downpour. She wrapped her arms around herself, watching as a few drops of the Paper Witch's blood ran down the mirror once more. The storm was growing worse, the wind outside rising to a desolate moan. The first flash of lightning split the dark beyond the tower window and seemed to crackle in the surface of the mirror.

It was a long, tense minute before the Lord of the Butterflies appeared, and when he did, his image was fuzzy, his reflection rippling as if in rough water. At last, it settled in the glass.

"Speak quickly," he said, his voice almost lost in a rumble of thunder. "We may have even less time than I thought."

Suddenly, Red wanted to be anywhere else. She swallowed the feeling down as Shane pushed forward, holding up the butterfly ring. The Paper Witch stood beside her with the hairpin laid reverently across his palms. The little butterflies shivered on the ends of the delicate chains.

"We have it," Shane said, swiping rain out of her hair with a damp sleeve.

The Lord of the Butterflies frowned. "That's not what I sent you to retrieve."

"What are you talking about?" Shane demanded. She leaned in until she was practically nose-to-nose with the man, every angry word fogging the cold glass with her breath. "It has to be. It was the only ring in her tomb. I pulled it from her hand myself!"

A shiver crawled along Red's spine at the thought of the Witch Queen's skeleton being disturbed. She had never liked dead things.

The Lord of the Butterflies wasn't impressed. "It may be my ring, but all of the magic has been drained from it. It's useless for fixing the hairpin."

Shane's face was livid, her hands curling into white-knuckled fists.

"How it that possible?" Perrin asked. Red could barely hear him over the rain lashing the old stone walls.

"Only Aurora herself could have done it," the Lord of the Butterflies mused. "She was quite clever at making use of other people's magic. I wonder what she could possibly have needed such a vast store of *my* magic for, though . . ."

The Paper Witch suddenly looked very pale. "I believe I can answer that question, great lord," he said slowly. "She used it to make a curse—a very powerful one. I know a girl who bears its mark."

A curse mark in the shape of a butterfly. Red knew immediately who the Paper Witch was talking about. So did Shane. The huntsman's jaw clenched so hard the muscles in her neck stood out.

"Fi."

The Lord of the Butterflies sighed heavily, his bright red robe flaring around him as he shrugged. "It's a pity you didn't bring this girl with you. I might have been able to use that magic—even in the shape of a curse. As it is, there's nothing I can do."

It couldn't be. After everything they'd gone through— everything *Shane* had gone through—it couldn't have been for nothing. That horrible squeezing feeling in Red's stomach had become a vise around her chest, and she almost couldn't breathe against it as she stared at the huntsman.

Shane's shocked expression should be morphing into anger. She should be yelling and threatening and overturning the tables, swearing she'd fix everything. Like she always did.

Instead, Shane just stood there, looking away. Looking defeated.

For a second, Red was teetering on the edge of a precipice, all her fear threatening to swallow her. And then she was feeling something else—molten-hot, boiling anger that seared through her and burned the fear to ash.

Shane came through for everyone—always—whether they deserved it or not. They couldn't turn around and repay that by failing her.

Red stomped forward, elbowing Shane out of her way and snatching the hairpin. "So that's it?" she demanded, staring down the ancient Witch in the mirror. "You're giving up? That's not good enough!" It felt like the storm was shouting with her.

"Red . . ." Shane said, laying a heavy hand on her arm. Red shook her off.

"I'm not talking to you," she snapped, brandishing the pin at the Lord of the Butterflies. "You! You're supposed to be the most powerful Witch of all time, and we need you! Aurora's descendants need you. Aurora's kingdom needs you. So don't you dare tell me there's nothing you can do. We'll find the girl, and we'll get the magic back—all I'm asking you to do is complete this pin. Fix it at least partway!"

"Partway?" Something glittered in the Witch's eyes. He looked amused and fascinated all at once, as if they had his full attention for the first time. Red recognized that look. It was exactly how the Spindle Witch had looked the first time she heard Red sing and recognized something she could use.

A deafening roar of thunder split the air, sounding like it was right on top of them. The candles wavered madly in their braces. The Lord of the Butterflies smiled.

"It's always those who know the least about magic who have the most interesting ideas," he said. "Perhaps because they know no limitations. What you ask may be possible, but there's something you need to understand. It isn't merely raw magic that makes these spells so powerful. The Lord of the Butterflies infuses each of his creations with a sliver of his own magic, giving them a life of their own, so to speak. Like me." He waved a hand airily at his own form in the mirror. "That butterfly has been completely drained. To restore the spell, it would need to be given new life."

"Like yours?" Red asked. "If you're also a sliver, can't you just—go in there?"

"Deliciously ruthless," the Lord of the Butterflies purred. "Your tiny mind can't even begin to understand the complexity of my existence, and yet you're willing to sacrifice me for your own ends."

Red's heart lurched uncomfortably.

The dark-haired man laughed. "Don't misunderstand. I wholly approve, and I am more than capable of fulfilling this request. But I'm in here, and the butterfly pin is not. I'll need one of you to serve as a conduit for my power to leave the mirror."

The Paper Witch swept forward. "I would gladly volunteer to assist you . . ." he began.

"No. You," the Witch said. His gaze was locked on Red. She felt the pit drop out of her stomach.

"Me?" Red repeated.

"You're the one asking for a favor," the Witch pointed out. "Besides, I have a sense this isn't the first time you've been a conduit for a magic greater than your own."

His words shook her to the bone. Red stared at the mirror, feeling all the shadows pressing in around her until they could have smothered her. She wondered what the Lord of the Butterflies saw when he looked at her. Maybe he sensed the blood magic that had bound her to the thorn rod and the Spindle Witch for so long.

The Paper Witch looked between Red and the Lord of the Butterflies, his face tight with worry. "It's up to you whether you are willing to take this risk."

"Not a chance!" Shane broke in with a snarl. "This has bad idea written all over it. And I've had enough of trusting our future to deceptive Witches."

"Shane, stop," Red said, tugging on the girl's elbow. "I can do this. I need to do this."

She was surprised how much she meant it. Red's moral compass was long since broken; she wasn't even sure it could point her toward what was right anymore. But it had pointed her to Shane. Shane was the best thing that had ever happened to Red. She was good and true and sweet in a way nothing in Red's life ever had been.

As long as Red's heart pointed to Shane, she had the sense she would never go astray again.

"She can do it." It was Perrin's voice. When Red looked back, he gave her an encouraging smile, along with a wink only she understood. "Take it from another member of the club."

Shane shook her head, at a loss. "He's not even promising it'll work," she argued.

"Will it?" Red demanded, turning back to the Lord of the Butterflies. "If you use me as a conduit, can you fix the butterfly?"

"I thought I was just going fix it *partway* and you were going to finish it yourself," he pointed out, smirking.

"You know what I meant," Red insisted.

The man huffed out a short laugh. "Nothing can take the place of my magic. But, yes, the hairpin will be whole again—brought to life, as it were. And the butterfly will be able to siphon my magic back from that girl. Assuming you ever find her."

"Okay," Red said, nodding too hard. Her head felt wobbly on her neck, and she wondered if anyone else could tell she was trembling. "What do I do?"

The Lord of the Butterflies looked pleased. "You'll need to shed a few drops of blood on the mirror to start."

Red could hear Shane growling behind her, but she ignored it. The Paper Witch was already at her side, offering his small dagger. Red held out her hand, trying to swallow down the sudden lump in her throat. She wished Cinzel were with her.

The Paper Witch's fingers were soft, and he gave her a reassuring squeeze before nicking a tiny cut into the pad of her index finger. It stung. Red watched in fascination as a few pearly red drops splashed down onto the mirror, sliding into the grooves.

"Good," the Lord of the Butterflies whispered. "Now slide the ring onto the hairpin."

Shane reluctantly pressed the ring into Red's hand, giving her a significant look. The single butterfly seemed to flutter in the flickering light.

The rain was howling now, the roar threatening to drown out everything else. Quills and inkpots rattled on the shelves. Red's heart almost leapt out of her chest when a sudden surge of rain slapped against the shutters, rattling them like cage bars. The Lord of the Butterflies was still smiling, a wide, eager smile that stretched across his face as he leaned forward in anticipation. His glittering eyes bored into Red.

"Now stab the pin into your palm."

A shock of thunder split the air as he said it. Red was certain she was the only one who heard him. Fear seized her chest, and she hesitated. Stab herself with a weapon powerful enough to stop the Spindle Witch? The spell wasn't finished, that was the whole point, and yet . . .

"You're going to come this far and then quibble over a little discomfort?" the Witch asked coldly.

"Red . . ." She could hear the worry in Shane's voice.

She couldn't fail at this—she wouldn't. Red lifted the hairpin. The sharp end gleamed like a knife. Before she could think too hard, she jammed it down into the palm of her hand, piercing right through the ugly mark left by the thorn rod, still raw and red and barely healed.

Thunder crashed around the tower. The shutters blew free of their braces, banging against the stone wall, and half the candles went dark. Red shrieked. Her entire body was suddenly crackling with pain, white hot and searing, radiating from the center of her palm where the pin had pierced her.

Distantly, she could hear Shane screaming her name. It felt like she was falling, slipping backward into blackness, into herself. She couldn't tear her gaze away from the mirror. The Witch's eyes flashed like the whole of the storm raged inside them, and then, just as suddenly, it was inside Red, too, filling her with power, with pain, the lightning rippling right under her skin. Her throat closed over a scream.

The Lord of the Butterflies was too powerful to contain.

Even a faint sliver of him was tearing her apart from the inside.

Then Red's body was gone, and the world was blackness. She wondered in horror if she had lost consciousness or maybe even died. But there was still a smooth voice in her ear.

I suspected you had been touched by powerful magic. Is that her, then . . . your Spindle Witch?

The darkness was gone, but it had been replaced by something far worse. Red could feel the Lord of the Butterflies rifling through her memories, dragging her through each one until she ended up before the Spindle Witch again and again.

Red saw herself receiving the thorn rod, on her knees before the veiled figure as the Witch forced the thorns deeper into her bloodied hand, binding it to her with golden thread.

She saw herself using that rod to summon the milky-eyed crow, whispering into its windswept feathers the secrets of Witches she'd spied on.

Or worse—selling them out to the silver-eyed assassin and letting the Wraith do the dirty work so she could steal their relics and treasures and present them to her master. All the worst regrets of Red's life on display.

Through it all, the specter of the Spindle Witch hung over her. She was too real to be just a memory. Red knew suddenly she'd been here all along, lurking in the darkest parts of Red's mind, haunting her like a ghost. A cruel painted smile and those beautiful golden threads that made monsters. Monsters like Red.

She hadn't lost consciousness, because she realized her eyes were open. The Lord of the Butterflies had disappeared from the mirror, leaving her staring into her own tearstained reflection. Perrin was wrong. She couldn't do this. She had been responsible for bringing so much pain and darkness into the world—shedding a few drops of blood couldn't wash that away.

The pain of the thorns in her palm was as sharp as the day she'd first let the dark power ensnare her. She had welcomed that little piece of darkness inside her, and now she would never be free of it. After everything she'd done, she was still snarled in the Spindle Witch's golden threads.

The Lord of the Butterflies's voice was in her head again.

That's a nasty bit of residue she's left in you. I think I'll take it with me when I go.

Red didn't understand what the Witch was saying, didn't understand what was happening, only that she was falling again.

No—she was on her feet, standing in front of a cracking mirror. Whatever was falling was inside her, a great swirl of power like the torrent of a river rushing through her and then draining away. She felt like she was being wrung out. A crack slid along the surface of the mirror, fracturing her reflection. The noise of the storm returned at a fever pitch, the rain pounding harder than her hammering heart.

A great fork of lightning split the sky, lighting up the tower, and the mirror gave a sickening crunch. Then, all at once, Red was herself again—just herself—cold and shuddering and dizzy from the wound in her palm. But alone.

It felt like an eternity had passed, but it must have only been a few seconds. She stumbled back from the mirror, and Shane caught her.

"Red!" she yelled.

Red shook her head, her vision hazy. The only brace of candles still burning had toppled over, sputtering against the stone floor. Perrin rushed to close the shutters while the Paper Witch righted the brace, removing one candle to relight the rest.

"Are you all right?" Shane demanded, spinning Red around.

Red had to swallow to find her voice. "Yes," she croaked. "I think so." Or she would be, as long as it had worked.

She looked down at her hand, her face twisting in horror. The butterfly pin was whole, as promised—three glittering butterflies now dangled from the chains, the empty band of the ring hanging uselessly on the stem. But the pin itself was driven all the way through Red's palm, the sharp tip gleaming where it protruded from the back of her hand. Drops of blood slid down her wrist to the floor in a steady *drip, drip, drip*.

"Get it out," Red begged, thrusting her hand at Shane. "Just get it out!"

"Okay, just calm down. I don't want to hurt you." Shane's face was pinched with worry. She wrapped her fingers gingerly around the pin. "On three," she said.

Red nodded mutely.

"Three," Shane said all at once, yanking the pin free. Red shrieked out a gasp, but she felt better the second the sharp tip was out of her skin. The empty ring band fell to the floor, clinking against the stone. The Paper Witch picked it up and studied it thoughtfully.

"Let's see the damage," Shane said, slowly uncurling Red's fingers from around the wound. Red was almost too afraid to look as Shane wiped away the blood to reveal—

Nothing.

There was no gaping hole, not even a scratch or a scab. But there was a scar. A ragged circle-shaped scar marred the center of her palm, so smooth it looked like she'd had it for years. It had completely obliterated the worst of the marks from the Spindle Witch's rod.

Red gaped, thinking about the Lord of the Butterflies's final words: *That's a nasty bit of residue . . . I think I'll take it with me.*

She glanced over at the mirror. The glass was cracked from end to end, the surface only reflecting their splintered faces. Red felt lighter, freer—like the Lord of Butterflies had scraped away the last remnants of the Spindle Witch from her heart. She turned the butterfly pin this way and that, watching the firelight ripple in the little jeweled wings. He was in there now, she supposed, but she had a feeling he wasn't going to be answering any more questions.

"Do you think it worked?" she asked breathlessly, turning to the others.

Perrin closed his eyes, swaying on his feet as he looked at the pin with an entirely different set of senses. "It feels complete to me," he said with a shrug. "But I don't think we'll know for sure until we try to use it."

"And that is the last time any of you will admit that to anyone outside this room," the Paper Witch warned. "We are all in need of a little hope right now. The ritual was a success, and the butterfly has been restored. I think we may finally stand a chance."

Shane suddenly looked miserable again. "We don't," she

said dully. "Because I lost Fi. We have no idea what she's doing—if she's even still alive . . ."

"Don't say that." The Paper Witch fixed Shane with a stern look. "Filore is a very resourceful girl. She may yet surprise us. For now, we can try to contact her ourselves."

"How?" Red asked.

"Through Perrin." The Paper Witch waved at the boy, who was currently staring thoughtfully at the wax dripping down the side of a candle.

Perrin's eyes widened, as though he was just as shocked as any of them to be called out. "Me?"

"You," the Paper Witch agreed. "Your dream magic has the potential to be every bit as powerful as any of the Great Witches of Andar. You should be able to jump into the dreams of someone like Fi, with whom you already have a connection." The Paper Witch shook his head as Perrin hissed, a hot splash of wax striking his hand in his distraction. "Though it may require a little more . . . *focus* than you've achieved so far."

"If Perrin can contact Fi, then maybe we really can finish this." Red wrapped her hand around Shane's, holding the completed hairpin between them.

Shane's fingers curled around the pin—then she jerked back, shaking Red off.

"*Maybe*," Shane repeated, her lip curled. "That's all we have—*maybe* and *if*. Face it—I lost the only chance we had of defeating the Spindle Witch when I let Fi go *again*. This is just a useless piece of junk!"

Shane threw the pin. It bounced against the stone floor.

"Hey!" Perrin protested, bending over to retrieve the precious relic.

Shane was already gone, the door banging behind her as she strode out of the tower, heedless of Red calling after her. Red shot one look back at Perrin and the Paper Witch and the broken mirror, then rushed after Shane into the rain. Within seconds, she was soaked.

"Shane!"

Her voice was almost drowned out by the storm, but she had a feeling Shane heard her and was just too stubborn to turn around. Red hurried as fast as she could, but Shane was quickly getting ahead. Red's boot plunged into a puddle, and her patience snapped.

"Shane, stop!" she shouted.

Shane shot her a dour look over her shoulder. "Give me one good reason."

Red huffed, trying and failing to push a dripping lock of hair out of her face. "Because it's wet and I'm in a skirt and I've got mud up to my ankles. And it's not fair to make me chase you down."

She had a feeling that wasn't the argument the huntsman was expecting. Shane blinked at her. Red could just imagine the picture she made, bedraggled, with sopping curls plastered to her face, stuck in a puddle and holding fistfuls of her long skirt out of the muck. Shane's lips quirked a little, just a twitch of a smile.

"I guess there was a good reason buried in there," she muttered.

Red sighed, relieved that Shane was walking back toward her. She took another slippery step herself and nearly ended up flat on her back—but Shane was there, close enough for Red to catch herself against the girl's shoulder. Shane didn't seem angry anymore; she seemed resigned, and that was worse.

Red bit her lip. "Look. I wanted to say . . ."

"*I told you so*?" Shane guessed with a dark chuckle. "Because you did. You knew this was impossible right from the beginning. And you tried to warn me. I just wasn't listening."

Frustration boiled in Red's chest. "You're not listening now!" she accused. Shane looked lost and bitter—she looked like the girl Red saw in the mirror, and she couldn't stand it. Without thinking, she reeled away and pushed Shane as hard as she could, sending the other girl stumbling across the road.

Shane caught herself against a rough stone wall, head whipping up in surprise. "You pushed me."

"Shut up!" Red warned. She stalked over to Shane, grabbing the front of her coat. Her fingers were cold and shaking, but inside, she was nothing but anger, hot enough to ignite. "You don't get to say those things, and you definitely don't get to give up! Not after dragging me here. Not after promising me a life and a future together. I didn't want to believe in any of it—in you—but I do now. And I'm begging you not to take that away from me."

Shane stared at her. Her voice, when she spoke, was oddly rough. "I didn't think I was getting through to you. Not after . . ."

The Eyrie? Her father's death? Ivan's secrets? Red could remember a hundred moments Shane had reached out to her, and she had wanted to reach back, but she just hadn't been able to reach far enough. So she'd let go—she'd let Shane go. But not anymore.

"You weren't getting through. At first." Red let go of Shane's jacket, resting her fingertips on the girl's strong shoulders. "But . . . you make me want to be brave, Shane. You're the first person who ever took a chance on me. The only person who ever told me I'm worth something."

"You are," Shane said, and though the words were so soft Red could barely hear them, they still made her heart flutter like it had wings. She gave Shane a playful shove.

"I know that *now*. It just took a while to sink in."

A lot of things about Shane had taken a while to sink in. Like the fact that she really was as straightforward and loyal as she seemed, and that she meant every word she'd ever said. And most of all, that she was the only person in Red's life who'd never made a promise she didn't intend to keep.

Red swallowed, holding on to the wet collar of Shane's coat. "Shane, I . . ."

"Yeah?" Shane pressed.

The words were on the tip of her tongue—the feelings that had been growing inside Red every day until they were almost overwhelming. But she didn't want to say it, not on a night like this, in the dark with the rain beating down on them and the wind howling in the empty streets. Those words were too delicate to cut through the storm and too important to waste. Red would hold them inside herself for now, until she was sure Shane would hear them the way she meant them.

Red pulled back and wrapped her arms around herself, pouting. "I'm wet and I'm freezing," she said matter-of-factly, as if that was all she'd ever meant to say.

Shane snorted. "Well, that's what you get for chasing somebody into the pouring rain."

That was the Shane she recognized. Red dug her heel into the toe of Shane's soggy boot, making her yelp. "That was your opening to invite me to stay in your house again, with your nice warm fireplace," she explained. "Unless you're planning to leave me and Cinzel out here to fend for ourselves."

Shane gave her a searching look. Red had a feeling the other girl could see everything she'd been about to say written all over her face. But Shane didn't push it—just let out a long, slow breath, her tentative fingertips brushing the back of Red's hand.

"I want you to stay," Shane said, swallowing hard. "And not just tonight, but from now on." Red's heart skipped at the intense look in those gray eyes as Shane leaned in, pressing her forehead to Red's shoulder. "I'm so tired of important things slipping through my fingers."

Red rested her hand on the back of Shane's neck, pulling her closer. "Me too," she whispered against her ear.

They stood like that for a long minute. Red closed her eyes and let it all in—the rain and the wind and the heat of Shane's body against her, burning like an ember everywhere they touched. The storm had softened, but she could still hear the raindrops pattering around them, so cold she never wanted to let go.

"I'll stay as long as you want," Red promised. When Shane lifted her head, she tweaked the huntsman's nose. "But, just so you know, Cinzel and I are a package deal."

"I'm not sharing the bed with a wet, muddy wolf," Shane grumbled.

Red laughed. "We'll see." Somehow, she felt warmer already.

17

Fi

FI SAT ON the ocean shore, watching the receding waves carry shells into the sea. Briar sat next to her, close enough that the trailing end of his coat brushed her leg. They weren't dressed for the ocean. Briar wore his long velvet coat, and Fi was in pants and a vest—just like the day they met.

Fi didn't look up at him. She wasn't ready yet. She wanted to enjoy this peaceful moment, even if it was just a dream.

She had always loved the shores of Pisarre, bright with white sand and sparkling pink shells, the cries of seabirds carrying on the salty breeze. She and Briar had never gotten to see it together—one of so many things they had missed. The sky was filled with brilliant golds and soft pinks, the orange glow of the sun dipping beneath the white tips of the waves as they chased each other over the horizon. It was the most beautiful sunset Fi had ever seen.

She stretched her bare feet out, digging her toes into the

sand and leaning into Briar. His coat was soft, just the way she remembered, and she pictured herself and Briar visiting this place. He would yelp when she splashed him, because he was still a prince and he wouldn't be ready for the cold water. But then he would splash her back, maybe even tug off his shirt and dive under the waves, pulling Fi with him. And she would give him a hard time, probably through a blush she couldn't quite fight down, because it was ridiculous to swim fully clothed, and then . . .

Then they would sit like this, side by side, and when Fi looked up at him, he would have that dazzling smile she'd grown to love.

Fi looked up. The bone creature sat next to her, nothing of Briar left. Massive claws had taken the place of his feet, glistening nails burrowing into the sand like half-buried shells. The velvet coat flapped over a brittle rib cage attached to the joints of his jutting spine. His skull head with the massive curling horns tipped as he looked down at Fi. Only a hint of red glowed in his eyes, even that malevolent spark almost swallowed in the empty sockets.

He lifted one clawed hand, seizing the golden thread that trailed from his empty heart. This time, the thread disappeared through the sand, into the waves, leaving with the tide.

Where does it lead? Briar's voice begged.

FI SHOT UP in bed, clutching her head as the world spun dizzily in a whirl of roses and gauze. She ripped back the white curtain and stumbled to her feet.

It took her a minute to remember where she was. Her

eyes raked over the white stones and the sea of red roses that spilled through the window, choking her with their heady perfume. A small window was set into the far wall, the very same one Fi and Briar and Shane had escaped through at the beginning of this adventure, what felt like a lifetime ago. This was Briar's tower, the one he had slept in for a hundred years in the castle of Andar. That was what the Spindle Witch had meant when she told Briar to *take her home*.

Fi waded through the roses and pressed her palms against the stone of the window frame, looking out over the castle shrouded in spiderwebs. The outer courtyards were dotted with fires and plumes of smoke from Witch Hunter camps, more than she cared to count. Fi had no idea how those extremists had been convinced to join the Spindle Witch. They seemed scared to take a single step into the castle, but she heard them through the windows, howling like dogs in the night. She hoped the giant cave spiders would pick off a few of them.

Beyond the Witch Hunters lurked the Forest of Thorns. The night was clear, full of stars, and Fi was reminded of the speckles of shells in the sand of her dream. She blinked hard, but she couldn't shake the feel of Briar's coat, the heat of the sun on her skin, and mostly, that voice ringing in her ears.

Where does it lead? Where does it lead?

Fi slammed her hands over her ears, jerking away from the window. "I don't know!" she screamed into the room. Through the haze of the swaying curtains, Fi could almost imagine there was still a figure in the bed, sleeping there, unwoken. It was torture. "I don't know what you want!" Fi yanked at the curtains. "I can't save you, Briar, so stop it— just stop asking!" She ripped the last of the curtains down and then slumped to the floor with the cloth in her arms, staring at the empty bed.

No tears pricked at her eyes, but she suspected that was only because she'd cried herself out days ago. That first night, Fi hadn't understood where Briar was taking her until he dropped her here, in this achingly familiar tower she'd seen so often in her dreams. Her first thought was that she was locked in the tower itself—a fitting punishment given what she knew of the Spindle Witch's own life. But to her surprise, the door was unlocked. She'd crept down the stairs, intending to flee.

She made it all the way to the vast front entryway, her footsteps echoing as she raced through empty rooms and hallways, before she realized the truth of her prison—and she should have realized so much sooner, because those hallways had not been empty the first time she walked this castle. They'd been strewn with sleeping bodies.

Now the slumbering people were serving a different purpose. And Fi had met her true jailor—though not in his own body.

The second Fi's hand closed over the door handle, two women grabbed her from behind, a fair-skinned woman in rider's livery and a tan lady in a jeweled gown. Their movements were jerky and forced, their eyes blank. The rider dragged Fi back by the waist while the glittering lady fastened a hand uncomfortably tight around her arm. Fi kicked out, managing to slam the woman in the knee. Those dark eyes didn't so much as blink. All she was doing was hurting the people of Andar.

Together, they dragged Fi as far as the stairs before dumping her onto the floor and turning away, slumping lifelessly into an alcove in the wall.

"I see you've met my little puppets."

She heard the voice before she saw him, a man in a rich blue tunic striding down the stairs. Even without the shimmer of his crown, she would have recognized those features that were so much like Briar's, soft blond hair and the shadow of laugh lines on his slack face. One of the fingers on his right hand was conspicuously crooked, as though from an old break badly set. This had to be Briar's older brother, Sage, the king of Andar. Or at least his body.

When he looked at her, his eyes weren't blue, but shining silver like something watched her from behind the king's face.

"Who are you?" Fi demanded, backing away.

"Not someone you can escape that easily," the man warned.

At his nod, a dull-eyed man in guard's livery appeared behind Fi, grabbing her elbows tight enough to bruise.

"Much better. I hate being forced to run in a new outfit." The body thief cracked the king's neck sharply, watching the play of muscle and tendon as he curled his fingers. "And these things get so stiff just lying around."

Fi's blood curdled at the thought of someone *wearing* the people of Andar, putting them on and discarding them like clothes. "So you've stolen that body," Fi said. "Are you some kind of Witch?"

"You can call me the Wraith," the man offered, which she would take as a yes. "I doubt we'll meet in person, but I just wanted to greet the castle's newest guest. And to assure you that you're not alone." There was menace in it, an unspoken threat.

Fi swallowed. "And what about them?" she asked, tossing her head toward the slumped figures in the alcove.

"Little more than tools." The Wraith gave a careless shrug. "I can only occupy one body at a time, but the people of this castle are just so empty I've found it doesn't take much more than a suggestion to move them around."

His silver eyes cut to the figure at her back, and the man let go of her, walking jerkily away. Fi resisted the urge to rub at the ache in her arms. She wouldn't give him the satisfaction.

"So you're here, what—to watch me? To stop me if I try to escape?" Fi asked.

"I could." The man sneered. "But something tells me I won't have to worry about that with you. You seem like the intelligent type. How far do you think you'd get?"

Fi's hands curled into fists. Even without the Wraith's puppets in her way, giant spiderwebs still covered the castle like a shroud, the deadly arachnids lying in wait on every tower and wall. Beyond them were the Witch Hunters, bored and ruthless. And even if she somehow survived that, all that waited on the other side was the Forest of Thorns and the monstrous wolves—and this time there would be no Shane to watch her back, no Briar to light up the dark, no Paper Witch to guide her out.

"What a lovely expression," the body thief crooned. "I'm glad we see eye-to-eye." With one last mocking wave, the man left, taking Sage's body with him.

Fi had retreated to Briar's tower—the only place with any good memories at all. Then she'd cried in Briar's canopy bed until the dawn light swept through the window.

It had been three days since then, or maybe four. It was easy to lose track here. Another time, Fi would have given any-thing to explore the castle of Andar, but she could barely make herself leave Briar's bed, much less the tower. The silver-eyed Witch always seemed to be watching her, slumbering figures coming awake all at once to stare at her with that glowing gaze as she passed.

The silver-eyed Witch always seemed to be watching her, slumbering figures coming awake all at once to stare at her with that glowing gaze as she passed. She could see the Spindle Witch's gold threads glimmering around their necks, keeping them under the Sleeping Curse. Trapped just like she was.

There was no escape. And worse yet, just as the Wraith accused, Fi wasn't even really trying. She'd found a path, through back hallways and flights of forgotten stairs, to a door set in the outer wall. She got all the way to unlocking it before she realized she could never delude herself into going out. She wasn't Shane, the type to throw herself at impossible odds. She was a pragmatist, a planner, a chess player. And she was out of moves.

Fi stared down at the mark on her palm with a twisted smile. She'd been right all along. She was no hero of Andar, no destined savior of Briar Rose. The bone spindle had chosen her by mistake. It was an unbearably bitter thought.

There was only one thing she hadn't tried yet. By night, Briar haunted the rooftops like a grotesque gargoyle. From the castle's highest windows, Fi had seen him perched up there, his gaze following her even through the thick walls.

Fi slipped into her boots, stealing down the dark stairs. She passed two slumbering figures whose eyes sprang open like silver lamps as she made her way to a lower tower with a parapet, where she knew she'd be able to reach the roof. Her boots chuffed against the stone as she reached the top of the stairs, the door at the top opening with a gentle creak. It was a clear night, the light of the waning half-moon glowing on the high spires and making the almost invisible threads of the spiderwebs shimmer.

"Briar?" Fi called.

She walked to the edge of the wide embrasure. One side looked over a sheer drop into the courtyard with the broken statues of the Great Witches. She could see dark shapes moving among them—crows, dozens of them perched on the Witches' gray marble shoulders and the spine of the castle wall. Fi made her way along the edge until she could climb up into the gaps between the wall's teeth and jump down to the slanting roof of one of the lower buildings. She wobbled on the slick shingles, her arms thrust out to catch her balance.

"Briar Rose!" she called into the night. Almost at once, she heard the familiar sweeping of the giant wings. Briar let go of a towering spire roof where he had been perched, taking off and flying toward Fi. Her hair and shirt flapped with the force of the wind as he landed next to her. Shingles broke beneath his clawed feet, sliding to the edge and falling to the courtyard far below.

"Briar?" she asked, inching toward him.

It was impossible not to notice the way his face had sunken in, the great wings and bone claws longer every time she saw him. He stood silently before Fi, his empty eyes locked on hers without even a spark of recognition. Fi reached up to lay a hand against his face.

"Tell me you're in there," she begged. "Tell me there's still a connection between us—that everything we had wasn't just some mistake."

His cheek was cool under her palm. His lips unmoving.

Fi would have given anything to have the old Briar next to her right now—the Briar who would have told her it didn't matter if they were destined or not because he loved her anyway and he always would.

"Please," she said. She fisted her hand into the lapel of his soft coat. "I need your help. I can't get away from here without you."

Briar's head tipped as he looked down at her, the white horns gleaming.

"That's right!" Fi said, feeling the prickle of tears after all. "It's me—it's Fi. Help me, please."

The black wings creaked, stretching as Briar prepared to fly. Hope rose in Fi's chest, a sweet, warm feeling that made her want to throw her arms around his neck. It was crushed as Briar shook Fi's hand away, spreading his wings and taking off alone.

She tumbled back on the slanted roof, losing her balance in the whirlwind of Briar's flight and sliding toward the edge like the broken shingles. The ground yawned beneath her. Fi scrabbled at the slick tiles, trying to get a handhold. She had the feeling that, if she fell, Briar would not be swooping back to catch her this time.

At the last second, she managed to dig her heels in, dislodging the final row of tiles as she caught herself. One of her heels dangled in the empty air, and Fi pressed herself back against the roof, breathing hard. A fall from here would certainly shatter both her legs, or worse. She didn't even have her rope anymore.

Part of Fi felt like she was still falling, still reeling. Even Briar was truly gone. She was utterly alone.

When she could breathe again, she looked at the long climb up the slippery roof and then glanced down instead. She could see some kind of balcony there—not directly below her, but just to her left—and it wasn't too far a drop. Fi inched along the roofline. When she was in the right spot, she lowered herself until she was dangling by her fingertips and then swung back and forth, clearing the railing and dropping onto the balcony.

The hard landing sent shudders through her body. She straightened quickly, shaking it off. A glass-paneled door etched with flowers separated the balcony from the room beyond. Fi pushed against it, wondering if she would have to shatter one of the beautiful panels to get in, but the door was unlocked.

She ducked inside, determined to return to the tower and never come out again. Then she got a look at where she was.

It was a library—the great library of Andar that Briar had wanted to show her. She couldn't make out everything in the dark, but her eyes drank in the gleam of lacquered shelves and the ceiling soaring over her head, chandeliers tinkling in the soft night breeze. The library was two stories high, and from the second floor, Fi leaned out over a sturdy railing, turning her head to take it all in. The shelves were endless, and every one was crammed with books, more than she could count—more than she could read in a lifetime.

This was the true treasure of Andar, the only prize she'd wanted when she and Shane first set off on their quest. Fi relaxed into the banister, breathing in the familiar scent of dust and old pages and linseed oil for polishing the shelves. Books always made her feel like she was home.

She picked her way down the twisting staircase to the ground floor, trailing her hand along the smooth cherrywood balustrade as she descended. A pair of unlit candles waited in a wall niche, and Fi smiled her first real smile in days. This was a problem she was prepared to solve. She pulled the flint and tinder from her pocket and then stopped, staring at the rock and curl of iron in her palm.

Having these with her wasn't destiny—it wasn't even luck. It was Nenroa knowledge. She always carried them. As she raked the flint against the iron, she could almost feel her father's hands wrapped around hers, teaching her to strike a perfect spark the very first time.

Fi lifted the lit candle high. She wasn't sure what she was looking for—a distraction, an escape, an answer. She had found all those things in books before. She rounded a sweeping shelf and found herself face-to-face with another wide glass door, this one leading out onto a lower balcony.

Her candle flickered, and for just a second, Fi could have sworn she saw a flash of something moving in the glass. She rushed to it, holding the candle close. There was nothing there, and nothing outside.

She didn't trust herself right now, dreaming about bone creatures, surrounded by spiders and thorns and the silver-eyed Witch who was everywhere at once. Maybe her mind was just playing tricks on her.

Fi turned away, trailing her hand gently over the books as she headed farther into the library. She loved the feel of them under her fingers—the stiffness of the casings, the way the leather was stretched over them with painstaking care. She imagined she could almost hear the stories whispering to her just by running her hand along the spines . . .

Wait.

Fi froze in the center of the library, spinning around as she looked at the hundreds of thousands of books—hundreds of thousands of *spines*.

"In the forest of spines, where the thorns gather . . ." Fi whispered the beginning of Camellia's riddle, staring wide-eyed into the dark. This was the place the Rose Witch had been pointing to—this library. Whatever the Spindle Witch was looking for, it was right here.

In spite of everything, Fi had solved another piece of the puzzle. It wasn't destiny that had led her here. She'd found her way into the library by chance. By mistake.

But not all mistakes were misfortunes, were they?

Fi's hand clenched around the flint and tinder in her pocket. Even if the bone spindle had chosen her by mistake, did that really change anything? No matter how she ended up here, she was here now, and what mattered was what she chose to do next.

That was what she had always believed. What her parents had taught her, what she had learned studying history and outsmarting ruins. The choices she made would determine who she was and what she could accomplish—not some spell, not some prince, not some destiny, and certainly not the Spindle Witch.

Fi didn't have much hope left, just a little, just a spark. Sometimes, a spark was enough.

18

⟫⟫⟫ ⧫ ⟪⟪⟪

Shane

SHANE RAISED HER ax high, bringing it down through a particularly dense patch of pine. Branches splintered and pine needles exploded in all directions with a satisfying crunch. Would it have been easier to go around? Probably. But Shane was in the mood to hack something apart.

They still had no leads on the whereabouts of Fi and her Butterfly Curse. Shane was having a rough time finding an outlet for her rage among the peaceful people of Everlynd. All the soldiers of the Red Ember were either on guard duty, patrolling for Witch Hunters, or patching up the sad little huts so no Witches would get drenched in the next big storm. She'd been sorely tempted to invite herself along every time Captain Hane set out to patrol for Witch Hunters, but she always stopped short at the last second. What if Perrin found something while she was gone? What if Red needed her and she wasn't here?

Shane wiped sweat from her forehead, listening to a pair of blue jays jeering at each other overhead. Perrin and the Paper Witch spent every day locked in the tower, working on Perrin's dream magic. Not that it had gotten them any closer to Fi.

The only thing Perrin seemed to be getting out of it was the bags under his eyes, and all Shane had was one creepy night when Perrin had appeared in her dream as if through a heavy mist, calling out for Fi. Long after he disappeared, his voice echoed in Shane's dreams. She'd had nothing but nightmares—first of Briar as the bone creature dragging Fi by a golden chain, and then of Fi with her own flesh melting away as she became a creature of the Spindle Witch.

She'd started awake so suddenly that she elbowed Red in the pallet next to hers. Red yelped, waking Cinzel, who started whining and howling at the top of his mangy lungs until nobody got any sleep. She just hoped it meant Perrin was close to harnessing his powers; four people and a wolf under one dilapidated roof was a pretty tight squeeze.

Her ax stuck in the gap of a thick, stubborn branch. Shane lifted her boot, kicking the branch until it splintered away. She ducked through her newly forged path in the trees. Maybe she couldn't go out with the patrols, but that didn't mean she couldn't scout around the camp. That's what she was doing—scouting. Not taking her ax for a walk because the Paper Witch had politely but firmly suggested that she blow off some steam *elsewhere*.

Tempers were running a little high these days.

A sound beyond the trees caught Shane's ears. She stilled. Something was tearing through the underbrush, moving fast.

She hadn't actually expected to find anything out here,

but something was definitely coming her way. She adjusted her grip on the ax, holding it like a proper Steelwight weapon instead of a cudgel.

The forest had gone quiet, the blue jays vanished. Shane listened hard. She could pick out bootsteps between the cracking of branches and the rustling of brush. Someone was in this forest, running.

She caught a glimpse of a red tunic first, followed by a flash of dark hair. Then a man stumbled through the aspens in front of her, dirty and ragged and breathing hard. Shane's mouth fell open as he skidded to a stop, lifting his head to reveal very familiar features.

"Armand Bellicia?" Shane said, shocked. She was lucky she didn't drop her ax and sever a few of her toes.

"Fi's partner . . . Shane," he said between pants. "I am so glad to see you."

She glanced back as though there might be *another* Shane standing behind her that Armand was talking to. She had honestly never thought she would see this particular snaky bastard again, much less scrambling around in the backwoods of Andar. She opened her mouth to demand an explanation, but Armand wasn't even looking at her anymore. He was looking desperately over his shoulder.

"They're after me!" he warned, and Shane realized there was still something moving through the trees—something much bigger than the weasel-faced heir of Bellicia.

"Who's after you?" she began.

A creature made entirely of bones burst through the trees, toppling the thin aspens and snapping the branches off bushy pines. Armand yelled and threw himself out of the way. Shane swore under her breath, swinging her ax out before she even got a proper look at the thing.

Her blade slammed into a thick skull that must have belonged to a bear or a wolf. The rest of its body was malformed, with too many rib bones and long hind legs that made its gait sickly and uneven. Long teeth pitted with yellow grime grinned out of its sagging jaw. It looked like the bones had been chosen haphazardly, pieces of many different creatures jigsawed together and held fast by—

Golden thread.

Shane's ax had chipped the skull and thrown the creature backward a few steps. It shook the blow off, the bones rattling as it straightened with little more than a deep gouge under its eye socket.

"They're undead. They belong to the Spindle Witch!" Armand yelled from where he'd hit the dirt.

"Yeah, I worked that out!" Shane growled.

The creature leapt forward, snapping its bone jaws. Shane caught it with the flat of the ax, heaving the monstrous beast away. Its malformed back legs scrabbled in the grass, and Shane darted in before it could recover, swinging her ax wide and smashing it into the body this time. Curved ribs splintered and burst. The creature's jaw gave another disconcerting rattle, and it lunged down at Shane, its teeth almost closing around her shoulder. She dodged just in time. Muscles clenching, she slammed her ax handle into the jaw, breaking the joint.

Its mouth hung loose in its socket now, and the entire chest cavity was nothing but a mess of splintered bone. Still, it limped toward her. Shane swore under her breath.

She had a feeling there was only going to be one way to

end this. She dug her heels in, turning the ax to favor the blunt back of the blade. The creature's feet scratched through the dirt, like a bull readying to charge. Shane held her ground. The bleached skull lowered, and the creature launched itself forward, barreling toward her.

Shane waited until the last possible second, then threw herself to the side, bringing the ax down with all her might over the creature's head. This time, the skull shattered, chunks of bone pelting Shane while the rest of it crumpled to the ground.

The body was still moving. She lifted the ax again, bringing it down over and over until the segmented spine was nothing but bone chips and dust. The creature had stopped twitching finally, but she struck it once or twice more, just to be sure.

Shane wiped a shaky hand across her face. She really hated everything to do with the Spindle Witch.

Armand got to his feet, glancing around warily. "That wasn't the only one."

A scream rang out from the direction of the Everlynd camp. Shane's guts lurched. She chambered her ax on her shoulder and took off through the grove, running as fast as she could. She could hear Armand's footsteps thundering after her. She doubted he was coming along to help—more likely he needed protection. Shane didn't know how the little lordling was even here, much less how he'd gotten on the Spindle Witch's bad side, but she did know that was a one-way trip.

Shane leapt through the last line of trees and reached the edge of camp at a dead sprint. Screams and shouts rang in her ears. Two of the bone creatures had gotten ahead of her, and they'd gone straight for the nearest houses, overturning carts and baskets of wild apples in their rampage. They were both a hodgepodge of animal pieces, as tall as horses with a snarl of ill-fitting ribs. Shane's stomach went queasy imagining the stockpile of bones the Spindle Witch had to be sitting on to create these.

Some people were fleeing deeper into camp. Others had taken up weapons and were trying to face the creatures down. Shane was glad to see Captain Hane among them, the tall, dark-haired leader of the Red Ember smashing a long plank of wood against one of the creatures' legs. The board splintered with a crunch. Captain Hane dove out of the way of the monster's bristling claws, her brown skin glistening with sweat. A group of men and women trapped on the roof they'd been rebuilding threw buckets of hot tar, splattering the bone faces with gashes of black.

Shane lost track of Armand as soon as they hit the houses, but she had much more important things to worry about. The second bone creature had someone cornered against a house, and as soon as she was a few feet closer, she could see it was—

"Red!" Shane ran straight for her. Red had thrown her arms around the monster's muzzle, desperately holding the clacking jaws shut while Cinzel snapped at its bony ankles. Red's wild eyes locked on Shane's. Then the creature wrenched its long neck, and Red shrieked as she was flung off, her head cracking against the stone wall.

"Red, hang on!" Shane smashed the blunt of her ax right into the creature's shoulder socket and skidded under its bristling ribs. She hauled Red to her feet. "I've got you."

The creature lunged again. Shane barely had time to drag a dazed Red out of the way, pushing the unsteady girl behind her. It slammed into the stone wall of the house skull first.

For one second Shane thought it had taken itself out—but the creature only unfolded slowly from a pile of bones, knees creaking and joints snapping. The little golden threads glinted in the sun.

If an ageless corpse with a cracked face could laugh at her, Shane had a feeling that's what it was doing right now.

"Still with me, Red?" Shane asked. She didn't dare take her eyes off the bone creature, but she snaked a hand back, searching for the other girl's.

Warm fingers wrapped around hers. "I'm alive," Red groused, dusting her ragged skirt. "Now stop pawing at me and finish that thing off." She squeezed Shane's hand once and then pushed her back into the fight.

"Any idea what these things are?" Captain Hane shouted. Shane risked a glance over her shoulder to see the woman throwing her ruined plank of wood aside and drawing her broadsword.

Shane shook her head. "Undead . . . somethings. You can't kill it. You just have to keep hacking until it's in small enough pieces."

Luckily, they weren't alone. The street was suddenly thick with the soldiers of the Red Ember, men and women in swirling red capes clutching pikes and staffs as they charged the creatures.

Shane hefted her ax and joined the fray. She ducked the snapping jaws and went straight for the base of the bone monster's neck, knocking the cracked skull off with a few expert swings. The soldiers made quick work of the rest. Soon both creatures were just ugly piles of tar-streaked bones. Shane slung her ax onto her back and leaned on her knees, taking a second to catch her breath. She looked up at Captain Hane through her sweaty bangs.

"A little present from the Spindle Witch," she panted.

Captain Hane nodded. Her expression was grim. "Bone creatures were said to be among those that ravaged Andar a hundred years ago when the Spindle Witch waged her war."

"Fantastic," Shane muttered. "Here I was just thinking we weren't outmatched by quite enough yet." She kicked one of the shattered bones while Captain Hane turned to the soldier at her side.

"Scout the forest. Make sure there are no more of them. We've had enough surprises for one day."

As the man headed off, Shane noticed a familiar figure among the people of Everlynd, his nose wrinkling as he considered the crushed apples splattered over his expensive boots. Shane crossed the street and hauled Armand out of the crowd.

"You owe me some answers," she growled.

Captain Hane crossed her arms, looking Armand up and down. "Who's this?" she asked, unimpressed.

"He's a . . . someone I know." Shane wasn't even going to imply Armand might be an acquaintance, much less a friend. She turned back to the lordling and shook a finger in his face. "Now that I've saved you at least twice over, you better tell me how you got here."

"You can thank your old partner for that," Armand sniffed.

Shane's hands fell back to her side. "Fi?" She couldn't believe it. "You were with Fi? How? Why?"

Armand scoffed. "Not by choice. I was threatened."

"Oh, like I care," Shane snapped. In fact, good for her partner. If Fi had been letting herself get jerked around by her ex again, Shane would have had to kick her tail for a whole new reason. She snagged Armand by the collar, giving him a rough shake. "Where was she? Is she okay?"

Armand's expression twisted into a grimace. "Last I saw her, she was fighting the Spindle Witch. And losing." Shane's stomach twisted like he'd jabbed a knife in it. Armand pushed a hand through his hair to hide his shudder. "Some horrible bone creature threw me into the river, and when I washed up, there were more of them waiting for me. I've been running for my life since."

Shane jerked him down to her height. "You left her there to fight alone?" Her voice was low and dangerous.

Armand just gave her a flat look. "I was *washed away by the river*," he repeated, enunciating every word.

Shane barely heard him anyway. Her mind was roaring like a hurricane. Fi was still all right, or at least she had been recently. And, most importantly, she was fighting the Spindle Witch, just like she'd promised.

"It's not over yet . . ." Shane said, almost to herself.

Armand shook her off with a snort. "It is for me. I want no part in any of this. Have a horse prepared for my journey back to Bellicia, and I will happily get out of your way."

Armand had probably lived his whole life getting off the hook that easy. It wasn't happening this time. Shane yanked him back by the sleeve, more than a little satisfied by the sound of that expensive coat ripping.

"You're not going anywhere until you've given a full account of what you saw to anyone and everyone who wants to hear it."

Captain Hane stepped forward. "Starting with me. I have

a feeling the council will be very interested in what you have to say."

Shane was glad to let the woman have him. She watched with satisfaction as Hane marched Armand toward the tower, most of the Red Ember soldiers following her. Nikor could rake him over the coals like he'd been salivating to do with Red.

Red.

Shane jerked her head around. Where had Red disappeared to? She'd lost track of the other girl in the scuffle. She hadn't seemed that badly injured, but Shane couldn't banish the image of Red's skull cracking against the wall.

A few soldiers were pulling debris from a collapsed house while the camp's healers tended to the wounded. The tar-stained bones from the creature she'd pulverized gleamed in the sunlight. But there was no sign of Red, or Cinzel. Shane wouldn't put it past her to slink off and lick her wounds alone.

She caught the arm of a young blond man—Soren, a soldier of the Red Ember and Nikor's cousin. That nasty expression must run in the family.

"Did you see what happened to Red? The girl with the wolf. She was right here."

"You mean the Spindle Witch's traitor," the man spat. "Maybe she disappeared after bringing her creatures down on us."

"Red had nothing to do with this. Those creatures were attacking her, too, if you bothered to notice." Shane was horribly tempted to break a nose for the first time in a while.

Soren sniffed, shrugging her off. "Maybe she called them, or maybe the Spindle Witch sent them to kill her. Either way, no one is safe with her around."

Shane had no time to waste putting Soren in the dirt right now. A pit had opened up in her stomach. Something was wrong.

"Red!" Shane yelled, moving away from the knot of people, twisting her head to look up and down every street. Then she heard it—the low, tense whine of a wolf. And there, in the distance, a flicker of crimson disappearing around a corner.

Shane cursed, leaping over the scattered bones and racing after her. Where was Red going? Their little house was in the opposite direction.

"Red, hey!" she called. But the figure just kept walking. In fact, Shane was pretty sure she'd sped up. Not running from the battle. Running from *Shane*.

She caught Red at the outskirts of the camp. Shane banked around a corner and found herself in a narrow alley, a twisted apple tree bursting through the cracks in a crumbled wall. Fallen globes of fruit crunched under Red's boots.

"Red, stop!"

Red paused, her back stiff. Her curls were disheveled, her long skirt ripped along the hem. Only now did Shane realize Cinzel wasn't padding obediently at her side but yanking at her torn skirt, whining helplessly around a mouthful of cloth.

Dread pooled in Shane's stomach. She reached for Red's shoulder and barely leapt back in time as a dagger flashed from Red's sleeve, nearly slicing off her fingers.

"Miss me?" The voice was Red's, but the glowing silver eyes piercing her belonged to someone else entirely. Shane's guts gave a hard lurch.

"Wraith," she hissed.

Cinzel pressed against her legs. Shane unslung her ax and pointed it at the Wraith. "Get out of that body right now."

"Or what?" The Wraith blinked Red's pretty eyelashes. "I don't think you're going to touch me in this skin. And I'm very comfortable here." He flicked the dagger easily from hand to hand.

The stench of rotting apples was so thick Shane was choking on it. Or maybe it was a memory she was choking on: Red's ashen face when she'd told them about the Spindle Witch's assassin. She couldn't stand the thought of that monster crawling in Red's mind.

"Red," Shane said through her teeth, "I know you're in there. You have to fight this—shove that creepy Witch out and come back to me."

"How touching. She can't hear you, of course, after that knock she took to the head. But I can just imagine what she'd say." The Wraith's eyes gleamed as the face in front of her softened into a horrible bittersweet smile that Shane could just imagine the real Red giving her. "Shane, please—you have to stop the Wraith. Even if you have to hack me to pieces."

"Stop it," Shane growled.

The Wraith stepped forward, holding Red's arms wide as though he were daring her to do it.

Shane could feel Cinzel shivering against her, whining in confusion and fear. Her pulse thudded in her head. She should force him out of that body—smash her ax handle into the girl's leg and snap her knee. But this was *Red*.

Shane's grip tightened on the ax. Then it slipped from her hands, thudding into the dirt.

The Wraith tossed Red's hair back, smug. "That's what

I thought. I'm taking this little traitor back to the Spindle Witch, and there's nothing you can do to stop me."

Shane ground her hands into fists. "Just because I can't kill you in there doesn't mean I can't stop you."

She lunged all at once, driving Red back against the wall. Red's elbow clapped off the hard stones as they grappled for the knife. But she didn't yelp in pain. She just laughed—a low, vicious laugh that was nothing like Red's.

"Get out," Shane hissed. Then she almost lost her grip as Cinzel seized her coat in his teeth, wrestling her away. "Mutt, I'm trying to save her!"

"Your helplessness is delicious." The Wraith's voice dripped with glee. "How many bones do you think you'd have to break to stop me from taking this body? A leg? Both legs? Here—I'll get you started."

He twisted Red's hand cruelly in Shane's grip until she could feel the bones straining, Red's fingers bent back against the wall, her wrist tight enough to snap.

"Stop it. Hey!" Shane shouted. But he just kept bending.

Shane let go. The Wraith cracked his elbow right across her jaw. Shane staggered back, tasting blood on her lip.

Red's body uncurled, holding the knife at her own neck. The Wraith took a step toward the end of the alley.

Shane swiped blood off her lip, eyes blazing. "I'll hunt you down. I'll never stop until I find her."

The Wraith took another step, tracing the knife down Red's throat. "What do you think will be left of her by the time you do?"

Shane's heart stuttered. Then a voice soared above her.

"Hold her, Shane!"

A figure vaulted over the broken wall.

"Perrin!" Shane called in relief.

The Wraith spun toward him. Shane seized that moment of distraction, catching Red under the arms and hauling the girl back against her chest. The knife jerked toward Red's neck. Shane grabbed the blade barehanded, flinging the dagger away.

"Looks like I'm just in time," Perrin said breathlessly, darting under the apple boughs. He met Red's furious silver eyes. "You didn't think you could use that kind of magic here without someone noticing, did you? I'll show you what real dream magic is." Then Perrin's eyes darted to Shane. "No matter what happens, don't let go."

"Not a problem," Shane promised, holding her tight.

Red was the one person she would never let go of.

19

‒‒‒»»⟫ ⟪«««‒‒‒

Red

RED FELL TO her knees in the cage of thorns. Her hands tore at the dark vines until they bled, her breath loud and fast as she fought uselessly against the bars.

She knew the cage wasn't real. But that didn't ease the sting of the thorns slicing her palms or the ache of the cold seeping up from the silver mist at her feet. Fear clawed at her throat. Her own shadow felt like it was dragging her down, growing longer and darker until it was a chasm at her back.

Red knew what would happen if she fell into darkness here. She would belong to the Wraith forever. Or at least until he got bored and threw her aside, a puppet with her strings cut. Worse, Red knew with every fiber of her being that the Wraith would use her to hurt Shane. She'd felt the malice in him as those icy fingers crawled into her mind and she lost consciousness.

The last thing she remembered was squeezing Shane's hand. Her head was throbbing as she pushed Shane back into the battle and slumped into the wall, watching that rust-red coat flare as Shane fought the way absolutely no one else fought. Even against the creatures of the Spindle Witch, she knew Shane was going to win. Shane always won.

The dark arms of unconsciousness were almost welcome, until she'd felt that prickle on the back of her neck, like something scratching its way in. Another mind overtaking hers. The dark magic she had feared for so long wrapped around her like an icy mist, the cold filling her lungs until she thought she'd drown in it.

Red had clung desperately to consciousness, but it was too late. The Wraith stretched under her skin, lifting Red's hand and dragging it a little too hard through Cinzel's fur, making the wolf whine. Everything she loved in the palm of his hand.

The next moment, she found herself in this prison of thorns. The brambles twisted around each other in snarled knots, gleaming like a tangle of golden thread. Red had no idea whether this prison was conjured from the Wraith's mind or her own nightmares. There was a part of her that had never left the Forest of Thorns, after all.

Red screamed in frustration, smashing her hands against the bars. This wasn't fair. Her connection to the Spindle Witch was finally broken. After everything she and Shane had been through, the Wraith didn't get to twist her and make her a puppet for that dark magic again.

A long mournful howl sounded behind her. Red froze. Her hands clenched tight into her pooled skirt.

The moon was suddenly glinting through the jutting branches above her. Only it wasn't the moon. It was a winking coin, spinning as though flipped high into the air. Red remembered it all too vividly—the silver coin shining between the Wraith's fingers as he sneered at her in a stolen body, the night he told her the secret to taking over minds.

Everyone has a nightmare inside them, Red. At least one thing that chews them ragged in the hidden recesses of their mind. Let it consume them, and they're yours forever. His eyes glowed as he looked her over, teeth bared. *I wonder what yours would be.*

The wolf called again, closer, and Red curled into herself. The Wraith had trapped her here, but the wolf was Red's nightmare—Red's heart, calling mournfully through the mist.

If she turned around, she knew what she would find. The white wolf, Shadow. The monster that led the pack in the Forest of Thorns.

Even as she thought it, Red felt hot breath on her neck. A low growl thrummed in her ear. She forced herself to focus on her bleeding palms, on the sting of the thorns. The Wraith could only control people who couldn't assert their will. If Red could wake up, she could escape. But this was no ordinary dream. And the white wolf that stalked her was no ordinary wolf.

Regret. Remorse. Guilt. *Loathing.* All the things that chewed her ragged in the dark.

Red felt the prickle of teeth on the back of her neck as the wolf's giant jaws creaked open. Hot saliva dripped onto her collarbone. Red hunched forward in terror and despair. When she turned around, when she saw the wolf, it would become real. And Shadow would drag her into the Wraith's grasp forever.

White fur tickled the edge of her vision.

"Red!"

A flash of golden sand swirled around her, chasing away the mist and the cold and the jaws of the wolf. Red jerked her head up as Perrin appeared on the other side of the bars. His tan robe sparkled as if woven from shifting grains of sand. Perrin's eyes were wide, but he shot her a reassuring smile as he yanked at the cage of thorns, struggling to wrench it apart. "Hold on," he said, voice tight. "I'm going to get you out of there."

Red struggled to her feet, watching in horror as Perrin cut his hands to ribbons on the thorns. The wolf at her back was gone, but she could still feel the mist roiling around her—the icy will of the Wraith trying to keep her here. She grabbed Perrin's hands.

"It's no use," she told him.

"We haven't even tried yet!" Perrin protested.

Red shook her head. "The Forest of Thorns is unbreakable here—because it's from my mind." That was how dream magic worked: the more you believed something, the truer it became. The Forest of Thorns in Red's nightmares was absolute. And so was its hold over her. Even as she thought it, the vines slithered over her arms, the thorns bristling as they grew thicker and higher.

"You can't give up," Perrin said urgently. "You've got a dream Witch on your side, remember?"

He backed away from the cage, lifting his hands like he was cupping something between them. Sand, Red realized, watching the golden flecks pour from one palm to the other as he turned them over and over like an hourglass.

Perrin threw his hands toward her. Sand spilled out of his billowing sleeves, hissing like a great storm as it smashed against the thorns. The cage shivered, a few of the twisted branches crumbling to black dust. Red's heart surged. But when the last golden grains blew away, the Forest of Thorns still stood around her—impenetrable, inescapable. Silvery mist curled around her leg like a shackle. Her body felt numb, the cold overtaking her inch by inch.

Red gasped. The Wraith's mist was coming for Perrin, too, slithering around his feet.

"You have to go," she begged. "He's too strong here. You'll be trapped."

Perrin's expression was grim. "Not without you," he insisted, summoning more golden sand.

Before he could form the hourglass, dozens of silvery white hands shot out of the mist. They wrapped around Perrin's arms, grasping his tan robe and wrenching his shoulders back. The sand poured through his fingers.

"Perrin!" Red screamed.

Perrin fought to break free. But the hands were too strong, yanking him down to his knees. He didn't even have time to gasp before long silver fingers wrapped around his throat. The mist rushed in Red's ears like the laughter of the Wraith.

Red couldn't stand it. "Just leave me here and go!" she begged, her desperate eyes locked on Perrin's. Shane might have cracked Red's heart open, but Perrin was her very first friend, and she couldn't stand to lose him, either. "Please— he's going to consume you."

Perrin's eyes were wild as he fought the silvery hands trying to pull him under. Then he sucked in a deep breath and closed his eyes. When he opened them again, he was smiling.

"It's all right, Red." His voice was soft and sure, as if he could no longer feel the mist hands crawling all over him. "I understand now. This is magic that can only bind you through fear. But fear is just one tiny part of the unconscious mind. Dream magic is supposed to be so much more than that. It's supposed to be beautiful."

His eyes sparkled as he said the last. Red watched in awe as Perrin surged to his feet, throwing his arms wide. The hands exploded away from him, just tendrils of mist evaporating into the air.

Perrin raised his hands again, his palms facing each other as he formed the hourglass. Something shimmered on his fingertips. But it wasn't flecks of sand spinning between his hands this time—it was water. Blue droplets glittered around him like falling rain. Everywhere they splashed down, the darkness ran like watercolor, the shadows rippling away into a shining lake that stretched out from Perrin's feet.

This time, when Perrin reached for Red, the cage of thorns collapsed around her, nothing but a cold, hard rain. For one moment, she was lost in the gale. She thought she heard the Wraith hissing in her ears, promising this wasn't over, but she wasn't sure whether he was talking to her or to Shane, somewhere outside the dream. Then Perrin's fingers closed around hers, and he pulled her out, into the sun.

Perrin stood surrounded by water, his robe glimmering blue like the sky reflected all around them. He looked radiant.

"Perrin . . ." Red's breath stuck in her throat. "What is this?"

"The true form of my dream magic, I think." Perrin raised his hand, staring at the drops of water sparkling on his skin.

Water, not sand. Red swallowed. "So the Paper Witch was right about your power."

Perrin laughed warmly. "He usually is. Though don't tell him I said that."

His head tipped, as though he were listening to something in the distance. His eyes grew wide, and he wrenched around, staring at something Red couldn't hope to see.

The dream wavered around them. The water shivered under Red's feet. Then she was plunging through the surface, the pressure closing around her like a vise. She wrenched up with a gasp, back in her own body again. Only the squeezing wasn't gone, because it wasn't part of a dream. It was Shane's arms wrapped around her, holding Red fiercely.

Red blinked up through her disheveled curls. The three of them lay in a graceless heap at the foot of an apple tree, someone's knee digging unpleasantly into her spine. She and Perrin must have squashed Shane as the dream magic pulled them under.

Shane's worried face hovered over her. "Red? Perrin? Somebody say something so I know that slimy, silver-eyed bastard isn't still holed up in there."

She looked a little worse for wear, a smear of blood at the corner of her mouth. Red trembled. She'd done that—or rather, the Wraith had, in her body.

Red reached up to trace Shane's bloody lip. "It's me," she promised. "I'm back."

Shane's eyebrows drew together. "Tell me something only Red would know."

There were a hundred things on the tip of Red's tongue—the secrets she'd shared with Shane alone, the promises Shane had made her even before Red deserved them. But she knew the perfect one. The moment at the card table on the border of Darfell, when she had breathed into Shane's ear, *You never let go of a lady once you have her*.

Red flicked a wild strand of hair out of Shane's face. "You're terrible at poker because you always wear your heart on your sleeve," she said fondly. "And you have a mean right hook."

Shane huffed a laugh into her hair. "I disagree with the first one, but the right hook I'll take." Then Shane hauled her in, and Red found herself crushed against the girl's shoulder. Shane's grip was shaky, as if she'd been holding on until her muscles ached. But she smelled of apples and sunlight, and she was warm—so warm after the icy cage of thorns.

Whatever else the huntsman might have said was lost when Cinzel tackled them, trying to lick both their faces at once.

"Seriously, I thought you were a goner. And so did this mutt, obviously," Shane muttered, pushing Cinzel's slobbery head away from her.

Red pressed her cheek into his soft fur. "I would have been, if not for Perrin."

She craned her head around to share a smile with Perrin. But he hadn't moved, his body slumped against the trunk and his eyes shut tight.

Red's stomach flipped. "Perrin? What is it?" She shook

his shoulder, and Perrin sprang awake, gasping like a fish out of water.

"I had her for a second!"

"Had who?" Shane wanted to know.

"Fi!" he said, his voice hushed. "It was just for a moment, but . . . I saw her. In the dream. I think I can reach her again."

"You're serious," Shane breathed.

A huge grin split Perrin's face. "We might actually have a chance. We did it!"

His excitement was infectious. Red threw her arms around his neck in a grateful hug, while Cinzel crooned and circled them, his tail whapping Perrin's face.

"No, you did it," Red whispered. "And you saved me. Thanks, Perrin. Or should I say Dream Witch?"

Perrin laughed. "Hey, what are friends for?"

20

Fi

FI ENTERED THE castle library, clutching a wide silver serving tray in both hands. She had made a short detour to the kitchen to snag the shining tray, ignoring the silver eyes that marked her passage. She couldn't care less what the Wraith thought she was up to.

Fi's nighttime trip to the library had put a thought into her head that she hadn't been able to shake. Either her instincts were right and she was going to get some answers, or she was about to look very foolish.

The great library of Andar was even more beautiful in the daytime. The bookshelves were all made of cherrywood that shone in the light streaming through the wide picture windows. The curved balcony of the upper level traced the contours of the room, and spiral staircases led between the floors, the steps decorated with light and dark woods patterned with intricate medallions. The library had been designed so that everything flowed together, the bookshelves curving around corners and topped with sinuous whorls. And there were roses everywhere, carved deep into the banisters and adorning the scrollwork of the windows.

Fi tried to take it all in at once. Every corner was crammed with books, their pages bound in blue and red and rich green vellum, the titles traced onto their spines in precise thread. In the nooks between shelves, she could see sturdy tables and long satin-cushioned benches made for lounging, not to mention the wide, deep windows that Fi knew she could curl up in for hours with a stack of books at her side.

She craned her head back to study the chandeliers cast of gleaming gold, each one hung with hundreds of translucent gems shimmering in the sunlight. At first, Fi thought they were crystals, like the ones she'd occasionally seen in the manor houses of Darfell, but then she noticed the little rainbows being thrown across the wall of the second floor. The pieces had to be glass. It seemed odd for such a rich library to have only a simple glass chandelier, but then again, the rainbows were lovely, and they added to the magical atmosphere created by the rose motif. Fi felt like she was wandering in some great garden of books.

She almost tripped down the stairs, staring up at the chandeliers instead of watching her step. The serving tray banged against the railing as she caught herself. There was a pattern of vines and roses carved into the high ceiling. Fi let her feet wander as she followed the whorls of vines, great bursts of roses blooming from every coil—except in one spot. In the center of the great library, the ceiling writhed with vines, but the roses in bloom had disappeared, leaving only buds and slightly parted petals.

Fi's pulse picked up. She'd seen that before—in the hidden room of Aurora's tomb.

It had to be a clue. In the tomb, the lack of roses had hinted that Aurora was not in the black coffin. Fi wondered what it meant this time. She tugged at her earlobe, pondering the roses and the tomb and Camellia's riddle until her neck was sore.

Out of ideas for now, she headed for the part of the library where she'd been the night before. She passed through rows and rows of books, moving faster when she recognized the giant glass door that led out to a low balcony—the one where she could have sworn she'd seen a flash of movement.

Figuring out the first line of Camellia's riddle had restored a little of Fi's faith in herself. She was no longer so sure the movement had just been a figment of her imagination. After thinking about it all night long, she had come up with a guess about who could have been reflected in the glass. That's what the serving tray was for.

Fi stopped in front of the door. Its frame, made of the same cherrywood, was built into a lattice of crisscross diamonds, each set with a piece of glass. Fi ran her hands along the pattern, wincing at the thought of what she was about to do. Then she lifted the serving tray and used it to splinter the delicate wooden crosspiece at one joint.

Once the wood bowed in, Fi shrugged off her vest and wrapped it over her hands to protect them while she worked the piece of glass free. She placed the glass on the serving tray and slipped her vest back on, heading for a dark alcove under-neath a curl of spiraling stairs. As far as she knew, the Lord of the Butterflies could only hide himself inside mirrors, but all glass could be a mirror under the right circumstances.

Under the stairs, she found a little desk tucked against the wall. Fi set the shiny tray upright on the scarred surface, hold-ing it in place with a heavy book. Then she leaned the square of glass against it, pushing the cool diamond flush against the polished metal until the glass turned opaque. Fi's hazy reflec-tion stared back at her as she sat down.

"I know you're in there," she said. At least, she hoped he was. She held her breath as the silence stretched out.

Then the reflection shuddered, and suddenly Fi was sit-ting across from the Lord of the Butterflies. He looked older than before, and weary, with worry lines carved deep into his forehead. His long gray hair hung limply around his shoul-ders, almost invisible against his jet-black robe. The scars over his left eye were lighter and thinner, faded with age.

"I suppose I have no need to hide from you," he said, looking Fi over. "You seem remarkably unsurprised to find a Witch lurking in the window of this castle."

"I've met one of you before," Fi explained, leaning for-ward. "But I'll admit I didn't expect you to be in this particu-lar library."

"And why is that?" he asked curiously.

Fi sucked in a breath. "Because of this," she said, raising her hand to reveal the Butterfly Curse.

The man's eyes widened, first in surprise and then in inter-est. He lifted his own palm, revealing the twin mark flutter-ing on his skin. "I see you know a little about my situation," he said, lips twisting into a bitter smile. "I was banished for many, many years before I made my way back to Aurora's castle. This is the last piece of myself I left anywhere."

"And you never got rid of the curse?"

"No." The Lord of the Butterflies rested his chin on his hand. "I suppose you were hoping for a different answer."

Fi clenched her palm against the desk, crushing down the disappointment. "I'm more interested in what happened to you. If you're the last sliver of the Lord of the Butterflies, then you must know the whole story. Everything that happened in Andar."

This was what Fi really needed—information, history, facts to fill in the gaps. And the Lord of the Butterflies might be just curious enough to give them to her.

"What were you and Aurora to each other?" she asked, thinking of the letters in Everlynd's library and the memory Aurora had shown her. "Were you lovers?"

The Lord of the Butterflies chuckled. "Nothing so ordinary," he promised, a little gleam coming back into his one piercing green eye. "We were something much rarer—kindred spirits in our thirst for knowledge. Specifically, knowledge of magic. I was the more powerful Witch—even her teacher for a time—but Aurora was so clever. I never knew what to expect from her."

Fi was fascinated. This wasn't just a piece of a man trapped in this mirror; it was a piece of lost history. "And the Spindle Witch?" she breathed. "Where does she fit in?"

"She was the wedge between us." The man shook his head. "My greatest pleasure at that time was researching new forms of magic. Aurora often came along on my investigations, though

259

her ministers would have preferred her moldering away on her throne. One day, we found ourselves in a dead valley beneath a black tower ringed in bones. And in the tower was a girl."

A chill ran down Fi's spine as she thought of the tall spire and the lonely window. "I've seen it," she whispered.

The Lord of the Butterflies lifted an eyebrow. "Then you understand why we felt for her. She was a Witch, half-mad from talking only to the crows, but she had magic like I had never seen. To the little spider, snuffing the life out of things with her golden hair came as naturally as breathing."

His voice was fond, and Fi felt an unpleasant prickle on her skin. Here he was, the man she recognized from the letters—dangerously fascinated by the Spindle Witch and far too unconcerned about the consequences.

"Aurora and I agreed to break the enchantment that held her prisoner. It was ancient and intricate, binding her magic to that tower and to the earth itself. The answer seemed simple: sever the girl from her magic, and she would be free. But Aurora realized the truth before I did.

"The girl was dead. She'd been dead long before we ever found her in that tower. But her will to live was immense. And so was her magic." His eyes glowed with a strange, reverent light. "Her magic brought her back in the same way she could use it to animate skeletons and half-dead creatures. Alone in that tower, she forgot she'd ever died."

Fi's stomach lurched as she recalled the girl from Aurora's memories manipulating the corpse of the crow with her golden threads. *Who are we to decide what true life is or isn't?* the Lord of the Butterflies had said. So Perrin had been right when

260

he theorized that consuming magic was what had kept the Spindle Witch alive for centuries.

"So you and Aurora fought about what to do with her," Fi guessed.

"Bitterly," the man said with a sigh. "I had been working on a relic to sever the girl from her magic—a pin to place in those lovely, magical locks. But if her magic was the only thing keeping her alive, then by severing her from it, I would kill her."

"The butterfly hairpin." Fi couldn't believe it. She'd held that hairpin—turned it every which way, even tested the sharpness of the pin on her fingertip, never guessing it was a weapon that could have killed the Spindle Witch.

Something of her thoughts must have shown on her face.

"It doesn't work," the Lord of the Butterflies told her dismissively. "I left the enchantment unfinished. I couldn't imagine destroying her." He turned his head, his gaze suddenly very far away. "You see, if I ever loved anyone at all, it was *her*. All she wanted was to be free from that tower and the incessant hunger she'd felt all her life. Aurora wouldn't allow it as long as she had to devour others to live. So I took matters into my own hands. I began researching a new kind of magic, a series of spells that would allow me to drain the power from the enchantment, the tower, the earth around it—everything."

Fi's breath stuck in her throat. "You created the Siphoning Spells *for* the Spindle Witch. To set her free. Even though you'd seen the tower, the valley of bones."

The decision to let the Spindle Witch out—that must

have been what he'd written about with so much vehemence in his letters, insisting that Aurora couldn't change his mind.

Fi shook her head in disbelief. "Why? You had to know what she would do. How many people she would kill."

"You sound like Aurora," the Lord of the Butterflies said, and Fi got the distinct impression it wasn't a compliment. Seeing that feverish gleam in his eye, it wasn't hard to picture the young Witch who fancied himself a researcher and had rationalized away all the harm the Spindle Witch would do. With that cold dispassion, he could justify anything—even unleashing a monster that would turn entire kingdoms to dust.

"But Aurora stopped you," Fi said.

The Lord of the Butterflies gave her a wry smile. "I see you know some of this story already, so I'll skip to the end. I was much more powerful than Aurora—I assumed I had nothing to fear from a Witch of her caliber. Then she sent me a certain letter opener with a swallowtail handle."

The mark on Fi's palm ached. She felt it all over again, the agony as the Curse of the Wandering Butterfly burned into her skin.

"She used my own magic against me," the Lord of the Butterflies said, sounding impressed. "As I said, she was quite clever. Though, as her former teacher, I suppose I share a little of the credit."

Fi closed her fist around the butterfly mark. "But, in the end, the Spindle Witch got out of the tower anyway."

He shrugged. "Unfortunately, the wheels had already been set into motion. I'd taught the girl to strengthen her magic by tying her hair into twists and knots. From there, she taught herself to spin, growing ever more powerful while the enchantment Aurora and I had tried to dismantle grew weaker and weaker. It was only a matter of time."

Fi's head was a whirl. He had told her so much; whether she could use any of it was a different matter. But she had one lingering question.

"Why did you come back and leave a piece of yourself here?"

"You are so young." The Lord of the Butterflies sighed heavily. "With age came a wisdom Aurora attained long before me. A terrible hunger lives inside the little spider. She consumes life and magic to survive, but it never fills the gnawing hole inside her. Nothing can—because no matter how much magic she consumes, she can never truly live again." He tapped his fingernail against the table. "I understood too late what Aurora was trying to tell me: siphoning is far too dangerous. It's a magic that never should have existed."

And Fi had gotten the Spindle Witch that much closer to finding it. She felt sick, knowing she had delivered Camellia's riddle and the Rose Crown right into her hands. If the Spindle Witch managed to put it all together before Fi did, she would carry the guilt of everything that happened next—but probably not for very long, because she doubted the Spindle Witch would leave anything alive.

"As to why I put myself into the glass of the library," the man continued, "I guess I was just hoping to see her one last time."

Fi wasn't sure who he meant, Aurora or the Spindle Witch. Before she could ask, the man held up a finger.

"Someone's looking for you," he murmured, with a secretive smile. Then Fi felt her head sliding down to pool on the desk in front of her, her eyes slipping helplessly shut.

FI STOOD IN the darkness barefoot. The dream was familiar by now, and she reached down, picking up the golden thread that trailed away into the blackness. She definitely hadn't nodded off; the Lord of the Butterflies must have made her fall asleep. He'd said someone was looking for her. Could he mean Briar?

Her bare feet slapped against the stone as Fi began to wander, waiting for the rattle of bones. Instead, she found herself walking through a pool of mist, silvery and cold, and then at last Fi heard a voice calling her name. It wasn't Briar. It was . . .

"Perrin!" she yelled. She forgot following the golden thread, letting it trail behind her as she wandered farther into the mist, searching for the boy.

"Fi!" She heard him calling, closer now.

Fi ran, her nightgown swishing around her. The mist rose up before her like a wall. She closed her eyes as she burst through, only to find she was suddenly sitting across from Perrin in a little rowboat. Inky water stretched out around them, the weather-worn craft lilting gently on a calm lake. She could only see snatches of it through the mist, but she thought she recognized it. Evista Lake from Everlynd.

Perrin leaned toward her, a deep blue robe shimmering around him like water. "Fi."

"How is this possible?" she asked. "Are you really here?"

She was desperate—so desperate for this not to be some kind of trick.

"Yes!" Perrin said excitedly, leaning forward to seize her arms. "I'm here inside your dream. I did it—I'm dream walking. This is my medium." He waved an arm at the lake and the rippling water. Fi's mind flashed back to the dream journey she'd shared with Briar on this same lake and the island of gold sand created by the magic of the original Dream Witch.

"Are you all right?" Perrin asked, looking her over anxiously.

"I'm not hurt," she promised, squeezing his hands. "But I am locked in the castle of Andar. I can't get out. And I didn't defeat the Spindle Witch." Her heart clenched as she said it, wondering if Shane was somewhere on the other side. The boat trembled as though it might capsize.

"It's okay. We have a plan." Ripples spread through the water as Perrin sat back, steadying the craft. "We've found something that can sever the Spindle Witch from her magic."

Fi's breath caught, the conversation she'd just had with the Lord of the Butterflies playing in her mind. "It's that hairpin, isn't it? The one Red and Shane found."

Perrin shot her a look. "You're oddly knowledgeable for someone trapped in a castle."

The details of Everlynd from Fi's memories were starting to bleed through the mist, lanterns winking on the distant shore. "There's something important I have to tell you," Fi said quickly. "That pin—it's incomplete."

Perrin shook his head. "At some point, you are going to have to tell me how you're doing this," he muttered. "The pin *was* incomplete, but we fixed it—mostly. Now we just need you to finish it."

"Me?" Fi repeated. "I'm no Witch."

"No, but you do have some of the Lord of the Butterflies's magic in that curse mark on your hand," Perrin explained, waving his own palm for emphasis. "All you have to do is touch the pin, and the spell will be complete. So we just need to get you out of the castle."

Fi's heart leapt at the idea of being freed from this prison. But that would leave the Spindle Witch here alone, with the Rose Crown and the riddle, just a hair's breadth from the Siphoning Spells. Everything the Great Witches had sacrificed themselves to keep safe. She had to stay.

"No," she said. "Don't get me out. Get the hairpin inside. If there's a chance to sever the Spindle Witch from her magic, it will be in here, where she's least expecting it."

Perrin seemed to glow for a moment, rippling as though he might wink out of the dream. The water around the boat became choppy and uneven, and the shores disappeared into thick white fog.

Perrin's voice was muffled, and it took Fi a moment to realize he wasn't talking to her. "That's what she said—I don't—one at a time!"

Fi smiled. Suddenly, she could picture exactly who was on the other side, clamoring in Perrin's ear. She reached out a hand, snagging his wavering form.

"Tell Shane I'm sorry," she said. "And that I'm really on the right side this time."

Perrin nodded, a wide smile stretching across his face. His hand slipped through Fi's, suddenly insubstantial, and she looked around, willing the boat and the swaying water to hold. There was only a tiny circle of Perrin's dream left, the mist closing in from all sides.

Perrin jerked forward, making the boat rock. "Shane says we can be there in six days," he said, hurrying as though he, too, knew their time was almost up. "And it won't just be us, Fi. We'll convince the Witches of Everlynd to march with us, too. Can you be ready on your side?"

"I'll be ready," Fi promised.

"Good," Perrin said with a sigh. "I didn't really know how we were going to reschedule this if you said no. Six days, Fi," he confirmed. "The attack will start at dawn, and Shane will get you the pin as fast as she can."

"I can help with that," Fi said. Perrin had started to disappear little by little, his blue robe running like drops of water. "There's a door beneath the eastern tower," she said, remembering the outer gate where she'd given up on her escape. "I'll make sure it's unlocked. Follow the blue pennants, and there's a path straight to the library. I'll be there— and so will the Spindle Witch. Tell Shane to be careful."

Perrin chuckled, even as the rest of his body began to shimmer. "Shane says she doesn't want to hear that from someone who threw herself off a cliff."

Fi choked on a little laugh. That sounded exactly like Shane.

"I don't think I can hold this any longer," Perrin admitted. The mist was so thick Fi was breathing it. Then her eyes widened.

"Wait!" Fi said, grabbing him. "Can you do one more thing for me? Can you put me in Briar's dream? There's something I need to ask him."

"Fi, it took everything I had to find you. Making a connection with him, too . . ." Perrin was little more than a translucent body with uncertain eyes, held together as precariously as a raindrop.

"But there's *already* a connection." Fi lifted her hand, the one that was always tangled in golden thread. "Briar's at the other end," she promised. "Please, Perrin."

"I'll try," he whispered, and even though he was almost invisible, she could make out the crease of his smile. "But I've only been a full-fledged dream Witch for a few days, you know."

The golden thread rose from Fi's hand, hovering in the air. In the space between heartbeats, Fi felt like she saw Perrin in the boat, and then a flash of the glorious dreamscape of Evista Lake, and then it was like the water was rising all around her, a great torrent of rain surging up from the ground. It surrounded her in a rush. The last thing she felt was Perrin's hand on her back giving her a gentle shove.

Fi stumbled forward into a dream she had never seen before. A baby wailed while a blond-haired woman in a high four-poster bed reached desperately toward it. The baby was ashen and weak, barely moving in the bassinet that spilled over with rich blankets.

"Please," the woman was begging, "please don't let him die. I would pay any price—just save my baby. Save Briar Rose."

The Spindle Witch swept over to the bed, her long black skirts trailing, and Fi realized with a start exactly what she was seeing. This was the moment the queen had bargained for the life of her child—the moment the Spindle Witch had betrayed Andar.

Fi took a step backward and collided with something

solid. The breath left her lungs as she looked up to find the creature with the horned skull beside her. The last flickering bits of red in the empty eye sockets were focused on the memory playing out before them.

"Any price, Your Majesty?" the Spindle Witch asked, eyes glittering.

"Any price, Spindle Witch," the queen agreed, sealing her own fate.

A smile spread across the Spindle Witch's lips. She reached beneath her veil, pulling forth a long golden thread and twirling it through her fingers. Tears streamed down the queen's face as she scooted to the edge of the bed, wrapping the baby's tiny hand in her own.

The Spindle Witch loomed over them. She looped the end of her golden thread like she was tying a knot and then reached down and slipped it into the baby's chest, right over his heart, her deft fingers pulling the end tight. She attached the other end to the queen.

She was draining the life from Briar's mother and giving it to him, Fi realized. The color drained from the queen as her life was sucked away, and the baby began to move again, his crystal-blue eyes opening. The Spindle Witch stood over the dead queen and the baby and cooed. Her golden braid slipped out from under the veil.

And then suddenly the baby was crying again, and the queen was alive in the bed, reaching for him. The memory had started over. Briar's mother begged for the life of her baby, and the Spindle Witch exacted her promise, reaching up under her veil and tying a golden thread around the baby's heart. The memory played over and over.

"I don't understand," Fi said, turning to the skeletal creature.

The skull head tipped, those last pinpricks of red burning into Fi. He reached for the golden thread stretching from his empty chest. Behind them, the Spindle Witch reached under her veil, pulling the golden thread, tying it around the baby's heart.

Where does it lead? he begged.

Suddenly, Fi understood what Briar had been trying to tell her all along.

SHE WOKE WITH a start in front of a dull pane of glass. Fi surged to her feet, knocking over her chair as she leaned into the desk, breathing hard.

Shakily, she put the chair back on its feet. Hours had passed, by the position of the shadows in the room, and it would be night soon. Fi didn't imagine she would sleep a wink. She had a lot to do in the next six days.

21

Shane

"THIS IS THE best and final chance we will ever have to beat the Spindle Witch. All that we have sacrificed and all we have waited for has been for this. The time is now."

The Paper Witch curled a fist in front of his heart as he spoke. Shane had never seen him looking so regal. He had donned a white robe with a silver sash, and his long hair hung loose for the first time in Shane's memory. He looked like Briar, like Aurora, like a Great Rose Witch.

Her eyes snuck over to the stunned faces of the Witches. They were gathered in the largest of the three towers, Everlynd's temporary headquarters. The Paper Witch had explained everything, including what they knew about the silver-eyed, body-snatching Witch, who had sealed his fate the moment he dared to lay a hand on Red. The only thing he'd kept back was the truth about the butterfly pin being untested.

A day ago, Shane wouldn't have dreamed she'd be standing here with Perrin and the Paper Witch, trying to convince the most important people in Everlynd to march on their own castle. A day ago, Shane hadn't known if her partner was alive. Now she knew that, and so much more, thanks to Perrin's new dream magic.

Shane didn't have any more doubts—in her plan or in her partner. But she seemed to be the only one who felt that way.

The tower was crowded with so many people that the strong oak tables and iron candle braces had been pushed together to make room for more to stand—but somehow nobody had a word to say. Shane's gaze moved along the table, jumping from person to person. The Seer Witch with her wizened hands folded in her lap, the Stone Witch with his head bowed, and Captain Hane, who was nodding cautiously, her arms folded over her leather jerkin. The clump of soldiers and guards standing behind her traded wary looks.

The only person willing meet Shane's eyes was Nikor, who sat slumped in a chair with his richly embroidered robes bunched around him. His hard expression as his gaze raked over the three of them told her he definitely wasn't on their side. Shane wasn't surprised. Nikor and the Paper Witch had some kind of bad history. Nikor's cousin and Perrin had some kind of bad history. All they were missing was Red, and then they'd have the trifecta of Witches the steward couldn't stand. Luckily, Red and Cinzel had opted out of the council meeting.

Shane gritted her teeth, fisting one impatient hand into her long red coat. The Paper Witch had warned her to let him and Perrin do most of the talking. In fact, his exact words had been *Yelling at the council, while highly satisfying, would be perilously counterproductive.* Shane agreed in principle, but she was dangerously close to testing that theory.

At least Armand Bellicia wasn't smirking at her from somewhere in this snake pit. After being thoroughly wrung out for information by Captain Hane, he'd been given one of Everlynd's precious few horses and sent back—ostensibly to warn the Border Guards in Darfell, but Shane wouldn't be at all surprised if he was just fleeing with his tail between his legs. She honestly hoped she'd never see that cockroach again.

The silence dragged out. Perrin shot a glance at the Paper Witch and then cleared his throat. "I know we're asking a lot . . ." he began.

Nikor scoffed. "You're asking the impossible. You want us to leave the camp undefended and march through the waste and impassable Forest of Thorns right up to the Spindle Witch's door. And we're supposed to do all of this on your say-so." He waved a dismissive hand. "A Witch who gave up his seat on this council, a boy who's yet to take his, and an outsider with no business in this room at all."

A growl was building in Shane's throat, but the Paper Witch waved her back. "You and I have debated this point many times, Nikor." His blue eyes, usually so cheerful, seemed a little dangerous as he stared the other man down. "The moment Briar Rose awakened, a war that was stopped in time for a hundred years began again, whether you like it or not."

"Spare me your proselytizing," Nikor spat. "Everlynd was among the first casualties of that war, and I hold you responsible for that, Paper Witch."

Everyone in the room stiffened. Shane could tell the memory of Everlynd burning was still raw. Nikor's fingers had wound into a fist, angry knuckles bulging.

"The last time we listened to you, we lost everything. And now you come here asking us to march out *tomorrow*. That doesn't even give us enough time to recall the farthest scouts or secure the city."

"There's no time," Shane snapped, sick of holding her tongue. "Were you listening to anything we said? It has to be now!"

Nikor's eyes burned into hers. Shane had a feeling he would have thrown her out of the tower himself if it didn't require getting out of his chair. The Paper Witch settled a firm hand on her shoulder.

"Time favors the Spindle Witch more than it favors us," he said, looking at Captain Hane. "Her forces are only growing stronger."

"I'm all for haste," Hane agreed. "For every Witch Hunter we catch on patrol, there are more running off to join the Spindle Witch. She's got us badly outmatched already."

"Well, then, by all means, let's march right into the teeth of it," Nikor hissed sarcastically.

"Temper, temper," the Seer Witch said mildly, but she didn't disagree with him.

One of the soldiers behind Captain Hane, a hard-faced man with a grizzled beard whose pale skin was marked with scars, stepped forward. "I'm sorry to speak out of turn, but there's something none of you are addressing. Even saying the soldiers make it through the thorns and the Witch Hunters and those monsters of bone—what are we supposed to do then? You said the people of the castle are likely being controlled. You expect us to kill our own countrymen?"

"You won't have to." This time, it was Perrin who stepped forward. In a midnight-blue robe that swept from his shoulders, he looked more impressive than usual, striking and powerful. "It's not going to come to that, because I'm going to go in ahead of you and wake them all up. They're only able to be controlled because the Spindle Witch trapped them under the sleeping curse cast by my great-aunt, the Dream Witch. I'm going to break it for good."

A murmur of disbelief rushed through the room. For the first time, the ancient Stone Witch raised his head. "You, Perrin?" he asked, regarding the young man thoughtfully.

Perrin nodded. "Yes. I've discovered my medium, and my magic is stronger now than I ever imagined. I can do this—and when I do, I won't be Perrin any longer. I'll be the next Dream Witch."

That seemed to shut everybody up. Shane felt hope rising in her chest, her eyes darting around the room as Captain Hane leaned on her fisted hand, glancing back at the grizzled soldier who had spoken up.

"It's a good plan," Hane said.

The man gave a hesitant nod. "It is . . . except for the part where this whole plan hinges on a girl my son's age being able to defeat the immortal Spindle Witch."

The Paper Witch spoke before Shane could break the no-yelling embargo again. "The weapon left by the Lord of the Butterflies is very specific," he explained patiently. "It can be wielded by no other, and even if it could, there's no one I would trust more with this task. I wasn't the one who chose her—the Rose Witch and the enchantment on the bone spindle did. That should mean something to all of you."

Shane waited with bated breath as the members of the council bent their heads together, talking in low voices. A heavy feeling sank in her gut as she watched Nikor shaking his head at Captain Hane, the Witches quietly withdrawn, the soldiers arguing in hushed tones. Fi was an outsider, too, and for many of these people, Andar was just an old story. Fear of the Spindle Witch loomed over them. With every second that passed, Shane could feel them losing.

"It's such a risk . . ." someone whispered.

Shane didn't even know who said it, but that was all it took to push her over the edge. She strode forward and slammed her hands down onto the table, making the candles and the council members jump.

"What is wrong with you people?" Shane shouted. "You're arguing over nothing! You've already lost Everlynd. You're living in a crumbling, burnt-out hole, struggling just to stay alive. Are you going to let the Spindle Witch chase you from one end of Andar to the other until she's killed the last of you off?"

Her words hung in the air like a crack of thunder. Shane was about ready to flip the tables and get right up in Nikor's face when Perrin brushed past her, mouthing, *I got it from here.*

"I know we're all frightened of the Spindle Witch," Perrin said. "And Nikor's right—I don't have a seat on this council yet. But my parents did. And you listened to them. Because deep down, no matter how terrified you are, you know they were right." He spun to address the entire room.

"We're not just the last survivors of Andar, hiding away to save ourselves. We're more than that. We're the seeds of Andar's rebirth. And if we give up on this fight now, everything we've been working to preserve all these years will be for nothing."

The Paper Witch added one last plea. "You have a friend inside the castle, and you have a weapon that could defeat the Spindle Witch. You will never have another chance like this one."

Shane was tired of giving them chances. She'd made up her mind. "I'm heading out tomorrow, even if I'm going alone."

Perrin threw her a look. "Well, you won't be *alone*."

"I will fight with you," the Paper Witch said.

"And so will I." The Stone Witch got slowly to his feet as he spoke, and Shane almost imagined she could feel the earth rumbling far beneath them, taking their side. Or maybe that was just the rush of excitement she felt as Captain Hane rose, too, giving Shane a quick smile.

"We'll be with you," she promised. The soldiers behind her were nodding, too, even the man with the grizzled beard. Suddenly, everyone in the room was agreeing, rising from their chairs and clapping each other on the shoulders.

All eyes turned to Nikor. The steward sat with his fingers steepled, pressed against his brow. Shane knew she was asking for trouble, but she couldn't stop herself.

"It seems the people of Everlynd have spoken," she said.

Nikor's eyes flashed with outrage. But it faded fast, the ember of an old and tired anger withering as he rose reluctantly to his feet. "It seems they have," he agreed. His rich cape flared as he threw a hand in Shane's direction. "To the castle, then. And to victory!"

Shane almost couldn't believe it. She and Perrin traded a very undignified thumbs-up that made the Paper Witch shake his head.

"Then it's decided," the Paper Witch said. "The Stone Witch and I will make a path through the Forest of Thorns."

"I'll head to the castle to break the sleeping curse and free the people trapped there," Perrin added.

"And I'll get the weapon to Fi so she can destroy the Spindle Witch once and for all," Shane finished.

Captain Hane met her eyes. "We'll hold her armies off for as long as it takes," she said, the words a little grim.

"And we'll all hope this girl is worthy of the faith you're putting in her," Nikor muttered, apparently unable to resist getting the last word.

Shane didn't care. The old coward could gripe and grumble all he wanted, because in the morning, she'd be marching for the castle—with the full might of Everlynd behind her, just as they'd promised. She'd won the first battle, and she'd be damned if she lost the next one.

She just had to talk to one more person.

22

Red

RED HUMMED SOFTLY to herself, stroking her hand through Cinzel's coarse fur. They were tucked up in the little house, and Cinzel was asleep on his side in front of the fire, his great floppy head resting on Red's pooled black skirts. His paws twitched as he dreamed about chasing something, and he let out a little whine. Red soothed him with her voice, murmuring a small snatch of an old lullaby. Her fingers dug into his shaggy pelt until she could feel the soft fur of his undercoat. His ear twitched in satisfaction as she gave him a vigorous belly scratch.

Cinzel was more like a dog than a wolf sometimes. Red had made him that way—maybe more so than she had ever realized.

Her fingers stilled in the white fur as her thoughts drifted back to the Snake Witch. Red had thought she was nothing like her ancestor, but now she was starting to wonder.

She imagined the young Witch from Perrin's memory with her hands cupped protectively around the little stoat. The towering figure depicted in statues and paintings with her snake familiar wound over her arm. The monster the Witch Hunters spoke of, enchanting beasts to obey her will. The woman who stood on the bank of a lake, entrusting her heart to another.

Which one was the real Assora?

There was an old story Red's father used to tell her called "The Witch in the Bell Hollow." It was about a Witch who lived in a house overgrown with bluebells and morning glories, a house so beautiful no one believed the woman inside could be ugly. But she was—ugly and rotten and wicked, like all the Witches in her father's stories. She lured travelers to her hovel with the sound of the wind chimes hung round her door, all of them strung of tiny ivory finger bones. Until one woodcutter's daughter got the better of her and left her to die, strangled by the bindweed hidden among the morning glories. Proof that the evil had been inside the Witch all along.

The High Lord of the Witch Hunters had been obsessed with stories where Witches got what they deserved. For every action, a consequence. Red knew better than to believe her father's stories, but the more she'd learned from watching Perrin and the Paper Witch, the more she realized that powerful magic had its own consequences. And Red was not immune from them.

She stroked her hand down Cinzel's long leg, scratching in between his toes. She'd always known that, when she hummed or sang, she could make animals understand her feelings—talk to them without words. But what exactly was she doing to them? Had she bent Cinzel and his brother to her will? Had she transformed them into something they were never meant to be?

The thought left her cold despite the crackling fire. Red bent over the wolf, pressing her forehead into the soft fur. "Are you happy?" she whispered.

Cinzel didn't say anything, just gave another sleepy grumble. Red closed her eyes, breathing in the musky scent of his fur. All those dark days when she was a child, haunting the Forest of Thorns like a ghost, Cinzel was the only thing that gave her the strength to keep going. She wanted to believe he felt the same.

She sat up when she heard the door opening. Cinzel raised his sleepy head and climbed to his feet, his tail swishing in recognition. Shane was back, and that meant the council meeting was over.

Shane's face was serious, one hand shoved deep into her pocket. Red wondered if it had gone badly. She got up slowly, brushing Cinzel's fur off her skirts.

"What happened?" she asked. "Did they refuse?"

Shane shook her head. "No, they agreed. We head out tomorrow."

Tomorrow. Red's stomach lurched. It seemed too soon.

"That's exactly what we wanted, right?" she said, forcing the uncertainty down. "So why the dour look? If you keep frowning, your face will get stuck that way." Red reached up to poke at the frown lines between Shane's eyebrows. Shane caught her hand.

"I have to ask you to do something," she said, squeezing Red's fingers. "Even though I don't want to."

Red swallowed. Her heart was beating in her ears like a warning drum, too fast and too loud. She wondered if Cinzel could hear it, too. Red could feel him vibrating, his whole body humming with protective instinct.

"For us to defeat the Spindle Witch," Shane began, "for the attack to even have a chance, Perrin has to get to the castle ahead of the soldiers. I need you to take him through the Forest of Thorns."

The words hit her like a blow. Red closed her eyes. Her ribs felt like they were caving in, crushing against her heart. But her terror at the thought of returning to the forest felt strangely blunted. Somewhere deep down, she had known this was coming.

Shane touched her shoulder, that unbearably serious look on her face. "I'm sorry," she said, her voice rough. "No one else can do this. You're the only person who knows the way through."

Red shook her head. "It's okay. I always knew I'd have to go back someday. You see, I left something in that forest—something important."

Twilight was coming on. Though the sky was perfectly clear, she could almost imagine it roiling with black thunderclouds and pulsing rain—the sound she still heard in her worst nightmares. Her mind swam with the memory of dark branches, wicked thorns, and the rush of red blood.

"He's waiting for me," she whispered. "It's time I finished this."

Shane looked scared, which was strange. She was never supposed to be scared of anything. That was Red's job. "What are you talking about? Who's waiting for you?"

Red let out a long breath. "Shadow, the white wolf."

Shane's eyes flashed over her face. "One of those creatures from the Forest of Thorns? Your wolves?"

Cinzel pressed against Red, anchoring her with his warmth.

"Those wolves were never mine—not really," Red said, already lost in the storm that always waited in the dark corners of her mind. "They belonged to the Spindle Witch from the very beginning. All but Shadow."

RED HAD BEEN in and out of consciousness after her father drugged her. All she caught were disjointed images through her half-closed eyes—the lurch of being loaded onto the back of the cart with the wolf pups tossed after her, the thump of their soft little bodies colliding with hers, and then the sensation of being carried somewhere, her ragdoll limbs swinging below her as strong arms hefted her out of the cart.

It was the rain on her face that finally woke her. A violent storm was raging, bursts of thunder and a wild streak of lightning splitting the clouds with its forked tongue. Red lay in the wet dust at the edge of the Forest of Thorns, blinking up at the twisting black branches. Her mouth tasted bitter, like ash. Her whole body felt cold and heavy, and her head was hazy, like it was filled with cotton.

"Pity." Her father's right-hand man, Ivan, appeared over her, his heavy black cloak soaked by the spitting rain. "This

would have been so much easier for you if you hadn't woken up."
He drew the wicked saw-toothed blade from beneath his cloak.

Terror shot through Red like a bolt of lightning. This man
she had known her whole life was nothing but a monster, his face
transformed by the dark and the storm. The rain rushed in her
ears as Red struggled to move. She tried to call for her father, for
anyone who might save her—but her voice was so small, so weak
even she could barely hear it.

The blade glistened in Ivan's hand as he raised it high. And
then a blur shot between them—Shadow, the white pup, leaping
out of the thorns to sink his little teeth into Ivan's calf, eliciting
a hiss of pain. Ivan kicked the pup away. Shadow rolled in the
dust, his fur matted and dripping with mud, as Ivan cursed, looking at the bloody bite mark.

Red scrambled to her feet. She almost tripped over Cinzel,
still unconscious. She couldn't tear her gaze away from Shadow,
his tiny yellow eyes filled with the crackle of the storm. Then
Shadow howled, leaping for Ivan at the same moment the Witch
Hunter brought the blade down.

A splash of blood hit her dress. She screamed, thunder and
lightning burning the color into her eyes. She grabbed Cinzel up
into her arms and fled into the Forest of Thorns, sliding in the wet
dust and pushing herself through tiny gaps, not even feeling the
rake of the thorns as she went deeper and deeper, running away
from the horror and the sadness and the grief.

She had spent days wandering the dark knots of the Forest,
crying and calling out for her father and the mother she had never
known and especially for Shadow. Red clutched Cinzel's tiny
trembling body to her chest and waited desperately for someone—
anyone!—to rescue her. They were both half-starved by the time

the Witch in the black veil appeared, towering over Red, reaching out a graceful gloved hand to lift her out of the dirt.

"What an interesting creature has stumbled into my forest," the woman said, her deep red lips pressed together into a smile. "Get up, dear. I have something for you."

The Witch crooked her finger, and Red's heart seized in her chest as a white beast prowled out of the cage of thorns.

"I'm afraid he's not exactly as he used to be, but I believe this belongs to you?"

Red pressed her hands over her mouth. It was a monster with vicious claws and a bony spine jutting from its back, his fur rippling with a snarl—but it was still Shadow, and he was somehow alive, and Red would have traded anything for that.

The Spindle Witch put her fingers beneath Red's chin, tipping her face up. "Now, then. A favor begs a favor. Let's talk about what you can do for me."

THAT WAS THE bargain she'd taken, the one she couldn't refuse. She had let her love for Shadow turn her inside out, had cut herself up into smaller and smaller pieces for the Spindle Witch until she barely recognized herself. She'd even learned to use her magic to whistle commands to the monstrous wolves. And when she fought Shane and Fi and Briar in the Forest of Thorns, she had used the wolves to attack. She had almost made Shadow into a murderer with Shane's blood smeared across his jagged mouth.

She didn't know what Shadow would be anymore, now that she had betrayed the Spindle Witch. Would he still recognize Red, or would she just be the enemy? Would she have to kill him, finish what Ivan had started so many years ago? Leaving him alone in that forest, at the mercy of the Spindle Witch, had to be worse.

She only realized she was crying when Shane pulled her in, tucking Red's face against her shoulder. She held Red tight while Cinzel whined and pawed around her. Red buried her face in Shane's ragged coat. She'd never told that story to anyone before. The confession left her raw, the words ripped out of her.

"It's my fault," she whispered, pushing back until she could meet Shane's eyes. "It's my fault Shadow became that way."

Shane's hand tightened on her shoulder. "It's not your fault."

"You don't know that," Red insisted. "You don't know what my magic's capable of. Neither do I."

Shane's gray eyes were clear—so clear and sure as she brushed the tears away with the pad of her thumb.

"Yeah, I do. Because I know you, Red. I bet you loved Shadow the way you love Cinzel—fiercely, with everything you are. That kind of love could never turn someone into a monster. And I think the mutt will back me up on that," she added, as Cinzel bunted his furry cheek against her hip, crooning low and soft.

Red bit down a sob. She wanted to believe that. But she wouldn't know—not until she faced Shadow.

"I still have to make it right." Her smile twisted, rueful. "That's what you told me, remember? *You live with it by making it right.*"

Shane grimaced. "Gotta stop making speeches I'm going to regret later." She shook her head. "The truth is I don't want you anywhere near this battle. I want to tell you to get somewhere safe."

She hesitated—then she breathed out, and her hand slid down, tracing the straggles of curls that lay soft against Red's jaw.

"I love you, Red," she said seriously. "More than I've loved anyone. You came along and filled a part of me that I didn't even know was hollow. I don't think I can go on without you anymore. So we're going to have to do this—together."

Red sniffed, turning her face into that warm touch. "I'm afraid of failing," she admitted.

"So am I," Shane said. "And so is everyone else. Anyone who says they're not is lying through their teeth. But we can't give up. Especially me—or so I've been told." A fleeting smile crossed her lips.

That got a watery chuckle out of Red, but she still felt numb. Shane had just told her that she loved her—more than anything. She wanted to answer, but her heart was all twisted up inside her, a labyrinth of dark brambles and razor thorns.

"I don't think I could do it for anyone else. But I'll do it for you," she said. Cinzel whined, and Red knelt beside him. "We'll do it," she amended, catching Cinzel's jaw and pulling their faces close.

Maybe it was time for both of them to face Shadow.

"You won't be alone," Shane promised.

"Because Perrin's lurking somewhere in this house, eavesdropping?" Red teased, looking around. The four of them had been tripping over each other for days.

Shane chuckled. "No. He and the Paper Witch are spending the night in the tower—fussing with some Witch thing that I'll apparently only muck up. But you've still got me and the wolf."

Cinzel tilted his head up to look at Red. Then he darted in between them and shimmied out a hole in the stone wall, vanishing with a mischievous flick of his tail.

Shane laughed, rubbing the back of her neck. "Well, you've still got me."

Red got slowly to her feet. Her stomach was churning with so many things—exhilaration, and dread, and something else. Determination. She had the sense, suddenly, that Shane was a beacon, guiding her forward through the night. No matter what darkness Red walked through, she could make it if Shane was on the other side.

Red twined their hands together, trying to memorize the rasp and catch of her fingers sliding into the gaps where they fit so well.

"Don't leave me," she whispered, pressing her palm to Shane's.

Shane shook her head. "Not as long as I live."

"Clever of you to make that promise right before heading into a battle where we'll probably all die," Red murmured. She stared up at Shane, taking in all the parts of her Red had fallen for. Those strong hands that could still be so gentle. Those arms that never hesitated, whether they wielded her ax or wrapped tight around Red, holding her together. And that foul mouth that somehow looked so inviting now, her lips just parted.

How was it that a single smoldering glance from Shane could undo her so thoroughly?

Red was no stranger to desire. She had felt it before—the

tingling heat that radiated from her core. The soft gazes and heated exchanges in the dead of night that had made her feel less alone, if only for a single fleeting moment. Red was no stranger to playing pretend.

But this was different. If she kissed Shane now, it wouldn't be pretend.

Shane wasn't the type to play around with. Red knew that all too well. The huntsman would claim Red. Shane loved too fiercely to do anything else. Whether they ended up together forever or not, Shane would leave her mark on Red's heart.

Maybe that was what she wanted. To be claimed by Shane. To belong to someone. So that even if she never found a place to belong in this world, there would be one person who was home.

"Red . . ." Shane started. But Red didn't want to talk anymore. She hooked her arms around Shane's neck and pulled her down into a kiss, bold and sure and desperate—all the things she felt for this wild heart that had stolen hers. Heat crackled on her skin as Shane's fingers slid up her back into her hair, the kiss deep enough to make her shiver.

Red had wanted girls before, but she'd never needed anyone like this. Or maybe that was exactly wrong. She'd needed comfort before, and found it on dark nights in cold, forgettable places. But she'd never truly wanted. And now she did. She wanted Shane.

"Are you sure?" Shane asked, her eyes on fire.

"Yes," Red whispered. Then she gave in to the kiss, and to everything she wanted—one bright and burning moment to carry with her into the dark.

23

Fi

FI TOOK A deep breath to steady her nerves, walking purposefully through the castle toward the eastern tower—and beneath it, the little door in the outer wall. She was careful not to run or even walk too quickly through the silent halls lest she disturb the Wraith. The silver-eyed body snatcher mostly ignored Fi since she showed no signs of trying to escape, and Fi in turn had a little more freedom to move around without his puppets following her.

Still, she took a roundabout path, sticking to the back passages. The silence felt heavy as she ducked through lavish chambers upholstered with pearly satin curtains and rich carpets that sighed under her boots. She tried to avoid the rooms that she knew held the piled forms of collapsed people whose eyes would follow her as long as she was in sight.

Fi creaked open the last door and stepped into a stone hallway under a high arched ceiling, the little niches in the wall decorated with ancient porcelain vases. A line of royal-blue pennants led the way to a grand staircase, sweeping up three floors—and beyond that, the library. At least Shane should have a straight shot.

Unlike last time, the little gate room at the end wasn't empty. A burly guard stood vacantly by the door, a long sword belted at his waist. Fi cursed inwardly, forcing her shoulders to relax.

You're not trying to escape, she reminded herself. *So the Wraith has no reason to stop you.* She just needed to unlock the door. Fi bit her lip, walking past the puppet guard as casually as possible. His eyes sparked to life with silver, following her movement as she reached for the handle.

"Planning to take a little walk?" the Wraith asked. He leaned the guard's shoulder against the door, holding it closed.

"Hardly," Fi responded. It was too late to just casually turn the lock. She was going to have to do something else. Her hand slid into her pocket, crumpling the little page of notes she'd been scribbling about Camellia's code. Aloud she said, "Just hoping for a little air away from the stench of Witch Hunters."

She'd seen the way the silver-eyed Witch looked at the camps that littered the courtyards. Even inside his stolen bodies, his disgust was clear.

The guardsman crossed his arms. "A necessary inconvenience, I'm afraid," the Wraith said. "But I'm sure that trash will be the first thing the Spindle Witch cleans up—once she's done with your friends, of course." He smiled cruelly, and Fi saw her chance.

"Don't talk about them," she snapped, at the same time as she unlocked the door, yanking it open and slamming the edge into the guard the Wraith was wearing. He stumbled back, not quite fast enough to dodge. Fi had learned that it took him just a few seconds to acclimate to the new bodies he jumped into.

The grass and the crumbling courtyard peeked out from the open door, and Fi grabbed onto the frame. Instantly, the guard was on her. Her seized Fi by her collar, dragging her back and tossing her toward the wall. With his other hand, he slammed the door shut, turning the lock harshly.

"Go get your air somewhere else," he suggested. His silver eyes bored into Fi. "And don't let me catch you down here again."

Fi nodded, rubbing at her throat. She forced her expression to remain cool and blank as she quickly retraced her steps into the castle. When she was sure she was alone, she let out a heavy breath, sagging into the wall.

She'd done it. In the moment when the Wraith was distracted, grabbing for her, Fi had shoved her balled-up paper into the lock, jamming the strike plate. The silver-eyed Witch might have thought he locked the door, but it would push open easily with the slightest shove. And Shane would probably do much more than that.

Fi couldn't help but grin as she thought of her partner slamming through that door the next morning. She had already set up everything else. She'd even called the crows, speaking to them in hushed tones about the Rose Witch's riddle, a message she knew they'd take back to their master. Now all she had to do was wait.

Fi made her way back toward the high tower but paused halfway up a twisting staircase, her eyes drawn to a figure outside the window. Briar was sitting on the roof, in the same place Fi had found him before. His face was turned up toward the moonlight, his great black wings cascading across the roof behind him. He was almost the creature from Fi's dreams at this point, more monster than human.

Fi changed directions, climbing up the tower and then over the side of the parapets. She had to slow down when she reached the slanted roof with the slippery tiles, inching her way to Briar's side. He didn't turn at all, didn't even seem to realize she was there. Briar's skin was cold, and the moonlight left deep pits of shadow in the sunken hollows of his cheeks and eye sockets. But he was still in there somewhere, she knew, because she had never stopped dreaming.

Fi sat down next to the bone creature, letting her feet stretch out in front of her. The stars were beautiful overhead, and Fi closed her eyes, remembering the night when Briar had promised her forever and she had given him her heart. He still had it, no matter what happened. Even if there was no forever anymore—even if there was just this night and he was a monster.

"I love you, Briar," Fi whispered, leaning back on her hands. "And I promise nothing will ever change that." The bone creature remained still, unmoving as a gargoyle, but he didn't leave. Fi stayed with him late into the night, sitting on the roof and imagining.

That night, she dreamt of dancing with Briar in a hall of mirrors. The song in her ears was the melody from her childhood music box. This time, she was in the Red Baron costume, with the crimson mantle sweeping from her shoulders and the white porcelain mask, and Briar was the skeleton in the tailcoat. The tricornered hat with its red plume covered her hair, while Briar wore no mask at all, his face just a skull. They spun round and round, their reflections twisting one way and then the other. Briar's eye sockets were almost completely dark now, only the errant sparks of red flashing as they danced.

The bone horns gleamed. His claws slithered over her back as Fi spun gently in his arms, circling him once and then letting him pull her close. She slipped her porcelain mask off, throwing it aside. It shattered into a thousand tiny pieces that slid away from them and toward them and back again in the whirl of mirrors, a sea of broken glass seething at their feet. Briar dipped her, and her red cape trailed across the floor like a pool of blood as Fi leaned her head back as far as it would go. For a moment, Briar held her there, and then very slowly pulled her up until they were face-to-face.

The red had returned to his eyes. He reached up to tug at the thread in his chest. Fi laid her hands over the cold claws, stopping him.

"I know where it leads," she promised. Then she stood up on her tiptoes and closed her eyes, pressing a kiss to the side of the skull.

24

——≫≫ ≪≪——

Shane

THE FOREST OF Thorns was just like Shane remembered. Unburnable. Unbreakable. Impassable. The hulking black vines reared over her in a vicious snarl, thick boughs twining under and through each other in a labyrinth of gleaming thorns. The whole forest felt hungry and alive, like it was just waiting to swallow them.

Behind her, the sun was just cresting the horizon. Pink lines streaked the sky like faded scars. Dawn had come, and inside the castle, Fi was waiting for them.

"It's time," the Paper Witch called out. Shane moved back to stand with Red and Perrin, a restless Cinzel pacing at their feet. Red had traded out her usual dresses for a crimson tunic that flared at the waist under her wide belt, and Perrin wore a blue jerkin emblazoned with the white tower, a look of purpose on his face. One glance at Red told Shane the girl was still terrified, but there was a fierce determination there, too.

The army of Everlynd stretched out behind them. Captain Hane stood at the front of the battalion, wearing thick leather armor and carrying a massive broadsword. Shane liked the look of that. They'd decided against horsemen, but all the soldiers were armed with pikes and poleaxes, and they looked grim but ready, armor gleaming, everyone holding their breath for the first command. The red banners of Everlynd rippled in the dawn winds. Shane hadn't seen anything moving inside the Forest of Thorns yet, but she was positive there were enough monsters in there to outnumber them two-to-one.

All eyes followed the Paper Witch as he stepped forward. He wore a snow-white robe with long billowing sleeves, and he almost seemed to glow against the black thorns. The little bell in his hair tinkled with every step. Suddenly, Shane felt she was looking at a stranger, some powerful Witch who had walked out of the old stories, instead of a soft-hearted eccentric with a habit of picking up strays. The Paper Witch raised his hands to his chest. Then he hurled them toward the forest, and hundreds and hundreds of little paper triangles poured out of his sleeves, shooting toward the thorns like a great flock of white birds.

Shane gaped. She had caught the Paper Witch sitting up late by the fire every night of their march through the wastes, folding scraps of paper into tight little triangles and scratching nearly invisible symbols into the surface with white chalk. She just hadn't realized he'd made so many.

The paper flock hit the great wall of the forest like a wave.

Some pieces snagged on the thorns and fell to the ground, cut to shreds, but the rest sailed on, spiraling through gaps in the brambles. They vanished from her sight, pressing forward to find a path.

Sweat stood out on the Paper Witch's brow. Shane saw his knees buckle. Just when she thought he couldn't take one more second, an ancient hand settled on his white-clad shoulder. The Paper Witch turned to face the Stone Witch.

"It is enough," the old man said. In his threadbare robe of soft gray, the Stone Witch didn't look like much, but there was something unyielding about him as he stepped forward, the very ground seeming to creak under his ancient feet. Shane felt Red's hand slip into hers.

The Stone Witch knelt, burying both of his hands deep into the blackened dirt. Pebbles popped and rattled at Shane's feet. Then, with a yell, the Stone Witch ripped his hands free, splitting the earth. The trembling turned into a great roar, the ground beneath them shaking so hard that Red lost her balance and fell into Shane, almost toppling them both.

The two cracks the Stone Witch had made snaked toward the Forest of Thorns, following the path of the Paper Witch's birds. The roar was so loud Shane slapped her hands over her ears. The brambles began to heave, their great roots exposed as the soil slithered away. A giant slab of rock thrust up from the dirt, followed by another and then another, each massive swell of red stone breaking through the black vines and forcing them aside. Soon, a narrow channel zigzagged between the slabs, bound by sheer rock walls. The Stone Witch was literally carving a path through the cursed forest.

Shane swallowed. It was barely wide enough for three people to walk side by side, but it was a lot better than trying to float the whole army down the river.

The earth shuddered one last time, the forest groaning and then growing still. The Stone Witch sank to the ground, clearly spent. The Paper Witch looked just as bad, but he found the strength to turn to Everlynd's army once more.

"The path through the Forest of Thorns is made," he declared. "All that remains is to retake Andar."

A great cry rose up from the army, men and women shouting as the red sun broke from the eastern mountains and swept over them, igniting the white towers on their flags. Shane felt the tingle of the oncoming battle in her blood. But something held her back. She would move out with the army, but Red and Perrin would be taking another path, slipping through the thorns to reach the roses that spilled from Briar's tower.

Shane looked down at the girl she was still holding in her arms, only to find that Red was looking up at her, too, her eyes full of an emotion Shane didn't want to put a name to in case she was wrong.

"Look, when this is over . . ." Shane started.

"Oh, save it." Red pursed her lips, and then she seemed to come to a decision. "There's clearly never going to be a right time for this, and I don't want to have any regrets, so . . ." She tipped up on her toes, their lips inches apart. "I love you," she said.

Then Red fisted a hand in Shane's lapel, giving her a hard yank and bringing them together in a quick, passionate kiss. Just as quickly, Red let her go, backing away with a pink blush dusted across her cheeks.

"Now, don't you dare go and die and make me regret saying that," Red warned. She grabbed an open-mouthed Perrin and dragged him toward the forest. Cinzel loped after them with his tongue lolling out of his mouth like he was laughing.

Determination swelled in Shane's chest. Red loved her. Red *loved* her. She suddenly felt like she could take the entire Spindle Witch's army on by herself.

When she turned back, Captain Hane was looking at her, faintly amused. "We'd better move," the woman said. "It won't be long before they're all over us."

Shane nodded. She reached back and unslung her ax, her hands finding their familiar places on the worn handle. "Ready when you are."

The Paper Witch and the Stone Witch looked on, weary but resolute. Hane gave a short whistle. "Move out!" she shouted. Then she and Shane led the way into the channel, and the entire force of Everlynd's army streamed after them, weapons drawn and banners waving.

Shane was lost in a second. The stone channel banked one way and then the other, forking into side paths that ended abruptly in sheer walls, forcing them to backtrack. She could only trust that the Paper Witch's spell had flown true as she headed for the distant shimmer of the white castle. Thick knots of thorny black vines hung above her, suspended between the jutting red stones.

The silence made her uneasy. The Spindle Witch had to know they were coming—they hadn't exactly launched a sneak attack. So why wasn't anybody putting up a fight?

They were almost to the mouth of a narrow passage when Shane finally heard something—or rather, *felt* something. It was a rumble deep in the stone, powerful enough to rattle her teeth. For a split second, she wondered if the Stone Witch was casting another spell. Then she raced out of the passage and right into the teeth of one of the Spindle Witch's bone creatures.

The heavy skull could only have belonged to a gigantic bear. Each rust-colored fang was as long as her thumb. Far too late, she understood what she'd been hearing: the crash of massive bone feet hurtling through the rock maze. The blunt head wrenched toward her, and the creature lashed out with one burly arm.

"Shane! Look out!"

Shane dodged just in time. The yellowed claws hit the wall behind her in a shower of busted rock. She rolled under the massive shoulder joint and raised her ax, aiming for the back leg—only to find herself hurled across the channel as something crunched into her stomach, knocking the wind out of her.

A tail, Shane realized, gasping for breath. The misshapen bear had a tail, thick as a spinal cord. It cracked like an angry whip as the creature lurched up onto its back legs.

It was easily three times as tall as Shane. That wasn't saying much, since Shane was short, but Captain Hane was not, and the monster dwarfed her, too. Its immense body blocked the entire passage, trapping the army on one side and Shane on the other. Ragged clumps of sleek brown fur clung to its gleaming ribs, and Shane got the feeling this one hadn't been dead long. The stench of rot made her gag.

"Attack!" Captain Hane shouted. Three soldiers rushed the creature and were knocked back in a heap. Wood splintered as it crunched through pike staffs like they were twigs. "Work as a unit!"

"We can't get through!" a soldier yelled.

Shane cursed. The bear had them pinned down in the mouth of the channel. She had to lure it away or it would pick them off one at a time.

"Hey, over here!" Shane shouted. Then she squared her stance and brought her ax down right on its tail, severing a chunk as long as her arm.

The bone creature reared up, the rotten strips of skin around its throat rippling as it let out a long eerie moan. Shane threw herself to the ground and dove between the creature's legs, cracking her ax hard against the ankle and breaking off one massive foot.

"Shane, get out of there!" Hane shouted, struggling to lift one of the wounded soldiers.

Shane didn't need to be told twice. She turned and ran, ax swinging wildly in one hand, with the bear right behind her. It smashed into wall after wall, but that didn't seem to slow it down. If anything, Shane thought, it looked even madder than before.

She leapt a fallen slab of stone and burst out into red sunlight in a broad stone gully. She risked a glance up at the white castle, deceptively close behind a wall of thorns.

With a great crash, the bear plowed right through the stone slab. Shane tightened her grip on the ax. She was going forward. Fi was in that castle. They were back on the same side, finally, and nothing with an empty skull cavity was going to stop her from getting to her partner.

The bone creature lunged for her, its jaws so wide they

were practically unhinged. At the last possible second, Shane threw herself down, rolling beneath the enormous head. Then she drove the ax into the base of the skull—right where a knot of golden thread held it to the twisted spinal cord. The neck splintered, and the body crumpled around her, pelting Shane with a cascade of falling bones and bits of rotting flesh.

"Nasty," Shane muttered as she kicked her way out of the corpse, picking an especially slimy bit of *something* she wasn't even going to try to name off her shirt. But her victorious feeling evaporated fast. At least a dozen more of the Spindle Witch's creatures crowded in the passage ahead, every one a jumble of claws, limbs, and misshapen spines topped by pockmarked skulls. A skeletal stag pawed the stone, its antlers crawling with black lichen.

Shane's heart thudded. There was no way she could take on that many.

The stag charged, coming straight for her.

Raised voices rang through the gully. Suddenly, the soldiers of Everlynd were streaming out of the fork, surrounding her in a sea of rippling red cloaks. Shane felt a bolt of relief as a very familiar broadsword caught the stag by the antlers. She'd never been so glad to see Captain Hane's stern face.

"Good timing!" Shane called, a little hoarse.

"If you were one of my soldiers, I'd have your hide for that," Captain Hane shouted back, but Shane thought she looked impressed underneath it all. Hane wrenched the broadsword free, and a group of soldiers with pikes wrestled the stag away from them, hammering its flank. All around her, other soldiers were doing the same. Hane wiped her sleeve across her face. "At least we're getting close."

Shane followed her gaze. The castle soared above them, the white towers glowing in the sunrise. Red and Perrin should have reached it by now. If they could just take these bone creatures down, she'd be free and clear—

"Witch Hunters!"

Shane's guts lurched like someone had reached inside her and yanked. A new enemy was pouring into the gully—men and women in ragged cloaks, howling as they descended on the soldiers with brutal saw-toothed swords. The Witch Hunters fought like jackals, surrounding the soldiers of the Red Ember and taking them on as a pack. But the Red Ember was fighting just as fiercely. A whip of fire seared over the crowd as Soren drove the Witch Hunters back.

A sallow-faced Witch Hunter headed straight for them. Shane spun around to meet him, catching his strike before the saw-toothed blade sank into her shoulder. The tarnished sword screeched against her ax.

"Working for your worst enemy, you sellout?" she growled.

The man's eyes gleamed with feverish light. "There's no wrong side when Witches are killing each other."

"How about the wrong side of my boot?" Shane whipped her ax handle up into his chin before kicking his legs out and introducing the Witch Hunter's face to the dusty wedge of her heel. She hoped that crunch was his nose breaking.

"Take them down!" Captain Hane shouted, raising her broadsword high. She caught Shane's arm before she could join the fray. "Not you. You have to go on ahead. Can you break through?"

Shane gaped at her. "You're kidding! There's a horde. I'm not leaving you to—"

"Yes, you are," Hane snapped. "If you don't reach the castle, none of this is going to matter. Stop wasting time."

Another Witch Hunter raced at them. Hane whirled away, smashing the saw-toothed blade out of his hand with her massive broadsword and then driving the pommel right into his temple. The man dropped like a stone. When she looked back, her eyes were serious, just a hint of a smile creasing her face.

"We're all counting on you, Shane. Go."

Shane cursed as Hane plunged into the melee, but the woman was right. With a hiss of frustration, she jammed the ax into its straps on her back. Then she raced for the gully wall. She'd never get through the knot of the battlefield. She'd have to take the high road instead—literally.

The red stone bit into her hands as she began to climb, her arms burning with the effort. Gravel slid out from under her thick heel and almost sent her tumbling into the dirt.

She scaled the last few inches by the grit of her fingernails. From above, the battlefield was a swirl of red cloaks and flashing saw-toothed blades. A couple of Witch Hunters were climbing up after her, determined to be a thorn in her side until the end.

Shane's head pounded as she sprinted along the thin ridge of stone. The cold morning wind whistled in her ears. Every step was a gamble, the thorns bristling like a pit of spikes beneath her. She slid down a sandy incline and ducked an arch of dark thorns curled over the stone path, so low it nearly gave her another haircut.

The Witch Hunters were up on the ridge now, gaining on her. But that wasn't her biggest problem. Ahead, the Stone

Witch's rock pathway stopped, dead-ending in a sheer drop into a churning mass of vines. She could see some of the Paper Witch's little white birds impaled on the black thorns.

Shane eyed the Witch Hunters behind her and the drop into the black forest. The thorns gleamed in the bloody red light—but beyond the brambles, maybe ten feet away, she could see a slice of green grass, the castle achingly close now. She almost imagined she could hear Fi's voice urging her on. Shane clenched her teeth.

She'd come this far.

On the upside, she was about to leave her pursuers behind, because no one else, not even a Witch Hunter, would be foolish enough to try this. Shane sucked in a breath just in case it was her last. Then she launched herself, legs churning, over the chasm filled with thorns.

She almost made it. Arms wheeling, she plunged into the forest at the last row of brambles, shouting as she hit the ground and rolled down the dusty black slope. The thorns tore at her arms and legs like ravenous teeth—but then she was through, hurtling into the grass, the morning dew cold on her skin.

The white castle towered above her. Black specks circled one of the towers—crows, Shane realized with a jolt. She pressed her hand to the pouch tied to her belt, making sure the Lord of the Butterflies' precious hairpin was still in one piece.

Finally, the adrenaline hit her, cracking her face with a wide grin. She'd made it.

Shane pushed herself up and raced for the eastern tower. "Come on, Fi," Shane muttered as she hit the weathered door and jerked the iron handle, praying for a click—"Yes!"

Shane whooped as the heavy door sprang open, and she dashed inside. The hard part was behind her. With Perrin breaking the Wraith's hold on the castle, she was home free—

The guardsman who'd been slumped by the door lurched up all at once, pike flailing. Shane yelped as it smashed into the stone over her head.

Silver eyes glared at Shane from the guardsman's face.

The Wraith.

25

Fi

FI DIDN'T HAVE to guess when the battle began. She'd been up for hours, leaning into the railing of a balcony on the eastern side of the castle and searching for any sign of movement beyond the wall of thorns. Suddenly, the ground under the castle was shaking, a low vibration that hummed in the stone walls and made her teeth ache. Fi nearly tumbled over the railing as two great waves of stone erupted from the thorns, carving a path through the dark forest all the way to the castle lawn.

The Stone Witch, she thought. Perrin had been telling the truth: all of Everlynd was marching with them. They were too far away to see, but it wasn't long before she caught the distant sounds of battle, raised voices and the clash of weapons ringing through the clear morning air. Fi forced herself not to think about what Shane and the rest of her friends were facing. She had her own part to play.

When it was time, Fi turned and raced down the white

stairs into the castle, making for the library. She wasn't the only one moving. A handful of guardsmen had surged up, lurching and staggering down the stairs to reinforce the doors. Right at the center, King Sage's body stood at command, inhabited by the silver-eyed Wraith as he directed his puppets. Shane and the others must be getting close.

The library was just as she'd left it, silent and gleaming. Fi rushed to the closest window, and the red light of the morning rippled through the glass as she threw it open wide. It was only a second before the crow with the milky eyes settled on the sill, ruffling its wings and fixing her with its penetrating stare. Fi stared right back.

"I've solved the code, just as I promised," she announced. "Bring Briar Rose and Aurora's ruby, and I can give you everything you want."

The crow twisted its head as though listening to a distant voice. Then it shook its wings and took off, and as it did, the rest of the birds rose from a nearby roof, sweeping across the window like one sleek black shadow. Fi gripped the stone sill. Her limbs felt shaky and too heavy, and she was breathing hard even though she hadn't run for long.

As the seconds ticked by, Fi felt panic welling up in her gut. Her whole side of the plan hinged on pinpoint timing. Now she feared she'd waited too long, that the Spindle Witch wouldn't arrive in time. One miscalculation could kill them all.

Suddenly, there was a great rush of air outside the open window, and Fi stumbled back as Briar landed in the library, hunching under his bat wings. Fi stared into his dim red eyes and swallowed. She wanted to say something to him, just one more time before she might lose her chance forever—then the double doors banged open, and the Spindle Witch swept into the room, her eyes gleaming through the sheer lace of her veil. Nothing masked her pleased expression, and Fi couldn't help but shudder thinking of everything she had learned about the undead Witch. The chandeliers above them shivered in a cold breath of wind.

"So," the Spindle Witch began, "you've finally solved my riddle."

"I have." Fi was surprised how calm her voice sounded in her own ears.

The Spindle Witch pressed her ruby lips together, pinning Fi with a hard stare. "And I suppose you think that by calling me right now, you'll distract me from that pathetic rabble of an army outside? If you think you've improved their chances, you're sadly mistaken." The veil trembled around her face as she chuckled. "They were doomed the moment they set foot in my forest, and nothing you do here will make any difference."

"Sounds like you've got me all figured out," Fi said coldly.

She had lured the Spindle Witch here with Camellia's code because she knew it was the one thing the woman couldn't resist. Even if she thought it was a trap, even if she thought Fi was plotting. Her obsession with the Siphoning Spells was her greatest weakness.

The Spindle Witch's eyes narrowed. Her fingers twitched as though stroking invisible threads. "Well?" she demanded. "Where are they?"

"They're right here," Fi said, stepping back and waving her hands. "Hidden in the library."

The Spindle Witch clicked her tongue, disappointed. "Don't

lie to me, girl," she warned icily. Golden threads slithered between her fingers, shimmering in the new morning light. "You think I haven't looked here? I have searched every shelf, every book, every withered page abandoned here to rot. I came to Andar—became one of the four Great Witches so many years ago—all so I could gain access to this library. The library of the Rose Witches. It was the first place I looked for Aurora's secrets. But there is nothing here!" Her anger uncoiled like a snake, her voice hissing out the last words.

Fi backed away, not eager to wind up with those threads around her neck again. "It's concealed by magic," she said in a rush. "Camellia's code—it's like a set of instructions. *In the forest of spines* means—"

"Yes, the library," the Spindle Witch filled in with a dismissive wave. "Faster, dear."

Fi swallowed around the lump in her throat. *Faster* wasn't really part of the plan. On the other hand, her explanations always took forever—at least according to Shane. She could almost hear the huntsman's voice in her ear: *Boring, boring—can't I get, like, an abbreviated version of this? You're trying to put me to sleep so you can keep all the treasure for yourself, aren't you?*

The thought of her impatient partner bolstered Fi's confidence. She met the Spindle Witch's stare directly, refusing to flinch at the malice in those dark eyes. "The next line—*Where the thorns gather . . .*" She lifted a finger, pointing up. "See the carving on the ceiling? There's only one place with thorns but no roses."

The pattern had been easy enough to spot that first day; the meaning had taken a little longer. Over the last six days, Fi had spent hours lying on the floor staring at it.

"It's hidden in the ceiling?" the Spindle Witch asked incredulously.

Fi shook her head. "No, that's just the next clue. It's pointing to that chandelier, the one in the middle of the room." Right in the center of the barren vines—a great branching chandelier with gleaming gold arms and scrolls and pure-white candles surrounded by glass prisms. It hung suspended from a heavy chain that wrapped around a brace high on the wall. "We have to bring it down."

"Be glad I am amused by this little production," the Spindle Witch said. She flicked her fingers in a wave, and Briar got to his feet. His wings snapped as he shook them out, sending a breeze through the library and making the pages of the books whisper. The Spindle Witch looked down at Fi as Briar took off. "For someone who can only be guessing at what's hidden up there, you seem awfully confident you've solved this code."

"I'm sure," Fi said, trying not to let her voice waver. In the end, no matter how educated a guess, it was a theory until it was proven.

It was the rainbows from the chandelier that finally helped Fi put the puzzle of the library together. That was the piece that didn't fit. She had already guessed that the Spindle Witch had searched the library, and in a century, she would have found even the most well-hidden alcoves, false walls, and passages. That meant they weren't just looking for a secret cache where the Siphoning Spells were hidden. By piecing together the riddle, they were actually going to reveal the spells themselves—*reveal the hidden butterfly*.

A shriek of metal made Fi jump. Briar's long claws whipped out, severing the chandelier's chain and sending the ornate contraption of metal and glass crashing down. Fi threw herself backward as it clanged against the floor, smashing some of the dangling ornaments of glass that clinked and shattered like a thousand pieces of fine china breaking. Little bits of clear glass skittered across the floor, reminding Fi of her last dream of Briar and the sea of glass under their feet as they danced. Her eyes sought out Briar as the boy dropped to the floor with dizzying speed, his wings folding as he landed.

The Spindle Witch extended a hand. "You have your chandelier. What are you waiting for?"

Fi stepped forward, a little shaky. Broken glass tinkled under her boots. If the Spindle Witch had shattered the chandelier to intimidate her, it had worked.

The metal column at the center was as tall as her waist, large enough that Fi didn't even have to bend over to examine it. The chandelier was built of three concentric circles, each crafted from whorls of metal and delicate chains that rang with glittering glass. Fi reached through the curving gold bars. There was a setting at the top of the column, completely invisible from below, that looked almost like a stand, three little strips of iron forming a raised bracket. From this close, she could see the iron pieces had been engraved and hammered into the shape of leaves. The cup between them was the perfect size for the ruby rose.

In the tomb, the absence of roses had been a clue that Aurora was not in that coffin. In the library, the empty thorns indicated exactly where a certain ruby should be placed. Nothing was ever an accident, and Fi couldn't help but admire the intricacy of the puzzle Aurora had left behind.

The harsh splintering of glass under the Spindle Witch's boots brought Fi back to herself.

"I was right," Fi said, ducking out of the shimmering golden arms. "The rose goes right here." She held out her hand for the ruby.

The Spindle Witch studied Fi's palm. "I think I'll handle this part myself."

Fi bit her lip but backed obediently away. The Spindle Witch's skirts dragged across the floor, her eyes fixed on the chandelier as she reached a hand into her sleeve and pulled out the ruby. The petals seemed to shimmer with an inner light, and Fi realized with a little jump of her heart that Briar's head had jerked up, his eyes more alive than she'd seen them in weeks as his gaze followed Aurora's rose.

The Spindle Witch didn't seem to notice, all her focus turned to the prize she had been pursuing for centuries. Fi recognized the glint in her eyes now—not greed, but hunger. She was an undead creature, brought back by her own magic, who would devour the world to appease her rampant hunger.

"The shine of Andar's most precious rose . . ." the Spindle Witch murmured, holding the ruby carefully in both hands.

"Reveals the hidden butterfly," Fi finished the riddle. "And then you'll have what you've been looking for—the Siphoning Spells created by the Lord of the Butterflies and stolen from you by Aurora all those years ago."

The Spindle Witch paused, shooting Fi a sharp look. Fi's palms were slick with sweat, and she wondered if she'd pushed it too far, but then the Spindle Witch's expression melted into a smile.

"Clever," she crooned. "I don't know where you learned that, but I can guess—another fragment of my old mentor skulking around inside his little glass prisons? He's far too late to stop me."

Fi threw a glance toward the window to the balcony. She'd leaned the little diamond of glass against the broken frame. It seemed empty, but she wondered if the Lord of the Butterflies was lurking there, watching.

The Spindle Witch dropped the ruby into the setting. It slid perfectly into place, the inner glow of the gem growing brighter as it caught the smoldering red light of sunrise. The Spindle Witch watched expectantly, while Fi held her breath.

Nothing happened.

The Spindle Witch stood frozen, waiting, for longer than Fi had thought she would, but when she moved, it was all at once—too fast for Fi to react. Golden threads whipped through the air, seizing her and dragging her forward. This wasn't the Spindle Witch's usual attack—pinpoint threads that slithered around her neck and arms. This was an act of pure rage. The threads were all around Fi, snagging around her waist, wrenching one arm tight against her side and forcing her down. Her knees hit the floor with a crack.

"I am tired of your games!" The Witch spun a long thread around one finger, the end gleaming and sharp like a knife.

"It's not a game," Fi said, looking up from her place at the woman's feet. "There's just one more piece. The rose isn't shining yet."

"Oh?" The Spindle Witch looked at the ruby. The feverish hunger was back in her eyes, the desperation to get her hands on the magic of the Lord of the Butterflies. Her features seemed older beneath the rippling black veil, her eyes narrowed to slits and her lips twisted in a sneer. Her threads loosened, and Fi crumpled to the floor.

"The key is Briar Rose," she said, pushing herself up and rubbing at the deep red lines the threads had cut into her skin. "We need him."

"The boy prince?" the Spindle Witch repeated. She raised a hand to tug the bone creature closer.

"It's in the code," Fi said, trying not to look at Briar as he was dragged mercilessly through the broken glass. "The *shine* of Andar's precious rose. Aurora had light magic, and Briar does, too. The ruby crown might have been precious to all of Andar, but this riddle was written by Camellia, and no rose was more precious to her than her brother. Briar has to make it shine with light magic. It can't be completed without him."

This was it, the last piece. If the Spindle Witch allowed Briar to use his light magic, they truly were about to *reveal the hidden butterfly*. And then the clock would be ticking. Fi's plan meant walking a knife's edge between giving the Spindle Witch everything she wanted and stopping her once and for all. She'd tried the same thing once before and failed.

This time she was not counting on Armand Bellicia, though, or the remnants of a dark curse. She had the whole story—all the information, all the history. And knowledge was always more powerful than magic.

Most importantly, she had Shane at her back, even if her partner was currently cutting it way too close.

Fi had stalled as long as she could. There was about to be magic in the library—*real magic.*

26

<del>→→→</del> <del>←←←</del>

Red

RED RACED THROUGH the Forest of Thorns, kicking up clouds of black dust under her pounding boots. Cinzel ranged ahead of her, while Perrin followed close behind, his footsteps a comforting presence at her back. The twisted branches closed in around them at every turn, razor thorns dangling over their heads like vicious snares. It only got darker the deeper they went.

When they had first plunged into the forest, Red was almost flying, exhilarated by the kiss with Shane and all it promised. Her lips had been tingling, her stomach churning with butterflies, and her heart overflowing with that sweet, infectious hope Shane always gave her. But the Forest of Thorns had sucked that heady feeling away. Maybe it was the way the sinister thorns jutted out at every turn, or maybe it was the feeling of being caged inside a crisscross of dark boughs that reminded her so much of the Wraith's nightmare. Maybe it was just that Red knew what was waiting for her.

She twisted her head around, searching for the calcified white oak tree that would be her next signpost. She had grown up here—she knew every dark corner of it. But somehow it was like a different forest. She and Perrin passed through hollows and archways that she remembered perfectly, only to find themselves facing impenetrable walls of brambles. Again and again, they were forced to turn back and find another route. The Forest of Thorns didn't *grow* exactly, but it did shift, some areas becoming denser while others tore themselves to pieces. Red had never realized until this moment how much she counted on Shadow and the monster wolves to cut paths directly through the thorns.

She shoved thoughts of the white wolf away. *Not yet.*

She still had Cinzel's help. He hurried on ahead, sometimes wriggling under a wall of thorns that Red and Perrin could never hope to pass. But he always returned soon after, his soft belly fur dark with ashen dust, to lead them through another passage. Red hated those moments of silence waiting for him to come back. She didn't want to be separated from Cinzel—not here.

Red motioned for Perrin to slow down as they came to a dense cluster of thorns. A dark passage led into it, almost like a tunnel. Cinzel had stopped at the entrance, pawing at the ground and whining.

"Are we lost?" Perrin asked, rubbing his sleeve over his face. "Do we need to double back?" He looked a little worse for wear, his clothing ripped and sweat running down his neck. One spike had caught him at the shoulder and sliced a jagged hole in his blue jacket, the torn fabric stained crimson.

Red wasn't doing much better. Forging a path had left

angry welts over the backs of her hands and up her arms. She had a deep cut in her leg, bleeding sluggishly, where a thorn had seemed to leap out of nowhere, gouging her. She got the distinct impression she was no longer welcome in this place.

"We're not lost," Red said. "In fact, we're close. This passageway will take us almost all the way to Briar Rose's tower."

Red knew that because Shane and Briar Rose and Fi had once escaped her using this very passage. She shivered recalling the battle between the dark twisting thorns. They felt like someone else's memories or a horrible dream that she'd finally woken from. But it wasn't a dream. It had been Red's whistles commanding the wolves, Red's bargain with the Spindle Witch binding Shadow to a cursed half life. She couldn't run from that.

If Shadow and the other wolves truly belonged to the Spindle Witch, then Red wouldn't be able to command them anymore. But if, as she had begun to suspect, it was her own magic that had bent the creatures to her will, they would still do as she said.

"Red, you okay?"

Red blinked. Perrin was looking at her strangely, and Cinzel was circling her, nudging her hip. Red cleared her throat.

"Just trying to remember the way," she muttered, ducking into the tunnel. Perrin didn't look like he believed her, but he followed anyway, forced to bend over to keep from raking his head across the low ceiling. Cinzel wound through her legs, nearly tripping her. With every twist and turn, the light got dimmer until it was almost a complete blackout, only a few bright pinpricks speckling the ground.

Red didn't stop. She didn't want to give herself any more time to think about Shadow—or what she might have to do.

She navigated one step at a time, covering her hand with her sleeve and waving her arm through the blackness to make sure she wasn't about to run herself into the razor thorns. She felt Perrin's hand on her shoulder. Cinzel was somewhere ahead, his low call leading her on. Then she turned one last corner, and the glowing exit was right ahead of her. Cinzel darted out into the sunlight, shaking himself off. Red hurried gratefully after him. Perrin sighed and released her shoulder.

"A little too cozy for me," he admitted, rubbing his sore neck. But his face wore that familiar grin, and Red couldn't help smiling back. She could do this. She could get Perrin to the castle—

A howl broke through the dense thorns, long and mournful and achingly familiar.

Shadow.

Red froze. Cinzel's ears perked up. He padded to the edge of the clearing, tail softly wagging.

"That doesn't sound good," Perrin said, catching Red's arm. "We should get out of here."

Red couldn't speak. Her eyes were locked on the forest, waiting for the answering howls from the rest of the pack. It took a beat before the first one started, joined by another and then another, the eerie strains of all their voices echoing. The full pack was still a ways away, but Red knew they would be barreling through the thorns, heading right for her.

Shadow's howl had been closer. She could hear him now,

the crunch of jaws snapping, the branches breaking with a sound like splintering bone. He was just beyond them in the trees, his yellow eyes gleaming with fury.

Red clutched her heart, forcing herself to stand her ground. *The only way to live with it is to make it right.* Shadow deserved that, no matter what it cost her.

"We've got to move!" Perrin warned, tugging at her.

Red shook him off. "There." She pointed to the space between two twisted masses of vines. "The castle's that way, and not far—don't stray in the wrong direction and I'm sure you'll make it."

"I'm sure I'll make it, too," Perrin agreed. "Because you'll be right there guiding me."

The branches trembled as the white wolf drew near, pounding through the dust. He was too close to outrun now—and Red had to know. She had to know if she had bent the wolf to her will, if she had truly been one of the Spindle Witch's monsters.

"Just go!" she said, shoving Perrin and making him stumble back. "Everyone's counting on you. There's something I have to do. Please!"

Perrin took a few hesitant steps toward the opening, clearly torn, before cursing and ducking inside. Then Shadow exploded through the undergrowth, thorns and bits of vine flying in all directions. His long claws raked through the dust as he skidded around to face Red.

He was just as she'd remembered him: as tall as she was, rippling with fury, the sickening twist of his spine rising from his coarse white fur. Cinzel yipped happily at the sight of his brother. Then whined, dropping to his belly as the great white wolf growled, his lips curled back around yellow fangs.

"I know," Red said softly, when Cinzel looked at her in confusion. "Leave him to me."

Perrin was on his way. Soon, he'd be scaling the roses on the castle wall and breaking the sleeping curse inside. That would make this a victory no matter what happened to Red.

Shadow stalked across the clearing, and Cinzel slunk back before him, his tail tucked under his legs. Red held her ground. She brought her fingers up to her lips, sucking in a breath. She let out an earsplitting whistle, commanding the creature as she had for so many years.

Shadow kept advancing. Red's stomach lurched, but she raised her head defiantly, calling on every ounce of her magic— the magic of the Snake Witch. "Stop," she ordered the beast.

Shadow lunged, his enormous jaws aimed at her neck.

Red's eyes widened in shock. She had been sure—so sure that she could control the beasts, but Shadow hadn't listened. She had no power over him.

All she felt was relief. If she didn't have the power now, she never had. Shadow and the others had obeyed the magic of the Spindle Witch, of the thorn rod. Red was just another pawn—just a girl, and not a monster. She squeezed her eyes shut, silently apologizing to Shane for dying so foolishly just when things were getting good.

"Red!"

Her eyes sprang open just in time to see Perrin leap in front of her. He had grabbed one of the splintered branches from the ground, wielding it like a club, and he smashed it against the great wolf's head. The branch shattered against Shadow's heavy skull, throwing him back. Perrin's hands were bloody from gripping the branch. He tossed the broken club away, seizing Red's wrist and racing for the gap in the thorns.

"Perrin—" Red gasped.

"Friends don't abandon each other. Not to mention, our club can't really afford to lose any members." He pushed her ahead of him as he spoke, urging her to take the lead.

Shadow was getting up already, shaking his head. Cinzel growled at his brother, baring his teeth and then loping away.

Red didn't stop to look back. She seized Perrin's hand and dragged him into the thicket, banking down a spiraling side passage so narrow it seemed like the thorns would rip them apart.

Shadow crashed into the thorns behind them. Red ran as fast as she could. She slipped out under a bristling archway with Perrin and Cinzel right behind her, and suddenly she knew exactly where they were.

The gray husk of the carriage house loomed to her right. The giant pillars of twisting vines were getting thinner, the river whispering through the trees. She could see the white stone tower through the cage of the black forest. They were so close!

Shadow surged out of the brambles in front of her, and Red screamed. The white wolf bunched his muscles, ready to spring. But it was Cinzel who leapt first, his mottled fur bristling as he sank his teeth into Shadow's neck. The white wolf snarled, knocking the smaller wolf away with one enormous paw. Cinzel skidded into the dirt.

"Cinzel!" Red shouted desperately as Perrin dragged her toward the castle.

Cinzel scrambled up as Shadow's long teeth closed over the space his brother had just been. The smaller wolf raced after them. Shadow sat back on his haunches, a bloodless gouge matting his fur. He let out one long howl that made Red's blood run cold.

Red was side by side with Perrin now, trying to keep up with the boy's longer strides as they raced for the tower. The spill of roses down the white stones shone like rubies in the morning light. Red's heart leapt as they splashed through a shallow eddy of the river. The warm water seemed to surge up to embrace her, washing away the sting of the thorns.

Then three howls rose one after the other. Shadow's pack was right on top of them. Red darted a look at Cinzel. He was keeping pace, but she could see he was limping hard, favoring his back leg. She and Perrin could scramble up the roses, but it would mean leaving a defenseless Cinzel at the mercy of the pack.

Never.

She skidded to a stop, turning to face the forest.

"You have to go, Perrin," she said, as the monster wolves broke through the thorns. In a minute, they'd be surrounded.

"Red!" Perrin protested.

She grabbed his arm, pulling him down so they were face-to-face. "Friends don't abandon each other, remember? Cinzel and Shadow need me. And all of Andar needs you." She dredged up a smile. "Good luck, Dream Witch." Then she shoved him away.

"You too, Red," he said quietly.

Red didn't turn around to watch him climb. She didn't want him to see the tears in her eyes.

In truth, Red had never really had any friends before. But she liked Perrin, with his kind smile and easy, contagious laugh, and she liked the Paper Witch, with his seemingly endless patience. She even liked Fi, though she'd only known the girl a short while. And she loved Shane, more than she had ever thought possible. She had never had anything to miss before, but now she was going to miss it all so much.

The dark knot of fear and guilt inside her was slowly unraveling. Shadow hadn't sacrificed himself to save Red because she had forced him to with her magic. He had done it for the same reason Red was standing here now. To protect someone she loved.

The first of the wolves bounded forward, leaping the river and coming straight at her. Dark claws sliced the air as Red threw herself aside. She snatched a rock and pelted it into the monster's flank. A second later, Cinzel was biting at the wolf, tearing into its hind leg before backing away to stand in front of her.

Shadow had loped out of the trees behind his pack mates, but he kept his distance, trying futilely to lick at his wound. Red found his gold eyes, begging him to understand how much she'd loved him, how grateful and how sorry she was for everything that had happened.

Two monster wolves reached Red at the same time. Cinzel snarled, jumping at one, ripping hard at its shoulder joint before being tossed aside. He let out a pained yip as he hit the ground. Red ducked forward just as the other wolf snapped its jaws at her. She rolled under his massive ruff and surged to her feet, ready to run.

A shaggy body gnarled with bones blocked her path. Red

tried to skid to a stop, feet slipping in the wet sand as the wolf bit down. The massive jaws closed over her shoulder. She could feel the razor teeth stabbing her like a dozen knives, one sliding into her chest like a hot poker.

Red screamed in agony. It felt like she was being ripped apart from the inside out. She fell to her knees, held tight in the wolf's unforgiving jaws. Cinzel was howling madly somewhere, whining and crying. Red wanted to reassure him, tell him that everything would be okay. He could run away now—the wolves would let him go now that they had Red. But all she could do was scream.

The monster would crunch through her, bones and all, just like it gnashed through the Forest of Thorns. Red blinked through hot tears, the edges of her vision going black. Then suddenly the pressure on her shoulder was ripped away as the wolf was thrown backward, its body slamming into the tower.

Red looked up in surprise. Shadow stood protectively above her, his bristling fur soft where he had loped through the water. The white wolf had turned on his brethren and was fighting off the other monstrous creatures. Fighting to protect Red.

Blood poured down Red's shoulder. She sagged to the ground, reaching for that massive white paw.

"Shadow," she breathed. The wolf's ragged ears flicked back, and he turned his head. For one moment, the yellow eyes softened, and Red was ten years old again, holding her hand out to a hungry, mewling pup whose mother was gone. "Thank you, Shadow," she whispered. Then he leapt back into the fray.

Red blinked. The world was fuzzy at the edges, the sounds of the fight muffled. She could feel the blood sliding down her arm from the gouges in her shoulder, trickling into the river. She closed her eyes and sank into a memory, one of the few good ones she had from the Forest of Thorns—splashing in that warm water with Cinzel, the sunlight glistening on his fur, and the white wolf watching them contentedly from the shore. The water of the river was always warm and clear, a bright spot in the dark forest.

Now she knew what that river truly was. It was her ancestor, Assora, the Snake Witch—the remains of her body and the last of her will. That great magic had been surrounding Red all that time, keeping her warm. And if it was true that the Snake Witch loved beasts and monsters, then maybe she would have loved Shadow, too. Maybe she could even love Red.

Red dragged herself backward with her good hand until she could lean against the tower, among the roses. She didn't want to die in the forest. Cinzel limped to her side, the fur of his flank matted from a deep gash. He lay down next to Red, tucking his nose under her hand, and Red dragged her fingers through the wolf's rough coat. Shadow gave a long howl, biting and snarling as he fought off the other three wolves.

Red leaned back, looking up through the roses at the blue sky, and she smiled. High above, Perrin had reached the top. His blue jacket fluttered in the wind as he spread his arms wide, getting ready to unleash his dream magic.

She hadn't failed after all.

27

※※»»— «««※

Shane

DREAD POOLED IN the pit of Shane's stomach. Something was wrong—very wrong. The people of the castle were supposed to be awake by now and out of the Wraith's reach. Instead, she found herself fighting off a hoard of dull-eyed soldiers, their bodies controlled by a silver-eyed puppet master.

Something had happened to Perrin . . . and Red.

Shane ducked a vicious pike swing, diving out of the way as the vase behind her exploded in a shower of broken glass. The shards pelted her arms like a dozen tiny bee stings. The guardsman swayed over her. He didn't even flinch when Shane surged up and smashed her shoulder into his ribs. She darted around him and kept running, cursing as she felt the unmistakable breeze of his spearpoint whizzing past her neck.

There was no point in stopping to fight. She could only hurt the people of the castle, and no matter how many of them she tossed aside, there were two more waiting right around the corner. Worse, the Wraith could suddenly be inside any one of them. Something Shane had learned the hard way.

The dull-eyed puppets' movements were jerky and sloppy—not a challenge at all, except for their sheer number. The guard waiting just inside the door of the castle had swung his sword so wide Shane probably could have run under it instead of blocking. Then the guard's eyes sprang open, suddenly pure silver. When he'd moved again, he'd been twice as fast, his blade nearly skewering Shane through the ribs. She'd wasted precious time fighting the Wraith in that body, finally managing to fling his blade away with the hook of her ax and lock him in the gate room before she sprinted on.

The Wraith appeared twice more. Once in a knot of guards in the entry hall beneath the blue pennants. And once in the body of a lady in a fine muslin gown who leapt over the railing of the stairs with a dagger clutched in her hands. Shane hoped she hadn't broken the woman's wrist as they tumbled, but broken bones healed.

Now four puppets in the blue guards' livery had her pinned down, and Shane was quickly running out of options for breaking through without leaving someone dead. She was stuck in a long corridor with picture windows on one side and a dizzying three-story fall into the entry hall on the other. Shane threw a glance at the dark stairway to the upper floors. She was so close—

A woman with a long, thin sword lunged at her. Shane barely managed to block the blade and redirect it into the wall.

"I'm trying to save you people!" she shouted, breath ragged.

What were Red and Perrin doing? That awful feeling

seized Shane again, squeezing her throat, and she almost took a pike through the shoulder as her gaze shot to the window and the Forest of Thorns beyond.

She couldn't think about them right now. Red was going to make it—they were all going to make it. And when the people of Andar retold this story to generations of wide-eyed little Witches, this would be the moment they gasped in horror before it all turned around.

A great crash echoed through the castle, like something heavy hitting the floor far above her. Shane swore. She had to get to Fi!

In a second, they'd surrounded her. The man with the pike swayed ominously. The swordswoman lurched toward Shane, dragging the tip of her blade across the stones. At Shane's back towered a bearded man with a double-headed battle-ax, and beyond him, a reedy man with a sharp face, his heavy mace bristling with wicked spikes.

Shane flipped the ax in her hands. They were out of time. She'd have to break through by force—even if it meant busting a few legs. She was about to launch herself at the swordswoman when all four figures went still.

Footfalls rang out through the suddenly silent hallway. The guards in front of Shane moved dutifully aside to reveal a man in a rich tunic, a velvet cape in royal blue rippling at his back. A crown of beaten gold gleamed in his blond hair.

Even if Shane had never met Briar Rose, she would have recognized the king of Andar. That said, his resemblance to his brother was uncanny—even with his eyes glowing that insidious silver. He sauntered down the corridor, hands clasped behind his back.

"We have unfinished business, Wraith," Shane spat at the body thief. She hadn't forgotten the way he'd toyed with Red, or her promise to hunt him down.

"So we do." King Sage's lips pulled into a bloodless smile. "I was looking forward to killing Red in front of you, but I guess you'll just have to go first."

He was on her between one breath and the next. The Wraith wrenched the shining sword out from behind his back and drove it straight at her heart. Shane leapt backward, feeling the tip of the blade scrape the button over her breast. Too close for comfort.

The silver-eyed Witch lowered his sword, fixing her with a look full of glee. Shane realized why when the bearded guardsman reared above her, swinging at her unprotected back with enough force to split her in half. Shane barely got her ax up in time to block. The shuddering blow threw her sideways into the window.

So it wasn't going to be one-on-one, after all.

Ears ringing, Shane pushed herself up, pressing her back to the cold glass so they couldn't flank her.

"Face me yourself, coward," she spat.

The Wraith shrugged. "I embrace a broad definition of the term." He jerked his head.

Three of the puppets came at once. Shane ducked the whistling pike, catching the giant battle-ax against the pol of her own weapon. The swordswoman darted forward, stabbing at Shane in the gaps between their bodies. Shane tried to twist away, but she couldn't get far enough. The blade slid deep into her thigh, leaving a line of fire in its wake.

She wasn't going to last long like this. Knees shaking,

Shane drove her nails into her ax handle, using all her strength to throw off the man bearing down on her with the battle-ax.

She swore, looking at the gash in her thigh. At least it had missed the artery. She wasn't going to bleed out—not before the puppets killed her, anyway.

At least the reedy man with the spiked mace was hanging back. Maybe the Wraith couldn't control the weapon with enough precision inside a puppet to keep from hurting his other playthings. Shane would just count herself lucky it wasn't four-on-one.

She couldn't afford to hold back anymore. With a silent apology, she swung out, driving the blunt back of the ax right into the pike wielder's stomach and breaking at least a couple of ribs. His body slithered down the wall.

The swordswoman was right behind him. Shane flipped the ax handle up into the woman's chin. Her head snapped back with a crack. Praying she hadn't knocked out any teeth, Shane hooked her boot around the woman's ankle and put her on the floor, kicking the sword out of her hand. It clanged against the railing and plummeted to the entryway below.

Two down—or disarmed, anyway. Shane dodged another ax swing and rounded on the Wraith hiding in Sage's body instead. There was no point in fighting the puppets when the puppet master was right here.

Ax flashing, Shane threw herself at the king. The blade was inches from his neck when she realized Sage's face had grown dull and vacant, his eyes no longer silver. The Wraith was gone. It was only Briar's brother she was about to kill.

Shane's guts lurched. With no other choice, she let go of the ax, heaving the weapon wildly over Sage's shoulder. The blade passed close enough to slice a line of blood along the king's jaw. Too late to backpedal, Shane slammed into the unresisting body, toppling with Sage onto the floor.

The gash in her leg throbbed. Shane pushed herself up on her hands, panting. Her ax was ten feet away, and she was winded, her breath sharp and tight in her chest. But at least she hadn't decapitated Fi's future king-in-law. She'd apologize for the close shave later. She scrambled up and yanked the dagger out of her boot, stabbing it through Sage's cloak into the banister.

"Stay down," she warned.

Sage's body jerked against his pinned cloak, but he didn't seem coordinated enough to get free. That would have to be good enough. Shane had other things to worry about. If the Wraith wasn't inside the king . . .

Shane ducked without even waiting to see where the body thief had jumped to. The spiked ball of the mace whistled over her head, smashing into the wall with enough force to chip the stone.

"So close," the Wraith said. He rolled the shoulders of the reedy body, looking totally at home in the man's skin.

Shane threw herself forward, tackling him at his knees and knocking them both to the ground. The mace thudded against the stone as Shane wrestled with the Wraith, pressing her forearm into his windpipe and crushing out his air. His silver eyes bulged. Then Shane was grabbed under the arms and hauled backward by the swordswoman.

The Wraith got to his feet, retrieving the mace. Shane hurled her body from side to side, but the woman held her tight, one leg locked over Shane's to keep her pinned on the floor. She threw a desperate look at her ax. The wound in her thigh was a steady ache, her pant leg soaked with so much blood she could feel it dripping down into her boot.

The bearded guard cranked his ax back, ready to slice all the way through Shane into the woman behind her, by the looks of it. Shane struggled wildly. And then suddenly the wrenching force on her arms was gone, and Shane kicked out of the woman's hold, throwing up her hands to catch the ax . . . that never came.

Shane jerked her head up. The guardsman had sagged, the battle-ax falling from his slack hands. All around her, she heard painful coughs and gasps as the people came awake. From the corner of her eye, she saw the man with the pike desperately scrabbling to yank the golden threads from his neck.

Relief almost knocked her over. The sleeping curse was broken. Perrin and Red had done it!

All the figures had dropped to their knees, gasping and choking as they were released from the spell. All but one.

Shane stared with disbelief at the silver-eyed man holding the mace. "That's your real body," she hissed.

"How very annoying of you to notice that." A look of cold fury spread across the Witch's face. "Someone's gone and ruined my fun. But I can still finish you."

Shane's fingers longed for her ax. Her head was going fuzzy from the blood loss, her aches and pains from the fight against the bone creatures catching up with her. She staggered up and planted her injured leg.

It would hold—she would make it hold. Shane was forged

in Steelwight, and the War Kings of Rockrimmon did not falter.

The Wraith spun the mace expertly in his hands, the spiked ball spinning faster and faster as he advanced. Then he struck out, and Shane surged up under his arms, catching the mace handle on her crossed wrists and twisting. The Wraith shrieked in pain as the spikes dug into his forearm. From an inch away, she stared at those silver eyes, narrowed for the first time with fear. Then she lurched forward and slammed her shoulder into his breastbone, hurling him backward toward the railing.

He never made it. His body jerked strangely, a choked gasp escaping his throat as a sword point erupted through the center of his chest. The shining sword of the king of Andar. Sage had struggled to his knees, one hand raised as he stabbed the body thief who had been using his people. The Wraith's eyes went dull, and he collapsed in a heap.

Shane offered the king a grim smile. "Thanks for the assist, Your Highness . . . er, Kingship."

Sage's arm shook as he dropped the sword, ripping the last of the golden threads from around his neck. "I've been waiting a long time to do that," he said, his voice gravelly from disuse. And then, with a smile: "And anyone who saves my life can call me Sage."

"Works for me." Shane bent down to snag her ax and fought off a wave of dizziness, bracing herself against the wall. She wasn't going down. Not until this was over.

She shoved her ax into its straps and glanced back at the king getting slowly to his feet. "I have to go. But they could use you out there." She jerked her chin toward the courtyard and the Forest of Thorns beyond. Then she pushed down all her aches and started running.

Shane had somewhere else to be. She fumbled with the pouch at her waist and the precious butterfly pin inside, and then sprinted toward the library like her partner's life depended on it—because it did.

28

Fi

"THIS ISN'T WORKING. And my patience is growing *very* thin," the Spindle Witch hissed.

Fi felt like she might pass out. Her blood was pounding in her head, and every second felt like an eternity as Briar Rose stood with his clawed hand extended over Aurora's ruby, red sparks of magic crackling at his fingertips. The sparks left an acrid smell in the air. But no matter how much magic Briar forced into the rose, it refused to shine—in fact, it seemed to be growing dimmer, the carved petals looking lifeless now through the cage of the chandelier.

The Spindle Witch howled. She yanked hard at something Fi couldn't see, but she knew what it was now—the golden thread looped around Briar's heart. The one she had tied there when he was just a baby. Briar's sunken face twisted in agony, his black wings flailing as he collapsed to the floor.

Fi cringed as one wing smashed against a shelf and knocked a whole row of books into a heap.

Come on, Fi begged, willing Shane to arrive. Briar was being eaten away by the Spindle Witch's desperation to get what she wanted. Fi couldn't take this much longer.

"Enough!" the Spindle Witch shouted, tossing the boy aside. "I see his life is no longer of value to you."

"No, wait!" Fi threw out her hand. "Lose him, and you lose your only chance to get the Siphoning Spells."

"You're just trying to save your little prince," the Witch snapped.

"Just think about it," Fi begged. "What you're forcing out of him, it's not real light magic. It's poisoned by you—by all of your dark magic twisting him." She shook her head. "That creature can't help you. Only Briar Rose can."

She held her breath as the Spindle Witch looked between them, still holding tightly to the invisible thread. Her hand jerked, and Fi felt it like a blow, squeezing her eyes shut against a scream of pain that never came. Then she realized the Spindle Witch was turning her fingers the other direction, like she was winding something back. As she did, the color returned to Briar's face. The sharp ridges of his cheekbones softened under his pale skin, and a hint of sparkling blue shone in his eyes.

Briar still had his great black wings and the bone claws and horns, but he looked like himself again, just enough to give Fi hope. Briar's light magic wasn't gone—the Spindle Witch had just proved it could be restored, and that meant she had a sliver of a chance to get him back.

This time, when Briar raised his hand, pure-white light

sprang to the tips of his claws. That familiar magic made Fi's chest ache with longing. Briar's hand hovered over the ruby, the little sparks swirling around it. The rose drank them in like drops of water.

"More!" the Spindle Witch ordered. Briar concentrated all of that overwhelmingly bright light into the end of one claw, just like Aurora had done in the tomb, and pressed it against the ruby.

The gem began pulsing, glowing brighter and brighter. Fi caught her breath. Maybe it was an illusion, but she could have sworn the petals were actually opening, the rose unfurling right there in the chandelier bracket. Briar's light kept pouring into it, glistening on the folding petals like sparkling dewdrops.

Suddenly, the rose ignited, bursting to life and blazing beneath Briar's hands. Red light flooded the library, outshining the sunlight. Every window was aglow, light clinging to the whorls and patterns in the beautiful wooden shelves. The carved roses stood out in brilliant scarlet. The rest of the chandeliers caught the light, too, throwing it across the room like a thousand dancing petals. Fi watched in awe. This was the magic Aurora had hidden in her library—her secret butterfly.

Everywhere the red light touched, the room was suddenly full of golden writing in Aurora's elegant hand—down the pillars, across the floor, even scrawled along the polished shelves: hundreds of pages of the greatest secrets of magic, painted with light magic and visible only in the red glow of the rose. The Siphoning Spells weren't hidden *in* the library. They were built right into its foundation—the only way Aurora could be certain to keep them safe.

Fi spun in a circle, amazed by the ingenuity and the beauty of it. She could see sketches of channels beneath the feet of mountains, trees dissected by glowing rings. There were spells about severing magic and stitching it together. The Siphoning Spells were so much more than just the destructive magic the Spindle Witch would use them for. Fi wanted to read every single one.

Her eyes caught on the glass door to the balcony, where the Lord of the Butterflies had appeared. She remembered his grim face in the mirror, the sadness in his eyes as he spoke. Some magic was never meant to be.

The Spindle Witch laughed, a wild, feverish sound that made Fi's hair stand on end. She ripped off her black veil, and the blond hair that had been coiled around her head spilled down her back, the long braid trailing into her dark, lacy skirts. She was as young as Fi had ever seen her, her ghostly white skin almost pearlescent in the red light.

"Finally," the Witch whispered, running her fingers reverently down a line of glowing words. "I have waited so long."

Fi watched her closely. The Spindle Witch had eyes only for the spells splashed across the walls, but that wouldn't last. Fi had truly become expendable now, and so had Briar. If Shane didn't get here soon, Fi would have to grab the ruby from the stand and break it.

She inched toward the fallen chandelier. She was still a few feet away when a piece of glass glanced off her boot and skidded across the floor. The Spindle Witch rounded on her.

"What are you doing?" she demanded.

Fi stared back, frozen. The Spindle Witch could destroy her in a second. But she could destroy everything with these spells. Fi had promised Shane she was on the right side this time, and that was a promise she intended to keep.

Without thinking anymore, Fi surged forward, making a grab for the rose. Briar was on her in a second. His leathery bat wings encircled her like a cage, but Fi threw herself under his arm. She felt the wind of those bone claws over her head as she slid through the broken glass, straight for the chandelier. Pain rippled through her as the glass tore into her hip and shoulder. She hit the gold frame with a crash, and she scrambled to her feet, her fingers closing over the ruby. With one fierce yank, she tore it out of the bracket. The gem still shone like a beacon, but the golden words began melting from the walls.

"No!" the Spindle Witch shrieked. "You won't take it from me. I will not be denied again!"

Fi wrenched her arm back, ready to smash the ruby against the floor. She didn't get a chance before her wrist was seized in the Witch's crushing grip. Fi struggled uselessly. Her heart plunged into her stomach as she looked up, right into the unforgiving eyes of the Spindle Witch. Fi was about to die.

It can't end like this, she thought desperately.

"Fi!"

Shane's voice echoed through the library like thunder splitting the clouds. An ax flew through the air, spinning end over end toward the Spindle Witch. The Witch threw Fi aside to pull the bone drop spindle from her sleeve. She deflected the ax with a furious sweep of her arm. The Steelwight weapon crunched deep into a wooden rose.

"Shane!" Fi screamed.

340

Shane was on the second level of the library, racing for the balcony. Something metal glittered in her hand.

"I won't allow it!" the Spindle Witch rasped. She kicked the ruby out of Fi's hands, sending it skidding into the glass. Dozens of golden threads of her spun magic uncoiled from the drop spindle. She twisted them together into a knotted rope and sent it barreling toward Shane, catching the huntsman just as she reached the banister.

The mass of threads hit Shane square in the chest and flung her backward into one of the bookshelves with enough force to bring the entire thing down.

Shane gasped out a shuddering breath. Her gray eyes met Fi's, and even from halfway across the room Fi could see her grin as Shane raised her shaking hand, hurling the butterfly hairpin with all her might. Then she slumped to the ground. The metal glinted red as it passed through the light of the glowing rose. Heart in her throat, Fi forced herself up and lunged for it, snatching the pin out of the air.

Something happened the second she touched it. She felt suddenly hot, like her blood was pumping too fast, her heart buzzing against her bones. Her left hand was in agony, burning like fire. *The curse mark.*

Fi hissed against the pain, watching in shock as the butterfly on her palm began to move. The mark shivered, and then the butterfly unfolded from her skin, tearing its wings free one at a time. For one moment, the dark butterfly looked like it was made entirely of ink. It fluttered on her hand and then took off, trailing its long wings as it flashed in front of her face. For the first time ever, Fi thought it was beautiful.

The magic swallowtail alighted on one of the hanging

butterfly ornaments, opening and closing its wings. When it opened them again, it seeped into the metal butterfly, and the whole hairpin seemed to come to life, glowing molten red in the ruby gems. None of the butterflies were still anymore, each moving gently as though they were real creatures fastened to the ends of the chains.

Who are we to decide what true life is . . . or isn't? The Lord of the Butterflies's words rang in Fi's ears.

Footsteps clicked against the wood behind her. Fi whirled to face the Spindle Witch, raising the pin. It had been made for one purpose: to sever the Spindle Witch from her magic and end her cursed half life.

The Spindle Witch seemed to know it. She backed away, her hooded eyes locked on the butterflies.

"How clever of you to get your hands on that," the Witch spat. "But I knew you'd try something. You will never— *never*—outsmart me."

Before Fi could even take a step, the Spindle Witch plunged both hands into her sleeves, whipping out golden threads already woven into knots. With a flick of her hands, the threads flared out like a spider's web, stretching between the ceiling and the bookshelves and cutting Fi off from the Spindle Witch completely. She stared down at Fi through an unbreakable golden barrier.

"You won't get anywhere near me with that," she promised, gleeful. "I won't allow you to touch a single hair of my magic."

"Not a single one?" Fi asked. Then she whirled away from the Spindle Witch and drove the pin into Briar Rose's chest, right over his heart.

Briar gasped. The Spindle Witch screamed. The bone spindle whirred in her hands. Golden thread shot across the room, snaring Fi and yanking her away from Briar. It was too late. The hairpin was already sunk deep into his chest, the little chains jingling as the butterflies madly flapped their wings.

A golden thread sliced into Fi's neck, choking off her breath. She didn't care. She felt like she had stabbed her own heart as she watched Briar fall to his knees, his great wings thrashing. But this was what he'd wanted, what he had been trying to tell Fi all along, asking where the golden thread led. She finally understood.

That golden thread tied around his heart was the only chink in the Spindle Witch's armor. When she'd saved infant Briar's life, she hadn't done it with a spun thread from her bone spindle—she'd reached up under her veil and pulled one of her own hairs. She could have severed the magic, tied it off from herself like the Lord of the Butterflies had taught her, but then she wouldn't have been able to possess Briar Rose.

Her greed for the Siphoning Spells had made her impatient. She'd bound herself to Briar so she could control him, but that connection went both ways. The golden hair in Briar's heart led straight to the Spindle Witch.

Briar hunched forward, his claws raking the air over the pin. The little butterflies fluttered, their bodies glistening with a red luster. Even as she watched, Fi could see the magic starting to drain out of him. The sparks disappeared from Briar's fingers, and the glow in his eyes diminished until it was barely an ember. Fi stared into Briar's anguished face and prayed she wasn't going to watch him die. She wanted to run to him, but the Spindle Witch's threads held her tight.

The Spindle Witch. Fi wrenched her neck around, trying to see what was happening. If this hadn't worked—if she'd stabbed Briar for nothing—

The Spindle Witch was gasping hard, doubled over in pain. She had fallen to her knees, her black skirts pooled around her like rippling water.

She was *unraveling.* Like a tapestry unweaving line by line as Fi pulled a loose thread.

That was the only way she could think to describe it. The Spindle Witch's pale skin uncoiled from her fingertips, sagging to the floor as nothing more than loops of golden thread. Her unbound braid glistened down her back. Her eyes snapped with disbelief and fury and something else Fi never expected to see there—fear. The spindle jerked in her hands, and Fi gasped as she was dragged toward the Witch, the golden threads tight as shackles.

A storm of black crows circled the tower, shrieking. The Witch's hands were nothing but bone now. Fi lurched to her feet, struggling to get away as the threads pulled her face-to-face with the Spindle Witch. Cold eyes glowered into hers, those deep red lips twisted in a gruesome sneer.

"I may die," the Spindle Witch gasped out, "but at least I'll take your precious Briar Rose with me."

The threads holding Fi snapped all at once. Dazed, she stared at the place where the Spindle Witch had been. All that was left on the floor of the library was a mass of golden hair, a long black dress, and a small skeleton—a child's skeleton. The dark spire of the tower flashed through Fi's mind. She wondered if this was what the Lord of the Butterflies meant when he said a small part of the Spindle Witch was still trapped there. The girl in the storybook had died in the tower long, long ago.

It had been too late to save the Spindle Witch, but maybe not too late for Briar. Fi scrambled up and sprinted for the prince. Something glanced off her boot as she ran—the ruby, she realized. The gem was still faintly glowing, and Fi was struck with a sudden idea. She scooped up the rose and then threw herself to her knees at Briar's side.

He was laid out on his back, horrifyingly still. The black wings had sagged around him, ragged and torn—no longer held together by the power of the Spindle Witch. But he hadn't turned back into her Briar, either, and he wasn't breathing. Fi curled her fingers around the butterfly pin, pulling it out in one sharp jerk and flinging it away.

She pressed her ear against his chest. Nothing. The heartbeat that had given her hope so many times had gone silent.

"No." Fi's voice stuck in her throat, and the word came out like a sob. "No, please." Hands shaking, she clutched the glowing rose and pressed it against Briar's wound—the wound she'd given him. *Don't die here, Briar*, Fi begged, still choking on her tears. *Not when it's finally over*. The Spindle Witch was dead, Andar was saved, even the Butterfly Curse was gone.

"Please," Fi repeated, clenching her hand around the rose. "It's light magic—yours and Aurora's. Take it and come back to me."

Hardly breathing, she leaned forward to study his face. It was smooth, no longer twisted in pain. He looked almost like he could be sleeping.

Fi felt tears heavy on her eyelashes. They spilled onto Briar, rolling down his cheek as she leaned over him, pressing a kiss to his cold lips. She was back in that moment in the tower when she'd first come to wake the sleeping prince. Her heart leapt inside her chest, Briar's form so still under hers. Fi closed her eyes, hoping she would feel something, anything.

Then she did. There was something warm under her fingers. The rose was shining with a fierce glow, the light pulsing in its carved petals like a heartbeat. Brilliant white light trickled out of the ruby and into Briar, glowing under his skin like silvery veins. Fi remembered the spells of the Lord of the Butterflies: the currents of magic that ran through everything. If that was true, then they had to be in Briar, too, and in her, and in the magic Aurora had left in her rose. Maybe she and Briar weren't destiny, but Fi would give anything—all of herself—just to look into those sparkling blue eyes one more time.

The entire library seemed to hold its breath. The light grew stronger and stronger, until Briar was so bright Fi could barely look at him. It poured through his body, stretching over the ragged wings like glowing feathers. For one breathtaking moment, Briar's wings seemed to be made entirely of light magic, all the power of the rose burning at his back. Then it exploded in a shower of sparks, cascading over Fi and Briar like a fine silver rain.

When the light cleared, Fi was leaning over Briar—just Briar. No bones, no wings, no glowing skin. The ruby had gone dark, the magic spent.

Fi pressed a hand to his torn velvet coat. His heart beat steadily, so strong she felt like it was beating for both of them. Fi laughed. She pressed her lips to Briar's again, and this time, they were soft and warm and tasted like roses. She could feel tears prickling her eyes for an entirely different reason now. The Spindle Witch was gone, and she had saved Briar Rose. It was over. They had won.

Briar's blue eyes blinked open, and he stared up into Fi's face, tracing her features. He sat up slowly, and Fi matched him, leaning back on her knees, though she kept her hand over his heart.

"Briar," she breathed. Her voice was hoarse, and she could barely see him through the tears in her eyes, but she would know that dazzling smile anywhere.

"You saved me," Briar whispered. Then he frowned, his eyes clouded. "You must be the one destined to wake me from the curse. What's your name?"

Fi had no idea what expression she was wearing. Her face was probably blank, showing nothing, because that was how she felt—like something in her had shattered. She was looking right into his perfect blue eyes, but he didn't even recognize her.

It wasn't her Briar after all.

29

-->>> <<<--

Shane

SHANE'S HEAD THROBBED like she'd pounded it with her own ax. She blinked blearily up at a stone ceiling. Then the memories came rushing back—Fi, the Spindle Witch, the library, being thrown bodily into the bookshelf. Her head had cracked against the heavy wood as books rained down on her, and then everything went black.

Whatever she was lying on didn't feel like a bookcase, though. It felt suspiciously like a bed, and she could hear soft voices around her.

Shane shot up, throwing back the white sheet with a half-formed idea of finding Fi or Red, or both. The world lurched around her as she tried to stand, and she sat back down heavily.

"Not a good idea," a cool voice said from her right.

When the world resolved again, Shane could see that she was in some kind of barracks that had been transformed into a bustling infirmary. Women and men in swirling silk robes were scurrying between beds, leaning over injured soldiers in frayed red cloaks, while others carried buckets of water and armfuls of bandages. Shane even vaguely thought she recognized one of the gray-haired women as the Witch she'd passed in the hallways. These were the people of Andar, finally freed from the Spindle Witch's power.

Captain Hane sat on the bed next to Shane. The woman had a streak of black dirt across her face, and both her knuckles were bloody. One of her arms hung at an odd angle. A young woman in a blue robe stood beside her, dabbing at a cut on her chin.

Relief flooded through Shane. If Hane was here, having her injuries seen to, then the battle was won, because there was no way the captain would let anyone drag her off the battlefield before the fight was over. Pain spiked through Shane's skull again, and she sagged back against her pillows with a groan. For the first time, she noticed the thick white bandage covering the gash on her thigh.

"You with us?" Captain Hane asked, when Shane finally steadied. "From what I understand, you took a nasty blow to the head."

"How'd it end?" Shane wanted to know.

Captain Hane smiled widely. "In victory," she said. "You were right to have faith in your partner. I haven't gotten the whole story, but she defeated the Spindle Witch, severing her from her magic and ending her life. Without her, the bone creatures fell apart—the whole Forest of Thorns did."

The girl who had been treating Hane put her cloth aside, lifting her hands and holding them over the captain's twisted arm. She was a Witch, Shane realized. Her entire left arm was inked with silvery tattoos tracing a pattern that looked like vines, or maybe veins. The tattoos seemed to shimmer as she closed her eyes, her fingertips hovering over Captain Hane's skin. The bones didn't spring back into place, the cuts didn't disappear, but the ashen look left the captain's face, and she sat up a little straighter.

"Thank you," she said, before turning back to Shane. "It wasn't much of a battle after that. The Witch Hunters that didn't get away were rounded up, and young Perrin—or should I say the new Dream Witch—was able to wake the people of the castle."

"Yeah, I met the king," Shane admitted. "Well, briefly. In between fighting for our lives."

Hane crooked an eyebrow as if to say she'd be waiting for Shane's side of the story at the big victory celebration.

The Witch at Hane's side threw Shane a lopsided smile, a chorus of little bells tinkling in her hair. "You all are the first patients I've treated in a hundred years. Hope I'm not too rusty."

"You're a blessing," Hane said. "It's been generations since Everlynd had any Witches from the Order of the Azure Drop."

Shane's head could use a little of that magic, and then maybe some more blessed unconsciousness. She had a few more questions first, though.

"My partner Fi and Briar Rose—were they hurt?"

"No," Hane said quickly. "They are both alive." There was something restrained in the woman's voice, as though she were hesitating. It put Shane on edge.

"How long was I out?" she asked.

The Witch healer gave a little shrug. "Not long, I think. You're one of my new arrivals."

They were interrupted by another voice, a soft baritone Shane would know anywhere.

"You're awake," the Paper Witch called, making his way to her. "That is very good news." The relief in his face was palpable. He looked weary, one hand braced on the wall over her bed to hold himself up, though he didn't seem injured. Seeing him made Shane feel better. That was almost everyone accounted for.

"What about Red?" she asked.

"Red is . . . here," the Paper Witch said slowly.

"Here, as in—she's hurt?" Shane demanded. She lurched up, spinning head be damned. "I need to see her."

Captain Hane looked grim. The Paper Witch leaned down, pressing a hand on her shoulder—to comfort her or to restrain her, Shane didn't care. She wasn't lying in this bed one second longer if Red needed her.

"Where is she?"

"Shane," the Paper Witch said. His voice was soft, his eyes an ethereal blue. "Her injuries are simply too severe. The Witches have done all they can, but . . . she may never wake up."

He seemed like a stranger again, the mythic figure she'd first met in a tavern years ago, reaching out a hand to guide her into a new life. But he was wrong. There was no life for Shane anymore without Red in it.

"No!" Shane knocked his hand away. "Take me to her right now." Her feet hit the floor a little unsteadily, and she grabbed the wall for support, breathing hard. Her body was screaming, but she didn't care—she would crawl to Red if she had to. The Paper Witch gave her a searching look, then sighed heavily, offering his arm.

"This way," he said.

He led Shane to the back of the little barracks. Red lay at the end of a row of empty beds. Her dark curls spilled around her, stark against the white pillow. Her whole chest was cocooned in bandages, an ugly splotch of crimson already bleeding through over her shoulder, and her face was still, her warm skin turned ashen. Like she was already dead.

Shane ran. The world was spinning again, but this time, it wasn't because of her head. It felt like someone had reached into her chest and ripped her heart out. She fell to her knees beside the bed, grabbing Red's hand and squeezing it between her own. She could feel the girl's erratic pulse, but her touch was limp, her skin clammy with sweat.

"What happened?" she asked hoarsely.

"Perrin says it was the giant wolves," the Paper Witch murmured. "He carried her all the way here, screaming for help, or she surely would have died out there."

"We did all that we could."

Shane whirled at the new voice to find a stately woman standing over her. Her gray hair was pulled back in an intricate braid woven through with little bells, and her skin glittered with the same spiderweb of silver tattoos, stretching up her bare left arm all the way to her neck. A single shining teardrop was inscribed under her right eye. Her gaze was somber.

"The magic of the Witches of the Azure Drop is not limitless. Some wounds are simply too deep for us to heal. I poured my own magic into this girl. I felt her bones knitting, her body struggling to heal itself, but . . ."

"Don't," Shane snapped. "Don't say it."

"Shane," the Paper Witch admonished softly.

Tears had gathered in the corners of Shane's eyes, and they slid down her cheeks as she blinked at the still form lying in the bed. Red had only joined this battle for her. She had a sudden impossible wish: that Red had never met her, never betrayed the Spindle Witch, never let Shane take her hand if this was where Shane was going to lead her. Her heart thudded with an old memory: Red, sick and dying of poison, telling Shane her fate had been sealed long ago.

A small whine drew her attention. Cinzel lay sadly on the floor, his head resting on his paws. A wide swath of bandages covered his flank, and Shane could see blood matted into his white-and-tawny fur. He whined at Shane again, inching toward her on the floor. Shane swiped at her eyes.

"Come on, mutt," she said, patting the bed. "I know it was probably doctor's orders, but Red would want you with her."

Cinzel climbed onto the bed, squeezing himself against Red's legs, and then lay back down, eyes fixed on his unmoving human. Shane just dared the Witch of the Azure Drop to have anything to say about that. But the woman was silent. They all were, watching the figure in the bed. Half a dozen men and women in the same blue robes had drifted to stand around them, a silent vigil, and Shane wondered if they were all thinking what she was thinking—that every breath might be Red's very last one.

A thousand memories of Red flashed before her eyes—Red humming happily as she stroked Cinzel's fur, Red stomping down on Shane's toe, Red's eyes flashing as they argued, Red standing in the rain, soaked to the bone, telling Shane she didn't get to give up. Red looking up at her through those lashes in the dark—the feel of Red's love, Red's kiss on her lips. Shane couldn't lose her.

"Try again." Shane ground her teeth together, searching the faces of the Witches of the Azure Drop, her hands balled into fists. "Whatever you did before, try it again! She's not done—we're not done, and she's not giving up."

The Witches exchanged weary glances, looking to the older Witch with the shining silver tear. Her dark eyes never left Shane's face.

"Our magic is nearly exhausted," the woman told her, sweeping one hand toward the infirmary. "We cannot create life energy from nothing."

"Then take mine!" Shane begged them. Red could have her pounding head, her aching wounds, her bruised body, and her raw hands. She didn't have much left, but Red could have it—all of it.

The Witch still looked uncertain, her lips pursed.

"She's one of us," a familiar voice broke in. Perrin pushed through the crowd. He was covered in his own swath of bandages, but his eyes were steady as he stepped to Shane's side. "She's descended from one of our own. Red carries the name Assora—and the blood of the Snake Witch. If you won't do it for us, do it for her."

The Witches traded shocked whispers. The Paper Witch's

mouth fell open, one of the few times Shane had ever seen him truly surprised. So there were a few things he didn't know. His expression turned wistful as he looked down at Red.

"Perhaps this is a sign, Nezira," he said quietly, turning to the gray-haired Witch. "The descendants of all the Great Witches are gathered here. Three women known for achieving the impossible." He laid a hand on Shane's shoulder. "I also offer my life to save Red's."

"Count me in," Perrin added with a smile.

Nezira bowed her head. "I make no promises. But we will try."

The Witches inched closer. Their blue robes rustled as they formed a circle, linking their arms until Shane and Red were inside an unbroken river of silver veins. The tattoos shimmered as magic raced through them, like a great river of power flowing from one Witch to the next.

Shane had never actually *felt* magic before, but she could feel it now—a tingle on her skin like she was standing in an icy winter glade in Steelwight, every breath shivering with frost, the whole world silent.

The young Witch who'd been caring for Captain Hane stepped forward, shimmering with magic, and the Paper Witch inclined his head so she could press her hand to his cheek. He sagged the second she touched him, her tattoos pulsing with the silver glow as he added his energy to the spell. Perrin held out his hand to a tall boy with green eyes. Then all of that magic was in Nezira, her brown eyes warm as she reached out and laid one glittering hand on Red's shoulder. Shane watched as the magic flowed into Red, shimmering under her skin.

"Call to her," Nezira ordered.

Shane scooted as close as she could get, twining her fingers into those tousled curls.

"You have to wake up, Red," she whispered. "That future you wanted so badly, it's right here. I'm right here. You've always been so stubborn . . . Don't tell me this is the one thing you're giving up on." Tears streamed down her face as she pressed her forehead to Red's.

Cinzel licked Red's still hand. Suddenly, her fingers twitched.

"Yes, yes!" Shane shouted.

Nezira pulled her hand back, her face cracking into a smile.

Red's soft brown eyes blinking open was the most beautiful thing Shane had ever seen. She wrapped Red up in her arms and pressed their lips together, not caring one bit that a dozen Witches were watching. Perrin laughed and clapped the Paper Witch's shoulder. Shane would be laughing, too, but she was too busy kissing Red.

As Shane pulled back, Perrin threw himself onto the cot and wrapped his lanky arms around both of them, and Cinzel, too, and suddenly it was a group hug with a wolf in the middle of it, Red gaping in surprise while Shane just threw her head back laughing. Cinzel was bunting Red and slobbering all over Perrin's face, crooning his happy song, and for once, Shane didn't need Red to tell her what he was saying. She and Cinzel were thinking the exact same thing.

"Welcome home, Red," Shane whispered. And then kissed her again, just because she could.

EPILOGUE: PART ONE

›››» «‹‹‹

Briar Rose

BRIAR ROSE SAT in the window of the high white tower that had been his prison for a hundred years, his arms slung over his knees. Camellia's roses still covered the sill beside him, and he was careful not to catch the sleeves of his newly tailored silver-and-blue coat on the tiny thorns. He didn't remember what had happened to his old coat, but it was shredded—it barely qualified as a rag at this point. Still, he couldn't bring himself to throw it away. He'd had it mended with a smattering of darker blue patches and left it hanging in the closet of his old bedroom, right next to Sage's, in the castle of Andar, now free from its curse.

Everything Camellia had promised him had come true. This tower was filled with memories of her. Briar closed his eyes, letting a thousand images of his sister wash over him. The smile on her face as she tickled him mercilessly. The shriek of her laughter as she and Briar were pelted with snow after he foolishly challenged the Snake Witch and the Dream Witch to a snowball fight. The warmth of her arms tight around him as she promised he would be saved from the Spindle Witch's curse. Against all odds, Camellia had managed to keep that promise.

A light breeze ruffled Briar's hair as he looked out over the castle grounds. On that first day, when all of Andar had woken from its hundred-year nightmare, it had been to a bleak view of raging winds and black wastelands. But in the weeks since, all of the dust had blown away, revealing new shoots of grass and green plants rising from the ashes. The impenetrable Forest of Thorns had crumbled to nothing.

Now this window looked out on a line of ancient willow trees sweeping over the river, their skeletal trunks slowly healing, their branches rippling with a cloud of soft white blossoms. Blue and purple bellflowers sprouted from the dark earth at their roots, and Briar could hear birds calling in the branches. It would be many years before Andar was restored completely, but everything was still there, sleeping just under the surface.

Laughing voices pulled his attention to the base of the tower. Briar leaned out. A group of people was moving through the castle gardens below. Some planted rose cuttings and sachets of seeds along the wall, while others ambled beside the riverbank, clearing away dead bracken and hanging the willow boughs with a thousand tiny bells—Aurora's bells. A young Witch in the robes of the Order of the Rising Rain walked among them, twirling a stream of water in her hand like a sparkling ribbon.

Briar recognized the girl—he'd passed her sleeping form

many times as he walked the castle in his dreams—but the others were strangers. He wondered if they were from Everlynd or if these were the new arrivals from hidden enclaves and villages to the north and south, where some of Andar's people had escaped the curse. More were coming every day, some all the way from the neighboring kingdom of Darfell. As he stared out this bleak window for a hundred lonely years, Briar had never imagined that so much of Andar had survived.

The Witch girl slipped on a patch of mud, the thick stream of water gushing over one of the workers. She slapped her hands over her mouth to muffle her laughter as the man spluttered, wiping a sopping sleeve across his face. Briar laughed, too, but he ducked out of the window before they could spot him.

As he dropped to the floor, a sharp pain bit into his side. Briar winced. Under the coat, he had a strange blue-black bruise right over his ribs, crescent-shaped, like he'd been struck by something small and metal.

Briar pressed his fingers gingerly to the spot. He wasn't exactly sure why he was hiding it from his brother and the castle healers, except that it seemed like a clue—proof of whatever he'd forgotten.

No one was willing to tell him anything, but Briar knew something had happened to him—something bad. The first few days after he woke, all of his limbs felt stiff and painful, his whole body sore like he'd been trampled under a horse. And then there was his magic.

Briar lifted his hand. Tiny white sparks crackled on his fingertips, but they fizzled out almost immediately. He could no longer feel that great shining well of magic inside him. He wasn't sure if that was because he'd almost died or because of what he had become.

Briar had only been given the barest details of the final battle, but there was one thing no one could keep from him. When the hero of Andar broke the curse, Briar had not been waiting for her as the sleeping prince. He had lost himself to dark magic and turned into a monster, one who served the Spindle Witch.

Sage had told him not to think about it. Briar had tried to forget it—but how could he forget it when he didn't remember it in the first place? His mind was a jumble of images he didn't understand.

He looked over at the little vanity. The oval mirror was hidden by folds of gauze, one of the torn curtains from the canopy bed. Briar had covered it himself the first time he came up here to think, because for just one second, when he glanced into the glass, he swore he was looking into red eyes framed by curling white horns.

It was a memory, he was positive. One he might be better off not knowing—even it if meant never remembering *her*, either.

Briar pressed the heels of his hands into his eyes. There was a person at the center of all his splintered memories: a girl with dark hair and arresting hazel-green eyes. He had woken in her arms in the library, and he didn't think he'd ever forget that first glimpse of her: the desperate look on her face, the tears that had glittered like glass on her cheeks. Briar had always known he'd fall in love with the hero of

Andar—it was destiny, as strong and sure as any love in the old fairy tales Camellia used to read him. But now he barely knew her, this girl, his savior—Filore.

They'd only brushed past each other since that first moment in the library, Briar whisked away by his brother and the Witches while Filore stayed with her companions. The closest they'd come was three days ago, when he found her working alongside a handful of castle staff cleaning up the library. From the upper balcony, he'd watched as she picked up a fallen book, cradling it lovingly and smoothing her fingers down the bent pages.

That was the first time Briar had a flash of memory—an image of Filore up a ladder in another library, with a soft coat and a smudge of ink on her face, smiling so brightly that just remembering it took his breath away.

Since then, flashes of her just kept coming, to the point that Briar thought he must be losing his mind. He knew this girl— knew her well. Maybe even loved her. Camellia's spell might have led him to his destiny, but he couldn't even remember.

The bells were ringing in the castle spire. Briar dropped his hands from his eyes and straightened his rich blue coat, tucking the white silk blouse carefully into his belt and dusting off his dark pants. His hair was still faintly damp from his bath. Soaking in the lavish tub, he had gotten one of his clearest memories yet: the silhouette of the girl behind a canvas screen, lifting her palm to him. There was something hesitant about the gesture, something that felt important. He'd wanted to take that hand so much he found himself reaching out through the steam, closing his fingers around empty air.

Footsteps on the tower stairs shook him out of it. "Prince Briar Rose," called a soft voice, followed by the much more insistent, "Briar, you up here?"

The door swung open, revealing his brother Sage. At his back stood a soft-spoken man who had introduced himself as the Paper Witch.

"You know, there is no *fashionably late* to your own party," Sage said, raising an eyebrow. Briar still wasn't quite used to seeing his brother up and around instead of slumped lifeless in his throne. It made him grin every time.

"You didn't have to come all the way up here just to get me," Briar said.

"If you're insinuating it's too many stairs, I'll remind you I'm not that old," Sage said. His voice was stern, but Briar recognized the edge of a smirk pulling at his lips.

"You are a hundred and twenty-eight," Briar pointed out, smiling back. "I admittedly ditched most of my history lessons, but I'm fairly sure that makes you the oldest king Andar's ever had." There was a name at the tip of his tongue, but he tripped over it. *Filore.* He wasn't sure why he thought she'd know. Or why his body jerked toward the door like he couldn't wait to run and ask her.

"Well, in that case, I'm looking forward to the rest of my two-hundred-year reign," Sage joked.

Sage still wore his outfit from that morning's ceremony, when the steward of Everlynd had formally returned the golden ruling scepter to the king. Briar had stood beside his brother on the dais in the great courtyard, looking out at the cheering crowd and the restored statues of the Great Witches smiling down on them. A heavy blue mantle swept from Sage's shoulders over his intricately embroidered tunic, and a golden crown sparkling with sapphires sat on his brow. It suited him—far better than the golden circlet he waved in one hand suited Briar.

"You forgot this," Sage said.

"Right." Briar reached out hesitantly, but he didn't take it.

Sage stepped over to the vanity, throwing aside the cloth like it was nothing. Briar's heart lurched as the last layer of gauze was swept away, but only his own reflection stared back at him, blue eyes in a smooth face. He was pale, certainly—he'd gone a hundred years without sunlight—but not bone white. He was just Briar.

Sage settled the circlet on his head. "There," he said. "Now you look the part."

He squeezed Briar's shoulder as they stood together in front of the mirror, their reflection framed by Camellia's brilliant roses. Then Sage turned and headed for the door.

"I've got a few more things to take care of. Why don't you escort your great-grandnephew to the party?"

The Witch in the silver-and-white robes inclined his head as the king passed, then moved to Briar. "Your Highness," he said, the little bell in his hair tinkling like a laugh.

It was hard to offer his arm to a stranger who reminded him so much of Camellia. Worse, the Paper Witch was one of the people from Briar's missing memories. Those blue eyes watched him expectantly, as if waiting for something, though Briar had no idea what.

Arm in arm, they moved down the tower stairs and headed for the grand ballroom. Briar could barely believe it was the same castle. The once-empty halls rang with chatter and laughter and raised voices. Men in soldiers' tunics hustled by with heaping armfuls of bedding. The great entrance hall was filled with cots for all the new arrivals, and a group of children chased each other up the spiraling stairs, shouting joyfully as they replayed the battle for Andar. Briar took a corner too fast and nearly smacked into a tall woman with a cloud of dark hair who had been given the position of Captain of the Guard.

Even in his earliest memories, the castle had never been so full of people—or of hope. He even thought he'd seen a wolf padding through the halls the day before, its white tail twitching cheerfully.

Out the window, he caught a glimpse of the secret garden of the Rose Witches. The white marble of the memorial tree shone in the sunlight, painfully bare—but he could see the green wisps of rose vines curling around the trunk again, a few bright red buds just beginning to peek open. Briar looked at the man on his arm. The Paper Witch had been declared the new head of the Order of the Divine Rose, and there was no one Briar would rather the position went to than Camellia's great-grandson.

The Paper Witch caught Briar's gaze. "Have you remembered anything yet?" he asked.

Briar shifted uncomfortably. "Not really. Just flashes." He shook away the thought of the creature in the mirror. "Maybe it's better that way."

They had nearly reached the door to the ballroom. The Paper Witch paused, covering Briar's hand with his own. "You should not fear your memories, Briar Rose." He looked suddenly older, his smile melancholy. "Your actions at the end were not your own. Not all of us can say the same of the choices we made. Many regrettable things were done in the service of breaking the curse—but every one of them brought us to this moment, and I would like to think that is reason enough to forgive ourselves."

He had stopped them right at the top of the stairs. Through the doorway, the great ballroom shone like a painting—the tables gleaming, the blue pennants rippling, and the dance floor whirling with laughing couples, their voices ringing under the high ceiling studded with dazzling chandeliers. Dark oak columns framed a view of the wide balcony, all the doors thrown open to let in the dreamy blue twilight.

The Paper Witch smiled Camellia's knowing smile. "This victory would not have been possible without you, too. Don't forget that."

Briar shook his head. "You have a lot of Camellia in you," he told the man, as they were announced at the door. "And I mean that as a compliment."

The Paper Witch tipped his head, his crystal earring glittering. "I can imagine no greater praise."

They moved down into the crowd. The tables were filled with a hastily pulled-together feast—platters of ripe plums and figs and pomegranates salvaged from the gardens of Everlynd, baskets of golden bread from the fields to the south, and jars of candied honey and nuts that had survived a hundred years in the castle storehouses. There was even some dark wine that had been sent by the duchy on the border of Darfell, the casks stamped with the seal of Bellicia. More supply wagons were rolling in every day. The hodgepodge of summer fruits and vegetables and simple pies was hardly typical fare for a royal gathering, but nobody seemed to mind.

The mood in the hall was buoyant. A small group of musicians played a lively waltz, and couples spun across the floor, dappled by the light of the crystal chandeliers. People in their best finery and people in dusty traveling cloaks talked over full plates, Witches and soldiers poured each other drinks, and strangers hugged suddenly when they realized they were distant relatives separated for a hundred years. Briar tried to smile at all of them, hoping it was a noble, princely smile even though his cheeks felt rubbery and stretched.

A young man with dark, curly hair broke away from a circle where many of the older Witches were gathered. He was by far the youngest of the group. A wizened old Seer sat beside a man whose grizzled white hair was woven with little twigs and sticks, the sign of the Witches of the Wandering Roots. Briar recognized the court astronomer leaning heavily against the wall, his Celestial Stargazers robes glittering with embroidered stars. The young man flashed a wide smile as he approached, his blue robe shimmering around him like water.

"Dream Witch," Briar greeted.

The young man blinked in surprise. "I don't know if I'm ever going to get used to that," he admitted, sharing a laugh with the Paper Witch.

Briar rubbed his neck, blushing faintly. He didn't remember the Dream Witch's real name, after all.

"It gets easier," the Paper Witch promised. "And you've more than earned the title—as well as your new position on the Council of Magic."

The young man flushed a little. "Youngest Witch ever to hold a seat," he admitted with a teasing lilt.

"Perhaps I should have added, 'Don't let it go to your head,'" the Paper Witch mused.

"Never," the Dream Witch promised. He turned to include Briar. "Have you seen the girls yet? I heard Shane had some kind of robe called a kyrtill made just for this."

The Paper Witch gave a thoughtful hum. "Last I saw them, they were trying to make last-minute adjustments to Red's dress."

"Last you saw them . . . ?" the Dream Witch pressed.

"Let me rephrase," the Paper Witch said. "Last I *heard* them, Red and Shane were bickering loudly enough that I could hear them from the hallway. I decided to let young Prince Briar escort me instead."

Briar shifted his feet. He felt strangely cut out of the conversation. Sage had said the Dream Witch was a friend of his, and the girls in question, too. He should know these people, all of these people, but he didn't. A huge part of his own life was a mystery to him.

The Dream Witch craned his head as he was called back to the circle of Witches. "I should go. It's good to see you, Your Highness," he added, clapping Briar on the shoulder.

Briar gave him a look. "If we were friends, I'm sure I told you to call me Briar."

The Dream Witch grinned. "Must have slipped my mind," he said, with a friendly wink that reminded Briar of the boy's ancestor, the original Dream Witch. Then he headed back to the others, and the Paper Witch went with him, inclining his head to Briar before turning away.

Briar drifted into the room, at a loss. He wandered past the feast tables, his eyes catching on the long vines of blooming roses wound between the serving platters. Sage stood at the head of the hall, surrounded by a knot of councilors.

Briar declined an offer to dance from a pretty young woman in a pink gown, taking a glass of wine instead. He almost choked on the first swallow when the herald announced: "The heroes of Andar: Lady Filore Nenroa of Darfell, the huntsman Shane Ragnall of the Steelwight Islands, and the descendant of the Snake Witch, Red of Andar."

Briar spun around. Three girls stood framed in the doorway, the crowd cheering and applauding as they descended the sweeping staircase that was draped with blue cloth and tiny twinkling lanterns. The short brown-haired girl, Shane, threw Filore a victorious grin. And though Filore rolled her eyes, Briar could tell she was fighting not to smile.

Shane wore something fashioned after the styles from her home country: a long tunic belted and cloaked by a dark green mantle pinned to her shoulder. She moved like a fighter, pounding down the steps in heavy wedge-heeled boots.

The girl on her arm was even shorter, beautiful and curvy with a wild mass of loose curls that tumbled around her. She wore a red ball gown with a heart-shaped top and a wide gauzy skirt that swished as she moved. Briar's heart swelled to see them together, though he had no idea why.

Filore hung back at the top of the stairs, wearing a long sheath dress of midnight blue with short sleeves that dangled over her shoulders. Her brown hair was tied off in a small ponytail, the long silver ribbon trailing down her back. The dress flattered her, but mostly she just looked stiff and out of place—not like herself at all. Briar wasn't sure where the thought came from. He just knew that when he pictured Filore, it was always in a dusty jacket. Maybe with a wide-brimmed hat.

For one second, her eyes found his. Briar's heart leapt into his throat.

He didn't know how he knew these things. He didn't know why he wanted to break through the crowd and run to her, to sweep her into his arms, but he did, and he wasn't going to hide from that anymore—not from his memories, and not from the girl at the heart of them. If he didn't know Filore Nenroa, then he wanted to. Briar set his glass aside, making his way across the room to where she had disappeared in the crowds.

He stepped aside as Shane and Red swept past, already caught up in the dance. Red's dress fluttered around her as she spun under Shane's arm, the two of them moving flawlessly together. Shane broke from the steps of the dance, pulling her partner in so close Red squeaked in surprise.

"See, I dance just fine," Shane said. Briar couldn't see her expression, but he could see the way Red scrunched up her nose.

"I didn't say you couldn't dance—I said we wouldn't match!" she protested, clearly continuing some earlier argument. She pouted as Shane pressed their palms together, circling slowly. "Your costume is green and *rustic*, and mine is . . ."

"Perfect," Shane finished. They had turned all the way around, and Briar could see the broad smile on Shane's face, her eyes soft as she looked at Red. "And we fit together perfectly." She leaned in to catch Red's surprised lips in a kiss, and Briar turned away, feeling like he was spying on a private moment. Though, if they wanted privacy, he'd recommend somewhere other than the middle of the dance floor.

At last, he had spotted Filore. He ignored all the curious eyes that followed him as he made his way to the banquet table, where Filore had moved aside a plate of fruit and seemed to be inspecting the silver charger beneath it. She was bent forward, her fingers tracing the pattern of twining roses that ran around the edge.

"Found something interesting?" Briar asked, leaning against the table.

Filore didn't look up, distracted. "I think I've seen other pieces by this same artist elsewhere in the castle. See the whorls in the rose vines? They're almost like a signature. Some of this looks like Divine Rose script, but that can't be right—what spell would they bind into a plate?"

Filore circled a clump of roses with her finger, looking up absently. Then she straightened with a jerk, letting the charger thud back onto the table.

"Briar," she said, surprised.

Briar. Warmth surged through him when she said his name. He was mesmerized by the small dusting of pink on her cheeks. He liked that. He had a feeling he'd spent a lot of time trying to make her blush.

The scent of the roses swirled around him. Briar took a deep breath. This was destiny standing right in front of him. It didn't matter if he had his memories—all that mattered was that they were together, right now, and he had a chance to get everything he'd dreamed of for so long.

Briar held out his hand. "There is a dance floor . . . unless you're more interested in the flatware?"

Filore gave him a sharp look, but he could see the flush deepening in her cheeks. "Are you asking me to dance?" she wanted to know.

"Only if you're willing to risk it," Briar conceded. "I have to warn you, I'm—"

"A terrible dancer," Filore finished, arching one eyebrow. "I know."

She knew him, too. That agonizing pit of emptiness inside him was where a part of her was supposed to be, a part he'd lost. He had to find it again. Briar bowed with a flourish and brushed his lips against the backs of his fingers, surprised when Filore mirrored him. Then he took her hand and pulled her into the dance.

He kept to the edge, under the arched picture windows, where they wouldn't be in the way of other couples. Briar tried not to step on her feet, but it was hard when he could barely tear his eyes away from her. Filore was just as bad as he was—she kept turning the wrong way, bumping into his chest as they both tried to lead, and when they executed a jerky spin, he was very nearly elbowed in the face. Filore smiled, trying to untangle them without letting go of his hand.

That grudging little smile encouraged him. Briar dragged her back toward him, their palms gliding together, and then hooked his arm around her waist and pivoted into a twirl, loving the way Filore's eyes flared in surprise. He tripped over someone's trailing cape and almost took her down in a heap, but it was worth it to watch Filore throw her head back, laughing so hard she couldn't speak.

Briar couldn't speak, either. A thousand tiny slivers of memory couldn't compare to the happiness he felt having her right next to him, smiling and laughing in his arms. If he couldn't have those memories back, then he wanted to make a thousand more. He would take Filore to the library and let her tell him what she loved about history, he would round up all the flatware in the entire castle for her inspection, and he would dance with her until she was sick of him tripping over her feet. This was the love he had waited a hundred years for. He wanted to spend a lifetime laughing with her.

His heart was racing as they spun again, a breathless whirl across the floor that left him dizzy and Filore gasping. He drew her close as the music swelled. "There's only one way to end a dance like this," he whispered.

Filore's expression was intoxicating. "Don't drop me," she warned playfully.

Briar's mind was on fire with a memory—another night spent dancing, Filore in a skull mask and a red cape swirling from Briar's shoulders as they spun in front of a shining wall of mirrors. The moments overlapped as Briar bent Filore over his arm in a sweeping dip. She grabbed at his sleeve to keep from falling, and they straightened quickly, wheezing and laughing. He wasn't sure if he was remembering being in love with her or if he had fallen in love all over again.

Filore searched his face. "Come on," she said, tugging him out onto the wide balcony.

Briar followed. He took a deep breath of the night air, not at all sorry to leave the party behind. He loved his brother, and all the people of Andar, but the castle had always been a cage to him, even before he fell under the curse. Now the whole world was open to him. He could go anywhere, see anything—with anyone.

Filore leaned against the banister overgrown with roses, the lush blossoms climbing the wrought-iron rails and spilling onto the marble floor. The sun had long set, and the clear sky twinkled with stars. It felt like the stars were all around them, too—little bits of pollen and seed pods drifted through the air, lit by the silver moonlight. The wind sang in the bells strung through the willow trees. Filore's skin had a warm glow, and her eyes glittered as she looked out over the rest of the sprawling castle.

Briar moved to her side, their shoulders brushing as he rested his elbows on the rail. "We owe you everything," he said softly. "You saved all of Andar—and you saved me, Filore."

Her smile was wistful, as though that had been *almost* exactly what she wanted to hear. Briar's chest squeezed. He studied her face, desperate for the answers that were locked away inside him. Then suddenly the air was full of butterflies—tiny blue-and-white butterflies rising from the glistening roses and shivering in the air between them.

Filore's eyes widened. "Briar," she whispered. She lifted her hand, and Briar saw a small pink mark that looked like a scar on her palm. It almost had the shape of a butterfly, though it looked like it had healed a long time ago. The butterflies drifted upward, flitting away from them, and Filore's smile turned sad. Briar swallowed. Butterflies meant something to her—maybe everything. He couldn't let this moment end so soon.

Small wishes. Camellia's refrain whispered through him.

Briar felt something ignite in his chest—something he had thought he might never feel again. He lifted his hand, and, almost unbidden, his light magic jumped to his fingers.

The heat of it blazed in his veins. White sparks glittered in the dark between them. This was a memory, too—his magic sparkling like stars in Filore's eyes as she leaned toward him, her lips just parted.

"Briar, I . . ." she began. Briar held his breath.

"Prince Briar Rose!" a low voice called.

His magic fizzled and vanished. The call was accompanied by the sound of spoons clinking against glasses, the newly restored king proposing a toast.

"Filore . . ." Briar said, trying to ignore it.

"Your Highness!" the voice called again, more insistently.

Filore ducked her head, a rueful smile tugging at her lips. "You may not remember this, but your steward, Nikor, is a bit high-strung. He's not going to stop looking till he finds you. You're holding up the toasts." She reached up, tapping Briar's nose and then spinning him around, giving him a gentle shove toward the door.

Briar hesitated. "What about you?"

"I'm going to stay out here a few more minutes," Filore said, watching one of the butterflies settle back into the cradle of a rose.

"But I'll see you later, right?" Briar pressed. Lord Nikor stood in the doorway, gesturing impatiently for him to hurry.

"Absolutely," Filore promised, her eyes bright. "See you later."

Briar shot one last glance over his shoulder, drinking in the sight of her framed against the white curtain of the willows. Then he turned away. For just a moment, he'd thought about climbing down the roses with her and escaping into the

374

night. Why was he so sure that if he asked to her jump, she would?

THE PARTY DRAGGED on into the late hours of the night. Briar tried to find Filore once the toasts were over, but no matter how many times he circled the great hall, she was nowhere to be found. He wondered if she'd already retreated to her room. It was a few hours before he could get away from all of the lords and council members and new citizens of Andar who wanted to wish him well—but as soon as he could, he ducked out of the hall and headed up the darkened stairs toward the southern wing, where the guests of honor had been staying.

Briar knocked softly on the door. "Filore . . . ?" he called. He trailed off as the door swung back on its own, unlatched.

Briar's mouth went dry. The room was empty, the bed was made, and the desk was barren, as if no one had ever stayed here. No pack. No traveling hat. No hero of Andar. The only thing left was the blue sheath dress hanging in the armoire, its long ribbon fluttering in the breeze from the open window.

"Filore?" he called again, though he knew it was useless. He could feel panic crawling up his throat.

"She's gone, Your Highness."

Briar whirled to find a young maid standing in the doorway. She clutched an empty tea tray against her dress, bowing low.

"She left during the party. She'd been packed since this

afternoon, with a horse readied . . . I thought you knew she wasn't planning to stay."

Briar could feel the girl's concerned eyes on him, but he couldn't think of anything to say. His mind was a complete blank. The entire party—while they'd danced, while she'd spun in his arms, while he'd fallen more in love with her with every passing second—she'd already been planning to leave him.

He felt cold from the inside out. He recognized that feeling all too well. It was loneliness—the same bone-deep loneliness he'd lived for a hundred years, waiting for her. Briar barely felt himself stumble out of the room and begin walking.

He wasn't surprised to find himself back in the white tower. Briar sat in the window thronged in roses, scanning the empty horizon as he tried to make sense of this strange feeling of betrayal. Filore hadn't made him any promises, so she couldn't have betrayed him. But that didn't ease the bitter ache in his heart, like something had been ripped out of him. When she'd leaned toward him on the balcony, he'd thought . . .

Briar thudded his fist against the wall. What did it matter? She was gone. Even if he loved her, leaving was her answer. *Destiny, fate, choice, love* . . . It didn't matter what they'd had, because it was over. If that's what she wanted, Briar would let her go.

A perfect rose seemed to be glowing at the edge of the sill, winking with dewdrops in the silver moonlight. Briar reached for it, mesmerized as a droplet hung on the edge of a petal like a tear shivering from an eyelash. He hissed and yanked his hand back as something sharp bit into his flesh.

One of the thorns had pricked him. The silence rushed in his ears as Briar turned his hand over, watching a thick drop of blood well up on his finger and encircle it like a curl of scarlet thread.

A drop of blood, a drop of hope . . .

The words poured into his mind, and with them came all the rest of his memories, finally unleashed, surging through him like a great torrent—the bone spindle, the Paper Witch, Shane, Perrin, Red, Everlynd, and Fi. It was like he was reliving all their moments together—the dancing, the laughter, the arguments, the kisses, and the promise he had made her under a starlit sky just like this one: to give everything up, to leave with her and follow wherever she led.

Fi hadn't broken her promise. Briar had broken his. That was why his heart felt like it'd been ripped out.

He knew what he had to do.

"Thank you," Briar whispered, brushing the droplet from the rose. He wasn't sure if these roses really had any magic left, but he was sure it was his sister, Camellia, who had helped him remember.

Briar leapt down from the window and raced for the tower stairs. He was at least four hours behind her, with no time to waste. He was going after Fi, and this time, nothing would stop him.

EPILOGUE: PART TWO

Fi

FI LOOKED OUT from under the brim of her new brown hat as she rode into the small border town of Benthaven, the kingdom of Andar at her back.

Benthaven was little more than a few log cabins that doubled as shops and residences and a single squat inn with uneven windows. A cluster of shacks was tucked back into the swaying pines, and any number of trappers and hunters pitched tents in the foothills during the summer. It was dusty and imposing, and it reminded Fi of Raven's Roost—the town where she had met Shane and they had partnered up for their *one job* together.

The thought put a lopsided smile on Fi's face as she dismounted in front of the inn. She handed the reins of her horse over to a stable boy, along with a few coppers from her newly fattened purse. Being a hero had its perks. The boy grinned in thanks, disappearing with the dapple-gray mare.

Her body was stiff from the long ride and too many nights sleeping on the ground. Fi had been traveling for days, camping out under the moon and starting off early in the mornings as she headed for the border. But now that she was here, she couldn't shake the feeling that she'd left something important behind. Probably because she hadn't told Briar goodbye.

Fi's boots scuffed in the dirt as she trudged toward the door, the evening sky roiling with storm clouds. Briar didn't remember her or what they had shared; he had been like a different person in the castle of Andar, and Fi couldn't stand it. She wasn't running, though. She was just giving them both the space to find out who they were again.

Okay, she was running, but that didn't make it the wrong decision.

Fi knew she could have stayed in Andar. She'd been welcomed as their savior, offered every position from library keeper to a seat on the ruling council, which she was woefully unqualified for. But it wasn't what she wanted. For the first time in so long, Fi was free of the Butterfly Curse. She could go anywhere she wanted, *stay* anywhere she wanted, without worrying about hurting anyone. She wasn't ready to be tied to one place.

Briar had wanted to leave with her once, but he wasn't that Briar anymore. He was the prince of Andar again—a beautiful, willowy stranger with a gold circlet in his tousled blond hair. Fi wasn't sure she was still a treasure hunter, but she didn't want to be a princess, either, and that's what Briar needed now: a princess to help rebuild Andar by his side.

She had tried to bury her feelings for him and her memories of all they'd been. But how could she when he kept doing all the little things that reminded her why she'd fallen in love with him? Briar flashing that dazzling smile. Briar performing little magic tricks for the delighted children, making a small white spark leap between his fingertips. Briar, who was such an abysmal dancer but who made her laugh so much she never wanted to stop. Briar, whose bright, beautiful magic always lit up the darkest places.

She'd been on the cusp of telling him everything that night on the balcony—seizing his hand through the cloud of butterflies and asking him to go with her. But in the end, she couldn't be that selfish. She couldn't risk Briar coming with her out of some sense of obligation. She rode out of the castle courtyard with a deep ache in her chest, but it was worse to feel that ache when he was right in front of her. Briar, but not her Briar.

All she had left was her old promise. She'd been willing to walk away from Briar once before, because if they were destiny, then this wasn't over. She would come back to Andar one day, when she was ready, and if everything Briar had told her was true, then he'd fall in love with her all over again. She could hold on to that. Her only regret was that he'd deserved a better goodbye. They all had.

A fat drop of rain hit the brim of Fi's hat, and she hurried toward the inn, her brown coat flapping around her. She'd definitely want to book a room for tonight.

Fi took off her hat as she stepped through the stout wooden door into the common room. A wave of heat washed over her from the crackling fireplace. The floor of the inn was crowded with rough-hewn tables and chairs and a few bleached stumps set in a half circle around the fire. A set of narrow stairs led to the rooms on the upper floor. Harried servers bustled in and out of the small kitchen in the back, and a stern man who had to be the innkeeper stood at the long bar, polishing glasses.

Most of the tables were already filled—groups of men and women with the hard look of traders, and one trio of robed figures who could only be Witches on their way to Andar, their jovial faces bright as they clinked their cups in a cheer. Fi had to smile. She could see a few open tables in the back corner, and the room smelled heavenly, of spices and stew. Fi wetted her lips, wondering what the tea was like here.

She was about halfway to the bar when a chair suddenly scraped across the floor in front of her, almost taking her out at the knees. Fi whipped around to glare at the person who had kicked the chair out. Her eyes widened.

"Shane!" she breathed in surprise.

The huntsman sat kicked back with her feet propped up on the edge of the table. Her dusk-red coat sprawled behind her like a cape, and her hair was windswept. She grinned at Fi, arching an eyebrow.

"I ordered your usual." She waved at the table, where a slightly bent copper teacup waited in front of the empty seat. "Though I don't know why you bother," she added, taking a swig from her wooden mug. "Do you have any idea how far we are from a lemon grove?"

Fi dropped into the chair in front of the lemon tea, feeling like she was in some kind of dream. "What are you doing here?" she asked. Her first sip of tea was far too sour, and she wrinkled her nose.

Shane's smile said *I told you so*. "Please," she drawled.

"Who do you think you're talking to? I knew you'd try to run off and leave us all behind. It's practically your signature move."

"I did not run off and leave you behind! I left a note," Fi protested, feeling a little blush creeping into her cheeks. "No matter how you slice it, our *one job* is definitely over. Besides"—she ran a finger around the rim of the teacup—"you and Red seemed happy in Andar."

Shane dropped her feet to the floor, almost choking with laughter. "How does someone so smart miss something so obvious?" she wanted to know.

"I have no idea what you're talking about," Fi grumbled.

Shane shook her head. "Andar's not my home, and it's certainly not Red's. And I didn't stick with you all that way just for the treasure—well, at least not entirely, *partner*."

Fi's mouth went dry. For some reason, she felt a prickle behind her eyes. She told herself it was just the heat getting to her after the long, cold nights traveling alone. "Well," she said, favoring Shane with a little smile, "there is this job I was going to take on . . . but it's a big job, and dangerous . . ."

"My favorite kind," Shane said, leaning forward on her elbows.

Fi nudged the undrinkable tea away, matching Shane's pose and lowering her voice. "I'm going after the Lord of the Butterflies," she said, watching Shane's eyes widen.

"You think that creepy old Witch is still alive?" she asked.

Fi shrugged. "Probably not, but I have a feeling there are plenty more slivers of him out there, hidden in mirrors. I intend to find them all and put them to rest." Fi felt the phantom tingle on her palm where the curse mark had been. She brushed her thumb over the smooth, pale scar.

Shane whistled. "You're right—that is a big job. Sounds like it could take a long time."

Fi smiled at her partner's unsubtle attempt to pry. "Well, I plan to make a lot of stops along the way. Maybe even stick around in a few places. Who knows—it could take us all the way to Steelwight."

Shane grinned. "I've also heard Idlewild is an excellent place to spend the winter."

Fi rolled her eyes, smiling so wide it hurt. "You've heard that, huh?"

"Know anybody who'd put us up?"

Her parents. A rush of warmth and longing surged through her, so strong she had to close her eyes. She imagined them tucked up in the library at Idlewild, her father trying to keep his place in three different books at once while her mother unrolled a leaf of ancient parchment, her dark braid pinned back by a pair of crossed fountain pens. She could almost feel the warmth of the mountain sun on her face already, the walk up to the front door spilling over with goldenrod and orchids. And the way it would feel to throw her arms around them and to know, for the first time in so long, she was home.

"It was always going to be my first stop," Fi said, shaking her head at her blunt busybody partner who was always looking out for her.

Shane held out a hand. "So, what do you say? One more job?"

"One more job," Fi agreed, shaking on it.

Shane's grin was pure gold. It twisted as she looked at something over Fi's shoulder, her nose wrinkling.

"I should have warned you I come with a little extra baggage these days."

Fi only had a second to wonder before a hand slammed down on the table hard enough to make sour lemon tea splash over the side of the cup. That's what the master got for serving it without a saucer. Fi craned her head around to look at Red, who had come up behind her. The girl wore a scarlet skirt and blouse laced up under a black bodice. Her loose curls bounced as she tossed her head.

"Shane," she said indignantly. "They won't let us stay here. Even though I did exactly what you said and pretended Cinzel's a dog, we're not allowed to have any pets in the room. So I said he's *not* a pet, he's family, and that rude jerk at the bar told me Cinzel could sleep in the barn!"

"Okay. Relax, I got this," Shane said, getting up and rubbing her neck. "Who'd want a wolf in their barn?" she muttered.

Fi smiled. Shane sure looked happy for someone with a lot of extra *baggage*.

The huntsman kicked her chair back under the creaky table. "I gotta deal with this."

"Need a hand?" Fi asked. She had just gotten to her feet when the door burst open and slammed against the wall, making the patrons jump. A gust of wind swirled around the figure that stood in the doorway.

Briar Rose braced one hand against the frame, panting. His golden hair was wild and speckled with rain, and he wore a white blouse and dark pants under a very familiar blue coat, the rich fabric sewn with dark patches and tiny embroidered roses. He wasn't wearing a circlet.

"Briar . . ." Fi whispered. She felt frozen to the spot.

"Fi!" he yelled.

"Looks like you've got something more important to take care of," Shane said, pushing Red ahead of her toward the bar, but not before shooting Fi a very smug look.

Briar was fighting his way through the startled crowd, his blue eyes locked on hers. He ran the last few steps, and Fi found herself swept up into a tight embrace, nearly lifting her off the ground. Briar's coat was soft against her cheek. She could hear his heart hammering like he'd run all the way from the castle.

"I finally caught up with you, Fi . . ." he whispered into her ear.

Her heart melted when he said her name. Tears swam in her eyes, and this time, she let them fall, wrapping her arms around Briar's neck and fisting her hands in his coat. She could feel the other patrons watching them, the Witches asking each other in whispers if that was really Prince Briar Rose. But she barely heard them. Her whole world was Briar—Briar's warm arms and his soft coat and the scent of roses easing that great dull pain in her chest. She pushed herself back a step so she could look up at him, just to see the recognition in his eyes.

"You remember me," she said.

"I remember everything," Briar said, voice cracking. "Including something you seem to have forgotten. A promise we made to run off together."

Fi swallowed hard. It was what she wanted to hear, more than anything, but she had to be sure.

"Briar," she began, "you belong in Andar. If you want to stay, I won't hold you to that promise."

"Oh, Fi." Briar leaned down, pressing their foreheads together, and this time, when she looked into the depths of his blue eyes, she felt like she could see his love for her shining in them, taking her breath away. "I told you I already know where I belong. It's not in that castle—it's with you, wherever you go." He was so close—close enough that Fi could almost feel the brush of his lips with each word. "I know you already have a partner, but could you use a Witch?" He lifted his hand, a single finger sparkling with pure-white magic. "Even one who can only do a few tricks?"

Fi covered his hand with hers, smiling at the light pouring through her fingers. She'd never need a torch again. "That sounds incredibly useful," she promised. "I can't think of anything I need more."

Briar gave her a dazzling smile. Then he leaned down and kissed her, and Fi closed her eyes, sinking into him. She didn't know if Briar's magic was still crackling between their hands, showering them with brilliant sparks. All she knew was that this was a different kind of magic—the kind that meant Fi would never be alone again.

Maybe there was something to this destiny stuff, at least when you took it into your own hands.

ACKNOWLEDGMENTS

First, thank you to all the readers who went on this journey with Fi and Shane. Your love for these characters and this wild romp has been everything to me!

I'm so grateful for my agents, Carrie Hannigan and Ellen Goff. Working with you has been an absolute dream. Thank you as well to Rhea Lyons, Soumeya B. Roberts, and everyone at HG Literary—I can't imagine a more wonderful team!

Thank you so much to Rūta Rimas. You are a dream editor, and you made *The Cursed Rose* sparkle more than I ever could have imagined!

To everyone at Penguin—none of this would be possible without each and every one of you! Tessa Meischeid, you are a rockstar publicist who always goes above and beyond! To my wonderful copy editor, Rachel Skelton, designers Suki Boynton and Jessica Jenkins, Felicity Vallence, Simone Roberts-Payne, and the entire team. It has been an honor and a privilege to be part of the Penguin family.

To Fernanda Suarez for three of the most beautiful covers I

have ever seen. It was absolutely amazing to see these characters and covers come to life, and I've been blown away Every. Single. Time. You are incredible!

To Lindsey Dorcus for the most spectacular audiobook narration. You bring so much feeling and fun and humor to these books! I am so grateful to Nick Martorelli, Emily Parliman, and the entire Penguin Audiobook team.

Seeing translations of *The Bone Spindle* go out across the world has been an author dream. I'm so grateful to all the amazing publishers and translators who have worked on these books.

Another author dream come true was all the gorgeous *Bone Spindle* art! Heartfelt thanks and awe to @mmarsloud, @arz28, @meliescribbles, @alicemariapower, and @ornitoplatypus. I smile every time I look at these fantastic pieces!!

Special thanks to the Boulder Bookstore, the Tattered Cover, and the Wandering Jellyfish for the most fantastic author events and signings. I'm so lucky to have not one but three amazing independent bookstores so close!

To the phenomenal bloggers, bookstagrammers, and reviewers who reached so many readers! You are absolutely irreplaceable. Special thanks to TBR and Beyond Tours and Colored Pages Book Tours, y'all are epic!

To the most amazing group of Colorado authors who make this whole journey more fun! Meg Long, Jen Peterson, Olivia Chadha, Malia Maunakea, Megan E. Freeman, Olivia Abtahi, Ellen O'Clover, Tasha Christensen, and Jessie Weaver.

To Kyle, Christie, Sarah, Jennica, Claire, Mary, Suzanne, Carey, and all the early readers—every time I started to flag,

I remembered your lovely words. I'm so grateful for everything you've done for this series.

I remain forever grateful for my family and my wife's wonderful family. There is no end to how appreciative I am for all your support and love.

Finally, thank you with all of my heart to my partner, Michelle. There were times in my life when I thought I wouldn't get here. You believed in me even when I didn't believe in myself. You got me over the finish line every time I faltered. You truly are my lifelong rock!